MOVING FORWARD

MOVING FORWARD

Nombasa Jakavula

Nombasa Jakavula

First Printing: 2019

ISBN 978-0-620-84095-8

Nombasa Jakavula
27 Umtata Street Ext 6 Mfuleni
Cape Town, South Africa 7100

nombasajakavula@gmail.com

This is for my friends, Tope and Osborn.

Chapter 1

Sive exited her red Toyota Yaris and headed for the Northern Sun Restaurant door. She was dressed in a white sleeveless denim top, white shorts that revealed most of her gorgeous legs and white All Star boots. Her image in the blazing sun brought out the angel that she was. She beamed at a little boy by the restaurant door and ruffled his hair before disappearing into the restaurant.

Sive was a kind person with a generous heart. She would smile when passing by a person, whether a stranger or otherwise. Her life, her happiness, her hobby was all about loving others. Ten per cent of her salary, and sixteen hours a month of her time went to the Mfuleni orphanage centre.

She was meeting her friends, Mihle and Aviwe. As she entered the restaurant, their eyes met and they smiled at each other. Aviwe and Sive were childhood friends, and they met Mihle at Shoprite in Bellville where she worked as a cashier.

They talked about everything. Did I say everything? I mean, as humans, there's always that room in our hearts we take time to open.

Sive was twenty-five, and three years her friends' junior. Her tennis ball size breasts, slim waist and gorgeous legs made her structure look so perfect. She was a light skinned with big bright eyes and long eyelashes. Just like her father. She was so beautiful. Her toned skin and long black, relaxed hair against her yellow skin complemented her beauty.

Although Sive had a crush on a young teenager at the age of six, she had never had a boyfriend until she was twenty-five. For that, her friends would call her Virgin Mary when teasing her.

Sive worked at Dr Bob Khabba Clinic in Mfuleni as a TB doctor. It was a centre that treated HIV/AIDS and TB patients. She knew from the beginning that her career would fulfil her aspiration of helping people. She made a solemn vow to herself that no life that could be saved would be lost under her care.

However, only time would tell as it was her first year of practice. Things seemed promising, though.

1

There was another doctor at Dr Bob Khabba Clinic who only worked three days a week. His name was Jonathan. Sive called him Jonno. They became friends, but Jonathan believed that they had something more than just a friendship. Her friends were fond of Jonathan, thinking there was something going on between them.

Jonathan was mixed race. His mother was a black South African, his father a white from Germany. She got pregnant when she visited her aunt in Germany who worked for Jonathan's grandparents.

Unfortunately, his parents didn't marry each other. They married different people from their own races. Jonathan didn't fit in both families. He was either too white or less white, and that made him an outsider in both.

Jonathan grew up feeling lonely, lost and less loved. He looked different from his siblings on both sides. He felt like he was just a branch of a new race in his family. He grew up longing for the sense of belonging.

When Jonathan left his home in Johannesburg to attend university in Cape Town, he thought he was a step closer to getting his own freedom. He wanted to settle down with a coloured woman and have a family that he could fit into perfectly. He misunderstood Sive's kindness and thought the heavens sent her and told himself that he would never let her go.

Sive joined her friends at the table. She sat opposite them.

"There's something going on between Virgin Mary and that Jonathan doctor," said Aviwe, eyeing Sive with a smile that asks for her confirmation.

Sive glanced at her, and then brought her attention back to her cup of tea. She ran her finger slowly around the edge of the cup. She looked at Mihle biting her lower lip as she always did when she was in thought. Mihle blinked and broke the silence.

"Is there anything you wanna tell us, Virgin Mary?" They both were waiting to hear her reply. Sive cracked a smile on her tight face and exchanged glances between her friends. She then pulled her seat forward in a comfortable position. Her friends were staring at her without blinking, as if she was going to answer in sign language, and they didn't want to miss a bit of it.

"What is it...tell us girl?" Aviwe burst out in a curious voice. Before Sive could say a word, Aviwe threw out another question.

"Did you guys...you know..."

Sive interrupted her, "Whoa whoa whoa...you mean..."

"Yes, she meant exactly that," said Mihle.

"No, guys! Jonno and I don't have an intimate relationship. I love him as a friend. But I guess he got it all wrong."

Aviwe chuckled. "Well, we all did."

"Meaning?" asked Sive eyeing at her.

"We thought you guys liked each other."

"Guys, who's we?" asked Sive with a confused look.

"Mihle, I and other people."

"And who are other people?" asked Sive.

"Why are you looking so serious, girl?" asked Aviwe.

"No, I'm not serious. I'm just thinking," replied Sive.

"About?" asked Aviwe.

"About…" Sive didn't finish her sentence. She stretched her eyes at Aviwe, "you haven't answered my question, Aviwe."

"What question?" asked Aviwe, looking confused.

"Who are other people?" Sive repeated her question.

Aviwe squinted at her, looking even more confused. Suddenly, an expression of relief appeared on her face, accompanied by a smile.

"Oh, that!" said Aviwe, looking relieved now.

"Yeah, that. Tell me," said Sive.

"Your mom, Michelle…"

Sive interrupted her,

"Oh, now I get it why my mom has been lecturing me about condoms and stuff lately."

Aviwe burst out laughing,

"Really! Come on dude; tell us more about this condom lecture, we might attend."

Aviwe continued laughing, and the two joined. Sive turned to her purse, hanging on the back of her chair. She took out a packet of condoms and threw it on the table in front of them. When the choice condoms landed on the table, they laughed even more.

"What! Choice, of all condoms!" said Mihle, as they continued laughing.

Suddenly, Sive realised that they weren't alone, and she quickly grabbed the packet of condoms on the table. In the act, her eyes caught up with the eyes of a guy who was sitting next to their table. They both smiled at each other as Sive was putting the condoms back in her bag.

3

Sive's attention went back to her friends who were still laughing, talking about Sive's mom giving her condoms.

"Come on guys, we're causing a scene," Sive whispered.

"Causing what!" asked Aviwe, still laughing, "Are you serious! Who doesn't know about condoms in South Africa? We decorate everywhere with condoms. The next thing you'll see is people blowing them up for birthdays' and weddings," said Aviwe, still laughing.

"Exactly, exactly," replied Mihle laughing.

Sive chuckled, "You guys are crazy. Crazy, crazy."

"Whoa whoa, guys," said Mihle, "Earlier, Sive sounded like she was going to tell us what's going on between her and Dr Jonno." Mihle's eyes were swinging between her friends.

The guy at the other table was unconsciously gazing at Sive. When she looked at him, he rose up and dropped his business card on the table and left.

When the waiter came to clear the table he took the card, and when he was about to throw it in a dirty cup, Aviwe screamed.

"No, waiter! That's for me."

The waiter looked confused, staring at her.

"The card in your hand," she said, pointing at his hand.

He looked at his hand, then stretched it towards Aviwe to give her the card. He smiled and apologised, then turned back to the table and finished what he was doing.

When Aviwe looked at her friends, they were staring at her in disbelief. Sive stared wide-eyed at them and said, "And now!"

Aviwe raised up the card and said in a naughty smile, "I'm keeping it for you, my dearest friend."

Then she put it in her purse. Mihle shook her head, smiling. She turned to Sive.

"Ok, girl. We're listening."

"Yeah, yeah. We are," seconded Aviwe, zipping up her purse.

"Ok." Sive wore a serious face again. Her friends sensed that something was wrong. They were blaming her visit to Malawi for her new behaviour, "I thought Jonno and I were just friends since we…"

"You thought!" said Aviwe.

"Yeah," replied Sive.

"Come on girly, we don't want your thoughts but facts."

Mihle interrupted her in a low, concerned voice, "Let her explain it in her own way." Mihle smiled and continued, "or this could end up like the Malawi story."

A smile emerged from Sive's face. Although she'd never told anyone in detail about what exactly had happened in Malawi, except that she found Chikondi dead, there seemed to be some beautiful memories attached to it. Her friends were waiting for the right moment for her to tell them everything.

Sive moved her lips back to their normal position and said, "Guys, this is not Malawi story time, but Jonathan's."

"But girl, we wanna hear all about it. Not just you found him dead and long buried…"

Mihle quickly stopped after she noticed sadness on Sive's face. Silence fell. It was the first time they had mentioned her visit to Malawi after she gave them a short version of the story.

Suddenly, Jonathan entered the restaurant and soon saw them. Aviwe and Mihle waved him over to join them.

Sive was in deep thought…deep enough not to notice anything. Those thoughts were cut short when Jonno's arm fell over her shoulder. Sive got a fright and turned, to her surprise, it was Jonathan.

Silence continued.

The two caught each other's gaze. This time, it happened under the observation of her friends. Their lips were only two to three inches apart.

Jonno's heart pounded, yeaning to taste those lips which appeared to be sweet in front of him, while Sive was still caught in a moment of surprise at seeing him there.

Sive wasn't seeing things the way others did until she felt Jonathan's warm breath on her neck, and then quickly moved backwards. She exchanged nervous glances between the three, and then dropped her eyes to her cup that was already empty.

The silence became more awkward.

Jonathan moved his eyes between the ladies, and then cleared his throat to break the silence. He was standing on the other side of the table, next to Sive, facing Aviwe and Mihle.

"How are you ladies?" he said cheerfully, his eyes running between the two ladies in front of him. He was happy because, now, other people had witnessed the connection between him and the woman his heart fell deeply for.

"We're doing great. How about you, Jonno?" replied Aviwe.

"Good, good," he replied, moving his eyes to Mihle.

5

Jonathan slowly moved his arm away from Sive's shoulder to draw her attention, which didn't work since she was sitting like a statue in her chair.

Mihle noticed that there was tension from Sive's corner and initiated a conversation that had nothing to do with her relationship with Jonno or the untold Malawian story.

"How's work, Jonno?" said Mihle, trying not to show her nervousness.

"Wow, working with a wonderful woman like this one," he said pointing at Sive with a smile that showed content, "work is great. Marvellous. In fact, it's a blessing. She is the kind of soul that brings peace and…hope to every life she touches. And I thank God that she came into my life."

Aviwe interrupted him.

"Are you two toget-"

Mihle elbowed her not to finish what she was saying. However, everyone got exactly what she was trying to say. Sive sat up straight to shake the tension. The three of them moved their eyes to her direction. When all eyes were on her, she glanced at her gold watch.

"Guys, I have to be somewhere."

She threw her phone into her purse. Aviwe interrupted her, looking confused, while Sive looked very calm and relieved.

"But we…"

Mihle interrupted Aviwe. She got it that Sive wanted to run away from the situation.

"Ok girl, see you at church tomorrow…if you're going." Mihle just said what came first to her mind, because Sive wasn't even a church person.

Sive looked at her friends with a wide smile as if something was amusing her. She then gave them a wink and started walking towards the door. She took a few steps before she heard Jonathan calling her name.

"Sive! Wait!"

She stopped, facing forward. Jonathan moved towards her, holding his car keys in his hand. He stood beside her.

"Are you ok, dear? You're not yourself today, what's wrong?" he asked, looking so concerned. Sive slowly curled up her cute lips into a soft smile that increased the throbbing of Jonathan's heartbeat each time he observed it.

"I'm fine. It's just that I have to be somewhere," she replied, trying to get her nerves under control. Jonathan's face was suddenly covered in sadness.

"Are you seeing someone?" he asked, with a perception of jealousy in his voice. He remembered that Sive refused to kiss him when he had taken her to the movie the previous weekend. He was convinced that the man he was going to see now was the reason.

"Yes, I am."

"Is it someone I know?" he asked with sadness in his voice.

"Yes."

"Who…who's that?"

Sive wanted to tell him that he wasn't her man; what she did with her life was none of his business. However, she held herself. She was planning a date with him to set the record straight between them, in a polite manner.

"My mom. I'm visiting my mom," she replied in a soft voice. Jonathan extended his lips in a wide smile of relief.

"Oh, you're meeting your mom. That's great. How's she, by the way?"

"She's well, thanks for asking."

Sive glanced at her wrist once more, "I have to go now. See you at work Monday."

When she started walking, Jonno held her arm, "Can we meet for diner later, please?"

Sive was getting tired of his behaviour. They were just friends for heaven's sake, not a couple. Even their friendship was only born yesterday. They hadn't known each other for long. Firstly, he tried to kiss her, and now, he was acting like a jealous boyfriend.

"I can't go. I'm sorry Jonno. I feel like staying home tonight."

"I can keep you company. Watch a movie…"

Sive interrupted him, "No, Jonno! I want to be alone tonight."

There was a sharpness in her voice. She turned and walked away. Jonathan called her but she ignored him. He followed her. Sive got into her car and drove off.

Jonathan watched Sive's car running towards the junction joining Adderley and Strand Street, before taking a right turn and disappearing. Jonathan was convinced for a moment that she was going to her mom's place since she took a turn to Belleville where her mother lived.

Nevertheless, she wasn't going to Belleville. She was going to Kuils River, where she lived. She wanted time to herself.

Jonathan quickly got into his car and drove off without saying a word to the girls. He followed her, wanted to see if she was really visiting her mother. He was afraid of losing her to another man because that was what he couldn't handle. His obsession over Sive was growing each day, and Sive was gradually noticing it. On the way, Sive decided to go to the orphanage and spend the day with the kids.

Mihle and Aviwe left at the restaurant, discussing Jonno and Sive. Although the tension between them was confusing, they were seeing them as a cute couple that could have cute babies.

Jonathan was very handsome. He was tall and thin, light-skinned and broad-shouldered and well educated… the whole package. Although Jonathan was cute with Sive, a Nigerian boy took Sive's heart.

It seemed like Sive was trapped in a long-distance relationship. First, it was Chikondi, who lived in Malawi. And it didn't end well. It ended in a tragedy that tore her heart apart.

Sive and Gabriel, the Nigerian guy, met on Facebook and they had been chatting for three months now. The connection between them was getting deep… too deep.

Jonathan drove straight to Belleville, Thandi's-Sive's mother- residence. He saw from a distance that Sive's car wasn't in her mother's driveway. His jealousy increased his heartbeat. He pulled his car off at Thandi's driveway and got out. He jogged to the front door and rang the doorbell. He was nervously tapping his right foot, waiting for the door to be opened.

The door soon opened.

"Good morning, Mrs Tikolo."

Jonathan and Thandi had never met. Thandi had seen him only once, but how could she not recognise him since he was the reason she offered her daughter condoms… choice condoms.

"Morning, Jonathan!" She replied warmly. A joy overwhelmed him that his 'mother-in-law' recognised his name… that was a plus.

"May I please talk to your daughter, ma'am?" he asked politely, making sure that he scored some points.

"I'm afraid not. I haven't seen her for days. She must be busy these days."

"But she told me she was meeting you."

There was sadness in his voice. The thought that she was seeing some other man was troubling him.

"No, we had no plans to meet today. Maybe she will come later," said Thandi.

"Ok, thanks ma'am," he said and jogged back to his car. Jonathan told himself that he couldn't rest until he found her. He went straight to Sive's place, but she wasn't there. He called her, but her phone was off. The thought that she was with some fella grew even stronger, and he couldn't bear it. He could even imagine what they might be doing.

Jonathan's heart became ill, and Sive was the only cure to that illness. Life was meaningless to Jonathan without Sive. Life without her was worthless, and he believed in his heart that they belonged together.

Jonathan threw his head on the steering wheel, and stayed there for a moment. He then lifted it up, turned the key and drove off.

***

"Hmmm, I guess these two are dating," said Aviwe, her naughty look was challenging Mihle's opinion on the matter.

"I want to agree with you but, something feels…so weird," said Mihle, looking thoughtful.

"Weird! Do you even know the meaning of the word, girly?" Aviwe replied in a controversial tone.

Mihle looked at her and smiled.

"I'm not going there with you, girl. We both don't know what's going on between Jonno and Virgin Marry."

Aviwe turned to her purse and took out a lip-gloss and rubbed her lips. She then put it back in her purse. Mihle looked deep in her thoughts.

"Girl, it's time for us to get the hell out of here," said Aviwe. Mihle didn't reply, still looking miles away.

"Hello!" said Aviwe, waving her hand in front of her, "I'm talking to you, you fool."

Mihle chuckled, curling up her lips in a smile and then back to normal.

"She needs us. Something is definitely not ok with her," said Mihle.

"You mean Sive?"

"Yes."

"But she always talks without being dug up, what's different this time?"

Mihle gazed at her friend for a moment before replying, "She has been through a lot lately…"

Aviwe interrupted her.

9

"A what! You mean losing a person she'd never even known?" She rolled her eyes and continued, "Oh please."

Mihle laughed, collecting her stuff on the table.

"But I still think she needs us to be real friends to her like she has always been to us."

Aviwe looked so thoughtful and said as she was moving her seat backwards to clear her way, "I guess you're right. And maybe if we could help her get things off her chest, it might help."

"You mean the Malawi story?" Mihle asked.

"Yes."

"And Jonno's." Mihle added.

"Whoa whoa, what about Jonno… he's all she needs. They're good together. In fact, perfect. All we owe them is our support. Sive is twenty-five, turning twenty-six soon. She can't be a virgin forever. Besides, they say if you stay a virgin past a certain age," she pursed her lips in a naughty way, and added, "which I think its twenty-five, you get weird."

Mihle laughed, "What! Where did you get that? That's nonsense," said Mihle, still laughing as they made their way to their cars.

Mihle stood by her car with a door open. She was smiling, looking at her crazy friend who was checking a message on her phone. Probably one of her booty calls. Aviwe was a loose woman, if not confused, somewhere there.

When Aviwe lifted up her eyes, Mihle was staring at her. She was smiling at her tenderly, "What now, you fool!" She asked, opening her car door.

Mihle burst out laughing, "If you knew the meaning of that word, you would be calling yourself that." She continued laughing.

All of a sudden, the laughing stopped, and seriousness replaced a smile on her face. Aviwe noticed through the window that something wasn't okay with her friend. She rolled it down.

"And now?"

"I miss Sive. She would be laughing her lungs out at your craziness right now," she reinstated the smile. "Her absence is a spice missing in our friendship," she added.

Aviwe released a soft smile, "I know. She's always been like that. When we were kids, we had never fought in her presence. Certainly, she has a gift of maintaining peace," said Aviwe.

"I agree."

Aviwe's lips twisted in a naughty smile. "That's why I'm planning to send her to Israel…"

Mihle interrupted her with a laugh. "You must be kidding me?! Israelites should find their own Sive, not ours."

They both laughed as Mihle got into her car.

Chapter 2

Sive had a wonderful time with the kids. They played many games, sang and danced. She was a great dancer with a lovely sweet, soft voice. Kids were very fond of her, and she loved kids so much that being around them was enough of a spiritual fulfilment for her.

Sive left the centre after 8pm, exhausted. She had plans to chat with Gabriel on Facebook that evening.

Gabriel wasn't handsome at all. He was too dark with big hands. He was neither thin nor big, just in the middle. Besides his looks, Gabriel was a good, loving and caring man. Sive fell deeply for his pleasant character before she even met him.

His looks blinded most women from seeing how wonderful he was. South African women had used Gabriel for material stuff to a certain point that he lost confidence in himself, and trust in women.

When Gabriel was 12 years old, his mother died. His father and a mean stepmother raised him. Sometimes, being mean to someone who's too kind is just a waste of effort.

Gabriel came to South Africa in pursuit of a better life, four years ago at the age of twenty-six. He worked as a manager at Ackerman's Clothing Store. Gabriel and Sive were planning to meet soon. They wanted to take their relationship to the next level.

When Sive was waiting for Gabriel's call to inform her to log in on Facebook, a doorbell rang. She went to answer.

Guess who that was. Jonathan.

Sive was shocked to see him at that time, but she didn't want to read too much into it. She stood on the door that was half opened, kind of blocking his way in. She was holding a door handle with one hand, and a doorframe with the other. It convinced Jonathan Sive was hiding someone behind that door, and he became more anxious to get in.

"Are you going to let me in, Sive?" he asked softly.

12

Sive looked at him and felt bad for her earlier behaviour. When she was still staring at him, Jonathan held her hand that was holding the door, looking into her eyes, moving inside. He pressed his front against hers as he was moving in.

He wished that moment was legitimate.

Jonathan was relieved to see an empty couch behind the door, only occupied by her cell phone.

"Oh, you're alone?" he asked nervously.

The question slipped out of his mouth, pushed by the fear of losing her to someone else, not knowing that he had already lost her. Worse, to a foreigner. Anyway, he was half a foreigner himself. Sive looked at him, thinking maybe letting him in was a mistake in the first place.

"Can I get you something to drink?" she asked, walking to the kitchen.

"Yes, please."

Sive came back. She was in a short, pink gown. She handed him a glass of cold drink and put her bottle of natural water on the floor, next to her. She sat on the far end of the couch. Avoiding sitting next to Jonathan, not realising that she was giving him a perfect view of her sweet legs.

Sive turned and looked at him. "What's so important that can't wait until tomorrow, Jonathan?"

"I want us to talk about us," he replied, turning his body at Sive.

"Us, Jonathan! Who's us?" she asked coldly.

"Me and you…what we have, Sive…"

Sive interrupted him.

"What is it that you think we have, Jonno?" she asked in a low voice, trying to calm herself down.

He tilted his head like a puppy, stared at her for a moment, and then replied, "Our love. I love you deeply, and I know you feel the same way. I can't live without you…my love. You're the last thing on my mind before closing my eyes at night and the first when I open them in the morning," he sadly explained his feelings for her.

Sive felt sorry for him when she looked at his confused, pretty face. As handsome as he was, Jonathan wasn't the man Sive wanted to spend her life with. As plain as Gabriel was, he was that man Sive's heart throbbed for.

Sive sighed exhaustedly. She pulled herself to the edge of the couch and nervously rubbed her hands together trying to calm herself down. She then locked her fingers and rested her chin on them. She closed her eyes and lifted her head up, trying to gather all the manners she could to be polite to her friend.

"There's nothing going on between us, Jonno. We're just friends and colleagues, nothing more. I love you as I love anyone else. You're a good person, and I love to be your friend...please..."

"Friends!" he laughed nervously, and then continued, "we're not friends, Sive. We're lovers. Why are you denying our love? We belong together," his voice got rougher, "and no man can take you away from me...do you hear me?" he said in a shrill, angry voice. Shaking in anger.

Sive was quiet, staring at him in disbelief. She wasn't sure whether she was dreaming. She knew him as a nice guy. Surely, there was a lot she didn't know about him, and no one could associate Jonathan with that kind of behaviour.

Jonathan buried his face in his hands and sniffed, and then wiped his face with his hands. He lifted his face up and looked at her. He put on an innocent face and moved closer to Sive. Sive moved a bit away, forgetting that she was already at the edge of the couch. She fell on the floor on her buttocks. Jonathan flew after her.

Sive was so scared of Jonathan. Her breath was trapped in her throat before screaming, trying to run away from him. She didn't know that he was only trying to catch her. She thought that maybe he was trying some stupid way of showing her his love for her.

Jonathan landed in between her appetising legs. He scooped her up off the floor with both hands and put her on his chest and held her tight. His head was resting on hers.

"I'll never hurt you, Sive. All I want is for us to be happy. I won't do anything against your will," he whispered those words when he saw that she was frightened.

Sive was still buried in Jonathan's arms when her phone rang. She knew it was Gabriel, and was afraid to answer it. She buried herself in his arms even deeper although that wasn't where she wanted to be. When the phone stopped ringing, she slowly moved away from Jonathan's arms. She went back to sit on the couch.

"Are you okay?" Jonathan asked, getting up from the floor.

Sive nodded, and then stretched her hand to reach the bottle of water. She took a sip and put it back on the floor.

"Are you okay?" Jonathan repeated his question.

14

Sive nodded again.

Sive wasn't sure whether she was or wasn't. She lifted up her head, looking at the time on the watch against the wall. It was 22:27. Her wish was for him to leave so she could bury herself under her blankets.

While Sive was quiet, trying to figure out how could she escape the situation, someone knocked on the door. She jumped, and headed for the door. She opened without even asking who it was. All she was praying for was someone to rescue her.

Now she was sure that Jonathan was obsessed with her, but she still wanted to handle it in a way that wouldn't embarrass him.

"Uncle Phiwe!" She said, cracking a smile of relief.

With his fifteen years of experience as a crime investigator, Phiwe sensed that something wasn't ok in that house. He ran his eyes passed Sive to the young man on the couch and back to Sive again, quietly investigating the situation.

"Evening *mtshana*, are you okay?" he asked, holding her shoulder and looking into her eyes, eliminating her chances of lying.

Sive just stared at him.

Phiwe just pushed the door closed with the other hand and walked past her and settled on the couch, next to the young man. He bent forward, staring at the young man.

Sive was nervously standing on the same spot. She didn't want her uncle to find out what was going on.

What was that exactly? That this guy frightened her, or they were dating? Maybe both.

The secret that Jonathan was obsessed with Sive was safe with her. But the question was, was she safe with the secret? Anyway, she was sure that she wouldn't let her uncle leave without her.

"Evening...do we know each other?" asked Phiwe.

"I'm Jonathan, Jonathan Sidloyi. Sive's boyfriend," he replied, without hesitating to mention that he was Sive's boyfriend.

Phiwe frowned in disbelief. He turned to Sive.

"I didn't know that you…"

Sive quickly went to the kitchen, avoiding her uncle's question.

"Let me get you something to drink, Uncle," she said nervously and hurried away.

Her uncle noticed that his niece was nervous. He thought that maybe it was because he found her with a man, and he decided to let it go, and said what brought him there. Sive came back with a glass of Coke and gave it to her uncle.

"Thanks, *mtshana*," he said receiving his drink, "Your mom is worried about you, and she asked me to come and check up on you...what's wrong?"

"I...I...don...maybe..." she stammered, without completing a word. She was stuck in the middle of trying to explain and just stared at her uncle for a moment.

"Please, take me to my mom's," she burst out in a nervous voice.

Phiwe was then convinced that something was wrong.

"Ok," he replied, looking thoughtful.

He finished his drink, and then gave an empty glass to Sive.

"Get your stuff so we can go, *mtshana*. It's getting late," he said, glancing at his watch.

Jonathan was quiet. Looking impressed, maybe because he introduced himself to Sive's uncle who was playing a father figure in her life.

Sive quickly went to the bathroom, grabbed her toothbrush, and slipped it into her gown pocket.

"Shall we go?" she said, looking relieved.

When Phiwe turned around, all the other rooms were already dark.

"So quick?" he asked, surprised.

"Yeah, I'm tired. I want to go to sleep," she replied.

They walked out. Jonathan signed her that he would call her the following day, as she was walking to Phiwe's car.

She got in the car, next to her uncle. Phiwe glanced at her just to check if she was ok, and then turned the key and drove off.

Both were quiet. Sive looked miles away, looking through the window. Questioning whether she was really handling Jonathan's behaviour the right way. Her uncle was also caught up in his deep thoughts, trying to figure out what was going on between the two. When he was tired of wondering in the dark valley of his own thoughts, he turned to Sive.

"Were you fighting with your boyfriend?"

"No, uncle."

Phiwe didn't want to interrogate her like one of the criminals at work. He decided to let her mother deal with the situation. Maybe it would be easier for Sive to open up to her mother.

Phiwe glanced at his watch. It was 22:45.

Sive and her uncle had a great relationship. They discussed everything and laughed a lot together.

In that evening, all that was gone. She hardly smiled; all she was doing was blinking her big eyes more than usual. She didn't know the right way to tell a sick man who's obsessed with a woman that the relationship was only a fantasy…it only existed in his head.

***

Thandi's house was dark. Phiwe pulled his car over, jogged to the front door, and rang the bell. When he turned around, Sive was just behind him.

Suddenly, the lights flipped on, and then Thandi's voice.

"Who's there?"

"It's me, sis. Phiwe."

Thandi quickly tied her gown straps and nervously opened the door. When she saw both of them standing on her doorstep, her nerves escalated to the next level.

"What's wrong? Is my baby ok…?"

"I'm ok mom, all I want is to sleep," she said as she was pushing herself in front of her uncle and then went to her room.

Sive didn't switch the lights on; she just threw herself on her bed next to the clothes that were neatly folded on one side.

Her bed in her mother's house had its own special way of comforting her. It felt like a mother's arms to a baby. She breathed a sigh of relief, and then fell fast asleep.

Two siblings, Phiwe and Thandi, were talking softly on the couch, whispering so Sive would not hear. They didn't know she was already passed out from a dose of Jonathan's twisted mind.

Thandi's buttocks rested on the edge of the couch, listening to her brother.

"I found her in her house with a man…her boyfriend," he said, expecting Thandi to be surprised, too.

"You mean Jonathan?" she asked, still nervous.

"Yeah. I didn't even know that *mtshana* was seeing someone," he said surprisingly.

"She didn't tell me either. But you know news travels fast," she explained, feeling relieved now. She realised that nothing bad had happened although she didn't understand why she had come to sleep over. "But I like him, he's a good young man," she added, smiling.

17

"And I don't," said Phiwe coldly.

"Why?" she asked surprisingly. "Did he do anything to hurt my baby?" she added, her face covered with seriousness.

"When I got there, they looked like they were fighting."

"What do you mean, was she crying or something?" she asked, looking concerned.

"No."

"Then?"

"It was just the feeling I got…"

Thandi interrupted him with a laugh.

"My dear brother, thanks for everything. But I don't want to go there with you, more specifically, where your suspicions are concerned."

"That will be my cue to leave my dear sister… it's getting late. I guess Smamkele is getting worried now."

"How's my nephew by the way?" she asked smiling.

"He's fine, thanks for asking," he replied, walking towards the door, followed by his sister. She watched him jogging to his car with a smile on her face.

Phiwe got in his car and turned the key, and then turned to his sister, "Lock the door while I'm watching; I won't leave you standing there. I can't afford to lose you to the crime of this country."

Chapter 3

Smamkele, Phiwe's son, was two years younger than Sive. His mother died of heart-related disease after they drove him out of the house for being gay. They made it clear to him that their Christian values wouldn't tolerate his filthiness.

On her twenty-third birthday, as usual, Sive went to share her birthday cake with homeless people on the street. She spent a day with them, listening to their stories.

When Sive was serving them cake, she noticed two young men joining the crowd. She went to serve them, and that's when she noticed a tattoo of Africa on the arm of the other man. Her heart pounded.

"Sma," she called him in a low voice, doubting her eyes. The moment felt like a dream. The young man lifted up his face and looked at her. It was, indeed, his cousin, Smamkele.

Sive embraced him. He was thin, shabby and shaking…probably from drug craving. He was in an unrecognisable condition that tore Sive's heart apart. She held her tears from falling; she wanted to be strong for him. She realised that he needed a strong shoulder to lean on.

Smamkele was like a brother to her. They grew up so close, playing together every weekend. They attended the same schools, from primary to high school. They shared their problems…their dreams.

Sive turned to the people. "Goodbye guys. See you next time," she said, taking Sma's hand, she started walking.

They took a train to Mowbray where Sive stayed. They didn't talk until they got to Sive's place. Sive put her bag on the study desk at the corner of her living room by the small window. She took off her gold watch that was her birthday present from her mother, and put it next to the bag.

She patted Sma's shoulder as she was passing the couch he was sitting on, "I'm coming,' she said, and disappeared into a small passage leading to a bathroom and a single room.

"Come this side," she said, standing on a bathroom door. Sive gave him a clean towel and her tracksuits to change.

"I'll be in the kitchen if you need me, preparing something for you to eat," she said, and then left.

She didn't even bother asking him what he would like to eat since the options in the kitchen were restricted. She had only sausage, eggs and some tomatoes. When he'd finished bathing, Sive brought him his food.

"Eat, before your food gets cold, little cuz."

Smamkele started eating, and you could tell that food wasn't always present where he'd been.

"I've been missing you, cuz," she said, smiling at him. "How have you been?" she added.

Smamkele looked at her for a moment without saying anything. His eyes were full of sorrow. Then he looked away. Sive saw in his eyes that he was quietly pleading for help.

"What is it, Sma? Tell me. You know you can always tell me anything."

Smamkele shook his head, and said in a sad voice, "What is love?"

Sive tilted her head and looked at him with eyes full of love. She smiled and said, "Love keeps no records of wrong." Smamkele turned and looked thoughtfully at her.

"I know you've been wronged. But this is your own life… your dreams that you're ruining here."

"I know I let myself down… I messed up, big time."

Sive smiled tenderly. She was so happy that he acknowledged his mistakes. She believed that it was his first step to making things right. Sive's smile made Smamkele feel loved.

"You can always get things right, cuz," said Sive in her soft, angelic voice.

Smamkele lowered his eyes and his face looked hopeless. Sive cupped his chin and lifted his head up. "You can do this, Sma," she said in a soft, encouraging voice.

"I feel like I've reached a point of no turning back," he said hopelessly.

"But we can always change how we feel, Sma," said Sive, holding his hands.

He pulled his hands away from her.

"Who will I do that change for? No one loves me. I'm filthy just like my dear Mom said," he replied in a high, angry voice.

Tears welled up in his eyes.

He was in deep pain. Sive hated to see him like that, but she wanted him to get things off his chest.

He wiped his tears with his hand.

"You'll change for nobody but yourself. You love yourself…and I love you so much. No words can express the way I love you," she said sincerely.

Smamkele felt a hint of hope deep inside. He knew his cousin was the most reliable person in the entire universe. However, he also knew that she did not know how filthy he was…filthier than his parents thought.

"But I'm filthy," he said in a sorrowful voice.

"Do you think being gay makes you filthy? No sexual orientation makes us filthy, my dear…"

"If that is so, why am I homeless, with no one?" he asked angrily.

"Human imperfection," replied Sive.

Smamkele lifted up his eyes and said. "So imperfect that parents lack love for their own children?" he asked, his whole body trembled with pain.

"Sometimes we shouldn't focus on the wrong people did to us, but on how to ease the pain they caused us," she said, smiling.

Smamkele looked at her, thoughtful. And then, looked away, digesting Sive's words. He sensed some truth in it, but his thought of being filthy clouded his mind. He knew his filthiness and wasn't sure if Sive could take it farther than being a gay.

"I know it's not you talking, Sma, but the fear and confusion."

There was silence.

"Yes, I'm hopeless. My life has turned upside down in a blink of an eye. One moment I was planning my future, the next I was on the street…homeless and addicted to drugs."

He paused and glanced around, trying to hold back tears.

"And above all that…HIV positive," he dropped the second bomb.

Quickly the tears rolled down his cheeks.

Sive felt a pit in her stomach, and then, started doubting her ears. But she told herself that she had heard him clearly.

Sive paused before replying.

"How do you feel about all this?" She asked, looking at him.

"What kind of a question is that? What do you think?" his voice raised up in anger. "This means that my life is over at twenty-one…twenty-one! Do you hear me?"

He shouted at her. Tears all over his face.

"My father will never take me back…do you see how filthy am I? Like a pig in the mud…do you see, Sive!"

He rose up from his seat, walked across the room, stood by the window, and watched the raindrops running down the window. Smamkele trusted Sive with all his heart. Although he knew that Sive would never let him down, he still wasn't sure if he could turn his life around.

"Can you take a filthy pig into your house?" he asked in a low voice, still looking at the window.

Sive got up from the floor in front of where he was siting and moved towards him. She took his arm and turned him around. Without saying anything, she put her arms around his lean body and embraced him. She took a step backwards, still holding his hands and viewed his miserable face.

"You can't give up on yourself now."

Smamkele lifted up his eyes at her, and then pulled his hands away from hers and placed his eyes back on the window.

"You're so strong, Sma. You can beat this."

Smamkele turned and looked at her, and said angrily, "I'm craving dope as we speak."

"I know you won't get clean overnight. You need help."

Smamkele just looked at her without saying anything.

"Excuse me, I'll be back in a minute," she said, and disappeared into the small passage.

When she got back, Sma was gone.

"Sma!" Smamkele!" she called him, looking around the house, but there was no single sign of him. She ran out of the house to look for him on the street. There was no Sma. The street was empty.

She went back inside, thinking that maybe he went to the shop to get something.

Sive glanced at her wrist, and quickly remembered that she put her watch on the desk. When she got there, there was no watch. She just knew what had happened. It crossed her mind that he might not come back and she decided to go and look for him the next morning.

"I won't give up on you, Sma. You can strip me of everything I have, I don't care."

Sive spoke to herself, standing in the middle of her small living room. She went to the kitchen and had got supper started. She left the pots simmering on the stove and went to curl up on the couch. She was exhausted.

Unexpectedly, she fell asleep.

When she was dreaming of rescuing Sma from drowning in a horrible sea, someone knocked at the door. She woke up and walked to the door.

It was Sma, as wet as he was in the dream.

Sive noticed guilt on his face. She threw herself on him and hugged him. They both became wet. They looked at each other and laughed at their madness as old times. It was their first laugh in months. They took turns in taking a bath and then changed into pyjamas.

They ate their supper. Sma was sitting on the couch, and Sive made herself comfortable on the floor next to her dear cousin.

"You look more relaxed now," she said with a friendly smile, trying to stir up a conversation.

Sma smiled, eating his food.

"You do know that I love you so much, right?" She said, tapping his lean thigh. Sma smiled at her.

Suddenly, the thought of stealing her watch hit his mind and the pain cut his heart so deep…and then, the smile on his face faded away.

"What's wrong now, Sma? Did I say…?"

"No, it's not you," he said, putting his plate aside. Sive put hers aside, too, and looked at Sma.

She had a good feeling that he was about to say something positive.

"I want help."

"What kind of help, cuz?"

"I wanna get clean," he replied, in a low seeking for help voice.

Sive threw herself at him and held him tight.

"Thanks, cuz," she said, smiling happily.

After making some calls, Sive told Sma that they were leaving tomorrow afternoon. Although education was important to her, she decided to skip classes the following day. Sma's life was more important than anything that could ever happen in her life. She didn't want to give him time to change his mind.

When Smamkele woke up, Sive was already back from picking up the car from her mom. They went to buy some things for Smamkele.

23

Suddenly, Sma and Sive were standing with his small suitcase in the middle of her living room, holding hands. Hope was written all over their faces.

"I can and will do this, right to the end," he said.

"I and my love for you will stand by you and with you all the way," said Sive.

"Thanks, cuz, for everything."

Sive replied with her angelic smile. They unlocked their hands, Sma grabbed his luggage, and off they went.

When they arrived at the rehab, Smamkele was expected. A tall, big man welcomed him.

Smamkele looked at Sive. They hugged each other.

"Be strong. You're bigger than this, and I know you'll overcome it," she said embracing him, "I'll visit you if they allow me to."

"Well, we'll send you a message when you can visit him. For the first few weeks, you're not allowed," said the tall guy.

They moved their eyes from the man and placed them on each other.

"Thanks sis, for everything," said Sma.

"Hurry up, you're meeting your doctor in five," the man said, taking a few steps to show Sma his room.

"Goodbye, sis," Sma said, took his luggage and followed the man.

Chapter 4

When Thandi walked into Sive's room, she found her sleeping peacefully. She stood over her, watching her lovingly. She removed the clothes on the bed, took a blanket and covered her legs, and then left.

Sive woke up the next morning, brushed her teeth and went to her mother's bedroom. She found her bed neatly made. She called her.

"Mom!"

"In the kitchen, baby!" she replied.

When she got there, she found her making breakfast, pancakes with cream and scrambled eggs. Sive's favourite.

"Hmmm, smelling yummy, my wife," she said, smiling. That was how she called her when serving her food.

Thandi chuckled, and said, beating the eggs, "Soon, someone will call you that. I bet that that Jonathan doctor couldn't wait to marry you."

There was a smile of amusement in Thandi's face. Sive's face quickly lost its smile; she then moved her eyes away from her mother's and placed them on a chair in front of her. She pulled it out and seated herself for breakfast. Suddenly, her mother remembered what her brother had told her.

She switched off the stove and turned to her.

"What's wrong baby; did he hurt you in any way?"

"No mom, he didn't."

"Then why did you wear a serious face when I mentioned his name?"

"Please mom, drop it. There's nothing wrong," she said, faking a smile, trying to deceive her mother.

Her mother stared at her, trying to read her mind. Sive felt uncomfortable under her gaze because she knew she was lying.

"Bring us food, old lady," she said smiling, trying to change the subject.

Thandi smiled and started dishing up for both of them.

"What would I do without this lovely, gorgeous lady…God bless her," Sive said, smiling at her mother, picking up the fork.

Thandi smiled at her, and then said, "Thanks, honey." She then picked up a small portion of egg with the fork and put it in her mouth. She lifted up her eyes and looked at her daughter. "Baby please, tell me about this young man in your life."

"Mom, there's nothing to tell. When there is, you'll be the first to know," she said, rubbing cream on a pancake with the back of a fork.

"Why are you so defensive, baby?" she asked with eyes demanding an explanation.

Sive couldn't lie anymore; she put down her fork and bit her lower lip, looking at her mother.

"Yes mom, there's something going on between me and Jonathan which is not good. But I'll tell you about it some other time."

"What is it, baby? Tell me, I have a right to know if he's hurting you. Have you lost your virginity to him, tell me I…"

"Whoa, Mommy, I'm still intact."

Thandi gave a smile of relief.

"Ok my angel…if you say so. I'll drop it, for now. Do you hear me young lady? For now!" She said smiling, pointing at her with a fork.

"Yes, old lady, I heard you," they both laughed and continued eating.

The phone rang. It was Thandi's. She looked at the screen, frowned, and put it to her ear.

"Hello?"

"Hello Mrs. Tikolo, how are you?" The voice replied.

"And whom am I speaking to?" Thandi asked.

"I'm Jonathan, ma'am. May I speak with Sive, please?"

"Ok, dear," replied Thandi, and then gave the phone to Sive.

"Hello."

"Hi baby, can we meet today?" said Jonathan.

"No Jonno, maybe later. I'm catching up with my mom now," said Sive, pretending she was fine…but she wasn't at all.

Jonathan was starting to breathe heavily down her neck. Sive decided to have lunch with him the following day and talk things through.

"How about having lunch together, tomorrow?" she asked.

"No Sive, tonight. I need to see you tonight."

"Ok. I'll be home by eight tonight," she calmly replied.

"Ok, I'll be there at eight-thirty."

Sive held the phone in her hand, looking thoughtful. She didn't like the coldness in his voice, but she was meeting him anyway.

"Is everything ok, honey?"

"Yeah, old lady," she replied, wearing a deceiving look.

Silence fell.

Sive cleared her throat and said, "Mom, you have never really told me about my dad. I mean my real dad."

Thandi paused before answering, cleared her throat.

"Do you mean Sizwe wasn't your father?"

"You know what I mean Mom, and you know that I loved him with all my heart. He loved me like I was his own. Although I was still too young when he died, I still remember the good times we had."

"But I didn't love him. And he knew that," Thandi confessed.

"What do you mean, Mom?" she asked incredulously.

Thandi looked at her daughter with a half-smile on her face.

"Yes, but you were too young to notice anything. He was a very good man, he loved us with all of his heart…but, unfortunately, my heart belonged to someone else. Your father."

Sive was looking at her mom attentively.

"But mommy, why did you marry someone you didn't love?" she asked, confused. She didn't understand how a lady as beautiful as her mother could settle for someone she didn't even love.

Thandi was quiet for a moment, and then replied.

"Because the one I loved was dead. Died in a plane crash on his way back home, coming from visiting his tiny adorable daughter for the first time…and it was his last time as well," she said, with a sadness covering her face.

"Did he love you, Mommy?"

Thandi paused before answering.

"More than anything. I felt his love without being told." She curled her lips into a smile that was inspired by the sweet memories of her life with Gerald, Sive's father.

A very short, beautiful life.

"We met at Baragwaneth Hospital during my first year working as a nurse. He was a doctor from the US, and he only spent one month there." Thandi's lips curled up in a sweet smile. "He was the most handsome man I ever met in my whole life...not to mention his kind, generous heart," she smiled at her daughter, and added, "you're an exact copy of the man who only exists in my heart now."

Sive was looking at her mother attentively with a happy smile.

"I'm glad you finally told me about my real dad," she said, glittering with that smile that took Thandi back to those sweet days with Gerald.

"I didn't tell you before because I didn't want to confuse you. But now, you're a big girl."

"And I had the best life a child could ever ask for..."

Thandi interrupted her.

"You only did because you were the best child a parent could ever ask for. Thoughtful and mature for your age."

Thandi broke off a piece of pancake and rubbed it in the cream and put it in her mouth, and continued, "And I thank God every day for the precious gift he gave me, unwrapped. Because if you were another kid, you would have acted stupidly when you found out at the age of fifteen that Sizwe wasn't your real father."

"I love you, Mom, and I know you have always loved me with all of your heart. And you raised me the best way you know how...and I'll always be grateful for that."

They both smiled and held each other's hands.

Sive pulled her hands away from her mother's, poured herself a glass of juice, and looked at her.

"How about this, Mommy?" she asked, holding up a jar of orange juice.

"Yes, please," she replied.

"You'll definitely need more than just one glass of juice, old lady. 'Cause I wanna know every bit of this romantic story," said Sive, making herself comfortable in her seat.

"This is the moment for you to know all about yourself, young lady. How you came into existence," she said, curling her lips up in a naughty position, sipping her juice.

"And I love every bit of it...you may proceed, old lady," said Sive, sipping her juice.

Thandi smiled and continued, "I was in the kitchen one Thursday afternoon, making myself a cup of tea. He came in. After a warm greeting, he asked me for a cup of tea. I made him one, and we started chatting."

"So, that's how it started? A relationship?" she asked curiously.

"Yea, and after that, we were all over Johannesburg, exploring every corner of it."

"How old was he?"

"I was twenty-three, and he was thirty-one."

"So, you were together just for only one month?"

"No, my dear, less than that. When we started dating, he had been in Johannesburg for more than a week."

"So, it was just a little more than a two week relationship."

"Kind of."

"No, old lady. Not kind of…exactly that," said Sive, and they both laughed.

"So, when was I conceived, on the last week of his visit?" she asked curiously.

"No dear, on the last night…and it was so beautiful. We never did it again. When he came to visit us, I had just given birth, so it was off limits. Besides, we were so overwhelmed by the joy of having our cute baby," she said smiling, feeling the joy of that moment.

"Did he love me, Mommy?"

"More than his own life. Gerald loved kids so much, and that love was extended to its limits for his own. You were in his arms the entire time of his visit. Changing your diaper. Preaching his undying love for us," she replied with a tender smile on her face as if she was looking at Gerald.

"Was he going to marry you, Mommy?"

Thandi didn't answer the question; she gazed at her and then said, "Come with me, dear."

Sive followed her into her bedroom. She sat on the bed while her Mom was busy looking for something in her wardrobe. She pulled out an old jewellery box behind the clothes. She opened it while she was still facing away. She took something out and placed it back. She turned to Sive, holding up a beautiful diamond ring. The morning sun rays from the window hit it, and it glittered.

"That's what he gave me, on his knees. Asking my hand in marriage," she said confidently.

Sive stretched out her hand to receive the ring from her mother. She looked so amazed. She locked it in her hand for a moment. Then, slowly moved her eyes to her mother.

"Why didn't you tell me that you had something from my father all these years?" she asked surprisingly, and then continued, "All along I thought you had a terrible story to tell." Sive smiled, and continued, "I'd never thought of something this beautiful…or anything close to it," she said, opening her hand and looking at it again.

The lovely view of it in her hand made her realise that Gabriel was the man she wanted to spend her life with and have children with. She gave it back to her mother.

"You can have it if you want," she said, standing by the bed, next to her.

"No, Mom. This has more sentimental value to you than to me. You have beautiful memories attached to it. He was your man, and I can't rob you of the only thing you have left of him."

"No, no my child. He left me with a wonderful gift. One I can't live without." Sive extended a beautiful smile on her face, knowing that she was that wonderful gift. "A product of our love."

Sive replied with an ecstatic wink. They both laughed.

Thandi put the ring back in the jewellery box and took out a small photo. She put the jewellery box back where she had taken it from. She turned to Sive.

"You can have this one, honey," she said, giving her a photo of a young handsome man. "This is your dad," she said.

Sive looked at the photo for a moment, smiling.

"He was really handsome, Mom, a knock-out."

"And you're a knock-out too; with good morals…Jonathan is a very lucky man."

"And you are also beautiful, Mom," she said, smiling at her mother.

Her mother extended her lips into a beautiful smile, inspired by those sweet memories.

"That's how you came into existence, my angel," she said.

"And I thank God that I was born to you. I'll raise my kids the way you raised me. You're the best mom ever. You were still young when you lost your partner, but I have never seen you with a man." Sive frowned at her mom. "How did you manage to abstain from sex that long?"

Thandi chuckled.

"I didn't abstain."

"How did you do it then?"

Thandi looked at Sive in silence, and then replied.

"Sometimes I would pretend that I was working night shift or do naughty stuff when you went to visit my parents. I respected you more than anything in this world."

Sive smiled,

"You are such a good mother, a role model."

A doorbell interrupted them.

Sive looked at her mom.

"Are you expecting someone?"

Thandi shook her head.

"Maybe Jonathan, baby," she said, walking to answer the door.

Chapter 5

"Baby, your friends!" she wailed.

"Good morning, ladies," said Sive.

"Morning," said Aviwe, running her eyes all over Sive, teasing her. "Are you ok, upstairs?" she added, pointing to Sive's head.

"What time is it?" Sive asked, glancing at her bare wrist; she then smiled at her friends to give her the time.

Aviwe glanced at her watch, making sure that her fingers were all visible.

"Huh!" Sive said, rubbing her eyes for better vision, "I just can't believe my eyes, is it real or am I just dreaming!" Sive asked excitedly.

Soon Mihle noticed a ring on Aviwe's finger, too. Her eyes bulged out surprisingly.

"Is it what I think it is?" said Mihle, her eyes running between her friends for confirmation.

"Yes, my darlings. Sbongile dressed up this finger," replied Aviwe happily.

"You mean, you're engaged?" Sive's mother asked, excitedly.

Aviwe nodded, "Yes, Mrs. T, I'm engaged to be married," she said, raising up her hand for everyone to see the ring.

Sive smiled at her friend and said, "I'm so happy for you, my friend. When did this happen?"

"He took me out to dinner last night. That's where and when it happened…in a Western way," she said, rolling her eyes.

"Let me sit down for this wonderful news," Sive said, pulling her friends to the couch.

Aviwe was a dark beauty. She was tall and slender with a character that wasn't pleasant at all. She was working as a nurse in Gooterskuur hospital. She was a flirt and a party animal that'd never been home.

Aviwe would sometimes take Sive to parties. Although Sive was a great dancer who could keep the party alive all night, she had better things to do than be a frequent partygoer. She'd rather relax at home for the next day's activities.

Sive was involved in a lot of activities that had something to do with helping others…mostly orphans.

Mihle could also not go out anymore. She was a mother of two young girls, and she was staying with her boyfriend, Zuko.

Although Sive was happy for her friend, she was also afraid that she might be making the biggest mistake. Sive swung her body to face Aviwe.

They all knew that Aviwe wasn't ready for a serious commitment…including Aviwe herself. But very few women could say no when a man goes down on one knee with a diamond ring in his hand.

"Baby girl, are you sure this is what you really want?" asked Sive, concerned.

Mihle was looking at her very attentively. She was asking herself the same question. They both knew how Aviwe was. She treated Sbongile like trash. It's so true that looks matters to guys. Definitely, Sbongile was marrying Aviwe's looks. Like many men, he was holding on tight to a very mean woman just for her physical beauty.

Even men who preach that beauty of a woman lies inside make the same mistake of falling for looks in the meanest woman and live a miserable life.

"What kind of question is that? Of course I am," she said, bored and defensive, exchanging glances between the girls.

Aviwe knew exactly where Sive was heading with her question, and she didn't want to go there. Sive knew that the marriage was just part of her mission of taking toying with Sbongile's feelings to the next level.

"Indeed, what kind of a question is that, Sive? Marriage is every girl's dream. Aviwe got an opportunity to achieve that dream…"

Sive interrupted her mother who was bringing them something to drink when she heard Sive's unreasonable question.

"Yes, I agree with you, Mom. But only when a girl has turned into a woman…"
Aviwe cut Sive off.

"Whoa! What do you mean by that?" Aviwe was getting angrier. "Are you trying to tell me that I'm not good for…"

Mihle interrupted Aviwe.

33

"Don't act like a child, Aviwe, you know exactly what Sive means." Aviwe narrowed her eyes at Mihle. "And I agree with her. You can't act immature and mean to Sbongile like you do and expect to be a good wife. We're friends, and we're supposed to look out for one another."

Aviwe laughed sarcastically and said, "Friends! I don't think so. Friends support one another, not criticise one another. You're just being jealous…"

Sive interrupted Aviwe who was more defensive than rational.

Thandi was still standing in front of them, looking confused. She turned and walked away, leaving the girls when she realised that there was so much she didn't know.

"Baby girl, if we think you're making a mistake we should correct you."

"Yes, that's what friends do," said Mihle.

"Oh, really! So, have you already corrected your friend" she said, pointing angrily at Mihle "who's been staying with a man for years, who has no intentions of marrying her, not to mention having two illegitimate kids?"

Thandi came rushing from the corridor, interrupting an angry Aviwe.

"Keep it down girls. I guess you should drop…"

"They're treating me as if I'm a bad person."

Sive cut in. "No one said you're a bad person."

"Shut up, you imperfect perfectionist! You pretend to be a perfect person but you're not. You pretend to be a virgin when you're busy sleeping with Jonathan behind our backs, you hypocrite!" Aviwe said angrily.

Everyone was silent as a grave. Sive was quiet for a moment. She looked at Aviwe.

"There's no reason for you to throw accusations," said Mihle.

Aviwe turned to Mihle. "It's so crazy that you are even a part of this conversation, you know, Mihle," she said angrily.

"Argument," Sive corrected her, and then lifted up her glass of juice.

Aviwe just glanced at Sive and then brought her eyes back to Mihle.

"Are you jealous?" asked Aviwe.

"Of what!" asked Mihle, her face frowning, showing that she wasn't happy at all.

Sive shut her mouth. She thought it was time for them to open their eyes on issues surrounding their lives.

"That Sbongile has done what your loser boyfriend has never even thought of?"

"Whoa, whoa, Aviwe, this isn't about me, but you," said Mihle.

"We let you make your own mistakes, why can't you do the same for me…if you think I'm making a mistake?" Mihle glanced at Sive to rescue her from the oncoming attack. Unfortunately, Sive saw the attack as the right method to bring Mihle back to reality that Zuko was over her, "You gave birth outside marriage, not even once, but twice. You're staying with a man with no intentions of marrying you…Who would bother buying the cow when they get milk and meat whenever they like," said Aviwe angrily.

Sive was listening to their argument without interrupting.

"Why are you treating me like this, Aviwe?" Mihle asked sadly.

"Treating you like what? It's time to put our secrets on the table, right?" Aviwe chuckled sarcastically, and continued, "So be it…before playing some stupid Dr Phil to other people's love lives, please, make sure yours is in good shape."

Mihle stared at Sive hopelessly.

"How many times has he cheated on you with other women? How many times have you cried yourself to sleep at night? Do you think a man who could marry you can sleep next to you without touching you?"

"Aviwe…"

"Don't Aviwe me!" said Aviwe, throwing her hands in the air, angrily. "Before you tell me what to do about my life, get yourself out of that hell, dear friend."

"You have diverted this conversation in a different direction, Aviwe…"

Aviwe interrupted Sive.

"Oh yeah, Miss Perfect! Do you think you're perfect, Sive? You're more confused and sick than perfect," she said, looking at her, ready to open her files.

Mihle was sitting quietly and ashamed. She knew all Aviwe said was the truth…but a bitter one. Although Mihle knew she meant nothing to Zuko, packing her bags and hitting the road was the hardest thing for her to do.

"Who said that I'm perfect?" Sive said in a low voice.

"You act as if you are," replied Aviwe.

Sive chuckled and said, "What's your problem? What is it with you and this whole attitude thing?"

"You're one of my problems, Sive. Do you think your virginity gives you the right to judge others?"

"Who did I judge? And which virginity are you talking about…the one Jonathan has taken?" Sive asked calmly.

"You slept with Jonathan, didn't you, Sive?"

"I don't owe you an explanation, Aviwe. What I do with my life is my business…"

"Get off my case, then!" Aviwe replied.

Sive tilted her head and looked at Aviwe.

"I know and you know that you enjoy toying with Sbongile's feelings. Can you please try not take your selfishness to the next level by marrying the man you know you don't have any love for? Please, be mature about this. What happens when you brought kids into that situation?" Aviwe was now becoming calm, trying reasoning. "Remember, we're friends, my dear friend. We know almost everything about each other, our strong and weak points. All I'm trying to say is this, give this some thought," said Sive.

Aviwe curled a soft smile on her lips.

"I hate to admit that you're right, and what I hate even more is that you are always right," she glanced between her friends and continued, "and I'm sorry for being a jerk."

"It's ok, girl. Arguing is not a symbol of a bad friendship," replied Sive, glancing between her friends. "Right, Mihle?" she continued. Mihle looked at Aviwe and then Sive.

And shrugged, "I don't know," she was still torn by the blades of truth.

Aviwe caught Sive's eyes.

"You haven't apologised to Mihle," she said, looking at Aviwe.

Although Aviwe knew that all she said was true, she turned to Mihle and cleared her throat.

"I'm so sorry, Mihle, for shouting at you. I shouldn't have done that…but what I said was true. And I hate it, I hate the way he treats you."

Sive smiled softly when Aviwe looked so worried.

Mihle forced a smile on her face.

"It's ok, Aviwe. Yelling and shouting is the only language I know…that's how we communicate in that house. Everything you just said was true." She then closed her eyes.

Soon, tears rolled down her cheeks.

She took her purse, opened it, put her hand in, and shuffled around for a tissue.

Aviwe noticed that she was looking for a tissue and took one out of her purse and gave it to her.

"Thanks," she said, sniffing.

Aviwe smiled.

Sive was listening. She didn't want to interrupt.

Mihle sniffed, "I'm not happy at all…and all the time, except when I'm with you guys, to the point that even my kids' noises drive me insane. I feel worthless," she said, sniffing, in tears, her body trembling in pain.

"Why don't you leave him? He doesn't deserve you," asked Aviwe.

"It's difficult to just pack up and leave with two kids. Who's going to marry a woman with two kids? And a woman who's as ugly as I am," she said, wiping her eyes with the back of her hand.

"Why do you think you're ugly?" Sive asked.

Mihle sighed. "Zuko tells me that daily, even my kids tease me about that sometimes."

"You can't believe everything he says, he just wants to drain out your self-esteem," said Sive.

"You just want to make me feel better. If he's lying, why then when we go out does every guy would want you or Aviwe? Not a single one wants me?"

Sive smiled.

"Let me tell you something, my dear friend. Decent guys go for decent women that they could build a serious relationship with, and there are very few decent guys out there. Those guys who are after us at those functions are only in it for a fling or a one night stand because we always wear revealing outfits. And dance like cheap prostitutes in a cheap brothel while you sit there decently, only moving your upper body to the beat," explained Sive.

"So, we're hoes?" asked Aviwe, laughing, trying to cheer up the atmosphere.

Sive moved her eyes from Aviwe to Mihle.

"If you feel the way you do about your relationship, what are you planning to do about it?"

"Nothing. I have two kids with him, and kids need to grow up with both parents," she said, trying to build up some confidence.

"Have you ever asked yourself why they say that?" asked Sive.

"Because they have to grow up the right way," replied Mihle.

"Do you think growing up in an environment where their parents lack respect for one another is the right way?" asked Sive, trying to show her that what she heard could be profitable if it could be done the right way. Poisonous if it's being done the wrong way.

Mihle took a deep pause before replying.

"No."

Her face was gaining another expression, a better one than before. She intended to give what Sive was about to say deep thought. She knew she was getting somewhere.

"Then why don't you do what's right for your kids?" asked Sive.

"What is it, Sive? What's the right thing for my kids in this situation?" She asked, looking confused.

"What do your motherly instincts tell you to do?" Sive asked.

Mihle shrugged, her eyes yearning for help.

Sive waited for Mihle to say something but she just shrugged.

"Kids are the foundation of the future. If a foundation is built wrong, the entire building will collapse and harm innocent lives. We always complain that the world is crazy, but we do nothing to make it better…instead we're contributing in making it worse. Exodus 20: 5-6, *I bring punishment to those who hate me and on their descendants down to the third and fourth generations. And I show my love to thousands of generations who love me and obey my laws.* That's the truth my dear friend…"

Aviwe interrupted with a laugh,

"Since when do you love the Bible?" Aviwe asked.

"And since when do I hate it?" replied Sive with another question, smiling.

"Oh please, give me a break, buddy. We all know that you hate the Bible, you always criticise it…"

Sive interrupted her, "Hold it right there, pal. When I disagree with you on something doesn't mean that I hate you. We just have different opinions on that particular matter. You see?" She replied.

"Hmmm, anyway…what does this whole God punishment thing have to do with Mihle's issue?"

Sive sighed and then took another sip of juice.

"As complicated as the bible could be, people are trying so hard to live their lives based on it although they lack the understanding of interpreting it the right way for its purpose…"

"The same bible you refer to as a person?" Aviwe asked, eyeing her naughtily.

"A good person," she corrected her, and then sipped her juice.

"Whatever, but you don't see it as many of us do."

"Of course, I'm not many of us…I'm Sive. My opinion should be different from anyone else's. Or, that would be contrary to the fact that we're unique," Sive replied.

"Carry on," said Aviwe smiling, making herself comfortable in her seat.

"Human beings were created by God with an innate knowledge of right and wrong. And humans used it to create a bible. The Bible can be used wrongly if the person reading it has lost his or her innate knowledge of right and wrong. Therefore, someone with an innate knowledge of right and wrong doesn't need the Bible," said Sive, looking at her friends.

Thandi was standing quietly at the beginning of the corridor that was situated behind them. She didn't want to interrupt them by showing herself. She was surprised and so impressed by what she was hearing. It was her first time experiencing the spiritual side of her daughter.

When Sive was young, she was active in all church activities to an extent that her mother thought she loved church. But when she gained her independence, she replaced church with community services. She paid her tithes in the community. Everyone loved her…she was a gift to many lives, someone that could bring sunshine on a rainy day. The smile she wore everyday said more than just a smile…an exact copy of her heart. Her good heart.

"How does this religious explanation answer my question, Sive?" Mihle asked, looking confused.

Aviwe eyed her to answer Mihle's question.

Sive smiled. "My point is, parents must be careful about the way they raise their kids. Raising them well includes protecting them from any form of abuse, as it could have a negative impact on their adulthood. Most people that go in and out of jail for all their lives, it's because of their parents. You see, a parent committed a foul, and a child has to pay.

"So, are you telling me that I'm a bad mother?" Mihle asked, looking sad.

"No. That's not what I mean. I know you're trying your best…just that your best is not good enough…"

"How Sive, how? I'm trying my best to be a good mother," said Mihle angrily.

"I know you are, but how do you think the situation at home could affect your kids? Do you think raising them with their father whom you fight like cats and dogs with is better than raising them alone, in a healthy environment? How do you think you could bond and love your kids when you're either moping or at the highest tip of your anger? Kids learn from their parents," explained Sive.

"Are you trying to tell me that my kids are the punishment from God?" She asked angrily.

"Not at all. They're the blessings from above. Some of the smartest and cutest kids on the planet, that I don't wanna see suffer in their adulthood because of early childhood exposure to domestic violence," she said tenderly, with a smile of love covering her face.

Aviwe's face was suddenly covered with a guilty expression. She felt like Sive was referring to her situation, that she turned out exactly like her mother. Sive noticed a sudden change on Aviwe's face. She just flashed her a smile and then both of them brought their eyes to Mihle.

Mihle covered her face with both hands. She pressed them hard to block the tears from falling.

Suddenly, her shoulders started shaking in pain. Sive was waiting for her to say something. She knew she had a lot to say.

Aviwe was touched to see her friend in so much pain. She moved closer to hold her, but Sive stopped her. Aviwe moved backwards and leaned back.

When Mihle was done wiping her face, Sive continued.

"When parents misbehave in life, kids pay the price. God is love, and He wants us to love one another. And when we don't, we wrong Him. We definitely hate Him. And if you hate God, you hate yourself. And if you hate yourself, you can't love others and that leads to living a miserable life. And your kids are more likely to follow that path. A criminal's child is more likely to become a criminal. By engaging yourself in wrong doings, you're punishing your own children. A child is an example of his or her own home. That's what Exodus 20.5-6 means, not that God will literally curse them. People believe that God curses the sinners, but, I personally don't believe that. Hate and love don't belong in the same room," explained Sive.

"What do I do now?" Mihle asked desperately.

"No one is going to tell you what to do, my dear friend. It's high time you listen to your mind, rather than what your heart tells you to do," said Sive.

Mihle sniffed once, and lifted her eyes to Sive and said, "I have two kids."

"I know, and that's the reason why you have to use your brain on this. You have other lives depending, counting on you," replied Sive.

"I need to think," said Mihle.

Sive was happy; at least there was hope.

Sive smiled, and then they all embraced. Her chin was resting on Mihle's shoulder, and her lips on her ear.

"I love you…with all my heart, my dear friend," Sive whispered.

Sive's words brought a little light into Mihle's dark soul.

Chapter 6

Sive got up.

"Guys, I'm going to take a shower," she said, stroking her hair backwards.

"Go," replied Aviwe, and then frowned, "And by the way, why are you, of all people, still in your pyjamas at this time of the day?"

'Isn't it you guys who glued me to this couch all day?" Sive replied, standing in front of them.

"Oh, please, do you know what time it was when we got here?" Sive's face extended in a smile. "It was already afternoon. And you were still in this," she said, waving her finger at Sive's outfit, "freaking outfit."

Sive looked at her, half smiling. She knew if she answered any further, it might reveal the reason why she was there. And that would include Jonathan's name that wasn't too pleasant in her ears.

She turned and walked away.

"What is it, Sive?" Asked Aviwe, sensing something wasn't right.

Sive stopped, her heartbeat increased. She also sensed that Aviwe was noticing, if not knowing, something. She turned. "What?"

"Why are you here?" Sive widened her eyes, pretending to be confused. "At your Mom's. You never said anything about visiting your mom." Aviwe squinted her eyes at Sive as if she was studying her. "Besides; you left us at the restaurant without giving us a good reason. And now you're in your pyjamas, past four in the afternoon…this isn't like you."

Mihle's face revealed a deep hunger for Sive's explanation. Thandi, on the other hand, froze with a snow-white tablecloth she was dressing the table with, stretching her ears to hear the reason why her daughter was there.

When Sive was glanced around, she realised that all eyes were on her. She bit her lower lip, cooking a strategy to escape the question.

"I agree with Aviwe, you're not yourself lately. You have never kept anything from us before. You're the most open person I know, with no secrets…"

Thandi interrupted,

"That's how I know my daughter, not someone with secrets."

Sive glanced at them once more. "I haven't changed a bit. Not keeping secrets, I'll tell you when the time is right. I need to talk to Jonathan first," she said, brushing her long, relaxed hair backwards with the palm of her hand.

"Oh, you will tell us when the time is right?" said Thandi, pulling the tablecloth straight on the table. "Which means, there's something to tell."

"That's not good enough, girl. We wanna know what's going on," said Aviwe.

"Let's allow her to tell us when she's ready," said Mihle.

"I agree with you," replied Thandi.

Sive smiled and disappeared into the corridor.

"Baby, be quick, I'm serving dinner shortly!" Thandi wailed from the kitchen.

"Ok, Mom," she replied. "Mom, can I use your cosmetic drawer?" she wailed from the bathroom.

"Ok, baby!"

Sive appeared from behind the corridor walls, looking so beautiful. She dressed in white shorts, white top and white sandals.

"Wow! You're glowing, girl. What's the occasion?" Aviwe asked in a wide smile.

"I'm having lunch with my three favourite ladies, and then chilling with my girls later at one of their places…"

"That sounds good…in fact, great," said Mihle smiling. "Aviwe's place is great.

"I guess yours is perfect, Mihle," said Sive.

"But the girls will interrupt us," replied Mihle, trying to keep them away from her house.

Sive smiled.

"That's the reason why your house is perfect for us to hang out in. Girls are part of our lives; we're mothers," Sive extend her smile even wider. "Remember, it takes a village to raise a kid."

Mihle smile nervously. Sive winked at Mihle,

"And I miss them a lot," she said.

"Girls, lunch is ready!" Thandi said.

The girls moved their eyes to Thandi as she was speaking.

"Ok, Mom, we're coming."

Thandi prepared broccoli, carrots, mash potato and grilled steak. She liked cooking for her daughter.

"Hmmm, what nice food, Mrs T!" said Mihle.

"Thanks, dear," replied Thandi smiling at her, enjoying the compliment.

Sive was deep in thought, staring at the white wall in front of her, chewing slowly. She was thinking about Gabriel, and she didn't know what to say to him. She had never stood him up ever since they'd started chatting. If she had missed his call, she would always call him back the first chance she got. And now, she hadn't returned his calls since yesterday and she missed their Facebook appointment.

"Don't kill yourself, we're all here," said Aviwe with a naughty smile.

Sive caught everyone's eyes on her, and quickly recalled Aviwe's words, and then a tender smile appeared on her sweet face.

"I'm just thinking," she said.

"Who else could you be thinking about, we are all here?" asked Mihle, putting a piece of steak in her mouth.

Thandi smiled and said, "Jonathan."

She lifted her eyes at Sive, "You have to fix things with him before some young lady gives him what you don't."

The girls exchanged glances.

"Give him what you don't?" whispered Aviwe, while Thandi wasn't looking.

Sive wanted to ask her mom what she wasn't giving Jonathan. She then realised that being inquisitive could bring up Jonathan's name and the relationship that didn't even exist. However, she wasn't lucky enough, as Mihle spilled out the question.

"What does she not give him?" Mihle ran her eyes between them, and then continued, "do you know something we don't, Mrs. T?"

"Sive arrived here at midnight, with her uncle. In sleepwear. Which means she didn't plan to spend the night here...what made her make that sudden decision?" said Thandi, trying to give them a picture that something was fishy.

"Maybe she..."

Thandi interrupted Mihle.

"And, Phiwe told me that when he got there, Sive and Jonathan looked like they were fighting."

"Why?" asked Aviwe, glancing between them.

Thandi shrugged.

44

"Guys, please. Stop talking about me as if I'm not even here," said Sive, wiping her hands with a table napkin.

"Wait till you have your own kids and see if you can sit back and watch when you smell a wet dog," said Thandi.

"Ok, Mom, I'm ok. No wet dog…no nothing. Just relax," replied Sive.

"You and Jonathan…"

"Yes. Jonathan and I. We're ok," she replied.

Thandi looked at Sive. "But I'm not saying you should compromise your values for him. If he loves you, he will wait till you're ready," clarified Thandi, rubbing her daughter's hand.

Sive was already fed up about this whole Jonathan thing, and wanted to elude the topic. She rose up in her seat and said, "Guys, we're done. Let's get going now," she said, clearing the table.

"Don't worry about this my baby, just go, I'll manage," said Thandi, rising up her seat.

Aviwe and Mihle rose up. Aviwe moved closer to Sive and whispered in her ear.

"You mean when Jonathan touches what he shouldn't, instead of saying no, you run to Mommy?" she said, when Thandi was busy clearing the table. Mihle heard Aviwe teasing Sive, and they both laughed. Thandi lifted her head, trying to catch up, but, unfortunately, it had already passed her.

When Thandi's eyes met theirs, the girls thanked her for the lunch, hugging her goodbye. Sive kissed her mother and then they walked towards the door.

Thandi took the dishes to the kitchen.

Suddenly, the doorbell rang.

Thandi looked around while going towards the door. She thought the girls forgot something. She opened the door. It was her brother. Smiling.

"Hi, are you getting married again, what's this big smile for?" asked Thandi, holding the door.

"Is it a crime to smile for my baby sis?" he asked.

"No! Not at all, big brother. It's a pleasure. Get inside. I miss you," she said, pulling his hand to get in.

"Wow, what's wrong? I was here last night. Don't make it sound like you haven't seen me in ages," he said, following his sister. They sat opposite each other.

"Yes," said Phiwe, staring at her.

45

"What?" asked Thandi, looking a bit confused.

Phiwe smiled. "I know you wanna tell me something, so go ahead," replied Phiwe, taking his cell phone out of his jeans pocket and placing it on the glass coffee table in front of them. He pulled his body backwards to relax.

Thandi stared at her brother for a while, trying to sort the words into the right order in her head to tell him that she was seeing someone.

"What is it, Thandi, is my niece getting married?" he asked, getting curious.

"No, it's not about her, it's about me."

"About you? What about you?"

Thandi didn't reply, she just stared at her brother. Phiwe raised her shoulders.

"Talk...what is it?"

"I'm seeing someone."

Phiwe couldn't help it. He burst out laughing, "You mean you have a boyfriend, Thandi?"

"Yes. Is there anything wrong with that?"

Phiwe shook his head, "No! I'm just surprised, that's all." He laughed. "I had never imagined you dating, you know?" He pursed his lips. "You came home with a little more than a month old beautiful baby girl. And the next thing you married a random guy from our church, which I'm still not sure whether it was an arranged marriage or what. But what I'm sure of- you didn't date the guy..."

"But he was a gentleman...wasn't he?"

"Sure, he was. And he loved my niece as if she was his own."

Thandi nodded.

"I know you didn't love him. But what I don't get is this: as beautiful as you are, why did you settle for someone you didn't even love?"

Thandi pursed her lips, "That's life."

"Well, a part of it that I don't understand," said Phiwe. "But I'm glad you finally found someone you really love. Sive is a big girl now. You did a remarkable job in raising her. She's a very special young woman. The man that will marry her will get the full package. She's everything a man is looking for in a woman. And more." He looked Thandi into her eyes. "But I hope that man won't be that Jonathan."

"Why you don't like this young man, you don't even know him?"

"Never mind," he said, knowing that Thandi wouldn't understand anyway.

Thandi pursed her lips and said, "Anyway, it wasn't our place to choose a man for her. Sive has a right to choose a man she wants to spend her life with. Our place is to support her."

"But…"

"No 'buts', Phiwe. We should let her make her own mistakes."

"I just don't trust that man."

Thandi stared at him. "Is that the reason why you're here?"

"No, yes…not exactly," he said, not knowing exactly what it was.

"Why are you here?"

"I noticed that something was wrong with my niece yesterday, so I came to find out if she's ok."

"She's ok."

"Did she tell you anything?"

"No, not exactly. But they are having problems…that I'm sure of." She pursed her lips. "Maybe it's not anything they can't solve," said Thandi.

"What if he forced himself on her?"

"No! It can't be that. Jonathan is wise enough to know that's a crime. Besides, Sive would've told me. I know her," she explained.

Phiwe chuckled. "Once things get beyond the boiling point below these young men's waist, they tend to forget about the law," he said.

Thandi looked thoughtful. "I don't think it has gone that far, maybe he was just pressuring her to do it. And that's when you came in…"

"And what if I didn't arrive when I did, what would've happened? Do you see what I'm trying to tell you?" Thandi blinked constantly, trying to see things from his perspective. "That boy is not good…mark my words, dear sis."

A short silence fell.

"I still don't think it was that bad," she said.

"If you say so. Maybe my suspicions about him are wrong." He paused, looking thoughtful. "But why hasn't she told even Sma about her new man, they share everything," he asked, looking confused.

"How's he, by the way?" she asked, dodging the subject. Phiwe knew she was escaping the topic, and let her.

"He's ok, and I'm proud of him. He's doing well at school…and thanks to Sive and that American doctor you met twenty-six years ago. His seed is a first grade otherwise it wouldn't have produced such a wonderful soul." They both laughed.

Suddenly, Phiwe's face got serious.

"If it wasn't for my niece, I would be a lonely man today, with no wife or son. I'm so ashamed that Sive, as little as she was, was the only person who understood the situation and had a solution to it at the same time. All we did was destroy our family, and she was always there to stick it back together."

There was a short silence, and then he continued. "I always remember her words." He chuckled. "If you loved your son like a parent should, your wife would still be alive. She has never had peace in her heart or restful nights after you had rejected your own blood. Her conscience, the Godly side of her, beat her till her body couldn't take it anymore…that's what she said, and she was right," he said, sadly.

"Sometimes she said things and I don't even know where she got them from. I experienced her spiritual side today, that I didn't even know she had," replied Thandi.

"Some people are gifted…You were telling me about your new man, Thandi," he said, trying to avoid the topic that was reminding him of his worst mistake.

Thandi extended her lips in a beautiful smile.

"I met him in Water Front. He's a lawyer; his office is in Sea Point…"

"Wow! He's a real *Ngamla*," said Phiwe, and they both laughed, "How long have you been together?"

"Six months now."

Phiwe widened his eyes. "Wow, that long! Why were you hiding it, is he married, cripple or something?" He asked, teasingly.

Thandi laughed. "No. He's handsome and single," she said.
Phiwe frowned at her to carry on.

"I'm hiding it from Sive, I'm not sure how she will react when she knows that I'm dating. She has never dated, I don't think she could understand," said Thandi.

"You have been a good example to her of how a woman should behave, and I'm proud of you for that. Now, it's time for you to be happy. Sive is a big girl and I hope she will be happy for you." He chuckled. "Just tell her that you found a man and get that poor guy out of the closet."

Thandi stared at him in disbelief. She didn't know that her brother could be supportive.

"Yes," he said looking at her, "and that could ring a bell for her to work towards a marriage. She's about that age now, we want *lobola*…fifteen cattle at R15, 000 each."

"What!"

"She's worth way more than that."

48

"Your niece will rot single," she said, laughing.

"Wait for her to find a man. I'll release her at that settlement…or more. She's a virgin…"

Thandi interrupted him, laughing. "If she still is…"

"I'll go to jail for murder. My niece won't lose it outside of marriage, I know that," he said, folding his hands into a fist ready to punch someone.

"And who will you kill, your niece?"

"The bastard that she lost it to."

Thandi laughed because she knew who that bastard was.

"Let's forget about the future and focus on the present," she said.

Phiwe interrupted her. "Are you and this secret lover of yours?"

"Hah, you sound like he's on your hit list, too," she said, smiling.

Which doesn't mean he's not. One mistake…his leg is broken," said Phiwe, and they both laughed.

"I'm serious, sis; no man can mess with you or my niece and get away with it."

Thandi laughed.

"Don't be over-protective my dear…"

"I'm not over-protective, I'm just a cautious big bro and uncle," they giggled again.

"Paranoid big bro and uncle suits you well," she replied, still laughing.

Phiwe's phone rang. He glanced at it and then said, "It's your nephew. Probably wants to borrow my car.

Thandi looked at her brother tenderly.

"How are you two coping with everything?"

"Good…I guess," he said, and then placed his phone back on the coffee table. He sighed and glanced at Thandi and then forward again. "He has a new boyfriend." He paused for a moment for Thandi to say something, but she was just staring at him to finish what he was saying. He, then continued, "I love him. He's my son, but I'm still trying to get my head around all this….man sleeping with another man. I'm trying to put myself in his situation, lying in bed next to another man, naked. Not to mention touching." He took another pause. "No! Without even including the Bible…it's just not normal," he said, opening his heart to his sister.

"Maybe it is just not normal to us since we share a different sexual orientation. Maybe they feel the same about us, who knows?" She raised her shoulders. "If he's happy, be happy for him," she said, trying to make her brother understand.

49

"I see," he said, rising up in his seat, picking up his phone from the coffee table. "Let me go sis, this boy needs this car to take out his boyfriend," he said, trying to get used to the fact that his son was dating another man.

"What did you come here for?" asked Thandi, getting up.

"I told you, to check up on my niece. I can't let anything happen to her. How could I solve the mysteries of this life without her?" he asked, walking to the door, followed by his sister.

"Send my love to my nephew," Thandi said.

Chapter 7

Aviwe parked her car in front of Mihle's house. The girls were talking, except Mihle. She was looking sad, probably because she didn't want them in her place. It was a grave for her secrets. It was Vegas…what happens there, stays there.

When they got into the house, Zuko was sitting on the couch, watching T.V with a bottle of wine. He just glanced at them and then took a sip from his glass. Sive and Aviwe placed themselves on the couch on either side of their dear friend who was feeling suffocated by their presence.

Zuko looked at Sive. "How are you Sive, my angel," he asked.

Sive was confused whether "my angel" was supposed to be in that sentence, or it mistakenly landed in there. While Sive was caught in the midst of confusion, Aviwe answered.

"Hah, my angel! I wonder, have you ever called your own woman that?" She asked angrily.

Zuko threw his eyes at her in an attempt to answer, but decided to ignore her and quickly withdrew his eyes from her and placed them back on Sive.

Sive's shorts revealed her sexy, smooth legs. The influence of alcohol in Zuko's sight made the view even more pleasant.

"I'm fine, thanks. Yourself?" She replied.

Aviwe was browsing her phone, preventing herself from losing it as usual when she was around Zuko.

Zuko and Aviwe didn't like each other. The way Zuko treated Mihle annoyed Aviwe, and Zuko was annoyed by how she stuck her nose in his business. They were always at each other's throats.

Sive, on the other hand, was the kind of friend who didn't like fighting her friends' battles, but wanted to empower them to fight their own battles. She had never taken sides. She always said, even a perpetrator is a victim who also needs help.

"I'm good, my dear. You look, sexy…as usual," he said, sipping his wine.

Sive's beautiful legs distracted Zuko to the extent that he seemed to forget that they belonged to his girlfriend's best friend. He rose up from his seat and went to the kitchen, and came back with three glasses of soft drink. He put them down in front of the women.

"Ladies, enjoy," he said, walking back to his seat.

"Thanks, Zuko," said Sive.

"You welcome, my dear," replied Zuko, placing his butt back on the couch.

Sive moved her eyes to Mihle.

"How're you feeling, Mimz?" she asked.

Suddenly, Bridgette and Simanye emerged from the corridor. Sive flew from the couch and landed on her knees on a floral floor rag in front of them. She opened her arms and accommodated them both.

The girls were so fond of her, she was like a second mother to them. Sive loved them as if they were her own. They buried themselves in her chest. Their little heads rested on either of her breasts, and their tiny adorable bodies were covered by her arms. They stayed there for a while, and came out in a beautiful smile extended from one ear to the other.

"We heard your voice, Aunt Sive," said Bridgette in her bubbly voice.

Bridgette was a bubbly kid who loved outdoor activities. Sive would take them out when she had time. She liked spending time with them. She was like family to them. Bridgette even listed her as a family when they asked about their family members at school. The love she had for them, no doubt, she was.

"We're hungry, Aunt Sive," said Smanye in her sharp voice.

Mihle glared at Zuko, secretly. She didn't want others to see that.

"What! Where have you been leaving your kids...?"

Zuko didn't even finish his sentence.

"You're their parent too, why didn't you feed your own kids?" Aviwe asked angrily.

"Aviwe..."

Sive interrupted Zuko. She noticed that he was angry and annoyed, and there was no way that what was going to come out of his mouth could be good for kids.

"Guys, please!" She said, shaking her head to sign them to stop.

"But, Sive..."

"Please," she said in a low voice.

Zuko looked at Sive, seeking for justice, and then brought his focus back to the television set in front of him.

Sive turned her eyes to Mihle and smiled.

"Can we use your kitchen, Mommy?" she asked.

"It's all yours, my angels," she replied, forcing a smile on her tight face.

"Thanks, Mommy," said Sive glancing at both of them, signing them to say it with her.

She rose up off the floor and held their hands, and went to the kitchen.

"I want egg bread," said Smanye on their way to the kitchen.

"Me too Auntie…and orange juice."

"Me too, orange juice," said Smanye.

"Ok guys, tell me what do we do before touching food?"

"We wash our hands with soup and dry them with clean towel," they replied.

Sive smiled. "That's my babies. Let's go clean our hands," she said, and headed for the kitchen sink. The two followed.

When they'd done eating, Sive took them out for an ice cream in a nearby pie shop. Sive knew exactly how to entertain them.

When Sive got back with the kids, the three were fighting. Zuko was pacing back and forth, swearing. Sive wasn't sure at first who he was referring to.

"Girls, go to your room. I'll be with you shortly," she said, walking them halfway. She quickly turned to the three.

"Guys, please. Keep it low." She glanced between them. "Why are you screaming at each other like this?" she asked, standing in front of them.

Zuko quickly swung to Aviwe's direction. "I'm sick and tired of this stupid bitch," he said, angrily pointing at Aviwe.

Aviwe looked at Sive, and then swung her eyes to Zuko.

"Who do you call a bitch?" She shouted at him, angrily.

"You Aviwe, you…"

Sive interrupted him. "Guys! Keep it down. What's wrong with you?" She turned to Mihle. "Why is she crying?" She said, pointing at Mihle.

"Hello! Do you even have to ask! This bastard is making our friend's life miserable," said Aviwe, angrily pointing at Zuko. "That's it! Mihle is coming with me," she added, rising up from her seat.

"You can take her, but my kids aren't going anywhere."

Sive was quiet, trying to figure out the nature of their argument.

"Who do you think you are, Aviwe? Have you already sorted out your own miserable life? I wish that poor guy had a woman like this one," he said, pointing at Sive, "not a slut like you."

Aviwe moved forward. "What did you just call me?" she said, hitting the oak coffee table in front of her with the palm of her hand.

"Guys! This isn't about you, please, try to hold your horses about the way you feel about each other," she said, trying to stop the argument between Aviwe and Zuko. "And Zuko is right, you can't live her life for her. You have yours, let Mihle handle hers," she said.

"Amen, Sive!" Zuko said, impressed.

Aviwe gaped at Sive astonishingly. "How could you take his side, he treats our...your friend like trash?" she said in a disappointed voice.

"It's not about taking sides...it's about doing what is right..."

"Doing what is right! What is right Sive?" Aviwe said, hitting the table, shouting at her. "She's not one of your projects, Sive, she's hurting...can't you see! The tears she's crying aren't the tears of joy...in case you haven't noticed," she said, annoyed by Sive's reaction.

"Please, don't fight over this." Mihle interrupted them, still sniffing back tears. "I know you are both trying to help, and you both always have been there for me. You're the only family I have in this world," she wiped her tears with her hands and continued, "I lied to you about who I am. I'm not the person I said I was." Everyone was listening very carefully. They didn't want to miss a bit of the latter information. Even the television noise seemed interrupting.

"Can I please switch it off?" whispered Sive, looking at Zuko, pointing to the television set.

Zuko nodded.

"I didn't come with my family here. I came alone," she cleared her throat, and continued, "I don't have any family...I have no one, except you," she cleared her throat again and rubbed the palms of her hands and locked her fingers together and carried on. "My mother left me with a friend and went to get a cigarette and was never seen again. The state placed me in a foster home. I slept with my former teacher for the bus fare to get here," she folded her hands, fighting back the tears, "And prior to that, I was a virgin. On my twentieth birthday, I found myself on a bus to Cape Town. I met a good-hearted woman on the bus who offered me a place to stay."

Mihle breathe a sigh of relief that she finally had courage to reveal the truth about her background.

Although Sive had sensed that Mihle had family issues, she had never thought it was that bad. She felt sorry for her.

Aviwe was so angry…and angry with Zuko that he mistreated an orphan…someone who has no one. She was trembling in anger.

Zuko was told the story, but it wasn't in detail, since he showed no interest when it was told.

"After three days I found a job at Shoprite in Belleville as a cashier. A week later, I moved in with my colleague who was from Mozambique. She was a very good friend, but she went back home for good." She sighed. "And then a few weeks later, I met…Zuko." She pressed a hand on her face, covering her eyes, blocking the tears from falling. However, one tear managed to escape, followed by another. She couldn't help it. She cried.

"I thought in time he would learn to love me…I wished."

"It's one of those wishes that would never come true," said Aviwe looking at Zuko, challenging him.

Mihle glanced at Aviwe, and then continued. "I pretended to be happy although I had never been. I can't even confront him even when I want to. I'm afraid he might leave me," she moved her eyes to Zuko, and then continued, "I couldn't imagine life without him," she sighed, "I spent all my life in fear. First, I was afraid to face the world alone. When I met someone I thought I could face the world with, I feared to lose him. I lived my life for him, I put him before anything and everything…including my kids. But it didn't do me any good, instead it brought me misery."

She chuckled.

"We take like months to have sex, and when we do it, it's not passionate. It's just a session for him to ejaculate…"

Aviwe cut in and burst out in a shrill voice. "How could you do that to yourself, your life?"

Mihle just glanced at her and then looked forward and continued talking.

"I love Zuko so much, but I know he doesn't, and he'd never loved me."

The tears welled up in her eyes…uncontrollably. Her whole body was trembling.

Mihle turned to Zuko. Sadness grew into anger with every word that came out of her mouth.

"How could you? How could you treat me like I'm nothing...the woman who carried your seed?"

Her voice rose up with an increase in anger. It was her first time confronting him about the way she felt...in eight full years.

"I did everything I thought a woman was supposed to do to make her man happy...but it was never good enough for you. I went from being a submissive woman to becoming your doormat. I'm just a sex object to you. When you don't have any other woman to sleep with, you turn to me...no matter how I feel. Without protection. But when I tested HIV positive...it was my fault..."

Zuko quickly cut in.

"Whose fault is that, Mihle? Who had been the prostitute here...me or you?" he asked bitterly.

"Do you have the nerve to even ask that stupid question? Do you really compare her single mistake to your whole life chasing women or is just your stupid strategy to switch the blame!"

"Stay out of it, Aviwe," Zuko said angrily. He knew that with Mihle's disclosure everything was obvious with his own HIV status. That made him nervous and shameful.

Aviwe glared at him.

"Where my friends are concerned, I'm definitely involved. You're such a heartless bastard...'

Sive interrupted Aviwe. "Enough Aviwe!"

"Sive, this man," pointing at Zuko, "is wrong...so wrong," she said, yearning for Sive's fair judgement on the matter.

"But two wrongs don't make a right," replied Sive.

Aviwe glared at Zuko and then placed her eyes on her phone.

Sive moved her eyes from Aviwe to Mihle who looked so terribly hurt. In that moment, Sive made a vow to herself that she would stand with Mihle throughout her dark storm.

When Sive realised that Mihle was done talking and now was her time to say something, she kneeled down before her. She held her hands and let them rest on Mihle's big thighs.

Sadness covered Sive's face, feeling Mihle's pain...deeply. She squeezed her hands showing some love before rubbing salt in her wound in order for it to heal.

Sive cleared her throat and said, "You are a very smart woman, Mihle..."

56

'Smart!" Mihle laughed sarcastically. "Please, don't try to make me feel better 'cause it's not working."

"I'm not…please hear me out," replied Sive, rubbing the back of her hand with her thumb to calm her down.

They were all silent, listening to Sive.

Aviwe swung her body to face Mihle with her back resting on the corner of the couch. Zuko was sitting still on the couch with a glass of wine in front of him that was tired of waiting.

"We all make mistakes, whether we were raised well or not…or we had everyone in our lives looking out for us. It's natural to make mistakes. It's ok to make them…"

Mihle interrupted her. "Don't patronise me, Sive! What mistake have you ever made, your life is perfect…spotless!"

"This is not about me Mihle, it's about you," said Sive.

"I want you to answer my question."

Sive paused, sighed and said, "The reason why my mistakes are not visible is because I have never been in a relationship. If I had, things would be different. But I will explain that later, if there is a need."

Everyone was interested in what Sive was about say. "Do you think if you had never dated your life would be this messy?" asked Sive.

Mihle looked at her for a moment, and then shook her head.

"So, when I said you are a smart girl, I didn't say it just to make you feel better…I meant it."

Mihle was becoming calmer now.

"You're a very strong and intelligent woman. You have built your life out of nothing, without any backups. Sleeping with that man in exchange for a bus ticket to where you thought you could better your future…wasn't bad. No one is supposed to judge you for that. You're better than I am. I have always had my mom. Without any doubt, you'll make a good wife to some good man… someday."

Aviwe nodded impressively.

Sive turned to Zuko, who was listening tentatively. "I'm not trying to say you're not a good man, Zuko."

Before Zuko could say anything, Aviwe burst out and said, "Of course he's not! If Zuko is not an example of a bad man, then what is a bad man?" Aviwe asked angrily.

"I don't know. Maybe that question would be answered by the end of this conversation," said Sive, and took her eyes off Aviwe and focused on Mihle and continued.

"You're not a child anymore, my dear friend. You're a mother. Your children's wellbeing depends on you." Sive smiled softly. "You should make peace with the past. You should let go of your hurt and resentment. Forgive your mom for abandoning you. Forgive Zuko for treating you the way he did. And forgive yourself for all the wrong choices you have ever made that brought you pain..."

Aviwe interrupted her. "This is not some Dr Phil show, Sive! Where everything is done according to a book...this is real life. And in the real world people don't just forgive and forget just like that," she said, snapping her fingers.

Mihle moved her eyes from Aviwe to Sive.

"How could I forgive someone who has ruined my life?" she asked in a low voice fighting back the tears, demanding answers.

Aviwe bulged out her eyes at Sive demanding an answer, too.

"When you forgive someone, you don't do it for them. You do it for yourself..."

"And you want the perpetrator to get away?

"What good could you gain from vengeance?" asked Sive.

"To make them pay for their cruelty," replied Aviwe.

"Honey, the one who holds the grudge is the one who suffers the most. Resentment is a self-torture. The past can't hurt unless you hold on to it." Sive moved her eyes away from Aviwe and placed them on Mihle. "Let it go."

"Why did she dump me like a piece of trash? What kind of mother does that?" Mihle asked, her eyes glittering with tears.

Sive softly rubbed her thigh with the palm of her hand. "Baby girl, we can't judge her. We don't know her reasons, what she was going through at that particular time..."

"It doesn't matter what her reasons were... they won't justify what she did. Abandoning a four-year old child...what mother does that?" She said sadly.

"At least promise me that you'll think about it," said Sive, smiling.

Mihle just looked at her thoughtfully and then looked away.

"Are you trying to say she must carry on living with this monster?" Aviwe asked, hatefully pointing at Zuko.

"That's neither my decision nor yours to make, but Mihle's. Besides, they are both to be blamed. They both wronged their kids for bringing them into this situation," said Sive, looking at Aviwe who was looking at her incredulously.

"No, no Sive, you're being ridiculous now." She moved forward to view Sive closer. She thought Sive was losing it.

"There's a victim and a perpetrator here. Mihle's a victim, and you know that. Why do you punish her by blaming her for being abused?" Aviwe asked angrily, looking straight into Sive's eyes.

"I'm not punishing her. I'm only trying to make her see where she went wrong…"

"By taking the enemy's side?"

"I'm not taking any sides. Until you let go of this unnecessary anger, you can't be helpful to her. All it does is cloud your judgement," said Sive.

"Even a fool can see who's wronged who here."

"This situation has passed a point of who's wrong and reached the point of why and how he or she was wronged."

"Why would we ignore that point, because that's where the problem started?" asked Aviwe.

"That's your mistake…in fact, everyone's. We always think the question of who was wrong is the root of the problem while it is most of the time only the outcome of what has been done wrong in the first place."

Sive collected Mihle's hands and held them on Mihle's thighs. At this point, Aviwe's inquisition was declining.

Zuko had never expected that Sive could speak the way she did. He thought everyone would see him as the monster Aviwe said he was.

Being stuck in a loveless relationship ruined Zuko's life, too.

"What's the root of this problem?" Aviwe asked.

"Lust and the wrong usage of sex," she replied.

"Go on," said Aviwe.

"Mihle's main reason of sleeping with Zuko was to have the family she never had. Zuko, on the other hand, wanted to feed his lust. They never had a common goal…now, who do you blame?" Sive replied.

Zuko looked at Aviwe, yearning to hear her reply to Sive's question, but instead she replied with another question.

"Is it wrong to sleep with someone to create that kind of relationship?" Aviwe asked.

"Yes, it is."

"How?" Aviwe asked.

"It doesn't always have a happy ending when we use sex in exchange for something, including love. We need to be ready before we could have sexual intercourse with our partners. Having sex with someone in order to get something is technically prostitution, and you can't have peace and fulfilment in that. When we do something wrong, we know it through our conscience, and it always repeatedly reminds us until it destroys us."

Sive paused and had eye contact with Mihle. She felt a change in the tension in her hands as she was holding them.

Mihle's mind was absorbing every word Sive said for later review.

"Still not clear,' said Aviwe.

"Sex is a spiritual thing, something beautiful, sacred and can't be used filthy because it can fight back and ruin lives," she explained.

"I'm listening," said Mihle, in a low voice after she had been quiet for a while.

"Honey, you know that I love you…wholeheartedly. And I would never do or say anything just to hurt you." Sive started like that, and Mihle nodded.

'I know," she agreed.

"In my narrow understanding of relationships, you should have done things differently."

"I know I should have. Although I don't know how," she replied in a shaky voice.

"You should've started by making peace with your past."

"I was afraid to be alone…and I still am," Mihle replied.

"Life revolves around fear and love. It's natural to be afraid, but you don't have to make bad choices because of fear."

"Can I go back and correct my mistakes now?" Mihle asked.

"It is possible to make things right, but I can't tell you what to do," replied Sive.

Aviwe was boiling in anger at this point when Mihle didn't know what to do when there's only one thing to do…leaving that looser. However, she kept her opinion to herself, as she was afraid of Sive's reaction.

Sive turned to Zuko, still holding Mihle's hands and said, "You can't turn women into objects, Zuko. That's what you're implying by feeding your lust with them."

"I know I was wrong and I'm paying for that. Do you think I wanted my life to be like this?" he asked.

"What do you mean, Zuko? 'Cause you can stop what you're doing to her," asked Aviwe.

Zuko glanced at Aviwe and then placed his eyes back on Sive. "I thought I would have a family with someone I truly love. This situation is killing me, too. And all you've said makes sense."

"How could you be so heartless…?"

Mihle interrupted Aviwe. "Why didn't you ask me how could I be so careless with my life?" Mihle's eyes glittered with unshed tears. Aviwe didn't know what to say. She just gaped at her.

"Sive is right about everything she said. I had been blaming Zuko for this situation as if I've done nothing wrong. We were both wrong about the decisions we made, and now we're suffering…so are our kids," said Mihle.

"And what are you guys going to do now?" asked Sive. They both said nothing. "It's you guys who could come up with a solution that could be best for everyone involved," added Sive.

"Sive, I have thought about it over and over again but instead of coming up with a solution I just get deeper into the mist of my confusion," explained Zuko.

"Kids need to be raised in an environment filled with love and compassion. How can that be achieved if their parents can't stand each other?" Sive shrugged. "You have to consider them in your decision," she added.

"Thanks, Sive for not judging me. I've always known that you're a good person, but what I saw today made me put a stamp on it. I had never thought you could pass a fair judgement on the matter that involves your friend as a victim," said Zuko, impressively.

Mihle smiled and said, "Thanks my friend."

They hugged each other. Aviwe joined the embrace to comfort her friend.

Zuko was left alone on his seat and Sive was touched. She went to hug him. They released the embrace.

"Thanks, Sive. It means a lot," he said.

Sive exchanged glances between Aviwe and Zuko,

"I wish you guys could get along for the sake of the kids. If we could make a big happy family no matter what Zuko and Mihle's decision could be, it would have a great impact on raising these kids," she said.

"That sounds perfect to me," said Zuko.

"I agree," replied Mihle.

Aviwe looked away.

Sive glanced at the watch on the wall in front of her. It was 19:32. She was supposed to meet Jonathan at her place at 20:30 and had plans to call Gabriel and apologise for standing him up the previous night. Although she knew her man was a patient and an understanding man, she didn't want to take an advantage of that.

Sive got up. "Guys, I have to run. I'm meeting someone in less than an hour," she said, tucking her hands into her shorts pockets.

"Let me guess..."

Sive interrupted Aviwe.

"Oh please, don't guess."

"Starts with a J."

"Why do you keep your relationship a secret?" Mihle asked, looking much better now.

"Yes, I'm dating. But, I'll tell you all about it when the time is right," she replied.

"We already know that part. Have you already...you know?" asked Aviwe.

Sive laughed.

"No, I haven't."

Aviwe frowned sillily at her.

"But how come you know about these things?" asked Mihle.

"I'm an adult, Mihle. My virginity doesn't make me any less of that," she replied.

"Are you ok, girl?" Aviwe asked teasingly.

"I'm okay and healthy, and if you must know, yes...I get horny at times. However, I'm abstaining from sex until the right time. I wanna share that special moment with someone I'll grow grey hair with," said Sive.

"Have you forgotten that you already have grey hair, you fool?" Aviwe said.

They all laughed.

"These are only the signs of wisdom," replied Mihle.

"I always heard them saying that but as from today, I agree with them," said Zuko.

"I guess that holds some truth in it, look at people like Thabo Mbeki, Mrs. Jake. Those people are the people that inspire me…"

Aviwe interrupted Mihle.

"Whoa guys, those are the old folks, they deserve grey hair."

They all laughed.

"My mom said Mr Mbeki is always had grey hair. I'm not sure about the other one," replied Sive, and they continued laughing, "Aviwe, take me home, girl. I really have to go home now."

"As if you have someone waiting for you at home," said Aviwe.

"What if I do?"

"I'll take that as a yes," said Mihle.

"Whatever," replied Sive, laughing.

"Do you know that you still owe us the Malawi story?" Mihle asked.

"Hmmm, I'm bad debt lately. I guess we should go on a weekend getaway, all of us, so I can have enough time to settle all my debts," suggested Sive.

"That would be lovely. I guess I need that…a lot," said Mihle, extending a smile on her face.

Aviwe frowned at Sive. "And, who's all of us?" she asked, thinking that Sive would spoil a perfect plan by tagging Zuko along.

A smile lurked behind Zuko's eyes; he also thought that he was included. Although Zuko had a woman that made him forget about his messed up life, Sive was the woman that turned him on. He knew she was the stars, if not the sun to him.

"Us, and the kids," replied Sive.

Aviwe silently released a sigh of relief. Zuko quickly grabbed the glass of wine on the coffee table and went to the kitchen. He felt that the disappointment was written on his face and he didn't want them to see it.

Aviwe bulged out her eyes.

"Don't you think the girls will spoil the fun?" she asked.

"Guys, don't worry about the girls. They will be fully mine. I'll take care of them. Kids need to clear their little minds, too," Sive promised.

Aviwe put her hand on her waist and said, "I agree and I believe you, but…you'll be like, we can't say that in front of the kids," she said, imitating Sive's voice. "Do you think that's not gonna spoil the purpose?" She added.

"Not at all. Kids go to sleep early. We can have an adult talk in their absence. I want them there, if it's ok with both parents," replied Sive, glancing at Mihle and then Zuko who was standing with his back against the table in the kitchen…listening.

"Fine by me," he replied from the kitchen.

"I hope that's not the wine speaking, dude," answered Sive, pulling his leg.

Zuko and Sive laughed while Mihle and Aviwe just smiled.

"I don't have more than two glasses of wine a day," he replied.

"That's good," said Sive, and then brought her attention back to her friends.

Aviwe stared at Sive mischievously. "I'll call Jonathan to be ready to give you a baby tonight."

"Oh, please! Not now girl. I'm relying on Sive with my kids right now," she turned to Sive, "Please girl, just wait for me to pull myself together before you have your own child," said Mihle.

Sive smiled tenderly, imagining herself pregnant with Gabriel's baby.

"Just make sure that you do that fast," said Sive, blinking her eyes naughtily. Aviwe and Mihle bulged out their eyes.

"Are you planning to have a baby?" They both asked at once.

"Not just a baby…"

"Babies?" Asked both, surprised.

"No silly, a family," replied Sive confidently.

"Wow, has he proposed?" Mihle asked anxiously.

Sive laughed, and said, "Do you even need a proposal when you're in love?"

"Huh, please don't end up where I am, dear," said Mihle sadly.

Sive patted her shoulder. "Don't worry my friend, I won't," she grinned sillily at her friends. "Just pray for it not to end up like the Malawi story," she laughed, and walked into the corridor to kiss the kids goodbye.

Sive stopped and turned to Mihle before she could disappear into the corridor.

"Oh Mimz, let me go back to what you said earlier, about pulling yourself together. That's the spirit. I'm proud of you, girl. And I know you can do it," she said, and then disappeared.

Chapter 8

"I left my phone here," she murmured confused, pointing to the couch that had nothing except a True Love magazine on it. She nervously lifted up the magazine, but nothing. She stood there in front of the couch, trying to think.

"I'm not mistaken; it was here on the couch. I threw my phone here when I went to put the glass in the kitchen," she thought.

Sive was still standing there trying to figure out where the phone could have gone.

The doorbell rang. She went to answer it. To her surprise, her phone was in Jonathan's hand.

Quickly, Sive's mind told her exactly what had happened. The anger she saw on Jonathan's face made her realise how hurtful Gabriel was.

Suddenly, her heart was throbbing at the thought of hearing his sad, disappointed voice.

"Oh my God," she murmured.

"Don't even mention God's name after all the devil work you've been doing behind my back..."

"Devil's work!" she snapped.

"You preach love everywhere you go...I don't think people know how cruel you can be, you are such a hypocrite!"

"What!"

"A filthy hypocrite."

Sive sighed deeply and looked away. "Here we go again," she murmured.

Jonathan sighed. "How could you break my heart like this?" He said sadly. "I love you with all my heart...and there's no man that can take you away from me, even that Gabriel. Do you hear me?" he said angrily.

"Can we please sit down?" she said, turning around and placing her buttocks on the edge of the couch. Despite all of her emotions, she tried to be civil. Jonathan walked around the couch to sit next to her. Sive's phone was still in his hand.

"Do you love this guy?"

"I do."

"What about me…us?" he asked sorrowfully.

The pain in his voice touched Sive's heart, but she decided to be strong and bring him back to reality.

"What about us? We're nothing but friends, Jonno," she replied.

"Come on, Sive! Everyone knows that we're together. We love each other…Why would you wanna spoil that for some crazy Nigerian idiot!" he said bitterly.

"I love that idiot," she replied softly.

"Have you told your mom and your friends that you love another man, not me?"

"No. They think…"

"Because you know that we belong together," he said confidently.

"Jonathan, we're not together. I'm with Gabriel, not you. I love Gabriel, not you."

Each time she mentioned Gabriel's name, her ego asked her about Chikondi.

Jonathan calmed himself down. "I know you're not used to these things. I know you feel comfortable with him, 'cause he's miles away and I'm here. You think I will put you under pressure to do things you're not ready for," he moved closer to her and held her hand, and continued, "I'll never hurt you in any way. Please believe me. And don't let me lose you, please baby," he pleaded.

"I love you so much, but I'm not in love with you. I'm in love with another man. I'm sorry, Jonno. I didn't mean to break your heart, but…"

"You just did," he replied sadly.

Sive tilted her head at him.

"We can always be friends, even if I'm with Gabriel…"

"If you want me to throw up, say that again," he said, closing the small gap between them.

Thinking of last night's incident, Sive glanced behind her to see if there was more space to move a few inches away from Jonathan. She didn't want to end up on the floor with him on top of her. Like last night.

"Why do you hate him so much?" she asked.

Jonathan didn't reply.

"Did you talk to him last night?" she asked, praying for the answer to be no.

Unfortunately, the prayer wasn't answered…or wasn't even heard.

Jonathan looked at her face as if he was studying it. "Of course we did. We had a long talk and he promised to stay away from you. However, I don't trust him...not one bit.

"What did you say to him?"

There was an awkward silence.

"Oh please, don't tell me you intimidated him," she asked nervously.

"I did what a man does when some fool tries to steal his woman..."

"Oh please, I'm not your woman," she said annoyingly.

Jonathan studied her pretty face again. "Sive, you're my future wife. You'll end up with me. Not that fool."

He sounded so certain.

Sive was so tired of repeating herself like a broken record. She decided to zip her mouth. She nervously wiped her face and then brushed her hair backwards with both hands, revealing her pretty face. She gaped with her eyes closed trying to put her emotions back in shape. She felt the warmth of Jonathan's lips against hers.

Sive opened her eyes. He was kissing her. She tried to move away from him, but she ended up in the same spot as last night. Jonathan in between her legs and she couldn't fight him anymore.

A kiss wouldn't harm that much after all. She let it happen. When Jonathan noticed that Sive stopped fighting him, he thought she had come to her senses.

He licked her soft lips, gently. He then moved his head a bit up to look at her, looking for confirmation to carry on.

"Are you done?"

That was the response he got from her.

"Come on Sive, what harm could a kiss do?" he asked.

"It will give you the wrong impression."

"About?"

"Us?" Sive replied, trying to get up but Jonathan pressed her against the floor. She stopped fighting.

"What do you want from me?" she asked.

"All of you. I want you to be my wife...mother of my three kids. And I know you will be," he said confidently.

"Jonathan please, stop!" She screamed at him, angrily.

Jonathan got up on his feet and offered her a hand to get up. She ignored him, got up, and went to the kitchen just to get away from this sick man's sight. Her phone rang. Her heart was throbbing as she was walking to get it on the couch, next to Jonathan. She stretched her arm to get it. Jonathan grabbed it.

"No, don't answer his calls, by doing so you'll be giving him false hopes," he said, holding her arm.

"Wake up, Jonathan! You're giving yourself false hope. I love him. Not you," she said, very annoyed.

In silence, Jonathan rose up from his seat and slipped her phone in his jeans' pocket. "I don't think it's a good idea for you to have your phone now," he said, and started walking to the door.

"You leave that door with my phone I will have to report you to my uncle," she said angrily.

Jonathan stopped once she mentioned her investigator uncle. He didn't want to get the investigator suspicious or his plan to make Sive his could be ruined.

He turned around and forced a smile on his face as he was pushing his hand in his jeans' pocket. He took out the phone and gave it to Sive.

"I know I can trust you, my love," he said as she was taking the phone.

Sive wanted to scream when he said my love, but she didn't want to do anything that could keep him in the house any longer than he already was.

He then walked out of the door.

Sive quickly closed the door behind him. She pressed her back against the door as she blew out a long sigh of relief. She raised up her phone and smiled at it.

She chuckled.

"My uncle's name works magic. I'll use it all the time to break the spell. Look, I got you back," she said to her phone, throwing herself on the couch.

She went straight to Facebook. She thought texting Gabriel could be much better than calling him and hearing his voice.

Sive was so disappointed in herself and she couldn't imagine how disappointed Gabriel was. She was sure that Gabriel was looking at her differently now after what Jonathan had told him.

Although Gabriel didn't know how Sive looked, the connection between them was getting stronger and stronger each day.

Gabriel knew by heart that Sive was the only one for him. She was his strength when he was weak. Hearing her voice in the morning was fuel enough to keep him going throughout the day in a foreign land.

Sive had only one image of herself on her Facebook profile. How beautiful she looked on it convinced Gabriel that it was just a picture of some supermodel. Sive on the other hand knew exactly how her man looked…and he was handsome in her eyes. The only thing left for them was to meet in person and make it official.

Sive put her laptop on her lap and logged in on Facebook. She went straight to messages. She froze in front of it as she saw Gabriel's name written in bold black.

She thought Gabriel blocked her because of whatever lies Jonathan told him. Another part of her just couldn't believe that Gabriel could actually do that without confronting her. She quickly went to her blocked list… there he was.

"How could you, Jonathan?" She murmured.

Sive, suddenly, got thirsty. She went to the kitchen to get herself something to drink. She went back to sit on the couch and called Gabriel.

When his name appeared on the screen, her heart started to pound. She ended the call and threw the phone on the couch. She put her laptop on her lap and unblocked Gabriel and sent him a message.

"Hi babe," she started.

"Hi."

"How are you today?"

"Who's this?" Gabriel asked.

"It's me babes, Sive."

"How am I supposed to know if you're really who you say you are?" he then logged off.

"Baby, it's me. Please believe me," she pleaded.

When she was waiting for him to reply, her phone rang. It was him, and she couldn't run away anymore.

Sive sighed deeply, and then picked it up. "Could you please tell me what's going on in your life?" he asked coldly.

"I have a stalker, baby."

"Stalker!"

"Yes, my colleague is obsessed with me."

A short silence.

"But how did a colleague end up with your phone?"

"He stole it."

"How? You're not telling me everything, Sive. After he called me and told me that you're his woman and you are planning your future, your phone was switched off as if your plans were really in motion…what do you have me thinking, Sive?" He said in a sad voice.

"Baby, I know it doesn't look good at all…but it's not what it looks like. I love you, with my whole heart. Not him. You have to believe me," she explained.

"You don't know how much I wanna believe you, but it's difficult based on what he told me," he said sadly.

"Baby please, do. I love you. Only you."

Her cyclical 'I love you' accelerated Gabriel's heartbeat until it reached a level where he regained a trust in her.

Another silence.

"I do," he said.

"Really!" she replied happily.

"I do trust you, and I love you so much, Sive. Please don't break my heart."

"I won't break it. I'll melt both of our hearts into fine molecules of liquid," she said smiling tenderly at the other end of the line.

"Honey, that's the same thing…or even worse," he said laughing.

"You don't get it my love, do you? I wanna rebuild a new, bigger heart to accommodate all of our interests to weather the storms throughout our lives. I wanna love you like I gave birth to you, Gabriel," she explained.

Gabriel got emotional. Tears of joy he couldn't hide. They rolled down his cheeks. Although they say men don't cry, obviously, women have the power to have that rule broken.

Gabriel sniffed back tears to break the silence that fell at the end of Sive's words.

"Baby, are you alright?" she asked, concerned.

"Yes mama, I'm ok. And I haven't felt this good since my mom died…and it's been a long time." The knock on the door interrupted him. "Babes, someone is at the door. Just a sec." He walked towards the door wiping his tears with his hand.

"Hey man. How's it going?" He greeted his friend, James.

"I'm…" James stared at Gabriel. "Hey man, what's up? Have you been crying?" asked James, concerned. He thought it was the police officers who always harassed the Nigerians in Johannesburg, accusing them of dealing drugs.

"Me?" Gabriel asked, embarrassed.

"No, the fool with red crying eyes behind you," Gabriel turned around. "You, of course! Who else is in the room?"

Gabriel signed him to hold on, and then put the phone back to his ear.

"I'm sorry babes, I have to go. My friend James is here, I'll call you later, my love."

"It's ok babe, we will talk tomorrow. I also need a warm bath and a deep sleep".

"Tomorrow then, sweet dreams my love," said Gabriel, kissing the phone.

"Sweet dreams *Sanalam*," she replied, happily.

"And what does that mean?" he asked, smiling.

"Means my baby, in my language," she explained.

"That's lovely. I hope you'll teach me more of your language when we meet," they both laughed. "Love you, and good night."

"Love you more. Good night, baby," she said, putting the phone down.

Gabriel turned and looked at his friend.

"Oh please, don't tell me this terrible look on your face and your acting weird lately is because of that phantom girlfriend of yours," said James, staring at his friend.

Gabriel turned and walked towards a fridge.

"How about a beer?" He asked as he swung open a fridge door.

"Do you know what time is it now?"

Gabriel looked at his wrist, but it was clean. He stared at his friend to tell him what time it was.

James glanced at his cell phone.

"22:45, who drinks at that time?" He frowned at him. "Wait a minute, why do you even have that stuff in your fridge, you hardly use it?" He asked.

"What?"

James shook his head.

"This phantom of yours is not only wetting your eyes, messing with your mind too."

"Eish man," he said, slipping his hands in his jeans pockets and looking at him thoughtfully.

Although Gabriel was still standing by the fridge and James not far from the door, they were not standing far from one another.

Gabriel lived in a bachelor flat, on the fourth floor. It was painted sky blue. When you entered through the door, his bathroom was situated on your right with a white door that matches the ceiling. Then the kitchen area with a bachelor fridge and a small dark brown built-in kitchen cupboard that has a small counter with two red bar chairs. There was a black stove situated in the middle of the cupboard. At the end of the cupboard, there was a wardrobe in the same colour as the cupboard. It served as a wall that separated the kitchen and the bedroom area.

On the wall opposite the door there was a big window with a comfortable windowsill to sit on. Below the window, there was a two-seater black couch. His double bed with a dark headboard was situated between the couch and the wardrobe with its length against the wardrobe and the couch.

"Come on, man. Say something," said James, trying so hard not to laugh. When he saw his friend trying to explain but nothing came out of his mouth except the movement of his lips, he burst out laughing.

"Oh boy, you have to live a little. Step out of your dream world," he laughed, and shook his head like a little boy as he walked to sit on the couch.

"You don't understand my friend, I adore that woman…"

"Adore! Do you even know the meaning of the word?" James laughed. "Who do you adore…a woman you don't even know or even how she looks?" said James, sitting on the couch.

"Come sit next to papa boy, and let me tell you what you need," said James, who was two years younger than Gabriel was.

"I know what I want," he murmured, walking towards the couch. He threw himself carelessly on the couch.

"I don't care how much you think you love that phantom. I have some parties lining up for this weekend." He smiles mischievously. "I'm talking about real babes, nigga. And, we're going."

Gabriel scratched his bald head. And then looked at his friend and said, "I love her, bro."

"Has it crossed your mind that this…what's her name?"

"Sive."

"Yeah, that. Could be the ugliest woman on the planet?"

"Who cares about looks with a woman like her? She's what a real man looks for."

"Well, I'm glad I'm not a real man. Falling for these social media psychos."

72

"Sive's special, man. And I feel her deep in my bones."

James twisted a naughty smile on his lips. "She's your missing rib, man?"

"That's what I'm talking about, man." They both laughed.

"But don't forget what Adam's rib did to him."

"What did she do?"

"Drove him away from God," replied James, and they shared a giggle.

"My angel won't do that."

"Let's forget about your ugly, desperate psycho."

"Ugly or not, I love her," he said, throwing a piece of paper that was in his pocket at him.

James laughed, picked it up and unfolded it, ironed the creases with his fingers and read it. He looked at Gabriel and then laughed.

"Don't tell me that you have paid this much just to change your linen for that phantom. Maybe she's fooling…"

"Gees man, I got this piece of paper from Thembi. She wrote someone's contact details for me…look at the back, you fool."

They both laughed.

Silence fell.

Suddenly, Gabriel was caught in deep thoughts about his phantom. James cleared his throat to break the silence.

"We're going, right?"

"Where?"

"To the party."

"Yeah," he agreed, scratching his bald head.

"You might find some hotty."

Gabriel glanced around, pretending he was thinking his friend was talking to someone else.

"Me!" He laughed and continued, "I'm not a fine guy, remember? Even girls considered as plain in this country make a fool of me. All they want is my money and to be their sex machine. I also want a woman, like you and other guys of my age man. If Sive is a fake, however, it worth a try," he said sadly.

"That's why I want us to go out more often so we can expand your options. The bigger the sea, the more the fishes," said James.

"And sharks," added Gabriel.

They both laughed

"You have to come with a partner to Ajay's birthday party." He smiled. "But don't worry, I'll organise some fine chick for you."

"Hello Mr Organiser! You said you have three parties lined up for this weekend. Can't we choose one that doesn't require a partner?"

James cleared his throat. "I was just playing big my friend, we only have one, Ajay's birthday party," he replied in a mischievous smile.

Gabriel laughed, shaking his head.

"Organise that damn chick, because I'm coming."

"That's my boy," replied James, patting his shoulder.

"Can we go to Sandton to buy something that might attract those damn chicks?"

"Your word is my command, Sir. Saturday at nine am, I'll be knocking at your door," said James happily.

Gabriel smiled. "Thanks, man."

"Anytime, boy," he replied, rising up from his seat and heading for the door.

"What made you to drop by at this time?" Gabriel asked.

"You were acting weird today, so I came to check if my homeboy was ok. If I knew it was because of that phantom I wouldn't have bothered," he said laughing, walking out of the door. "See you man!" he wailed.

"Thanks man," Gabriel wailed back, locking the door.

He turned and leaned against the door on his back, looking up. His mind was, once again, invaded by Sive. He agreed to James that he would go with some random woman to their friend's birthday party. However, he knew he wouldn't cross the line with her.

"Sive, Sive, Sive. You are the core of my happiness…who are you?" he murmured as he was making his way to his bed, unbuttoning his shirt.

Chapter 9

Jonathan saw Sive's car entering the clinic. He waited for her by his black Jeep. Sive wasn't in the mood for Jonathan's twisted mind; she pretended to be busy in her car just to avoid him.

Did that work?

No! The crazy Jonathan waited for her with a smile that extended from one ear to the other. The smile got brighter as he saw her approaching him.

"Good morning, my love," He said cheerfully.

"Good morning, my dear colleague," she replied, as did not want to entertain his craziness anymore.

"How are you, my love?"

"I'm fine. Yourself?"

"I'm good. How could I not be when I started my day by seeing my favourite woman," he replied with ecstasy.

Sive didn't reply.

"You look gorgeous, baby."

Sive ran her eyes all over herself, trying to see what Jonathan was talking about. She was in her casual blue jeans, white sweater and black flat pumps.

She glanced at him.

"What's gorgeous about jeans and a sweater?" she asked, as they were walking into a hallway facing her office.

"I mean you…your face, you're glowing." Jonathan's beaming face quickly converted into a sad, long face. "Did that punk call you?"

Sive greeted her patients with a divine smile and flatly ignored Jonathan. She went into her office and Jonathan followed her in. She placed her handbag on her desk and turned to Jonathan.

"What is it Jonathan? I want to work."

Jonathan browsed at his wrist. "We still have seven minutes," he replied.

"Ok. Say what do you have to say so I can…"

"You didn't answer my question, sweetheart."

"What question?"

"Did that loser entertain you last night?"

Sive walked past him to the door. She swung it open as wide as it allowed her to.

"Get out of my office, Jonathan!" she said feistily, trying to scare Jonathan since she knew he didn't want the public to see the reality about them.

"I didn't mean to make you angry, sweetheart…"

"Out, Jonathan!" She cried. Her voice interacted with the passing of Michelle, and she stopped.

"Is everything alright guys?" she asked with a note of sarcasm in her voice.

Michelle wanted Jonathan for herself and wished that what people had been saying about Jonathan and Sive wasn't true.

"I want him out of my office," replied Sive.

"I won't go until she's answered my question," replied Jonathan.

Michelle looked at the receptionist dropping off patients' folders for Dr. Tikolo, and then glanced between the two and pulled Jonathan out of Sive's office.

"You heard the lady. Come with me."

"This conversation isn't over," said Jonathan, leaving with Michelle.

Sive called out for her first patient.

***

After work, before Sive visited Mihle, she went straight to the shelter to drop off some food she had collected for them.

Gabriel preoccupied her mind as she was driving. She loved him to the extent that she would laugh alone when she found herself in such thoughts. Although her feelings for Chikondi were still alive, she loved Gabriel.

Sive was content with her life, with who she was and what she was doing was making her happy. Helping people was her calling. Her humbleness made it easy for her to develop a friendship with everyone. A light soul anyone could connect with, and she wasn't afraid to make mistakes in life. She knew she wasn't flawless.

When Sive got to Mihle's house, the whole house was dark. She knocked, rubbing the cold off her arms. She glanced around, doubting if there was someone in the house. She knocked repeatedly, but no response.

"Anybody home!" She wailed. Still no reply.

Sive took out her mobile phone from her handbag and when she was about to press the first digit of Mihle's phone number, her phone rang. It was Jonathan.

"Hi," she answered.

"Hi babe, where are you? I've been..."

"I'm visiting a friend."

"Who, Aviwe or Mihle?" He asked curiously.

"It doesn't matter who."

"It does to me! Do you want that jerk to take your virginity and then go home; he's a foreigner for crying out loud."

Jonathan's obsession was escalating each day. He knew Sive would be his. Rain or no rain.

"Come home, I'm waiting for you and it's been long," he commanded.

"Jonathan, this is my virginity. Not yours. And I'll give it to whoever I want...but definitely not you," she replied, annoyed.

"Baby..."

"Bye, Jonathan!" she said dropping the phone.

Sive let out a long sigh of relief and put her eyes back on the phone to dial Mihle's number.

It rang again. She broke the tightness on her face from Jonathan's stressful conversation with a wide smile that covered her face.

"Good evening, my love," she said warmly as if she wasn't recovering from an annoying conversation.

"Hey honey, I miss you so terribly," he said happily.

"I miss you always, baby."

"Are you walking?"

"No, I'm standing at my friend's door, but I guess she went out."

Suddenly, a door opened. Sive lifted up her eyes to see who it was...it was Mihle, looking terrible.

"Baby, we'll talk when I get home. Love you."

Gabriel didn't even have time to reply; Sive hanged up the phone and turned to Mihle.

"What's wrong, my friend?" she asked, flipping the light on.

"If I had no kids," short silence, "I would've been buried a long time ago."

Another silence.

"It has never been easy for me here on earth," she added.

"What now, darling?"

"But I can't let my kids go through what I went through. I know how it like is to be all alone in this world."

"That's the spirit!"

"What spirit is it when you feel so weak and pathetic?" asked Mihle, her eyes glittered with unshed tears.

"At least you have something to hold on to. Save your kids from the misery of growing up without a mother. Just be strong for them."

"My kids have almost no one. They have no aunt, no uncle, no grandmother…and I'm not trusting Zuko to put them before his fun," she said gloomily.

"I'm their aunt," replied Sive, stroking her back. Mihle moved her head to look at her.

"I know. But I meant blood family."

"Honey, a family is not only approved by DNA, but deep love and connection. What if Bridgette is not your biological child? Something had happened at birth and you came home with someone else's child? Would the fact that you don't share the same DNA make you stop being her mother?"

Mihle shook her head.

Sive raised her shoulders.

"You see, your kids do have an aunt…me."

Mihle smiled.

"I know you're my everything, Sive. The sister that I have never had, the family that I never had, the friend that I never had. Please don't think I'm ungrateful…I'm too grateful for everything you've been to me. My strength, my eyes when I couldn't see, my light throughout the darkest tunnels of my life, my mentor."

Mihle couldn't hold back the tears anymore. "I don't know why you're not a priest," she added, breaking a smile on her miserable face.

"I don't like the feeling of being jailed up; the religious norms would give me that feeling. I like to be free in the world. I belong to the world." She shrugged. "Besides, what priests go clubbing?"

"As if you do that frequently."

"Even if I seldom do, I still do and priests don't."

"I see."

"But you didn't tell me why you're in this state," said Sive.

"I bet you don't wanna know."

"I do."

Mihle sighed deeply. "It's the same old story. My relationship is over."

"I thought you already knew that."

"Me too, until last night."

Sive bulged out her eyes at her to carry on.

"After you guys left, we had a conversation that could've turned into an ugly argument if I wasn't tired of fighting. I had never known Zuko could be that cruel to his own kids."

"What happened? What did he say?" Sive asked nervously.

"He wants us out by the end of the month. And I won't let him get away with this; I'm taking him to court…"

"I don't get it…how could he want you on the street?" she asked, confused.

Mihle shrugged.

"How did he put it? Did he say, 'I want you and the kids out by the end of the month?' What did he say exactly?"

"He told me he wants his house and he's going to buy us a Wendy house and place it in his aunt's back yard for me and the kids…a shack, Sive! So, his kids are only worth being raised in a shack to him while he lives in a nice house with some hoe?" she asked angrily.

"Calm down, dear."

"How! How can I calm down when Zuko wants to screw up my life like this?" She shook her buttocks making herself comfortable in her seat. "This is South Africa, maybe he's forgotten that. Thabo Mbeki said if you've been living with a man for more than three years, you're husband and wife…"

"I'm not a lawyer, nor into law that much, but I guess you should think it over. Going to court could be an extra burden on your existing misery…maybe you should compromise on this…"

"Compromise! Or let him walk all over me?"

"This guy is gonna buy a Wendy house that costs about R20 000 and go negotiate a place to put it and then pay child support."

Mihle was surprised how Sive knew what Zuko said. The way Sive put it made Mihle certain that when she told her she'd already known.

Mihle looked at Sive for a while, surprisingly. She then shook off the dirty thoughts that had crept into her mind. Now, she was thinking Sive could be the other woman.

It's human nature. When we hurt, we distrust others and push away those who care most about us. Where do you think that leaves us? In a deep, dark, sorrow grave.

"Why do you always take his side?" she asked.

"Open your mind, Mihle; I'm trying to help you here. I'm not taking any sides. Take a deep breath and think long and hard about this, don't make impulsive decisions. If staying with Zuko is getting more awkward, you can move in with me until he's got you a new place."

"You mean a shack!"

Sive told herself that she would pass that.

"Where are my girls?" she asked, smiling.

"Sleeping," she replied coldly.

Sive noticed that her friend was in the spirit to fight with her. She decided to cut the visit short.

Although Sive liked controversial topics, she didn't like fighting.

Sive hugged her friend goodbye,

"When you need me, you know where to find me. I've got to go now," she said rising up.

***

Sive closed her eyes and leaned backwards, facing up when she saw Jonathan's Jeep in front of her house.

"This is getting out of hand now," she murmured before pushing her car door open.

She got out of her car and walked confidently towards Jonathan's car to sort him out. She noticed before she reached his car that he wasn't alone. She quickly turned back to her car.

Jonathan quickly got out and ran after her and held her delicate arm. He gently turned her around to reach her other arm and gently pulled her towards him. He whispered,

"Please, don't embarrass me, he's my friend and he wants to see you."

Sive glanced at her watch. It was five minutes to eight. "At this hour, Jonathan? I need to rest, I have work."

"We won't stay long, I promise," he pleaded.

Sive blinked once and again, and then nodded.

Jonathan jogged back to his car and came back with his friend.

"This is Gerald, my friend. Gerald this is Sive, my girlfriend."

Sive smiled and extended her arm.

"Nice meeting you, Gerald," she said, shaking hands.

"Nice meeting you too, Sive."

Jonathan helped her with grocery bags to the house.

"Lovely name. My dad was Gerald, but he died shortly after my birth," said Sive.

"I'm sorry, I didn't intend to open old wounds..."

"Don't worry. It's ok. I don't even know him," she replied, opening the door.

They went inside.

"Take a seat," said Sive to Gerald, pointing to a brown leather three-seater couch that was standing confidently against a cream white wall. It was facing a dark brown entertainment unit that held a big flat screen T.V.

Behind the couch there was a big window running from ceiling to a laminated floor. A portrait of African indigenous people, about a metre squared situated on the wall opposite the door. There was a big red pot plant with big green leaves placed neatly in the corner by the T.V.

Sive and Jonathan went into the kitchen to drop the grocery bags.

"Gerald, what would you like to drink?" she wailed from the kitchen.

"Tea, please."

Sive shifted her attention to Jonathan, eyeing him for a reply.

"Sive, can I please sleep over tonight, I'll behave. I can even sleep in the other room," he pleaded.

"Jonathan, tea or coffee?" she asked pretending she didn't hear what he said.

"Please, baby," he insisted.

Sive glared at him. "Jonathan, we aren't lovers."

Gerald's entrance into the room interrupted her.

"May I have a glass of water, please?" Gerald said.

Sive smiled and got him water.

"Thanks, Sive," he replied in a cheerful smile that made Jonathan uncomfortable.

Sive made two cups, tea for Gerald and coffee for Jonathan. Jonathan glanced at his cup and stared at Sive.

"Coffee babe, after eight in the evening?"

"You didn't answer when I asked."

"It's ok, I'll drink it. But once I can't sleep I'll call you to keep me company," replied Jonathan, following Gerald to sit in front of TV. Generations, Sive's favourite show, was almost finished.

Sive placed herself in the middle of the couch with the guys on either side.

Gerald was a tall, dark well-built young man. He was in black jeans and a long sleeve white sweater.

Sive liked dark-skinned guys, and Jonathan was out of her league.

Gerald glanced around.

"You have a beautiful place, Sive."

"Thanks Gerald, I like simple things," she replied.

"That will stop once we get married. I'll spoil you rotten, a queen should be treated as such," said Jonathan, inviting himself into the conversation.

"Oh, you're planning to marry, too? That's nice, you'll make a cute couple," said Gerald.

"Yes. We can't date forever. We need to settle down and start a family, you know," he turned to Sive, "Right, baby?"

That was her cue to leave the room. She didn't want to embarrass Jonathan in front of his friend, and at the same time she didn't want to give him the wrong impression.

She quickly got up and went to grab her car keys from the kitchen counter.

"Where are you going babe?" Jonathan asked surprisingly.

"I have to get the car in the garage while you are still here guys, I don't wanna be out of the house alone after ten pm," she replied, nervously rushing out of the door.

"I agree, it's not safe for pretty faces like you to be out at night," he wailed behind her.

Gerald noticed that there was something weird about this couple. However, he thought maybe it was just his imagination. He moved his eyes from the door where Sive disappeared to Jonathan next to him.

"You have a really cute woman, Jonno," he complimented.

"Yeah, and that's why I won't let any man steal her from me."

"Is there anyone who might?"

"Yeah, some fool she met on Facebook."

"Is it a serious thing or just some harmless flirt?"

82

"No, it's serious. That fool is so into my woman, you know."

"You should warn Sive about these guys. What if this dude is some psycho who's after hurting young women?"

"That's what I'm thinking, man," said Jonathan.

Sive got in, rubbing her arms from the cold.

"Baby, put something warm on, it's cold," said Jonathan.

"I'm gonna take a shower and then cover myself in my warm pyjamas and watch Muvhango and then go to bed," she said, leaving out what she wanted to do more than anything…chat with the psycho.

"Oh baby, I promised you we wouldn't stay long," said Jonathan rising up from the couch, and turned to Gerald. "Let's get going man."

Gerald got up.

"Oh, by the way babe, we were talking about that Facebook psycho who's stalking you."

Sive glared at Jonathan.

"Social media is not safe anymore since there are crazy guys who try hurting girls," explained Gerald.

"Thanks, guys, for your concern, but I got this," she said.

"But…"

"Good night, Jonno," she said pushing Jonathan to the door.

They walked out, and she remained standing by the door.

"Lovely night guys," she said as they were walking to Jonathan's car.

"Good night, Sive!" Gerald called back.

Jonathan was quiet, feeling jealous.

Sive locked the door and then ran into the shower. She wanted to be available when Gabriel called to tell her to log in on Facebook. She quickly dried herself with a pink towel. She then put on a pair of summer pyjamas and a warm winter gown because it was a bit cold that evening.

When she started curling up on her couch, Muvhango came up on SABC 2. Then, her phone rang on a couch next to her…and it was Gabriel. Jonathan didn't steal it this time.

"Hey, honey," said Gabriel cheerfully.

"Hi baby," she replied happily.

"How are you, my love?" asked Gabriel.

"I'm fine, just missing you so much," she replied

The sound of it made Gabriel's heart throb with joy. Any man would be pleased to hear that he's been missed by the woman who stole his heart.

"And I've been missing you too. And how I wish I could see you and hold you," said Gabriel sincerely.

"That's what I've been thinking about since that Saturday incident."

"And?" He asked anxiously.

"And, I thought it would be nice if we could meet this weekend."

"You mean, this weekend!"

"Yes. I can leave here on Friday after work and spend the whole weekend with you, my love," explained Sive.

Gabriel put the phone on his chest and murmured a three-word prayer as he was lying on his back on the bed.

"Thank you, Lord."

Then the silence made Sive nervous, thinking that maybe she was moving too fast for his liking.

"What's wrong, baby? If you don't like the idea we can…"

"Don't like what? Are you kidding me? Baby, I'm thrilled! And thanks so much for trusting me honey."

"You're welcome."

"I'll buy you a plane ticket tomorrow and get myself together, ready to meet my queen…I'm so ecstatic," he said cheerfully.

"You mean you have some coasts that needed to be cleared by saying you'll get yourself together?" She said, sounding jealous.

"No babe. When I said there's no one except you who owns my heart, I meant every word."

"What did you mean exactly by what you said just then?"

"I just meant I need to be prepared for your arrival."

"Ok."

"Please baby, don't spoil my wonderful evening. I don't want you to be upset my love."

"I'm ok baby. Don't worry."

"Smile for me," said Gabriel.

Sive laughed.

"That's my girl."

"What're you doing, baby?" she asked.

84

"In bed baby girl, chatting with my wife. And you?"

"On the couch, in front of a blank TV screen, chatting with my handsome hubby."

"Why a blank screen, is it broken?"

"No, not broken. But who could let a TV interrupt when speaking with a hubby?"

"Do you love me that much, Sive?" he asked, her sweet words touched him.

Gabriel'd never been called husband by any woman before or given the respect he was getting from Sive. And that's why he didn't care about Sive's looks. All he fell in love with was her heart…her inner beauty.

"I love you more than you could ever imagine, and I'm glad you allowed me to come. I'll be a good girl."

"Giving your hubby all he needs?"

"Yes baby, all he needs."

"That's my girl."

In his mind, Gabriel thought about sexual entertainment. He knew Sive was a mother of a two-year-old boy whose father was dead. And she wasn't staying with her baby like most girls in South Africa. They don't stay with their first or all of their kids. They let their mothers raise them if they were born out of wedlock. Therefore, he had never even thought that she was a virgin.

Gabriel knew that if you want to impress women in South Africa you have to be sure of your game between the sheets, and how to dirty your pockets or you will kiss that relationship goodbye. He wanted to score all the points this time.

"When did you last call to find out about your son?" He asked.

"This afternoon."

"That's great. I would love to meet him too, soon," he said warmly. He didn't know that the boy was born to some woman and a man whom he shared Sive's heart with.

Although Sive loved Gabriel, she still had intense feelings for Chikondi. She had always had the feeling of wanting to go back to Malawi.

Malawi felt like her second home in her heart and it felt like she had unfinished business in that country.

Chapter 10

It was hard for Sive to accept that Chikondi was only her past.

"Definitely, you will when the time is right," she said with her fingers crossed. She didn't want to tell him all about her previous relationship yet…if it was considered a relationship at all.

"I wish you could love me the way I love you, Sive," he said with a perception of fear in his voice.

"Where is that coming from now, baby?"

"Fear."

"What fear, baby?"

"It just feels so good to be true," he said.

Sive laughed.

"If you could know how crazy I am about you, you would be relaxed."

"You are?" he asked anxiously.

"Yes, baby."

"What if you don't like me when you see me?"

"I don't think that could happen."

"What if my looks don't meet your expectations?"

"I love you, and that won't change, not over looks."

"I love you so much, and I don't wanna lose you."

"You won't."

"Baby can I ask you something?"

Sive's heart started pounding. She didn't want him to ask any further questions about the baby. But, she had to allow him to ask.

"Anything, baby," she said bravely.

"Would you settle down with a foreigner?"

"Baby, my heart knows nothing about foreigner, race. What it knows, is the beautiful people God created…so yes, I can."

"So, will you marry me?"

"That's my wish, if you could be my ideal guy."

"And, what's your ideal man?"

"I won't tell you. I just want you to be yourself, not to strive to be what you're not just to impress me."

"That's so unfair! What if I do all the things that annoy you?"

"That will mean we're not compatible partners."

"And don't you think it's a bit unfair?

"Not at all. What I think is unfair is when you strive to be who you're not just to fit into someone else's life…"

"What if that someone is your life?"

"If you have to change who you are, then, they're not your life."

"What's it then?"

"Application for a miserable life."

"How?"

"How long do you think you could put up with an act before your true colours appear? Do you think you could be happy pretending to be who you are not for the rest of your life?"

"I get what you mean honey, and I didn't mean I wanted to fake my personality, no. That's not who I am. I'm a very honest person when it comes to my personality."

"That's my boy." She yawned. "Eish, baby I'm tired. I want to sleep. Can we talk tomorrow?"

"Ok my love. I want to sleep, too. And I'm looking forward to meeting you, honey."

"Sure, we meet on Friday…sweet dreams babe."

"Good night, sweetheart," he said, kissing the phone.

Sive dropped the phone, smiling.

***

It was Wednesday. Two days before the internet love birds would meet. Sive didn't tell anyone about her trip to the city of gold, because she wasn't ready for their questions. Her plan was to meet them on Thursday, after work. Now, she was driving to see her uncle after a call that he wanted to see her.

Sive was a dog with two tails all week. The thought of visiting Johannesburg had thrilled her heart as if it was her first time visiting the city.

When Sive's mother was working in Johannesburg as a nurse, she had a friend who had a daughter, Sive's age. Her name was Lisa.

Sive would spend her school holidays in Johannesburg with Lisa's family. She made good friends with Lisa. She stopped visiting them when Lisa went to study in the UK. They still communicated on Facebook.

When Lisa got back she got married, and they last saw each other at her wedding just a little over month ago.

Sive had called Lisa to meet her at the O.R Tambo Airport on Friday evening. She told her the whole story and that she wanted her to be there in case something went wrong.

Simamkele opened the door. Sive smiled.

They hugged.

"How are you, cuz?" She asked, moving away from his arms.

"I'm ok. You?"

"Great."

Sive tapped his shoulder as she was walking towards her uncle who was sitting on the couch, reading a newspaper.

There was a guy about Sma's age busy in the kitchen, washing dishes. Sive waved to him and then focused on her uncle.

"Hi uncle," she said, taking a seat next to him.

"Hi *mtshana,*" he replied, not looking good at all.

"You don't look good. Is everything ok?" She said exchanging glances between the young men.

"I'm ok. But, there's something that I think we should discuss."

"Ok," said Sive with a concerned look.

"Your cousin," he eyed Smamkele who was standing in front of them, waiting to ask Sive if he could get her anything. "He wants to drop out of university and go to the US for something that has to do with his AIDS..."

"HIV," Sma corrected him.

"That's the same thing," said her Uncle, bored.

"Don't you approve of it?" Sive asked.

"Not at all. Why can't he be like you...doing things the right way?"

"What right way do I do things, Uncle?" asked Sive.

"You have finished school and you have a job. Your mom is proud of you...in fact, we all are..."

Smamkele interrupted him.

"You mean you're not proud of me, Dad?" he asked angrily.

Sive exchanged glances between them.

"I love you Sma, but..."

"But what dad! That I'm not like other people. Of course I'm not like you, Sive or any other person. This is my life you're talking about, which you know nothing about. I'm living with HIV, Dad. The sooner you accept it the better. I'm going to this HIV/AIDS awareness conference in US. I can finish my studies next year," said Smamkele, angrily.

Everyone was quiet, listening to Sma.

The young man in the kitchen was leaning against a cupboard, listening. He was aware that Sma's father wasn't happy with him staying there, and he had been staying with them for almost two weeks now.

"Life is not all about you and your feelings, Sma. Have you ever thought about me...my feelings in your decision making? No!" he folded the newspaper, threw it on the floor, and made himself comfortable in his seat for the long argument coming.

Sive was quiet, listening to both of them to understand what they were fighting about since Sma interrupted her uncle when he was trying to address the issue.

"Your sexual orientation is strange in this family and when I'm trying to adjust myself to this new experience, you start making things difficult..."

"How Dad...how?"

"I'm a Christian..."

"So?"

"Please Sma, let me finish."

Sma moved backwards to sit on the couch behind him.

"People talk. My son is gay, and he's living with another man under my roof. And now, you don't want to finish your studies to be independent," he said.

"So, you want me out?"

Sive intervened before her uncle answered.

"I don't see anything wrong with Sma's decision, Uncle. Sma is different from all of us..."

"Because of his strange sexuality?" he asked annoyingly.

"Because of everything that makes him who he is and that has an influence on how he does things. His journey to success doesn't have to be like anyone else's. Maybe not going to the US could be an obstacle to his success. Besides that, he needs to understand HIV/AIDS if he wants to live well with it."

Sive looked at Sma, leaving her uncle with a reasoning face.

"Uncle has a point. If one wants to live well with others, they should consider their feelings. Whether one's sexual orientation is gay or straight, they still have to respect their culture and parents. In our culture, we don't live with boyfriends or girlfriend under one roof as our parents. And you know your sexuality is rare…"

"You mean abnormal!" snapped Sma.

"Please, don't put words in my mouth, Sma. If you think abnormal is the best word to describe it, that's on you…"

"My Dad just said it now, in front of us."

"Said what!" Sive asked.

"That my sexual orientation is strange."

"Yes. That's a fact Sma," Sive replied.

"A fact!" Sma exclaimed.

"Yes Sma. Anything that is out of one's nature is strange to them. But it doesn't give us the right not to accept each other's differences," she replied.

Silence fell, and then Sive continued.

"There are fewer gay people than straight ones, and that, together with the Bible concept on the matter, makes people believe that homosexuality is a sin and a curse to the family and an insult to God. It's the same as when a family gave birth to a disabled child, they think they are being punished by God for the sins they had committed. Some feel so ashamed that they keep them away from the rest of the world, because disabled kids look different from the rest of the kids. All we need is to teach each other to tolerate each other's differences. God created man in different forms so they can understand one another…"

"What do you mean, created in different forms?" asked Uncle.

"Can we please go back to that later Uncle, if it isn't answered by the end of this conversation?" said Sive and then continued, "All I'm trying to say is that it's unfair to expect heterosexuals not to find homosexuality strange, and vice versa. Still, both have to tolerate one another." Sive looked around, and continued.

"If the Creator wanted us to be the same, there won't be any different races, humans with different body types, colour tones, etc. on earth…"

"What's your point mtshana?" Phiwe asked.

"My point is, we have to respect God's creation…"

"What's God's creation about Smamkele dropping out of school and sleeping with another man under my roof, mtshana?"

90

"I stated earlier that what he's doing in your house is unacceptable. He's causing you pain in your own house. If Sma wants to live in your house, he has to respect your rules. But, he's entitled to make his own decisions about his own life."

Sive moved her eyes back to Smamkele.

"When are you planning to leave for the US?"

"Saturday."

"You mean, this weekend?" she asked, realising that she wasn't going to be around when he leaves. Postponing her trip to the city of gold was not an option. She decided to say her goodbyes on Thursday.

"Yes. And I thought Owam could stay here till he found a place of his own…" Phiwe interrupted Sma.

"Do you hear what I just said? Smamkele doesn't care about my feelings, now he's…"

"Don't worry Dad, he's moving out."

"But Sma, you have to know your boundaries, boy," said Sive.

"I'm sorry, I realise my mistakes now," said Sma ruefully.

"You're apologising to the wrong person, dude." She pointed with her head to her Uncle. "You should be apologising to him," she added, cracking that magical smile of hers on her face, and continued, "It would be great if you guys could make peace before Sma leaves."

A silence fell.

"I've viewed Sma's decision from a negative angle. But now I see some good in it," he placed his eyes on Sive, "And you're right, *mtshana,* Sma is a man…but not in my house…"

"Definitely not in your house, old man," agreed Sive.

They all burst out laughing, except for Owam, probably distracted by the news that he only had two days to find a place to stay.

Phiwe continued, "It's hard to be a parent in a world where everyone is busy with other people's business. They force you to try so hard to be perfect until you find yourself drawn into the deepest depth of your imperfection. I didn't mean to be mean to you. I was just trying to be a good father. And you have my support, all the way my boy."

"That's my Uncle!" said Sive hugging him, "I know you're trying old man," she added.

"If you could see me chasing those criminals at work, you would call me young man."

They laughed again.

Owam didn't find it funny. He turned to the dishes and started drying them.

Owam was a nice, bubbly person with a sense of humour, but feisty. That night, that character was gone. He had a lot on his mind.

"But my son, you have to find your boyfriend a place to stay in two days…"

"Don't worry my cuz, a friend of yours is a friend of mine…Your friend can move in with me until he finds a place of his own."

"Really?" said Owam surprisingly.

Everyone looked at Owam. He was so happy, his eyes sparkling with joy.

"Yes. You can come with me, right now if you want," she replied.

Owam signed Sma to follow him to the bedroom. He hanged both of his arms on Sma's shoulders. He smiled and said, "Baby, I think it is a good idea if I could leave tonight and leave you alone with your daddy so you could repair your relationship before you go overseas. We can see each other every day during the day," he suggested.

Smamkele and Owam had been dating for almost a year now. They were so in love.

Smamkele agreed with his man and started helping him pack his stuff.

"You know that I love you, right?" Sma asked, folding a pink beach towel.

"With all your heart, yes."

"Exactly," confirmed Sma, wrapping the towel around his waist. He pulled him closer to him and stroked his face and then kissed him, "I'll be away for only few months, baby."

"I know love, but don't make it sound as if six months is nothing."

"Let's hurry up, I don't want to keep my cousin waiting," said Sma.

"She looks like a good person," said Owan, zipping his luggage.

"She's a great person, and very wise like an old woman who'd been through a lot in her life when she's only a twenty-five year old virgin…"

"Did you say, virgin?" Owam asked, surprised.

"Yes, a virgin," repeated Sma.

"A beautiful chick like that!" exclaimed Owam, pointing to the wall that separated the room and the hallway.

"Yeah. Do you see how perfect she is? I feel insulted when I am compared to her 'cause I'll never be that good," he kissed Owam who was standing puzzled in front of him. Holding his big, red bag. "But she's the one who understands human imperfection more than anyone," he said, taking the luggage from Owam and pulling it out of the room to the living room.

Owam was right behind him, in a pink and grey tracksuit top.

Phiwe and his lovely niece were chatting, laughing about criminals at his work.

A sharp pain hit Phiwe's heart when Owam emerged with his luggage, ready to go. He blamed himself for being harsh and heartless towards a boy who needed a place to live.

"Ready to go already?" asked Sive with a bubbly smile, looking at Owam and then quickly turned to her uncle and said, patting his shoulder, "Have a restful night, young man."

They all laughed.

"I always do after talking to you, and this night won't be any different. You're the best niece an uncle could ever ask for…"

"And the best cousin a cousin could ever ask for," Sma completed his daddy's sentence.

Sive rose up and walked two or three feet and stood in front of Smamkele.

"Go out there, baby cuz, and make us proud. You're the best…Do you know that?"

"Baby cuz… seriously, Sive! Are you aware that you are only a year and nine months older than me?"

"Still, that makes me a big sis, doesn't it?"

"Oh yeah, you win."

"My win is my cue to leave." She looked at Owam and tapped his luggage. "Dude, let's go."

"Sure," replied Owam, handling his luggage. Before taking his first step, Phiwe cleared his throat.

"I don't hate you Owam, my child, I hope you know that."

"I understand, Uncle. Don't worry, and I'm sorry for putting you in an awkward situation. What we did was wrong and against our culture of respecting elders like she," he pointed at Sive with his head, "said earlier…"

"That's exactly why I love you," Sma burst out.

"That…is against our culture of respecting elders, too. We're not supposed to express our love for our lovers in front of our parents," said Sive, pulling her cousin's leg.

They all looked at Sma and laughed.

"Sive, get out," said Smamkele jokingly.

Sive started walking towards the door with a wide smile on her face. Owam was behind her.

"Owam!" Phiwe intercepted him, "Thank you for your apology."

Owam nodded, and then continued walking.

Chapter 11

Sive and Owam got home after eight. She showed Owam around the house, and all the rooms had something in common…space. They were all spacious, and neat.

Sive showed him his room. It had a double bed covered in snow-white linen, with a dark built-in headboard. Each pedestal held bedside lamps. There was a dark brown built-in wardrobe with silver handles and a brown wooden-frame mirror on the wall by the door.

"This is your room, Owam."

He gaped at her. "Yours or mine?" he asked.

"Yours."

"Thanks…This is amazing!" He quickly took out his phone and called Sma. "Just booked-in; into a five-star hotel, babes." Sma laughed. Before he could say anything, "I'll call you later babes when I'm relaxed…in my suite," said Owam, and cut the call.

Sive was smiling waiting for him to finish.

Owam looked at Sive. "You have a cosy house, Sive," he complimented, rolling his eyes.

"Thanks," replied Sive. "Let me leave you to settle in. I'll be in my room if you need me, taking a shower," she said, disappearing behind the door, then quickly reappeared, thinking Owam might be hungry. "I didn't cook, if you're hungry there's a green salad and a chicken breast in the fridge," she said, leaning against a doorframe.

"I'm hungry but I'm not a goat, I can't eat leaves. I want to eat goat itself, not what goats eat."

They both laughed.

"You're funny. Well, you can look for the goat in the fridge and cook it…and please feel at home," she said and then disappeared.

Sive didn't cook; she had little time to cook in her busy life. If it wasn't work, it would be her chores at the children's home or at the shelter for homeless people or spending time with her friends or family. Now, there was an addition to her life, Gabriel. When she cooked, she cooked food that could last more than just a day.

Sive had a green salad and a chicken breast in her fridge. It wasn't enough for two, and since Owam didn't want it, she would have it for supper after a shower.

***

Bridgette heard the sound of Aviwe's car. She ran to open the door, hoping that it was Sive.

Aviwe went inside.

"Is Aunt Sive with you, Aunt..."

"Go to your room, Bridgette!" Mihle snapped at her daughter, "And she's not your aunt, do you hear me!" she said angrily.

Bridgette went to her room. She took her doll and slowly brushed its hair.

Aviwe brought her eyes back from where Bridgette had disappeared and placed them on Mihle's miserable face as she was sitting next to her.

"What is it, Mimz?"

"Everything."

"What's everything, girl?" asked Aviwe, stroking her back, just like Sive did when she was comforting them.

"Sive."

"What exactly did Sive do?"

Mihle wiped off the tears on her face with her hands.

"She's having an affair with Zuko!" Mihle burst out in anger, her lips quivering.

Aviwe felt a jolt.

"An affair...with Zuko?"

"Yes," replied Mihle.

"What made you suspicious Mimz, have you caught them kissing or something?"

"No, but she always takes Zuko's side over me. And, she definitely has a soft spot for him."

"If you talk about a soft spot, Mimz...she has it for everyone..."

"But why didn't she show that when she was giving you a hard time about the way you treat Sbongile?" asked Mihle, trying to make her see it the way she did. "It's different, Mimz. I'm her friend and Zuko isn't..."

There was silence.

"Sive said something that Zuko told me without getting it from me. Do you see what I mean?"

"But…"

"She spoke as someone who's discussed it with Zuko…"

"I guess it's not…"

"She pretended to love my kids and yet, made him abandon them. How could she do that…that hypocrite!" cried Mihle.

"What…what exactly are you trying to tell me?"

"He wants us out of the house by the end of the month, me and the kids. Do you even believe that?"

"Is that what Sive told you?"

"Yes," she replied without giving her Sive's exact words because her new perception of Sive made her trust her instincts.

Her degree of suspecting Sive was escalating in her mind. Aviwe didn't know what to believe, although she knew Sive's high morals, but she would be lying if she could say she'd never noticed Sive's soft spot for Zuko. If she didn't know Sive the way she did, she would have concluded herself that they were having an affair.

"Did you ask her how she knew?"

"No. I wanted to be sure first."

"And?"

"You were here when she made excuses for him. Making me the bad guy after all that bastard did to me…So, what do you think?"

Aviwe took her mind back to during the day, and she dwelled there for a while before she answered.

"I saw it," replied Aviwe.

Mihle bulged out her eyes to sign her to go on.

"Huh?"

"I noticed that, and if I didn't know better, I would have said she had a thing for him.

"As unbelievable as it is," said Mihle.

"But what are you gonna do, Mimz?

She pursed her lips.

"I don't know," and there was a perception of sorrow in her voice. "Why does my life have to be this cruel, full of deception? First it was my mom and now my best friend," she asked, looking at Aviwe for answers.

"Come on girl, don't talk like that."

"I have to speak like this." There was a silence again. "No one treats me fairly. Maybe I shouldn't have been born," she said sorrowfully.

"You'll be alright, just hang in there, girl," Aviwe comforted her.

Mihle looked at her with eyes sparkling with unshed tears, and sighed deeply.

"That's my daily song. If I could be given a rand each time someone sings it for me. I'd have been a millionaire by now, and probably not needing Zuko's house," she said, with a half-smile on her face.

Mihle pretended to be happy with Zuko. Now, her pain boiled down to anger. She felt the weight of her emotional bargain too overwhelming and blamed Sive for the collapse of her relationship.

Sive was Mihle's rock, her light. She'd always made Mihle's life problems lighter for her to carry. Without her, Mihle felt like a car with no fuel and for it to move forward, was nearly impossible.

"What are you gonna do, Mimz?" Aviwe repeated.

"I don't know…but I hate Sive so much right now," she replied, rocking herself back and forth.

"I understand, and I don't blame you. We need to keep our eyes open so we can confront her with something solid," suggested Aviwe.

Mihle lifted her eyes up at Aviwe,

"Thanks, Viv."

"We're friends, we can't betray each other…it's unacceptable," said Aviwe.

"Thanks again, girl," said Mihle. "I need to go and lay down. I'm tired." she cracked a smile. "Thanks for coming. I really appreciate when there's still someone by my side."

"We're girls, we're friends and we will always be there for one another. I know this is not my area of expertise. I can't be as good as Sive…"

"Don't even mention that filthy name if you don't want me to throw up," she said, forcing a smile on her face.

Aviwe smiled as she rose up on the couch, and patted her on the shoulder.

"Be strong my friend. Don't let these two love birds destroy you…"

"You mean the filthy love pigs?"

They both laughed. Mihle was relieved that Aviwe didn't take Sive's side.

"Love pigs, *chomi*," Aviwe repeated.

They continued laughing.

"Do you remember what I told you the other day *chomi*, and you said I was crazy?" Aviwe asked.

"Remind me."

"That if you stay a virgin past the age of twenty-five. You begin to act weird."

Mihle remembered and they giggled.

"So, you think she's not mentally ok?"

"Yes *chomi*, and now she just wants a service and it's not important who renders it as long as it is rendered. Your man, on the other hand, can even sleep with a pig as long as it's covered in pink lace."

They both laughed.

"You just make it too decent for his liking," said Mihle, "even if it is covered in mud, as long as it got that thing."

They both laughed.

Aviwe put her hand on her shoulder, smiling.

"It makes me happy when I see you can still laugh this much."

"You know I always laugh around you."

"Yeah, I notice that nothing has changed," she replied, opening her arms to hold Mihle. They stayed in each other's arms for a moment.

"Girl, let me go home, it's getting late. That man in that house will think I'm coming from some booty calls. He's getting more jealous by the day," she said, breaking away from her.

"How are you two, by the way? I'm sorry for being this selfish these days. All I care about is me and my dumb problems." She rose up. "How's the engagement going?"

"If we start that topic I will definitely have to sleep over," she said, grabbing her car keys on the coffee table and rushing out of the door.

Aviwe didn't want to give Mihle enough time to go deeper in her private life. It was a mess. She and Sbongile were always at each other's throat, and the restaurant guy was an addition to their problems. Aviwe was seeing him.

***

99

On Thursday afternoon, Sive got home from work. In her lounge, Owam and Sma were cosy on the couch with Owam's feet resting on Sma's thighs, stroking them. They were listening to Alicia Keys. The aroma of a roasted chicken was inviting every passer-by.

Sive greeted them warmly. "Afternoon, love birds."

"Hey, cuz."

"Hmmm, the aroma is mouth-watering, what are you cooking my *chom*?"

"Roasted chicken and steamed vegetables, my *chom*," replied Owam, rolling his eyes.

"It smells delicious…"

"I can guarantee, it is. I know my baby rocks in the kitchen," said Smamkele confidently.

"The smell agrees, cuz," replied Sive with an impressive smile.

"I can't wait to marry him. The benefits seem so endless," said Smamkele, smiling at his boyfriend.

"Makoti wa gay," said Owam.

They all laughed, thinking of the gay bride posted on Facebook a few weeks ago.

"How do you feel about this, *chomi*?"

Sive widened her eyes in confusion. "You mean the joke on Facebook about the gay bride?" Sive asked.

"No. About this," he said waving his hand at them, as they were cosy on the couch.

"Be specific *chomi*, this," she said, waving her finger at them, "could mean a lot of things."

"And, what those things are?" Owam asked.

"Like, how do I feel that you're dating my cuz? Or, how do I feel about you marring my cuz. Or, how do I feel that I found you cosy on my couch. Or, how do I feel about staying with a gay guy. You see, the list is endless," replied Sive.

"All of them," said Owam.

"I'm cool. If you guys are happy, I'm happy too."

"I mean, you wouldn't mind if me and your cousin got married?"

"Not at all. Why would I?"

"Please, don't act like a kid. You know what I mean."

"No, I don't."

"We are gay."

"So?"

"You know how people feel about gays," replied Owam.

"And I also know that people don't know what they want from others."

"Yeah, but, with us it's different. They don't even pretend to accept our union. They hate us, period," he said sadly.

"You don't need any acceptance from anyone. Your God loves you. All you need to do is to love Him with all your heart."

"How could I love someone who wants me dead?"

"Says who?" Asked Sive with her eyes bulged out.

"Come on *chomi*, you know who."

Sive widened her eyes even wider.

"The Bible," he said.

Smamkele was quiet; listening to the conversation between the two people he loved the most. He didn't want to interrupt. He knew whatever comes out of Sive's mouth was food for anyone's soul.

"Now you're talking my dear. It's some of the scripture writers that want you dead. And they managed to paint God as the bad guy."

"But they say the Bible is the word of God," said Owam.

"And what do you say?"

Owam shrugged.

"I don't know."

"If you don't know, who has to know for you?"

Owam didn't know how to answer that question.

"You have to accept and love yourself for who you are and stop worrying about how others feel about you. People will always have something to say…that's human nature." She glanced at her wrist again. "Guys, I have to go and see my friends."

"But this, to be continued," said Smamkele.

Sive went to take a quick shower and changed into blue jeans, a long sleeve sweater and white sneakers. She tied up her long, black hair in a neat ponytail.

"Guys, see you later," she said, walking to the door.

"I might not be here when you get back, cuz," said Sma, as Sive was walking towards the door.

"I don't care as long as I find my friend here."

"Do you enjoy staying with Owam?" Sma asked.

101

Owam was grinning from ear to ear. He was feeling at home already.

"Very. He's a good guy. If you don't marry him, you'll be a fool."

Owam's smile was getting wider.

"Hmmm, I like that *chomi*, say it again," said Owam, rolling his eyes.

Sive laughed and went out of the door and jogged to her car. She got in and quickly closed the door and inserted the key. When she was about to turn the key, she remembered that she forgot books she bought for Bridgette and Smanye.

"The books," she murmured.

She jogged back into the house. She used her key to open the door, she found lovebirds, passionately kissing each other on the floor. They were too deep into their romance. They didn't even hear her coming in.

Sive cleared her throat to signal that they had company. Smamkele, who was on top, jumped up.

"I'm sorry cuz, I thought you were…"

"It's ok Sma, I forgot something. I'll be out quickly."

She quickly went to her room to get the books.

Sive said, when passing Owam and Smamkele, still in each other's arms, "Resume," She smiled naughtily and went out.

"Get out, you fool," said Owam jokingly.

Sive laughed and said, "And I'll stay out, my dear."

"Yes, my child, until your elders are done with elderly stuff," replied Owam. They all laughed.

Smamkele was so happy to see his boyfriend and cousin getting along. Their friendship was growing by the second. They even called each other girlfriend or *chomi*.

Sive thought it was a good idea to tell at least one of her friends about her trip to Johannesburg. She thought telling Owam would be wiser since he wouldn't ask her any questions she couldn't answer. She planned to tell him when she got back from seeing Mihle.

"Don't sleep before I get back *chomi*," she said, looking at Owam.

"Are you going to meet some…," asked Owam, looking at her naughtily.

"What! My cuz doesn't do those things."

"How sure are you about that?" Owam asked, still looking at Sive.

"Too sure."

Sive was smiling holding the door, probably thinking Sma shouldn't be that sure.

"Did you see that smile, babe. It says it all," said Owam.

Sive pulled the door closed and jogged to her car.

***

Mihle's house was dark.

Sive raised her arm above her steering wheel to look at her watch. It was after seven in the evening. She got out of the car and jogged to Mihle's front door. She knocked several times without any response. She called Mihle on the phone.

Voicemail.

She tried Zuko's phone. It rang.

"Pick up please," she murmured.

"Hi," said Zuko.

"Hi Zuko, its Sive…"

"Hey Sive, how are you?" he replied warmly.

"I'm fine, and you?"

"I'm ok. How can I help you, dear?"

"I'm at your door, looking for Mihle, but it looks like nobody is in the house. Do you have any idea where they might be?"

"No dear, when I left home they were all there. Did you try her phone?"

"Voicemail."

Silence.

Zuko was thinking of where they might be while Sive was waiting for him to say something that might be a link to where they went.

"Ok Zuko, don't worry. I'll check if they're not at Aviwe's place."

"Yeah, that's what I was gonna suggest, too."

"Thanks for your time."

"Pleasure my dear."

Sive quickly went back to her car without ending the call, and neither did Zuko. She tossed it on the passenger seat and went to Aviwe's place.

Aviwe and Sbongile were arguing when Sive got there. She didn't want to get involved so she drove away. Sive was worried that she wouldn't see her friends before leaving for Johannesburg. Soon, she found herself unlocking her house door. Owam was watching Generations.

He glanced at her.

"You look terrible, why?" he asked, swinging his body to look at her as she was approaching him. "What's wrong, talk to me," said Owam.

Sive was silent for a moment, and then said, "I'm leaving tomorrow evening with my boyfriend to Johannesburg. I wanted to see my friends and spend some time with them before I leave, but no one is available…"

"All you should focus on is your trip with your man and think about anything else when you get b…," he bulged out his eyes, surprised, "Do you have a man, *chomi*! And he's here in Cape Town!"

"Stop interrogating me, all I'm telling you is that I'll be away this weekend," she said grumpily.

That's what secrets do, make people sensitive.

"But…"

"No buts."

Owam stared at her for a moment. "Is there something you're not telling me?"

"A lot, but it's not the right time for it," she said, getting her food from the kitchen. She came back with a nicely decorated plate of food. Owam was still gaping at from where she had disappeared.

"Hello!" she said, waving her hand in front of him.

"What did you say?" Owam asked.

"I have a lot that I'm hiding from you…"

"Why is that? I thought we were friends."

"Yes, we are..."

"But, friends trust each other…"

"This is not about trust, Owam."

Owam narrowed his eyes at her. "It's just not the right time to break open the box of lies I recently found myself in."

"But, Sma told me you're an honest and open person with no secrets."

"Underline, recently," said Sive, putting a piece of broccoli in her mouth. She chewed twice and then continued, "And I hate the person I've become."

"Then why you don't go back to your old self?"

"I'm kind of protecting someone…"

"Who, your man?"

"No."

"Who, then?"

"It's complicated," said Sive.

"Complicated…how?"

"Can we please change the subject?" said Sive.

Owam stared at her silently, and pursed his lips. "Ok. I'll drop it, but don't say I didn't warn you. Take care of lies before they take care of you, *chomi*." Owam said, curling up on the couch.

"Don't worry *chomi*, it's not like real lies," replied Sive smiling to comfort him.

"Lies are lies *chomi*, someone is gonna get hurt. If not you, it will be somebody else."

"Don't worry girl. These are not those type of lies. Just that…never mind."

There was silence.

Both of their phones gave a message alert. Both of them were smiling as they were replying.

Owam lifted up his eyes and saw a tender angelic smile on Sive's beautiful face. He pressed the send button and threw his phone back on the couch.

"I know that you're a new liar, but you can't deny that's your boo on the phone," said Owam, with eyes demanding an answer.

Sive stretched her lips even wider. "Yes, that's him." She confirmed. "He sent me his pic."

"Let me see his pic, girl," he said, stretching his arm to reach the phone.

"No!" she said putting it behind her back.

"Please *chomi*," he looked at her waiting for her to give him the phone.

"You won't get this phone, friend. Just give up."

He laughed. "I know beautiful girls like you have bad taste in guys. You're probably ashamed of his looks," he said, picking up his phone from the couch and looking at it, then threw it back on the couch.

"Ashamed, of what! He's a hunk girl, and I'm scared you might want to steal him."

"Oh chill girl, Sma is the whole package. He's honest, caring, loving, good-looking…and so awesome in bed. What else could a bitch ask for?"

Sive was looking at him, thinking about a taste in bed, although she wasn't ready for it.

"How does this guy taste in bed?" He asked, pointing at Sive's phone. He was now not sure whether he should believe that Sive was still a virgin.

Sive shrugged. "I don't know."

"Haven't you tasted it?"

Sive shook her head. "No."

Owam folded his arms and bulged out his eyes at her.

"I hope you're planning to break that treasure box in the city of gold."

"I'm not ready to take my relationship to that level, *chomi*..."

"What! If you're stingy with it girl he will find some generous girl."

"That will mean he wasn't mine. And he would leave me eventually whether I gave him all the goodies in the treasure box or not," she said confidently.

"Wow! I like the confidence girl. Although you sound like you're living somewhere there," he said shaking his hand, "in the mid-nineteenth century."

They both laughed.

Sive smiled and then said, "Let's talk some serious stuff now, girl."

"Ok."

"I'm leaving tomorrow evening. My flight departs at six in the evening. Would you mind taking me to the airport and picking me up on Monday morning, at seven again?"

"Cool! No problem," he replied cheerfully.

"Thanks, you're a star...darling."

"You're welcome," he said smiling.

"Ok, good night then. I have to pack my bags tonight," she said, lifting herself up.

"Not so fast young lady. I'm helping you pack your bags," he said getting up, "I know you won't get things right in that bedroom without a fashion guru."

Sive laughed.

"Ok. Come fashion guru," she said, pulling his arm and running, laughing into her bedroom.

Chapter 12

Owam was curled up on the couch, enjoying a cup of tea after cleaning the house when Sma knocked.

"Hey babe," said Owam, kissing Smamkele with a pleasant smile.

"Hi sweet thing, you look so happy," said Sma.

"'Cause I am."

"Is there any particular reason, my love?"

"I'm sharing a house with an angel," he replied, pulling him to the couch. Smamkele smiled.

"I didn't even have to ask, I know how sweet it is to stay with her."

Sma gazed at him.

"And what's more," asked Sma.

Owam cleared his throat. "Your cousin is going to Johannesburg, with her man…"

"Man!" Asked Smamkele surprised.

He nodded.

"What man?"

Owam eyed him. "It seems as if you don't know your cousin." He sipped his tea. "She's dating."

"Ok. Is it someone I know?"

Owam shrugged. "Maybe." He sipped his tea again. "I'm gonna be alone tonight."

"Ok, I can spend my last night with the love of my life," whispered Sma in his ear.

"Hmmm, sounds like a perfect idea," whispered Owam.

And, they kissed.

***

Sive was a dog with two tails all day at work. She was a little nervous, but mostly excited to meet Gabriel. In that moment, Chikondi was out of the picture. All she could see was Gabriel's smiling dark face.

Gabriel called her to check if everything was still going according to plan. Sive told him that she would be his guest that night. They were both happy about taking their relationship to another level.

Smamkele left Sive's house before Sive arrived. He wanted to be home when his father got back and tell him in person that he would spend the night over at Sive's place.

"Sive, harry up!" Owam wailed from the lounge.

Within a few minutes, Sive emerged from the corridor. She was dressed in navy blue skinny jeans, a red body top and red heels. She was pulling her pink luggage and a red clutch bag tucked under her arm. Her outfit revealed all her curves.

"I'm ready to hit the road."

"Wow! You're one to die for…you look so hot, *sana.*" He glanced at his watch. "Let's get going," he said, taking the luggage from Sive and pulling it towards the door.

Sive glanced at her watch that was placed nicely in between those fine accessories on her wrist.

When Owam reached the door, he turned and looked at Sive who was still standing, sending a short silent prayer, asking God to protect her.

"Come on girl, I'm not the one who's going on a romantic weekend here."

Sive chuckled. "I know. Let's go," she said, walking towards him.

Sive locked up the door and walked to the car; they took their seats and drove off.

***

Zuko was going to catch the same flight as Sive to Johannesburg. He was taking his side chick on a romantic getaway.

Mihle checked Zuko's phone while he was getting ready. She saw Sive's call that lasted more than thirty minutes. She felt a pit in her stomach. Her heart beat fast, and then slow. She exhaled heavily, and her mind started putting one and one together and came out with six.

Now, Mihle was convinced that Sive was the other woman. She hated her even more while Sive, on the other hand, was worried sick for leaving without seeing how she was doing.

Zuko pulled his small, black luggage, took out his phone, and went out of the door without saying anything to Mihle.

Mihle grabbed her car keys and told her kids that she was coming back soon. She locked them inside the house and hurried to her car. She flew the car to Kuils River, where Sive lived.

Mihle was shocked when another person answered Sive's door. Owam answered her without letting her in.

"Is Sive home?"

"She's on a romantic weekend getaway in Johannesburg with her man," he said.

"Her man!" exclaimed Mihle.

And now, everything made sense.

"Yes, her man." Owam replied.

"Who's that man?" Mihle asked, looking surprised.

"I don't know. Who are you, by the way?" asked Owam.

Mihle just glared at him, turned, and walked away. She got what she wanted.

Mihle got in her car, shoved in the key, and turned it on. She threw her arms on the steering wheel and burst out crying. She was in a terrible pain. Mihle knew that Sive's man was actually her man. She didn't know what went so wrong between them, their relationship that used to be like paper and glue. Everything was proving to her that she was right about Sive and Zuko. When she got home, she set everything Sive bought her and her kids on fire in the back yard.

The collapse of Mihle and Zuko's relationship affected their kids, too. Bridgette's teacher, Mrs. Owens had been sending Bridgette's parents one letter after another to talk about Bridgette's sharp drop in her school performance. But none had been replied to. For Bridgette, both school and home were hell. All she wished was to stay with her aunt, Sive.

Sive was missing them on her way to Johannesburg. She took at least one third of her travelling time thinking about how they were doing. She pressed the back of her head against the back of her seat, facing upwards. Her mind was just dwelling in the valleys of Mihle's life. For a moment, she forgot about why she was on that plane. She shook off the thoughts and focused on why she was flying to Johannesburg.

***

Sive arrived at O.R. Tambo International at fifteen minutes past eight. People were moving from Terminal B towards a big parking lot. Some were glancing around, looking for those who were picking them up.

Sive emerged from the crowd, bouncing up and down, swinging her lovely pair of hips from side to side. Her long black, flowy, relaxed hair was following to the rhythm of her steps. She broke out a joyful smile as her eyes met her pregnant friend.

Lisa and her husband were standing by a white BMW.

Gabriel recognised her from her single picture on Facebook. His heart beat a thousand times a second, and burst out.

"That's her, man!" he said excitedly.

"Who?"

"Sive."

James glanced around.

"I hope you're not talking about that lady in the navy jeans and red top?"

"Yeah, man."

James laughed. "That woman is surely a model who came here for casting in Sandton or something. That type is for guys like AKA, man…not someone like you and me. Don't fool yourself boy-boy," he said, laughing, patting his shoulder.

Gabriel's eyes were still glued on Sive, bouncing up and down, swinging her hips, smiling at a pregnant woman. His gut feelings were telling him she was the one.

"Your phantom can't be good-looking. If she shows up, she'll be an ugly, fat woman. Desperate to get a man…only if she shows up," he said, and then glanced around for a lost, ugly woman.

"Shut up! You're not helping, you know," said Gabriel, annoyed by the fact that his friend could be right that Sive might not show up.

Lisa ran to Sive smiling, her arms in the air. Sive dropped her luggage and spread her arms.

They embraced.

"Look man, I told you! She's meeting these people…not you," he said and then curled up his lips into a naughty smile. "Let's look for your date. Maybe she's a cripple and still straggling inside."

Gabriel glared at him. They burst out laughing.

"I don't wanna laugh man, but being around a lunatic like you, no one can help it."

"But you know I could be right, right?"

"Yeah," he replied in a low voice.

"Come on man, say it out loud. I can't hear you," James said, teasingly.

"Yeah, you could be right," he said louder.

110

"Yeah, thanks boy-boy."

"You're enjoying every bit of this, aren't you?"

"No, boy-boy. You know we're in this together."

Gabriel glared at him. "We're in this together, my foot," he said, and they laughed again.

Nathi, Lisa's husband who was walking behind his wife, picked up Sive's luggage from the ground, and then waited to greet her.

"Hi *sana*, it feels like a long time since we last saw each other," said Lisa, still holding hands.

"It is, *sana*. This is proof," said Sive, patting her bulging tummy.

"You are such a fool, do you know that?" Said Lisa, laughing.

"Why?"

"I was already more than three months pregnant on my wedding. Didn't you notice that?"

"Of course I did." Lisa bulged out her eyes in disbelief. Sive murmured in that smile that confirms 'I was lying.'

"Yeah, that's what I thought," replied Lisa, moving forward pulling Sive's hand, both laughing.

"Oh, Veve," that's how Lisa called Sive, "has your lover-boy called?" She asked.

"No. But I have already seen him..."

"Where! Have you talked to him?" asked Lisa anxiously.

"No, I want to see if he will recognise me," replied Sive.

"No man can't recognise a beautiful face like this," said Lisa, smiling at her.

"Don't make me blush..."

Lisa grinned and then frowned at her. "Where's he?" she moved her mouth closer to her ear and whispered, "The lucky fella."

Sive smiled, and moved closer to Lisa's ear. "Do you see those two guys by the red Toyota corolla?"

"Yeah, yeah."

"The one in blue jeans and a Manchester United jersey, that's him."

"Hmm *sana*, you can recognise him just like that," said Lisa, snapping her fingers and wearing a naughty smile. They giggled. "He's a giant," she whispered.

"What do you mean?" Sive whispered back.

"He's big. Are you not scared of those big, strong muscles?" Sive stared at her. "Yes, you're an amateur in this game, baby girl. You can't stand tough games like him."

Sive glanced at Nathi. Hoping he wasn't listening, but he was, and impressed with the conversation.

"What do you say, baby," said Lisa, glancing at her husband.

"Oh please, forgive me Nathi for being rude," she said, trying to dodge the subject. "I forgot to greet you. You know how I am around this crazy wife of yours…"

"Who's crazy?" Lisa asked, smiling at her friend.

Sive turned to her, frowning. "Shut up," they both burst out laughing.

"I'm talking to the sane insane," said Sive and then, turned to Nathi, "How're you doing?"

"I'm fine, thanks. And you?"

"I'm good, thanks…"

"Oh, please. Stop avoiding the subject."

"My dear, I love Gabriel. Giant, or not. Case closed," she said, and then they looked at each other and burst out laughing.

"Come on girls, what's so funny?" Nathi asked.

"Baby, please, keep your line open this weekend. We might be called to pick her up from Gabriel's place. I doubt if this amateur can handle that tough guy," she said laughing.

Sive blushed and Nathi noticed.

"Baby drop it. They're adults, I'm sure they can manage."

"Besides, nothing is gonna happen this weekend. No sex, on a first date…if that's what you're implying." Sive said, trying to be brave.

"Says who?" asked Lisa.

"Me."

Lisa clapped her hands twice. "Wake up girl! Which man can sleep in the same bed with a hot girl like you and lock his hands in his pockets?"

Silence.

Sive stared at Lisa with a perception of fear in her eyes. Nathi exchanged glances between the two friends and said, "If he loves her, he will wait until she's ready…"

Lisa interrupted him.

"Baby, don't forget that these guys didn't meet in some sacred place, but social media. Frankly, we don't know this guy and we just can't trust him like some saint from heaven."

Nathi moved his eyes to Sive. The look on her face was as if she was going to say, "Book me on the next flight back to Cape Town."

"Take my number and give me a shout if things are turning the wrong direction, I'll be there in a sec," he said, taking out his mobile phone from his jeans. Sive opened her clutch bag and took out her cell phone, and they exchanged numbers.

"Wait man," said James, seeing a tall, big and dark girl. Looking lost. She was coming from Terminal B.

The woman was dressed in brown long skirt, blue blouse and black flat pumps. She was exactly what James had in mind for Sive.

"Man, that could be her," he said anxiously.

"Where, man?" Gabriel asked, getting off the car.

Gabriel stared at his friend who was replying with a shrug.

"Call her man. If she picks it up, that's her."

Gabriel nervously patted all his pockets, looking for his phone.

James laughed. "Not now man," said Gabriel, annoyed.

"You put your phone in the car, man."

Gabriel got in the car, came out with his phone, and started dialling Sive's number. And then Gabriel's eyes were running between Sive and the other woman to see who would answer her phone, and James had that in mind, too.

"Is it ringing?" James asked.

After a short pause.

"Yes, it is."

Suddenly, the nerves made sweat run down his face. The other girl quickly opened her handbag and answered her phone while Sive was still holding hers in her hand, talking with her friends.

The call was cut before it was answered, and the girl looked more nervous than before while Sive was smiling and putting her phone in her purse.

"What now, man?" James asked, curiously.

"The call dropped."

"Maybe it's her battery or something. Go and talk to her, man." James suggested.

He shoved him in the back in the girl's direction. To both of them, Sive wasn't the woman they were waiting for…but some model who dates some superstars, and the other girl was Sive. The woman who took Gabriel's heart by storm, and the one they came to pick up.

No matter how bad her looks were, Gabriel's heart still felt the same about the woman he had known for months. He pulled himself together and started walking to the girl.

Smiling nervously.

"Hey."

"Good evening. Are you Gabriel?" the lady asked, nervously.

Gabriel's lips extended from one ear to another.

"Yes, I am," he replied happily.

The lady replied with a smile of relief.

"I was starting to get nervous when I couldn't see any sign of you," she said relieved.

"I'm here now, you're safe. I won't let anything happen to you," said Gabriel.

The perception of care in his voice confused the lady, and there was an awkward silence.

Gabriel smiled at her to break the silence, and said, "Let me help you with your luggage."

He put her luggage in his car trunk and then opened a car door for her.

He then threw the car keys to his friend.

"Get behind the wheel and drive us home, boy."

James grabbed the keys and shook his head, and then got in the car.

When Sive was walking towards Gabriel's car, Gabriel got into the car, next to the woman and drove off.

Sive stood there for a moment, confused. She took the phone from her clutch bag and dialled his number.

Gabriel's phone rang, in his pocket, he took it out. His heart throbbed as if it was going to break out of his chest. On the screen, "SWEETHEART" was written.

There was only one sweetheart in his life, and that, was the one he left at the airport.

"Sive!" he screamed.

"Baby, where are you?"

Gabriel turned to the woman next to him.

"Who are you, woman!"

Chapter 13

"Baby where are you?" She repeated her question.

"Where are you, sweetheart?" he replied with another question.

"I'm at the airport."

"Stay put, I'll be there in two," he replied, and then lifted up his eyes to James, "Turn the car back to the airport," he commanded.

"What's going on, man?"

"Stop asking a million questions, just do as I say man," he said nervously.

James laughed. "I know, you picked up the wrong woman, you fool," he replied, still laughing.

"That's not funny man."

"Yes, it is."

"Don't say that when you were the one who messed with my mind, you moron," said Gabriel. "Pull off!" he added.

"Wait man. Let's use that spot," said James. He pulled in next to Nathi's car.

Nathi was standing with his wife next to their car while Sive was standing a few metres away from them, holding her phone in her hand.

Gabriel jumped out of the car and rushed to his sweetheart. Sive flew to Gabriel, her arms flying. Her face was glowing with her angelic smile. She rested, wrapped in the big, strong loving arms of her man. She buried herself in his arms for a while and then looked in his eyes.

Gabriel lowered his head and let their lips touch.

Lisa smiled. The other woman was smiling, enjoying the moment, and forgetting that she was actually lost. The one who was supposed to pick her up didn't show up.

Nathi moved towards the love birds and said to Gabriel, "Man, this is our precious stone, you break it, you pay!" he was trying to scare him not to hurt her.

"If you knew how valuable this soul is to me, you wouldn't bother warning me. I won't let even a single teardrop fall from these beautiful eyes," replied Gabriel, looking into her eyes and then pulled her closer to his chest again and covered her tenderly in his arms.

Nathi went to fetch her luggage and came back with it.

"Here is her luggage; I guess we should get going now, man. It's getting cold, and it's not good for my wife's condition."

"Thanks man. I can take it from here," Gabriel expressed his gratitude.

"We'll go together so we can see where you stay. We can't take any chances," said Nathi.

"That's cool, man," replied Gabriel.

"After you, man," said Nathi, getting in his car.

Gabriel pulled Sive's luggage in one hand and held Sive with the other. He then saw the other woman's luggage and remembered that they still have the other mystery to solve.

James was standing with the other woman by the car, quiet. They didn't say anything to each other.

James couldn't take his eyes off Sive. He'd never seen such beauty before. He knew for sure that Sive was just one of the gold diggers Gabriel had met before. All she wanted was benefits from his friend and he told himself she would get that over his dead body.

Gabriel got Sive into the back seat. And then said, "I'm coming, my love."

Sive nodded with a happy smile. Gabriel went over to the other woman.

"Lady, who are you?"

Nathi was already running the engine, ready to drive off.

"I'm Tinashe, originally from Zimbabwe. I'm meeting Mr. Arendse. He said he would send a guy by the name of Gabriel to pick me up, so I thought it was you," she explained.

Gabriel chuckled. "Wow! What a coincidence."

When Gabriel was trying to help this woman, James called him,

"Gabriel! This man is looking for some woman."

The man walked to Gabriel and Tinashe.

"Who're you looking for, man?" asked Gabriel, trying to make sure if that guy was the right guy.

"A woman, by the name of Tinashe. My boss has sent me to come pick her up. She's from Cape Town," explained the guy. He wasn't sure whether Gabriel was her husband.

"And who's your boss?" Gabriel asked.

"Mr Arendse."

Gabriel looked at the woman. She nodded. He then took her luggage and handed it over to the guy.

"Ok Tinashe, go well," he said, waiving to the woman and then turned to his car, opened the door and sat next to his woman.

"Chauffeur, take us home."

James burst out laughing. "I heard that before."

"What!"

James turned and looked at his friend and laughed.

"Each time I turn around you have a different woman. Are you sure you're not Mr Zuma?"

"Baby, don't mind him. He's not only my chauffeur but a moron from hell as well," said Gabriel, kissing his beautiful woman.

James viewed them from the mirror in front of him, kissing with their hands all over each other.

"You were sitting like a statue next to your first lady…"

"Shut up, and drive! That's what I pay you for," said Gabriel, and then kissed his phantom.

Gabriel stopped kissing her and brought his attention to James.

"Oh man, please keep up with that white BMW behind the metre taxi behind us," he said, looking serious now.

"Why?"

"They're my in-laws, man. They wanna know where I am taking this angel."

"Is it already time for the bride's price negotiations?" James asked, teasing his friend.

"No, you fool. They wanna be sure if I'm not one of those scumbags who hurt women in this world. You know how we met. I don't expect them to trust me," he explained.

"Definitely! Not after you abducted that poor woman. What's her name again? Tinashe…yeah. Tinashe," he said teasing him.

"Shut up, you fool," said Gabriel and then brought his attention back to Sive. She was quiet with a smile, exchanging glances between these two crazy friends.

"You must be hungry my angel," he said.

Sive was staring at the movement of his lips. Hiding, and revealing those beautiful snow-white teeth. The craving for them tormented her thoughts and she moved towards them. Gabriel was watching this golden movement impressively and didn't want to contribute in making that magical moment happen.

When Sive's lips touched his, she licked them once or twice, before she inserted her tongue in his mouth. Soon, her body wanted to get closer to his. She dragged her body closer, and pressed it against his.

Gabriel couldn't hold his horses anymore. He kissed her back, sucking her tongue, squeezing her body.

James cleared his throat, interrupting them.

"Get a room!"

"I'm sorry, man," said Gabriel, both sitting up straight, facing forward like two naughty teenagers caught in the act of their naughtiness.

"Ma'am. Let me correct my friend's rudeness by introducing myself. I'm James, Gabriel's best friend.

"I'm Sive."

Gabriel was quiet, letting his right arm rest on her left thigh.

"Nice meeting you, Sive," said James.

"My pleasure," replied Sive, smiling.

Sive shifted her attention from James to Gabriel. She extended the existing smile on her face, and then rested her head on his shoulder.

Silence fell.

Gabriel was stroking her hair gently, using his fingers.

"I cooked your favourite meal," he whispered.

Sive looked at him surprisingly. "My favourite!"

Gabriel nodded. "Roasted chicken, broccoli and butternut," he said.

Sive smiled and said, "Thanks baby," and then buried her face in his chest.

Although Sive was thinking that Gabriel was the guy she'd been waiting for all her life, she had divided feelings. A part of her still loved Chikondi. His death was the worst nightmare of her life.

Gabriel could feel Sive's love and his heart was more than just contented with her.

The sound of an engine was the only sound in the car. James was focusing on the road to take the lovebirds home as he was commanded. Gabriel was holding his phantom close to his heart, where it belonged.

Sive was what Gabriel couldn't afford to lose.

***

Mihle called Jonathan. Her heart was as heavy as a piece of iron. Her life was a mess. Other than Sive, she was blaming God for everything that was going wrong in her life.

Sometimes when life is bitter, we lack the knowledge of who God is and start seeing Him as a monster that is responsible for our pain and suffering. Maybe we do know, but we don't want to take responsibility for our mistakes. We always want to have someone to blame for being the victims of our own bad choices.

Sive wasn't aware that she was her best friend's worst enemy. She was planning to help her throughout her hardship. Mihle, on the other hand, was putting all her effort into hating and bringing her down.

Although women could be emotionally vulnerable to sex, they still make things worse by using sex to get what they want. Including trapping men in a relationship that could never be good for anyone involved…and that was a mistake Mihle made. She thought she could find home by trapping a man into a commitment. Now she was suffering from the side effects of casual sex and the situation affected her whole life. Everything was just taking the wrong direction in her life.

"Hi Jonno. Is Sive with you?"

"No, I'm on my way to her house."

"Ok, bye then," said Mihle. She didn't even mention that she was away. She didn't want to talk about it…everything about it was disgusting to her.

***

Gabriel, Sive, Lisa, Nathi and James were following each other into Gabriel's place. They stood by the door. Gabriel was holding Sive's hand and Nathi's arm was wrapped around Lisa's fat waist. When James noticed that he was the only man with no woman in that house, he walked straight to the couch at the end of the room.

"You've got a nice place, man," said Nathi, feeling a bit trusting of the guy.

"Thanks boss," replied Gabriel.

"Guys, we have to go now. My wife must be exhausted."

"Thanks man, for everything." Gabriel replied.

Lisa broke off from Nathi, moved closer to Sive, and whispered something in her ear. And they both giggled.

"Let me take my man and leave you with yours, my friend," she glanced at her wrist, "It's few minutes to ten now, and way past my bedtime. No wonder my feet are killing me." She moved her eyes to Nathi. "You gonna give them the best treatment, baby."

"Anything for you, my love," replied Nathi, wrapping his arm around her waist, driving her to the door.

"I'll call you my friend," said Lisa as they were walking out of the door, leaving James and the lovebirds.

Gabriel closed the door and turned to Sive who was standing facing the door with her back to James. He held his queen's hands. He looked into her eyes, and then pulled her close to him and wrapped her petite figure with both hands.

Sive quickly felt a quiver and started shaking. She then lowered her eyes to Gabriel's chest. He gently touched her chin and lifted it up until their eyes met. Slowly, Sive lifted up her eyes to Gabriel's gaping lips. Soon, they were gaping at each other.

Suddenly, Gabriel, pounding with anticipation of what was going to happen, squeezed her waist as he was pressing her body against him. Slowly, he moved his lips to hers, breathing heavily.

"That's my cue to leave," said James, jumping up from the couch like ready toast.

Sive felt embarrassed and buried her face in Gabriel's chest.

"See you, man," replied Gabriel, kissing Sive's forehead and stroking her back.

"When a man loves a woman

Can't keep his mind on nothing else

He'd trade the world

For the good thing he's found

If she's bad, he can't see it

She can't do no wrong

And turn his back on his best friend," James replied with Michael Bolton's song, walking slowly to the door so he could reach the line with a message he wanted to send to his friend.

"Come on man. Stop sulking like a child, you know you're my best man," said Gabriel while James closed the door.

Gabriel quickly broke off from Sive and hurried after James.

121

"Where're you going, man?" asked Gabriel, walking behind him.

"Home."

"But you don't have a car."

"I'm taking this one," he said pressing a remote to open Gabriel's car.

"But…"

James quickly turned around,

"No buts man. What's important in your life now is your phantom, right?" he answered with a long face.

Gabriel laughed. "You're jealous, man."

"Jealous, no!" he replied pulling the car door open. "Do you think that woman loves you?" he asked, holding a door with one hand, facing Gabriel so he would hear every word he had to say. "That woman," he said, pointing angrily at the house, "is up to no good, trust me. She will hurt you, and leave you broken…I mean it in every definition of the word."

He then got into the car and shoved in the key. He looked at Gabriel again. "Do you think a woman as beautiful as her could be single and desperate enough to pick up any guy she could find on social networks?"

Gabriel was quiet, looking at James who had a negative perception of Sive.

"Wake up, man," he said warning his dear friend.

"I love this girl, man," said Gabriel in a low voice.

"That's the problem," he said, putting his hands on the steering wheel, "you're so much in love with this woman that you can't even see through her…she's a wolf in a sheep skin, careful man," said James.

"How?" asked Gabriel.

"How many kids does she have?"

"One."

"And the father?"

"Died."

"How?"

"What!"

"How did he die? Got AIDS and she's a carrier too…wake up man," he said, twisting the key.

Gabriel didn't reply. He turned and walked back to the house.

"Think about it, man. You have to send her back!"

Gabriel turned and walked back to the car. He pulled the car door open.

"I'm not sending anyone back. I love Sive with all my heart. AIDS or no AIDS, and I'm coming with her to the party tomorrow. And you will have to behave."

James looked at him and drove away without saying anything.

When Gabriel got back into the house, he found Sive on the couch, browsing her phone. She lifted up her eyes and welcomed him with a warm smile. Sive noticed that Gabriel wasn't ok when he cracked a smile from his sad face.

"Are you ok, babe?" she asked with her angelic voice.

Gabriel threw himself on the couch next to her.

"Yeah babe, I'm fine," he replied, extending his smile, embracing her body.

"Ok," she whispered, buried in his arms.

Gabriel released the grip of his arms around her body and moved away slowly to have full view of her gorgeous face.

Sive had always had that smile that locked beneath her skin.

"I love you," he said sincerely, stroking her pitch-black hair and everything James said about Sive faded away. All he was thinking about was how much he loved the woman in front of him.

"I love you more," she replied with that smile that knocks him off his feet.

Gabriel wrapped her in his arms, and squeezed her.

"Thanks, honey," he said.

"Ouch! You're breaking my bones, baby," she said laughing.

Gabriel released the pressure and kissed her on the forehead.

"You must be hungry baby," he said, moving backwards to view her face again.

Sive glanced at her gold watch. "I can't eat at this time. A cup of warm milk will be fine," she replied.

"Are you a baby now my love, you sleep with a milk?"

Sive laughed and glanced at her wrist again. "It's too late for me to eat now. Besides, milk helps me to have a relaxed night…sleeping like a baby."

"What! You get no milk here. Do you want me to be your bodyguard?" he said eyeing her.

"No baby. It's like a routine for me. I get a cup of warm milk before bed," she explained, laughing.

"Well, let me be your cup of milk. You'll drink me till you dose off," he said wearing a naughty face.

Sive got uncomfortable at first, and then shook off the tension and revealed her naughty face, too.

"And what is that supposed to mean?" she asked, biting her lower lip.

Soon, Gabriel's blood pressure went up, sweating just at the thought of the two of them in bed. Embracing.

He knew that with South African women you have to prepare for the best performance on the first night if you want to score some points. He had already noticed that Sive was thirsty for it and he was ready to quench all that thirst.

Gabriel moved slowly towards her mouth. He let their lips touch, gently. He sucked her lower lip, and then the upper one. He licked both of her lips until she gaped, and he tucked his tongue into her mouth.

Sive wrapped her arms around his body. The magnet of Gabriel's affection pulled the virgin closer to him without using his physical power, and soon, her heart beat against his.

Gabriel lifted her to the bed and continued kissing her. His hands were all over her body. He moved his hands slowly, down her neck, across her chest towards her left breast. He tucked his hand under her top and cupped her left breast.

Sive got uncomfortable when she was touched in that manner and her feelings for Chikondi resurfaced and she felt she was betraying him. She pushed herself up.

"Wait!" she said, pushing him back.

Gabriel quickly moved aside. "What's wrong, babe?" he asked worried, thinking that he did something to annoy her.

Sive sat up, pulling her top down and moved an inch away from Gabriel. She was looking nervous. She then rose up and hurried into the bathroom.

Gabriel noticed that something was wrong with her.

The feeling of betraying Chikondi was unbearable. She pushed the door closed with her buttocks and closed her eyes fighting back the tears. She whispered, "Chikondi is dead and life has to move on…why can't I accept that! Gabriel is a good man who deserves a woman who's fully committed to him; not some pathetic woman with divided feelings. I have to let go now."

Tears welled up in her eyes. Letting Chikondi go seemed like a very difficult thing to do.

It seemed like her feelings for Chikondi wouldn't let her go down the aisle with another man. Maybe going back to Malawi would help.

Sive tore off a piece of toilet paper and wiped her eyes. She looked at the mirror on the wall…she was terrible. She ran cold water, rinsed her face, dried it up with toilet paper, and went out.

When Sive got back, Gabriel was making a bed. The guilt of having feelings for another man was eating her up inside.

Gabriel lifted his eyes to start a conversation when he noticed her miserable face. Her eyes were red and wet. Gabriel could clearly see that she had been crying. He sat on the bed and pulled her onto his lap.

"You have been crying baby, what's wrong?" asked Gabriel, confused.

"No, yes, I'm ok. Just that, I'm not ready for…you know?" she replied.

It's ok my dear, we can wait. I love you so much," said Gabriel pulling her closer and embracing her.

He kissed her forehead, then rose up the couch, and moved towards the cupboard.

Gabriel opened one of the three pots on the stove, the biggest one. Suddenly, he turned to look at her.

"Are you sure you don't want anything, honey?" he asked, holding up a pot lid.

Sive gave him a smile that reminded him of what she asked for. He quickly said,

"Oh please, not milk. I don't want you to pass out on me sweetheart. We've so much to talk about…looking into each other's eyes."

Sive chuckled. "Give me a juice then."

Gabriel put the lid back on the pot.

"I won't eat either," he said, and then opened his small fridge.

"Orange or apple?"

"Apple."

Gabriel gave her a glass of juice, and then sat on the couch in front of her.

Being there alone with Gabriel made her wonder how life could have been with Chikondi. She had deep feelings for him, and in her heart, his son was hers.

Sive planned to tell Gabriel the whole truth when the time was right, but for now, she didn't want him to know she was a virgin.

Gabriel noticed that she didn't want to talk about her son and he assumed he reminded her of her ex. What Gabriel didn't know was that she was keeping secrets from him.

"How close you were with your baby-daddy?" he asked, trying to find emotions hidden in her mind.

The question took Sive off guard. She paused before replying.

"Our hearts were too close," she replied.

"Was he your first love?"

"Yes."

"Did you date someone after him?"

"Yes."

"Who?"

She pointed at him with her head. Gabriel smiled impressively.

"Did you only date one guy in your life except me?"

She nodded. "Yes."

Gabriel's face lost a smile. "What are your plans with me, do you love me?"

"If you're the right man for me, I would love to settle down with you and have beautiful kids," she broke a smile when she mentioned kids. She loved kids more than anything in the world.

"I asked this before, and I'm asking it now. What's the right man for you?"

"I said this before and I'm saying it now. Just be yourself. I don't want you to change who you are for me. I wanna fall in love with the real you. Not a fake that will change along the way and become something else that will make my life miserable."

Gabriel smiled. "I hope the real me won't chase you away, 'cause I need you."

Sive smiled and sipped the very last drop of her juice.

"Some more?" asked Gabriel.

"No, I'm cool," she replied, "But I wanna take a quick shower."

"Cool…do you mind if I join you?"

Sive bulged out her eyes at him. "No! That's not a good idea."

"Why?"

"That would arouse our sexual feelings, and I told you I'm not ready for that now."

"Meaning that you will want me?"

Sive looked at him for a while and then replied. "Yes, Gabriel. And I want you even now…"

"But?" he asked, afraid that Sive would say he wasn't what she pictured of him.

"We like one another, but we don't know each other. You need to know and understand the person before you marry them. Let's allow ourselves to know if we're the right people for one another before we get married," she replied.

"Honey, we're talking about making love and not marriage. I know it's a bit early for such commitment," replied Gabriel.

"Sex! That's what you mean?" she asked.

"Yes...sex is included," he replied hesitantly, not knowing if he was saying something to score him good points with her or not.

Sive chuckled.

"And what do you call a marriage?"

"It's when two people have said their vows before God that they will be together till death do them part," explained Gabriel.

"And where's God?" asked Sive.

"Come on babes, you know he's everywhere."

"Ok, I see," replied Sive, rising up. Gabriel intercepted her.

"What's a marriage to you, babes?" he asked.

"Sex. Sex is a marriage."

Gabriel bulged out his eyes at her.

Sive chuckled, and continued, "It's sex that touches deep into another person's spirit and creates a strong union that makes the two feel as one. Not a wedding ceremony or a marriage certificate," she explained.

"So, were you married to your baby-daddy?"

Sive looked at him without saying anything, and then started walking.

Gabriel grabbed her arm.

"Answer me babes."

Sive gave him a smile that weakened his knees.

"I'll only marry one man, and that man is in front of me," she said and then sat on his right lap, with her left arm around his neck. She then moved forward to kiss his lips. "If you could know how much I love you, you wouldn't be worried about a thing," she said, rising up his lap.

"Not so fast, young lady," said Gabriel, grabbing her arm and pulling her back onto his lap. Soon his tongue was deep in her mouth, and the question he was going to ask, how she could get pregnant if she'd never had sex with her ex...faded away.

Gabriel had never felt such affection with any other woman in his life before...he could feel it in his veins that she was exceptional, and James' perception of her was wrong.

Sive broke off from his arms and looked into his eyes.

"Let me go and have a quick shower, it's getting late," she said, leaving Gabriel who looked miles away. He was trapped in a moment of a combination of fear and disbelief that he finally found a woman who could voluntarily preach her love for him. Not just a woman, but a beautiful woman.

Soon Gabriel heard the sound of the shower running.

Chapter 14

On Friday, the day before Simamkele left for the US, he was lying on the bed with Owam. They were having their last chance for closeness. After an hour or so after Mihle left, there was another knock on the door while they were kissing.

"Ignore that," said Owam, breathing heavily on top of Smamkele.

"Answer it babes."

Owam pulled Smamkele.

"Answer the door, please babes," he said.

Owam glared at him and then got up and went to the door.

"Hi," he said to someone at the door.

"Hi," replied Jonathan in a confused expression.

Jonathan was more jealous than confused to see such a handsome guy in his woman's house. His jealousy had blinded him to see some elements of homosexuality in Owam because it wasn't hidden at all. Jonathan wasn't sure whether the guy was Gabriel.

"What are you doing here?"

"I live here, and who are you standing on my door, asking me that?

"Did she sell this house?" Jonathan asked Owam, who was looking at him with his right arm resting on his waist.

"No, we both live here."

"Where's she?"

"She went on a hot romantic weekend getaway to the city of gold."

"Damn it, that fool!"

Owam shrugged.

"Are you sure she went with a man, 'cause I'm her man?"

"She told me herself. She even showed me his picture on FB."

"Do you know that guy's name?"

Owam shook his head. "I don't know. All I know he's a tall, dark and strong with big hands. Do you know what they say about guys with big hands? She's probably moaning painfully underneath…"

"Shut up! It's not a joke to me," he said angrily.

"I'm sorry. I was just…"

"Shut up! Just…shut up!" said Jonathan throwing his hands in the air, walking away.

Jonathan was so hurt and hated Gabriel even more. The thought of Sive in his arms, stroked by those big hands was killing him. He was so sure that Sive would lose her virginity to Gabriel. However, he was convinced that Sive would end up with him, not Gabriel.

On Jonathan's way back home, it started to rain. His eyes started doing the same. He couldn't imagine life without Sive. He wanted her as his wife, the mother of his kids and his life partner. His heart was as heavy as a stone knowing that she was moaning underneath some foreigner. And he could feel its weight in his rib cage. It felt like the blood in her body was still.

"God you can't let her do this to me. Make her realise that Gabriel isn't the man for her…I am. You know I can't live if living is without that woman. She's my everything, dear Lord."

The prayer ended with his car entering his garage. When Jonathan heard the garage door close, he threw himself on the steering wheel, and soon his body was trembling in pain.

"I love Sive and I can't live without her," he silently said those words. He then lifted his body from the steering wheel, looking through his car window at the glass door that led into the house.

"Sive's mine…only mine. She has to be mine. I just can't sit and watch my life pass me by…Sive, you're mine babe. You're mine!" he screamed, shutting his car door and walking through the glass door.

**

Sive woke up the following morning topless, embraced in Gabriel's arms, on his side of bed, under his own blanket. Her bare, round and firm breasts pressed against his bare, big chest. Their legs tangled.

They had separated their blankets and put a pillow in between them the previous night. The pillow was on top of Sive's blanket in the morning.

While Sive was moving as she was waking up from her sleep, Gabriel opened his eyes. He was the one who first noticed that Sive was naked. His heart started pounding with fear that he might have done something he shouldn't have done.

When Sive saw the fright on Gabriel's face, she pulled her eyes to where Gabriel was staring. She screamed,

"No! What happened? I was in my pyjamas when I got into bed last night."

They both looked if their bottoms were naked, and they were still covered.

Gabriel looked at Sive thoughtfully.

"Are you sure you didn't take your top off?"

"And what would I do that for?" she asked, confused.

Gabriel shrugged. "I don't know, baby. I'm trying to figure out how it happened," he replied.

Sive stared at her bottom part that was covered.

"What is it baby?"

"Are you sure we didn't…you know?" she asked in a low, confused voice.

"What?" He quickly got what she meant. "No baby! We didn't, otherwise we would know."

Sive gave him a puppy look.

"I was just asking out of confusion."

"Maybe you felt hot in your sleepwear and just took it off without knowing," he said, trying to explain how it might have happened.

"It's ok baby, at least we did nothing," she said then buried herself in Gabriel's chest. "It feels good to be in here, anyway," she confirmed.

"Yeah babes, it does," he agreed, squeezing her body gently in his arms.

Gabriel loosened the grip of his arms and looked at her.

"Something awkward about this."

"What baby?"

"Were you trying to rape me, woman?"

"What?"

"You were the one who was found, naked…"

"Half naked," Sive corrected him.

"Yeah, on my side of the bed…in my blanket. What's up, babe? Do you wanna tell me?" said Gabriel teasingly.

Sive smiled sheepishly.

"Hey, don't get embarrassed honey, I'm just kidding," said Gabriel stroking her back. "I'm your man babe, if you want me…you want me. And that's ok."

Sive stared at him with those big, white eyes.

Gabriel chuckled. "I mean when you wanna be close to me."

They embraced each other.

"I love you, baby," said Gabriel.

Gabriel could feel the depth of her love without words being used. The way she looked at him, touched him, talked to him, all preached how deep her love was for him. They were so comfortable in each other's skin.

"It's been a few hours, including those we spent sleeping since we met. But it feels like I have known you all my life," said Gabriel, holding her in his arms.

"I feel the same, and I love you wholeheartedly, my love. I'm enjoying every moment with you. I feel I trust you to the point that I could tell you about my illness I just discovered," she said, with her face buried in her lover's chest, close to his heart where her name was engraved.

Gabriel didn't know that Sive was admitting that she unconsciously took off her clothes and got under his blankets, by saying illness. He thought of the AIDS James fed his mind with. Gabriel's heart beat faster beneath Sive's ear when he heard the word, "illness". He just thought about what James said the previous night. James's voice was once again clear in his memory. He just knew that James was right about Sive's HIV. He quickly remembered himself saying HIV or not he loved Sive, and now, the endless love was being tested.

Sive lifted up her head and looked at him.

"Baby, what's wrong?"

"What?"

"Your heart is pounding a million times a second…what's up?"

"Oh that? I'm just impressed with your words and felt so scared of losing you," he replied nervously.

Although his heart told him she had HIV, he loved her no less.

"Baby I'm preaching my undying love for you, and you still think of me leaving you?"

Gabriel kissed her passionately.

"I know my love. I was just being silly."

"I'm stuck with you, in case you haven't noticed," said Sive receiving a kiss.

"Stuck!"

In Gabriel's mind, it sounded as if she meant she was stuck with him because no one would want her with her condition. Soon, his smile was removed from Gabriel's face.

"Yea, baby. Stuck. The depth of my love for you makes me see no man but you. I wanna be yours till my face is covered with wrinkles," she expressed her sincere feeling.

When Gabriel realised that he got it all twisted, he squeezed her even harder against his chest.

"Ah baby, watch it! You gonna break my bones."

Gabriel laughed and loosened up a bit and then dropped a gentle kiss on her forehead.

Sive smiled softly.

Gabriel quickly rolled over her adorable body. Sive moved her legs apart and he made himself comfortable in between them, and his face against hers. The beauty of her breasts stole his attention for a moment, and then he stretched his hand to feel them. They were firm, but soft. He lifted his eyes to look into Sive's eyes.

"Can I have a taste, babe?" he asked softly.

Sive looked into his eyes, and nodded.

"Thanks," he replied kissing her voluptuous lips. He kissed her until she was loose and started moaning delightfully. Her legs spontaneously moved apart.

Gabriel made sure that their genitals were at least greeting each other and saved knowing each other better for another day.

Soon, Sive's hands were all over his baldhead, and the moans were taking on another level now.

In Gabriel's mind, there was no doubt that this woman loved every bit of it and she was ready to move to the next level. He then slipped his hand into her underwear, when his fingertip touched her private parts, Sive jumped and soon was on her buttocks.

"No! Baby, you..."

"It's alright now my love...I'm sorry," he said, his heart throbbing. He was so scared that what he did was a turn-off.

Sive looked at Gabriel's eyes and realised he was hungry for it, and she felt sorry for him. She hugged him and whispered in his ear,

"I know you want it baby, but I'm not ready."

Gabriel moved a bit away from her to view her face. He put his hands on either side of her face and said, "It's ok, my love. I can wait. What's important to me is that, we're here. Together."

Sive smiled naughtily, and said, "When we've started doing it, you can ask for it, anytime. Anywhere."

"Really! That's so sweet my love," replied Gabriel looking amused.

"Oh baby, there's another thing," he said, sitting next to her.

"What is it baby?"

Gabriel smiled. "I'm invited to a friend's birthday party tonight, and I would love if you could come with me," he requested.

"Baby, why didn't you tell me in advance so I could bring something proper to wear?"

"Don't worry; we can go get you something to wear, honey."

"You mean, spending your money on me?" she asked, surprised. She heard that guys spend on women when they want something. Therefore, in her mind Gabriel was still trying his luck to taste her cake.

"Baby relax. I'm your man. Aren't I?'

"Yes, but…"

"No buts, baby, just…"

"I didn't give you what you wanted, and you wanna spend money on me…"

Gabriel's smile faded and he gradually slipped off the bed, grabbed his gown from the couch and went to the bathroom. Soon water was running.

Sive quickly got off the bed and followed him into the bathroom. His face was covered in a towel, as he was drying it. When he removed it, he saw her beautiful breasts, and threw a towel on her.

"Cover up your body," he said and walked out of the door.

Sive followed him into the kitchen; her body was covered in a towel.

"Baby," she said in a low voice.

Gabriel turned and looked at her.

"Sive, how could you think that low of me? Sex is not what I'm after. I love you." His voice started low and rose up with each word coming out of his mouth.

Sive was standing still, listening.

"I love you, do you hear me? I love you damn it, with all my heart," and then lowered his voice. "What I feel for you is what I've never felt for any other woman. I loved you before I even laid my eyes on you. When I didn't even know how you looked. Yes, I have a desire to make love to you…to my woman. But, when you're ready."

"I'm sorry baby," she said, and couldn't explain any further since her explanation might reveal her ignorance on relationships, and that wasn't a good time for him to know that he was her first.

Sive slowly walked towards the bed and threw herself on it. She looked sad, bothered by secrets she found herself loaded with. Her friends and her mom didn't even know about her visit to Johannesburg or that she was even dating.

Gabriel knew her as a mother when she was merely a virgin. She kept Jonathan's obsession with her to herself. She thought she was protecting him from getting hurt without knowing that she was giving him false hope that she would pay for, dearly.

Sive was known as a transparent glass that can't hide anything. Now, she became a thick wall that hides everything.

Sadness on her face pained Gabriel's heart and he went to sit next to her, holding her hands.

"What's wrong, honey?"

Sive shook her head, "Nothing."

"Are you sure?"

Sive broke a smile and then nodded. "Yeah."

Gabriel tilted his head. "Please let me pay for your outfit, my love," he pleaded under the dose of love.

Sive looked him in the eyes, and something in them told her that she could trust him.

She nodded.

"Is that a yes?" He asked excitedly.

"Yes."

Gabriel embraced her and quickly got up. He pulled Sive.

"Get your nice ass off my bed and get ready," he said teasingly.

Sive laughed as Gabriel tapped her cute round buttocks.

"You rude baby, go and wash that mouth!"

They both glanced at the clock on the wall and looked at each other.

"It's five past ten!" they both shouted at once, ran into the bathroom and ran the water. Soon, they were both naked, and realised that they weren't supposed to be in that manner. They stared at each other uncomfortably, and then both burst out laughing and jumped in the shower.

Gabriel rubbed soap on Sive's back. He had a beautiful view of her curved body from the back where there were no eyes to distract him. He watched the foam of soap driven down her spinal cord to in between her buttocks.

Sive was enjoying it. She had never been in a shower with anyone, except when she was growing up with Sma. When they visited their grandparents, they used to shower together. Now those days were gone.

Gabriel turned her around and covered her with his arms. He kept her in there for a moment. Suddenly, the fear of losing her from nowhere invaded his mind. He slowly moved her away to look at her pretty face. He looked into her sparkling, white, big eyes.

"Please, don't leave me." He said with a voice that comes in between the walls of a deep pain.

Sive was looking at him, confused. She didn't know where all that was coming from. She didn't know that her beauty reminded him of how all his relationships ended. Women always left him. He couldn't figure it out how Sive with all her beauty could be different. He moved slowly to drop a gentle kiss on her tender lips, and then looked at her face again.

"I can't afford to lose something as beautiful as you are."

"Baby, I'm not going anywhere. I'll grow old with you." She curled up her lips in a naughty smile. "Unless a prettier woman could take my place in your heart."

Gabriel extended his lips in a happy smile.

"In that case, I should relax. You're forever mine, 'cause no woman is prettier than you are," he said, bending down to kiss her and then covered her in his arms.

"Let's get done baby." She said, feeling a bit uncomfortable to be so close to him in that manner.

"Yeah babe," he said swinging her under the water. She screamed, laughing.

Soon they were standing in front of the mirror with their bodies covered in towels, applying body lotion. Sive pulled off Gabriel's towel.

He chuckled. "You're such a naughty girl," said Gabriel, and then pulled her towel off, too.

They both giggled.

"That's how it was supposed to be when applying body lotion, right? Naked?" said Sive, busy rubbing lotion on her cute leg.

Gabriel looked at her, and stopped massaging his body.

"Exactly," he agreed, and then continued massaging his body.

When Sive looked at Gabriel, he was already dressed up.

"Wow! You look breath-taking."

"Thanks babe."

"You need a little bit of this now," she said, lifting a narrow bottle of a perfume and chasing him. Gabriel ran, laughing.

"Baby I can't smell like a girl," he said, opening a door trying to run away from her, and he bumped into James who was at the door, about to knock. He was returning Gabriel's car. Sive bumped into Gabriel's back and they all fell on the floor, just outside Gabriel's door; James, underneath, Gabriel on top of him and then Sive.

Sive and Gabriel were still giggling and Gabriel was trying to get the bottle of perfume from Sive. He knew if she could spray it on his clothes, the whole attire would be ruined.

"Guys, please get off me!" he yelled from underneath, pushing them away.

"Baby wait, wait," said Gabriel getting up, and then Gabriel offered James his hand to help him get up.

James glared at him.

Gabriel whispered, "I'm sorry."

"Are you crazy man?" he asked shaking dust off his clothes. "Now you're acting like a kid," he added.

"Is there anything wrong when a fella is happy?" asked Gabriel, happy.

"No , if…" he wanted to say if the happiness is gonna last, but he stopped himself and just continued shaking off the dust.

James turned to Sive and greeted her politely.

Sive smiled and replied with a sweet, warm voice.

"Good morning, James."

"I hope your first night here was good," said James smiling for the first time at Sive, and maybe for the last time as well.

Chapter 15

Gabriel and James were childhood friends. They went to the same secondary school in Lagos. James was the one who had always had good girls. Gabriel had never been that lucky. In fact, he had never had any luck when it came to girls. He always left with a broken heart if he was lucky enough to get one.

Although it was funny when they grew up, it changed to pain over the years. It bothered James so much that his friend couldn't get as much fun as the rest of their friends did.

It seemed like a disease with no cure.

Gabriel tried everything to keep a relationship, even throwing his money at girls, but nothing worked.

Sive picked up a perfume bottle cap from the floor and looked at him, still smiling.

"You're the best," said Gabriel amusingly.

"Oh, she kept you all night long?" Gabriel glared at his crazy friend. "I know that smile boy," added James.

Sive glanced between them uncomfortably. "We were just talking," said Sive, correcting whatever James was thinking. She then walked inside.

Both of them watched her walking away.

"Shit! She's a bomb, I must admit," said James.

Gabriel glared at him. "Shut up! She's my woman, man."

"Come on man, I was just admiring God's nature."

Gabriel pushed him. "Get out of my way."

James wasn't even in his way. It was just his own way of appreciating that his friend finally accepted Sive. What Gabriel didn't know was that his friend was not even close to accepting his relationship with Sive.

James chuckled.

"Hey! Catch," he said throwing his car keys, "your keys, man."

Gabriel caught them and put them in his jeans pocket. "Thanks man."

James smiled mischievously.

"Don't give those keys to that phantom for her birthday."

Gabriel smiled. "Shut up, you fool," then the smile on Gabriel's face faded away. "Are you still calling her that?"

"No man. I was just pulling your leg. You're a big boy so I decided to let you make your own mistakes."

"If it is."

"Yeah," replied James walking away.

"Hey man!"

James turned.

"Where're you going?"

"Catching a taxi home."

"I'll give you a ride home."

James pursed his lips. "Ok, sure," he replied and then started walking, following Gabriel into the house.

Sive was busy clearing the clothes on the bed.

"Leave that babes, we can do it when we get back," said Gabriel opening one of three wardrobe drawers, the bottom one. He ran his eyes between the items that were scattered there, including some belts, which he took one of. A black one. He then looked around, tucking his belt in his jeans.

"Honey, have you seen my wallet somewhere?"

Sive bent down and pulled out his jeans from the pile of clothes that were folded on the bed. She pulled out a dark brown wallet from one of its pockets, and gave it to Gabriel. "Here."

Gabriel dropped a kiss on her forehead. "Let's go guys," he said, approaching the door and James joined him. Gabriel turned back to get Sive's hand. She was still standing by the bed, watching them leaving.

"What's up babes? Let's go." He glanced at his cell phone. "It's twenty past twelve now," he added.

"Exactly, and I didn't eat anything since yesterday afternoon in Cape Town."

Gabriel sunk into a pit of embarrassment. He couldn't reply. His throat quickly went too dry to slip out any word.

James, who was just behind him, chuckled. "You shagged a hungry chick the whole night?" he murmured.

Gabriel glared at him. "Shut up, you fool," he said and turned to Sive.

"Can't we grab something on the way, babes?"

Sive nodded. "Ok, but my breakfast time has long passed.

"I know honey, I just got excited and…"

James got annoyed and interrupted him. "Got excited!" He chuckled.

"Shut up man!" said Gabriel looking at James who was annoying him.

Sive moved to Gabriel and stood in front of him, looking at his face. She blinked her big eyes twice and said, "Let's go."

Gabriel threw his arm around her waist and pulled her closer. "I'm sorry my love," he said holding her against his chest.

"Guys!" said James signalling with his head to go.

Gabriel took Sive's hand and walked towards the door. When they passed James, standing in the corridor, by the door, Gabriel gave him a slight shove in the back, trying to cheer him up.

"Get out my way, you moron," said Gabriel jokingly.

James laughed and said, "Throw the keys. I don't mind being your chauffeur till I get to my place. Beyond that, you get behind the wheel," he said, smiling at his friend.

James didn't want to ruin Gabriel's happiness, but he also didn't want to see him hurt again. He loved him so much that sometimes he crossed the line in protecting him. Gabriel quickly slipped his hand in his jeans pocket and threw the keys at his friend.

"You such a smart fool, you moron," said Gabriel, laughing at his friend's unspoken reply.

Sive laughed. "Can a fool be smart?" she asked.

"See! If you're not thinking of dumping this fool," said James, wagging his finger at Gabriel, "You'll definitely be having bad taste in guys," he added.

They all laughed.

A part of James wanted to trust Sive, but her beauty and the way Gabriel found her made him sure that she was just one of them. He was keeping an eagle eye on her and he was definitely sure that Gabriel had no future with her. He thought Sive was either HIV positive or in that relationship for a catch, but definitely not true love.

Sive looked at Gabriel, smiling. "My life wouldn't be the same without him.'

Gabriel looked at her with an impressive smile, and the James.

"Get behind the wheel chauffeur and do what you're paid for and shut the hell up," said Gabriel laughing, opening the car door for his queen.

James laughed and said, "I wonder how long you will pretend to be a gentleman?" he was looking at him, waiting for his answer.

"'Till I die," replied Gabriel confidently, and then walked around the car to get in on the other side.

After James inserted the key, he turned to look at Sive.

"You might come back from the party tonight singing another tune, my dear. There will be good guys there, nothing like this fool," said James, pointing at his friend whom he gave a fright because he knew that there would be some fine dudes there.

"Hey, tell me if you don't want me to come to that damn party!" said Gabriel, a bit annoyed.

James laughed and threw his hands in the air. "I was just kidding man," he said and drove off.

***

It was Saturday afternoon, a few hours before Simamkele's flight departed from Cape Town International.

Smamkele and Owam were cosy in bed, treasuring their last moments together. Six months is really a long time for people who love each other as much as Owam and Smamkele. They made love the whole day since Smamkele had packed his luggage the night before.

They loved each other so much. Owam was a good person with a generous heart, but easily got annoyed with people who had a problem with his sexual orientation. That was the reason he loved Sive so much. She had a great understanding of human nature.

Owam was a girl trapped in a pretty boy's body. He acted like a girl and Sive condoned that behaviour. She even called him girl and he was so delighted when he got called that.

Smamkele's soul was knitted to the soul of Owam like that of Jonathan to David. 1 Samuel 18: 1-4 describes the life of Smamkele and Owam. Their love was so special and inspiring for everyone knew what true love is except for some judgemental souls who consider their kind of love the only love.

Smamkele met Owam at an HIV/AIDS workshop at UCT, and they hit it off immediately. Owam was a very pretty boy with a bubbly personality. Apart from Sive, He was the reason why Smamkele accepted his condition.

Owam was the only one for him, and even the US would never change that…he would be his husband

141

"I'm counting only hours, then you'll be gone," he said, looking sad.

There was silence.

"But I'll be back my love. And, I'll never leave you again," he replied, stroking the side of his face with the back of his hand.

A pause.

"What if you meet someone better than me in the US…would you still think about me?" He asked, the fear of losing him torturing him.

"Baby, please. Don't do this now," replied Smamkele.

"I wanna know baby," he said.

"Baby, no one can take your place in my heart. You're the only one I want in this life. You're the best. No one would wanna lose a bitch like you," said Smamkele, gently pulling his nose.

Owam smiled. He loved it when his man called him a bitch. He knew that word would arouse both of their sexual feelings. Once that word was been dropped, all he could think about was Sma, making him moan…delightfully.

Owam smiled.

"Babe, please wait for me. When I get back I'll finish my studies and make you my husband."

"Promise!" Owam asked cheerfully.

"Promise," he said, kissing him.

Owam's face suddenly covered in sadness. "But baby I wish I could stay with *chomi* till you get back."

"That would be a good idea," replied Smamkele moving his upper body a bit away to view his face. "Talk to Sive, I don't think she would mind. She loves people, and moreover, you're her favourite person."

Owam smiled. "Don't flatter me, sweetie. Who's not Sive's favourite person? Sive smiles at everyone and everything on the street, from old people to little kids with running nose to puppies with rabies."

They both laughed.

"If you want to be treated with respect, mention that you're related to Sive Tikolo.

"Huh, I smell that my baby has used that privilege," said Owam, leaning forward to kiss him.

"More than once, my love," he confirmed.

They laughed.

"And soon, I'll be related to her by marriage and gain that privilege too," he said, moving his hand slowly across his strong belly towards his waist.

"Don't tell me you want some, babes," said Smamkele with sexy hungry eyes.

"I wanna have too much of it to hate it for the next six months," he said, slipping his hand in his underwear.

"In that case, I'm all yours my bitch," he said turning him over on his belly and stroking his buttocks, and then they made love. They started on the bed and finished on the floor.

Sweaty. And salty.

***

It was afternoon, and Aviwe was still in her blue pyjamas. She was curling up on her snow white leather couch, holding a bowl of cereal. She was staring at the air in front of her, stirring slowly with a spoon. She was lost in her deepest darkest thoughts of her childhood.

Suddenly, the loneliness clung to her heart. The pleasure of her wildness turned into an aloe juice. In Sbongile's absence, she realised her loss, and she knew in her mind that he wasn't coming back.

Sbongile had told her too many times to clean up her act, but she continued taking their love for granted.

Aviwe was always out with friends, partying while Sbongile was home cooking and cleaning on the days Zenande, their helper, wasn't on duty. She only worked two days a week.

Although Sbongile wasn't a sexist, he wanted a woman who knows her place, who's proud of being a woman. Not the one who's clueless of what she wants.

Aviwe's secret of taking her clothes off for every X chromosome was eating her up inside and destroyed her relationship with the man who loved her so much. Lucky for her, her conscience was slowly waking up from its deep sleep.

Aviwe's thoughts brought her back to the days when she would bump into her mother making love to a different guy each time. She was the only child her mother, Nolwazi, had raised. Nolwazi was a dark beauty with curves in all the right places, tall and slender.

Aviwe picked up her phone and dialled her mother's line.

"Aviwe, hi baby."

Aviwe's tears welled off her face. She couldn't say anything.

"Are you alright, honey?" Her mother asked.

There was silence.

Aviwe sighed deeply. "I've turned out just like you…just like you," said Aviwe coldly. Her voice was low. But clear.

Another silence fell.

Nolwazi just knew what she meant. She'd never wanted her daughter to end up like her.

"I can't get enough of sex. And I don't know how to treat a man," Aviwe said, breaking the silence.

"But you and Sbongile are engaged, sweetheart?" Nolwazi said in a shaky voice.

"Not anymore. He left last night."

"Baby, what do you mean?" Aviwe didn't answer. She was in deep pain. "He's gonna come back baby…he has to…"

Aviwe laughed sarcastically. "Who could come back for a woman like me, Mom?" She wiped the tears from her pretty face. "Open your eyes mom! He's not coming back. He's done with me…done!" There was an awkward silence. "Like mother like daughter, right?" she added.

"Baby, I'd never wanted you to become like me. I wanted you to become a better woman than I was."

"Charity begins at home, my dear mother. What were you subjecting me to when you changed men in front of me? Not to mention exposing me to sex at a very young age. I didn't even know who my dad was in those guys. When I asked who my dad was, you got angry and fought with me." There was a pause; "I need to know him now and I'll drag you to court if I have to."

A short silence fell. Both of them were crying on each end of the line.

"We should meet in person and talk about this, baby. I'll come to Cape Town on Saturday if it's ok with you."

"Ok. Thanks, mom."

"Bye baby."

Aviwe curled up on her couch, crying. Sive was the only person in her mind. If she hadn't gone to Johannesburg, she would go and talk to her. Sive had a gift of making everyone's emotional pain manageable.

All Aviwe wanted was to be in Sive's arms. She believed just being there could make a difference. In that moment, she forgot every bad thing Mihle fed her about Sive.

Aviwe quickly jerked herself up into a sitting position, picked up her phone from the couch, and called Sive. It went straight to voicemail. She stared at her phone for a moment, and then threw herself back into a lying down position. She cried herself to sleep.

***

Gabriel and Sive found themselves in Truworths clothing store, after walking happily up and down Sandton, hand in hand. They were wearing bubbly faces that said to everyone passing by…behold. They took pictures all around Sandton. It was the lingerie that made them realise they were in Truworths women.

A red push up bra with a matching panty stole both of their attention. They slowly moved their eyes away from it and looked at each other, wearing a naughty smile.

"It's beautiful," whispered Sive.

"Take it," Gabriel whispered back.

Sive put it on her arm and they continued going around the shop, looking for an outfit for Sive for the party that evening. They were both on top of the moon doing things together as a couple. Gabriel couldn't get his hands off her slim figure.

Sive found black shorts and a white blouse.

"Baby, this is perfect!" she said excitedly, holding up both items in one hand.

"Go fit them babes and see if that's what you want," said Gabriel, not happy at all about the outfit his woman had chosen. He was so uncomfortable with her displaying her legs.

However, he paid for it because that was what his woman wanted.

***

It was after three in the afternoon on their way back home when they were passing by a park, full of people. Sive looked at Gabriel.

"Let's join them," she said.

"What!" Asked Gabriel, confused.

"These people, at the park."

Gabriel glanced at his watch.

"Baby, it's already past three. The party starts at seven, remember? We won't have enough time to get ready," he stretched his lips into a smile, "You know how long you women take to get ready," he added.

Sive gave him a begging look.

"Ok baby. But we're not gonna be long," he said, pulling off the car.

145

Sive kissed him while he was trying to park his car, next to the latest model BMW.

"Whoa babes! Do you want me to hit this car? I will have to sell everything I have, including you to have it fixed," he said, parking his car.

"What!" she bulged out her big eyes at him, "You won't get rid of me that easily boy."

"You're my life. There's no way that I can get rid of you."

Sive smiled at him. "I wanna make a promise. But I can't until I have asked you something," she said looking at him, and then opened the car door.

"What promise you wanna make?" Gabriel asked, his heart beating fast.

"Get out of the car baby and enjoy the sunlight," she said, standing outside the car.

The sun was bright and the park was full of bright colours. People were walking up and down green trimmed grass, others sitting on the wooden branches that surrounded the park.

When Sive looked around, she saw a white vehicle decorated with different flavours of ice cream. She looked at him.

"Do you want an ice cream?"

"Yeah, I do."

Sive pulled his arm towards a vehicle.

"I want vanilla, and you babes?" she asked, opening her purse.

Gabriel quickly took out a R50 note from his jeans pocket and gave it to the big man in the ice cream vehicle.

Sive glared at him for overriding her paying for the ice cream.

"What, babes?" asked Gabriel, pretending he didn't know why she was glaring at him.

Sive closed her purse and tucked it under her arm again.

Gabriel collected the change, put it in his pocket, and then took the ice cream from the guy. She gave Sive the vanilla one and started licking the chocolate.

They walked quietly towards the wooden branch. When Gabriel started thinking Sive was upset, Sive turned and smiled at him.

Gabriel replied with a smile.

They both sat on the bench, not far from the ice cream vehicle.

"I always buy this flavour," said Gabriel, lifting up his cone. He chuckled. "I'm not sure if I know how others taste."

Sive squinted at him with a naughty smile.

"Someone wanna have a taste of my yummy ice cream," she said teasingly.

Gabriel replied with a smile full of affection. "I wanna follow your tongue route on that ice cream with mine," he said looking at her.

At that moment, his love for her went too deep. All he could think about was the positive things and not the negative. In that moment, in her eyes, he saw them growing old together.

With her, Gabriel felt like a man. A real man. Not some client who's forced to pay for every service rendered, even those that have not yet been rendered.

With her, Gabriel felt like he was at peace with the whole world. He was sure of his feelings for her and he didn't care what her intentions were with him.

Gabriel moved closer to the cone, looking into Sive's eyes. He then lowered her head to the ice cream and started licking it. He made sure that his tongue covered all the areas Sive's did.

Suddenly, Sive's naughtiness invaded her mind. She shoved the ice cream into his face and Gabriel was soon a mess. The ice cream was on both of his lips.

Gabriel smiled at her. "You're naughty."

Sive looked into his eyes. "Don't worry, I have something soft to wipe this mess with," she said, slowly leaning forward to wipe his lips.

Sive licked Gabriel's lips, starting with the bottom, and then the upper lip. She then moved backwards and observed his face. A dose of her affection was working on him. His lips were open for more and his eyes saw only her in that entire park.

"Is that all?" asked Gabriel.

Sive glanced over her shoulder. "We're not alone in this park, babe. When we get home, I'll take care of you," she replied, wearing a naughty smile.

"I don't forget such sweet promises, young lady," he said, smiling tenderly at his woman.

"And I don't make such sweet promises with no intention of fulfilling them, dude," she said, and then winked.

Suddenly, Gabriel remembered what Sive said earlier. The smile on his face faded away.

"You said earlier you will make a promise after asking me something…what did you mean babe? What is it that you want to ask me?"

Suddenly, seriousness replaced a smile on her face. She moved a bit away from Gabriel to have a full view of him when answering the most important question that would detect if Gabriel were her ideal man or not.

Gabriel could tell from the look on her face that there was some seriousness to this question, and his heart started pounding with fear.

"I'm listening, babe," he said. Sive perceived fear in his voice.

"How do you feel about gays," she dropped an unexpected question.

Gabriel was shocked.

"Gays!" he repeated shockingly.

"Yes. Gays. How do you feel about them?" Sive repeated her question.

"I have no problem with them. I love them like anyone else. But," Sive's eyes stretched in suspense, "There's something I love more about them. Their uniqueness. They're like two in one…a woman in man's body, or vice versa. That fascinates me a lot. We have one at work, he's very bubbly, loving and caring," he said, and then licked his ice cream.

Gabriel quickly raised his eyes at her. A thought that she could be a lesbian or bisexual crossed his mind. It was South Africa after all; anything is possible when it comes to it. The rest of Africa referred to it as a Gomorrah, but a Gomorrah that they flock to in numbers.

"Don't tell me you're gay."

Sive chuckled.

"No, I'm not." She licked her ice cream. "And what about disabled people?" she continued asking.

Gabriel jerked backwards on a wooden bench.

"Where are you going with this, babes?" asked Gabriel, afraid of giving her the wrong answers.

Sive smiled. "Somewhere. Please, answer," said Sive in a smile.

She was so pleased with Gabriel's answer to her first question. It accelerated her love for him.

Gabriel licked his ice cream, and then leaned forward to Sive.

"My love, we're all created by God, in his image, no matter how different we may look or think," he extended his lips in a soft smile that knocked Sive off her feet.

She now saw what he was getting to and her heart spontaneously accepted him, "I love everyone regardless of how they look or do things," he explained.

Sive looked at him for a moment, smiling. Tenderly.

Now, her heart rose with an excessive love for him. She tossed the remaining part of her ice cone in her mouth and rubbed her hands together. She rose up and moved to Gabriel. She put her leg in between his and moved them apart. She sat on his lap and threw her arm around his neck.

Gabriel wrapped his arm around her waist and let the other one with the ice cream rest on her other thigh.

They were looking in each other's eyes full of love.

Gabriel could read the depth of Sive's love for him. In that moment, it was written in her eyes. Even his doubting Thomas friend would see it.

"I love you with all this heart," she put her other hand on her chest, "that I have. And now, I can make my promise to you."

Gabriel's eyes widened spontaneously in suspense.

Now, Chikondi's feelings were buried under her love for Gabriel.

"We will grow wrinkles together. And I'll be the mother of your children, and grandmother of your grandchildren," she said sincerely.

Gabriel's lips were gaped in great shock. He couldn't believe his ears. He had never expected to get such sweet words from a lady, not at least someone as beautiful as Sive.

"Do you mean that?" he asked in a shaky voice. He got emotional but he told himself that he won't let his tears fall. Not in that place.

Sive smiled.

"I meant every word. God is my witness," she replied, looking into his eyes.

Gabriel moved his head to kiss her appetizing lips. When their lips touched, he pressed his lips on hers for a moment. He then wrapped both his arms around her body and squeezed her.

His head rested on her breasts while the side of her face rested on his bald head. Gabriel murmured with his mouth buried in between her sweet breasts.

"I love you."

Sive replied with a kiss on his bald head.

After a moment, Gabriel moved his head and looked at her. "Honey, what does this whole gay/disabled people thing have to do with this sweetest promise?" he asked, looking at her, confused.

Sive blinked her eyes twice and then replied. "My love, I know that we love each other. But, sometimes love is not enough to build a strong, healthy relationship."

"Still, I don't get it," he said, looking more confused.

Sive cleared her throat to organise the right words to explain herself.

"If we wanna settle down and have kids one day…"

"Oh dear, believe me I do," Gabriel quickly answered that before Sive could finish her sentence.

Sive grinned and murmured with her teeth tightly closed. "Me too."

Gabriel moved his head and dropped a soft kiss on her forehead. He then moved backwards to look at her pretty face.

"I – love – you – Sive – Tikolo," he said softly and slowly, looking into her eyes.

Sive moved forward to his ear and whispered.

"I love you more my darling," and then softly bit it.

Gabriel leaned forward to have a close look at her as she was sharing a word of wisdom with him. "Carry on my love, your man is listening."

Sive beamed and continued. "It's not marriage that raised the kids well, but the parents' competence and devotion in raising them well. And that has to start somewhere, which is pure and true love for them. When you love someone, you love them for who they are, regardless of their flaws…"

Gabriel interrupted her.

"Exactly like how I love this beautiful woman," he said, poking her flank.

Sive laughed and said, "You're interrupting me again. I'm not done with this talk."

They both laughed, and then carried on. "Anyone who feels ashamed of gays and disabled people is not good parent material at all. What if she or he gave birth to a gay or disabled kid, will they love them less or not love them at all?" said Sive looking into his eyes.

Gabriel nodded. "Now it makes a complete sense."

"Yes, baby. Childhood is the foundation of adulthood. If something went wrong in your childhood, you're more likely to collapse at a later stage. And that collapse contributes to the world's corruption," she then, put both of her hands on either side of his face stroking the roughness of his shaved beard with her right thumbs, "Let's contribute to making the world a better place for all of us by loving our kids with all of our hearts."

Gabriel nodded.

"You're that woman I've been searching for," said Gabriel, and then pulled her closer to him and covered her in his arms, "I want five kids my love," he added, pulling her leg.

Sive quickly broke away. "What!"

"Five kids, my love. We already have one," then he lowered his eyes to her belly, "You have to go another four rounds, tiny tummy," he said patting her flat tummy.

"No babes, two is enough," she replied.

Gabriel tickled her. She tried to move away from his fingers that were all over her body…she fell on the ground with her legs apart. In his attempts to catch her, Gabriel ended up on top of her, in between her legs. They were caught in a gaze of affection, and they were thinking the same thing…at the same time. Kissing.

Both of their lips were gaped. Gabriel got a confirmation from the look on Sive's eyes that she was yearning for a good, passionate kiss.

He then leaned forward, slowly and let his lips touch her sweet, voluptuous lips. He kissed her.

An old woman who was walking with a handsome young man stopped over them. She looked mixed race and no younger than eighty and you could tell she was pretty in her younger days. She was wearing a floral dress and a navy pullover, tucking a black purse under her arm.

The old woman cleared her throat, and then stretched her wrinkles on her face in a soft smile.

"Marry her," she said in a smile.

She looked around and then dragged her feet to the bench and sat. The young man was still standing.

"You look so young. How old are you?" she said, looking at Sive who was already on her buttocks next to her man.

Sive smiled. "I'm twenty-five, turning twenty-six next month, ma'am."

The old lady chuckled. "You're not too young. You have a deceiving look. I thought you were a teenager," she said, and then asked the young man to give her water.

The young man opened a bottle of water that was in his hand and gave it to her.

The old lady sipped and then brought her attention back to Sive.

"Maybe it's because of your extreme beauty. You're so beautiful, darling," she put the bottle of water on the bench and looked at Sive, smiling.

Sive glanced at Gabriel and he squeezed her hand.

The old woman glanced at the young man and cleared her throat again.

"Sit next to granny, my darling," she said, patting the seat next to her and then focused on the young couple on the ground again. She smiled at Gabriel and then switched her focus to Sive, smiling.

"What are your plans for this relationship?" she asked, her eyes running in between them.

"Settle down and start a family," replied Gabriel, without hesitation.

It was possible that it was just a dream that would never come true. It was too hard for Sive to get past Chikondi's death.

"Do you feel the same, my darling?" he asked, looking at Sive.

"Yes. I do."

"Why do you want to marry him?"

"He proved to me that he would love me and our kids, truly."

The woman swung her eyes to Gabriel, "And you, why do you want to marry her?"

Gabriel turned to Sive and viewed her pretty face for a moment. He leaned forward, dropped a light kiss on her forehead, and then turned to the old woman.

"The beauty you see on her face is nothing compared with the beauty inside. A wise woman like her is the best gift a man could get from God. I wanna marry a woman who could be strong for my children even when I'm gone. Life has no guarantees. Above all that, she makes me happy. I love her, wholeheartedly," he explained.

The old woman clapped her weak hands and the young man smiled impressively.

She chuckled and said, "You know exactly what you want my darlings." she sipped her water and looked at them, "and I have a very strong feeling that you'll grow wrinkles like mine," she lifted up her weak, wrinkled hand pointing at the wrinkles on her face, "together." She chuckled. "I got married exactly at your age," she pointed at Sive with her eyes, "I loved my husband with all my heart and he would lay down his own life for me," She stretched a soft smile, and continued, "He was a tall, handsome man with a generous heart. He was a doctor, and I was a nurse," she cleared her throat, "We met in England, he was a South African, and I was English. After two years of going out together, he'd come back to South Africa."

She sipped her water again, "After he left, I couldn't live without my better half and I did what the Bible says. I left my parents' house and followed him."

She coughed, covering her mouth with her wrinkled hand.

"Mind you, I knew no one in South Africa and I'd never been anywhere else in the world besides the United Kingdom. I was so scared, but my hope was in the person at the end of my journey. My boyfriend, Nicholas…"

"Was Nicholas expecting you?" asked Gabriel.

The old woman stretched her wrinkles in a beautiful smile, inspired by sweet memories.

"Oh yes, my dear. We planned it together. We both missed each other like crazy."

"And your parents knew about your trip?" he asked again.

The old woman's romantic story bought back Sive's memories of Malawi. She sighed deeply, questioning why she had to lose him. Why her story had to end up sadly.

Gabriel noticed sadness on her face. He leaned forward to her and whispered.

"Are you ok, honey?"

Sive forced a smile on her face and nodded.

"No. I called them when I arrived in Johannesburg. They were so angry at me…both my Mom and Dad. But they trusted Nick."

She sipped her water again and put the bottle next to her, on the bench.

"When I got to the airport in Johannesburg, Nick was already waiting for me," and suddenly a smile was replaced with sadness on her face, "And I expected a kiss and a hug, which I didn't get. He just stood there in front of me for a while, staring at my face. He wasn't sad, neither smiling."

Everyone was so scared that a sweet story was turning sour.

"And the gesture gave me all the wrong ideas," she continued, "When I started getting pale, he slipped his hand into his black pants pocket and came out with a little, red box. He opened it. Hah!"

She covered her mouth with her hand as if she was surprised, "It was a gold ring, decorated with beautiful, sparkling diamonds…it was so beautiful."

A beautiful smile emerged from her face, "He got on his knees and popped the question, in front of everyone who was there."

Soon her eyes were filled with unshed tears.

Telling the story took her back to that day, when she shed tears of joy.

"I cried, forgetting that I haven't even answered. A black woman, in her fifties said…say yes. And I said yes. He then got up, kissed me, and then buried me in his warm, loving arms."

The old woman stretched her wrinkles into a beautiful smile and continued.

"I heard the sound of clapping hands while I was buried in his arms. Two months later, I was Mrs Nicholas Roger. And God blessed us with three children," she said raising up three fingers, "Two boys and a girl."

The old woman turned to the young man next to her.

"This is Adam, my grandson from my middle born," she rested her weak hand on his thigh, "He always makes sure that I'm taken care of. Instead of going out and doing whatever you young people do, he took me out to be around nature," she extended her lips into a smile, "He's the fruit of my beautiful love with his late grandfather, Nicholas…"

"Oh, Nicholas passed away?" asked Gabriel sadly.

"Yes, my dear. He passed away three years ago, at eighty-three," she coughed and then had a sip of her water, "Although death is a terrible loss, my Nick had lived a complete life. He loved and was loved. He raised our kids with great love."

The old woman smiled and continued.

"Above all that, he witnessed each and every birth of our grandchildren and participated in raising them. He also had an opportunity to hold our first great grandchild," she took a last sip of her water, "Oh, my darlings, enough of my stories." She said putting an empty bottle on the bench, next to her.

"Wow! That was so wonderful and inspiring," said Sive smiling tenderly.

"Let me get you another water, Grandma," offered Adam.

The old lady looked at him. "No, thank you my dear. We're about to go home now," she said and then turned to Sive, "My dear, I know a wonderful thing when I see it. This one," she said pointing to Gabriel and Sive "is a good union…"

"Thank you, ma'am," said Sive impressively.

The old woman tried to get up off the bench. Adam helped her.

She turned to Sive again.

"I'm too old. Eighty-three years old. But, I won't join my husband before attending your wedding my dear. Call me on this number for an invitation, 011 2347654."

Sive took it down and then looked at the old lady.

"Thank you ma'am. I'm sure your lovely, romantic story didn't only inspire me."

Gabriel nodded.

Adam looked at Sive.

"Can we please exchange Facebook user-names to add each other? I would like to be at your wedding, too.

"It's Sive Tikolo. And I'll be glad to see you both at my wedding."

The old lady and her grandson started walking towards the boundaries of the park. Sive wailed.

"Ma'am! Please wait!"

The old woman took ages to turn around. Sive ran to her, and Gabriel followed, walking behind her.

"Can we hug?"

"Oh, my angel," she said spreading out her weak arms, "Come here."

Sive and the old lady were beautifully wrapped in each other's arms. Gabriel took the picture of the beautiful moment, and Adam couldn't resist.

They broke off, and the old woman dropped a kiss on Sive's forehead.

"Take care of you, my dear," she said and waved bye to Gabriel and then walked away, hand in hand with her grandson. Talking and laughing.

Sive watched them walking away, and then glanced at her watch. It was 15:50, and the party was starting at seven. They still had to drive for more than twenty minutes to get home.

Gabriel quickly glanced at her wrist too. He grabbed Sive's arm, ran to his car, and drove off.

Chapter 16

Mihle heard Sive's name in her kids' room as she was lying on the couch. She went to check. Bridgette was playing with her sister, pretending to be Sive while her sister was pretending to be Aviwe.

Mihle stood at the door, listening to them.

Suddenly, she burst out.

"Sive is not welcome in this house anymore; I'll kill her if she sets her foot in these premises. And I don't wanna hear her name again…do you hear me?" she said angrily.

Bridgette got up, climbed onto her bed, and curled up on it.

***

Gabriel was standing with his back against the kitchen cupboard. He gazed at her as she was walking towards him, wrapped in a red towel, coming from the shower.

"What's up, babes?" asked Sive looking at his face.

"I'm hungry, babes."

Immediately her mobile phone rang on the bed.

"Me too, love," she replied walking to answer it. Sive quickly turned around. "But we're lucky 'cause my man cooked yesterday. We just have to warm up the food."

She picked up the phone.

"Hey girl, how's it!" she said cheerfully.

"Not so well," she said in a down voice.

Sive slowly sat on the bed. "What's wrong?" she said in a concerned voice.

Aviwe was quiet for a moment, and then replied. "He moved out. Sbongile moved out." She sniffed tears. "I tried to stop him, but it didn't work," she said, trying to be strong.

"What happened?"

"We fought."

"About?"

There was a long silence. Sive was waiting for her to bring herself together and tell her what really happened.

"What did you fight about?" Sive repeated herself.

"Are you now interrogating me?" said Aviwe angrily.

"You know that I'm not. All I'm trying to do is help," said Sive in a low polite voice. "But if you don't wanna talk about it now, it's ok. We can talk about it when you're ready."

There was another silence.

"How are you coping?" asked Sive.

"Not well at all, we even fought physically."

"Sbongile hit you?" asked Sive, surprisingly.

"No, it was the other way around."

"But why, love? You know that violence doesn't solve anything, instead, it makes things worse."

"When I'm angry all I could think about is to fight, whether physically or verbally.

"But you can stop that."

"How?"

"By telling yourself you won't do it again. You're the only one who can change you."

"But it's not easy," said Aviwe with a shaky voice.

"Nothing is easy, baby. Was getting your degree easy?"

Aviwe shook her head. "No."

"Exactly! Please don't fight with Sbongile ever again. If he wants to leave, let it be," said Sive advising her childhood friend.

"I love him…so much," she replied with a shaky voice.

"I know, but you don't know how to love him. Until you learn how to appreciate his love, give him some space. In the meantime you'll find yourself."

Another silence.

"I guess you're right. "Short silence. "My mom is coming to visit this next weekend."

"That's a great thing. I miss her too."

"We're going to discuss something, and I would love if you could be there."

"If you want me there, I'll be there. That's what friends are for, being there for one another."

"Thanks. Let me not keep you, bye."

"You know I always have time for you, sweetie. Be strong. I love you. Bye…"

"Wait wait, wait!"

"Yes love." replied Sive.

"When are you coming back?"

"Monday morning."

"Ok, see you then."

"Ok. Bye."

Sive's conversation with her friend gave Gabriel a perception of how sweet Sive was, and, that was a plus.

Gabriel had already served the food by the time she finished talking on the phone.

"Honey!" Sive lifted up her eyes at him. "Do you want juice or something?"

"Wine."

Gabriel looked at her in surprise.

"What?" said Sive, bulging out her eyes.

"I thought you said you don't drink."

Sive eyed him. "I want wine," she insisted, with no smile on her face.

"Baby, I don't have it," replied Gabriel still looking astonished.

"Beer then."

Gabriel quickly remembered his previous relationships with drinking women, and how bad they were. Soon his ego reminded him that this was South Africa, where girls drink more than their fathers do.

"Baby, I don't keep alcohol in the house. I drink occasionally, remember?"

Sive burst out laughing, looking at Gabriel.

"What now, babes?" he asked.

"Did you see your face when I was asking for a beer? It was like I was asking for a gun to shoot a nun," she said, still laughing.

"You were not serious, right?" he asked.

Sive shook her head laughing. "No."

Gabriel let out a sigh of relief. "Thank God."

Sive put her hands on her waist. "Oh please, don't tell me it's wrong for women to drink," she said, looking into his eyes.

"No honey. It's just that I've dated drinking women in the past and things were not sweet at all. I was so happy when you said you don't drink."

Sive laughed. "Relax babes, I don't drink," she said, taking her food and heading for the couch.

Gabriel smiled looking at her walking to the couch, followed her, and sat next to her. He stared at her.

"What?"

"I just love having you around, honey," replied Gabriel and then he started eating.

"Hmmm, nice food, my love."

"Thanks honey," he replied, impressed.

Sive rose up in her seat and headed for the fridge. She poured herself a glass of grape juice and then held up the juice bottle.

"How about this, babes?" she asked.

Gabriel smiled sheepishly. "I'm sorry, honey; I forgot to give you something to drink."

Sive smiled. "It's ok. I'm the one who confused you with my jokes…"

"Do you call that a joke when it almost gave me a heart attack?"

Sive chuckled. "I'm sorry, babe."

Gabriel smiled.

Sive leaned forward and kissed him. He put his glass of juice next to his plate.

"Some people do have a really sweet romantic story to share."

Gabriel quickly got what she was referring to, and he lifted his eyes up. "You mean the old lady at the park?" he asked.

"Yes, her."

"The way she believed in us made me see a bright future for us," he said, looking at Sive with eyes full of love.

Sive sipped her juice and lifted up her eyes to Gabriel.

"I don't need anyone to convince me of a future with you. I know we belong together. That wise woman only said what she perceived. I truly love you."

Gabriel got emotional, and held her hands. A bit tighter. Controlled by deep emotions. Unshed tears covered his eyes.

He felt a valve in his throat, blocking a word from coming out to express his feelings. The unshed tears, shed. He pulled Sive to his chest and buried her there, in his loving arms. He then dropped the most affectionate kiss on the top of her head.

Both of their hearts were throbbing.

"Promise me you'll never leave me, Sive."

Sive broke off from him. She looked him into his eyes. "It's death that will come between us," she said, looking into his eyes.

Gabriel looked at her pure, innocent face for a moment. "Marry me," he said.

Sive's eyes widened in surprise, she thought of the general meaning of a marriage. It didn't occur to her that he was referring to her own meaning of marriage…sex.

However, she wasn't ready.

The word, marry, resurfaced her memories of Chikondi. She slowly broke away from him and slowly walked across the room.

Gabriel followed her. The tears were racing down her cheeks.

Gabriel held her arm, then, another one, looking into her wet, sexy eyes.

"Make love to me, Sive. Please," he pleaded.

Sive looked into his eyes with her mouth gaped. She wanted to say what Gabriel wanted to hear. Yes.

However, she was not ready to take their relationship to that level. Not with those unresolved feelings for Chikondi.

Sive had two choices, to move on…or mourn for Chikondi forever.

She shook her head. "I can't. I'm sorry babes," she said crying.

Gabriel wrapped her in his arms. "It's ok, honey, it's ok," he said comforting her.

Gabriel moved his arms from her and walked to the bathroom. Sive called him before he could reach the bathroom door.

"Gabriel!"

He turned to her.

"I love you."

Gabriel nodded. "I know, baby," he said and disappeared into the bathroom.

Sive paced up to the bathroom, grabbed Gabriel's arm, and pushed him so he landed on the toilet seat with his buttocks. She started kissing him unconsciously, trying to fight her demons.

Gabriel noticed that she wasn't herself. He moved her a bit away to view her face. It was red and her body was trembling in confusion and pain. He lifted her up and put her on the bed. He lay down next to her with her face on his chest.

Gabriel stroked her back, murmuring, "It's ok, my love. It's ok."

Sive drifted into a deep, relaxing sleep.

Gabriel glanced at his wrist and it was 18:04, just a little less than an hour before the party started. He moved his arms carefully underneath her and carefully placed a pillow underneath her. He then went to take a shower.

Gabriel wanted to be completely done by the time Sive got up. He wanted her to see him stunning in his new attire.

He started dressing up, and soon, he was in front of his wardrobe mirror. He was dressed in blue-faded skinny jeans, white T-shirt and a black Nike Sneakers. With his beard trimmed well, he looked so good and confident enough to take his beautiful lady out. He couldn't stay away from the mirror.

Gabriel opened his wardrobe door, took out his cologne, and put it on. Now he smelt as good as he looked.

Sive opened her eyes, and without noticing anything, she closed them again.

Gabriel went to sit next to her. He looked at her pretty face. He ran his big finger softly on her delicate facial skin.

"Wake up, sleeping beauty," he said softly.

"What time is it now?" she asked, stretching her body.

"Seven o'clock," replied Gabriel expecting her to be anxious, but she was calm.

Sive wasn't the nervous type. She could remain calm in an impossible situation. She lifted up her body to a sitting position, next to her man. She smiled.

"You're looking awesome, babes."

Now Sive was looking calm, her feelings for Chikondi probably went back to their place. At the basement of her heart.

"Thanks, hun," he said, dropping a soft kiss on her lips.

Sive sat down, in front of a mirror, blow-drying her hair.

***

It was ten past seven at Cape Town International. That awkward moment when lovers have to say goodbye to one another. Smamkele's flight was departing at eight o'clock that evening, and Owam was a bit emotional now.

"Don't do this, baby," said Smamkele, looking at Owam's unshed tears.

"Six months is definitely not a short period of time, what do you expect me to do?"

"To be strong, for me…for us."

Owam forced a smile on his face and hugged him.

"You know I'll be back for you."

"I know," replied Owam, smiling.

"And at least you're no longer lonely. Sive is your best friend, right?"

"Yes, Sive is the greatest person I've ever met."

"You see, with her, you have a family."

Owam smiled.

***

Sive liked her hair silky and soft but with a bit of a volume to extend her beauty. She liked it when the air blows her hair like washing hanged on the line on a windy day.

Gabriel was still glued to the mirror, but now, he wasn't observing his image, but Sive's. He finally moved away from the mirror and walked to the kitchen.

"Honey, have you seen my phone?"

"Check your jeans on the floor, babes," she wailed; the blow dryer was making a huge noise, it was difficult for him to hear.

"What!"

Sive turned the blow dryer off and raised up her head to look at him.

"In your jeans on the floor by the bed," she said, and then carried on.

Gabriel went to sit on the bed.

The phone rang in his hand. It was James. He went to answer it in the bathroom, running away from the noise.

"Hey man! I was about to call you."

"Where are you?"

"I'll be late ,man. I've tried the birthday boy, but his phone is off. Can you give him the phone?"

"I'm still home man. I'll be late, too."

James chuckled. "They say a woman can change a man, now I'm convinced. You've never been late, you are always on time," said James, not impressed at all.

"Shut up man, I'm not the host," he replied, trying not to entertain his attitude.

"Please, don't let her make you forget who you are."

Gabriel sighed. "I know you don't like her. But please, don't make her uncomfortable tonight."

"Yeah you right, I don't like that woman. Moreover, I don't trust her."

"You don't have to tell me that. I know, and it's killing me that my homeboy can't be happy for me..."

James laughed sarcastically. "You're living in a fool's paradise if you think that bitch is in for love."

162

"Bye. I don't wanna spoil my day with your nonsense," said Gabriel, and slipped his phone in his jeans pocket and went to check up on how far his better half was.

Sive was pulling up her black shorts when Gabriel emerged from the bathroom door.

"You have magnificent body, babe. Are you sure you're twenty-five?" said Gabriel impressively.

Sive looked at him. "And soon, I'll be twenty-six. You see, I'm aging," said Sive winking at him.

Gabriel chuckled. "You wish," replied Gabriel. Pouring juice in a glass and standing against the cupboard, looking at his woman.

Sipping his juice.

Soon, Sive was standing in front of Gabriel looking as pretty as a picture. She was wearing black shorts that revealed her stunning legs, a white blouse and black heels that brought her to Gabriel's ear. Her shiny, soft relaxed hair rested nicely on her shoulders. Her silver clutch bag was neatly tucked under her arm, and her leather jacket, on her other arm.

"Shall we?" she said confidently.

Gabriel extended a smile from one ear to the other. "Wow! You look splendid," he complimented, staring at the amazing view in front of him.

Gabriel took Sive's arm, turned her around, and then pulled her closer to him. He looked into her eyes.

"Am I allowed to say, I'm luckiest man on earth?" he said, dropping a soft kiss on her sweet lips.

"Oh yes, my darling," she replied slightly opening her lips to welcome in his soft, warm tongue.

The taste of his tongue weakened her joints. Soon, she dropped everything on the floor. The scent of her perfume turned Gabriel on the same way the fragrance of his cologne did to her.

Gabriel stuck his tongue in her mouth. Deeper. He then tucked in his hands under her blouse to feel her flesh.

Sive moved her body closer to him, and looked at Gabriel's face; she pulled him to the bed and pushed him to land on his buttocks on the bed.

Gabriel thought it was the time, and he didn't want to have the most wonderful moment with her, in a rush.

Sive took off his jacket, and started kissing him…passionately, slowly pushing his body to lie on the bed. Her hands were stroking the roughness of his cut facial hair while Gabriel's hands were caressing the softness of her body.

Everything about Sive turned Gabriel on.

She then whispered. "We have to go now."

"Are you serious, babes? Do we have to end it here?" said Gabriel, yearning for more than just a warm-up.

"Get up, you know we can't go further than this," she said, stretching her arm to help him get up. She then helped him put on his jacket and then dropped a kiss on his lips.

Sive went to the mirror to see if she wasn't a mess.

They then left for the party.

***

Jonathan's heart was in pieces. He couldn't think of anything else except Sive's being away with another man. Not to mention in his arms. It was the second night, and he didn't sleep properly the previous night. It was one nightmare after another.

In Jonathan's dreams, Sive had sex with this person, she fell pregnant, and they discussed their wedding.

When Jonathan woke up, he realised what that dream meant. He told himself that he had to act fast if he didn't want to lose her for good.

Jonathan was lying on his back on his bed, facing the ceiling. Both of his hands tucked under his head. He was a prisoner of his own thoughts, and he couldn't escape.

Not at that moment.

At that moment, the fear of losing her controlled his life. He knew he had to do something, and he had to do it fast before Gabriel got his claws in her life. He was willing to do anything to make sure that Sive was his.

When Jonathan was wondering about those desperate measures, his phone rang. He jumped up, almost hitting the ceiling.

Without looking at the screen, he answered.

"Hello!"

"Hey handsome!" said a woman's voice.

"Sive, is that you?" he said, sitting on the bed.

Although Sive's voice was different from the voice on the phone, he still thought it was her.

"No, it's not her. It's me, Michelle," she replied, cheerfully.

"What do you want?" he said coldly.

"I miss you. Or should I say, that wonderful night?" she said, trying to seduce him.

Michelle believed that feeding Jonathan with sex would make him love her.

"How many times do I have to tell you that I'm in love with Sive…"

"Come on, be reasonable. Sive would never make you happy the way I do. She's just a naïve virgin who's clueless of what men want."

Jonathan dropped his phone and went back to his lying position. He browsed through the pictures of him and Sive on his phone. All he was thinking about was Sive. He wanted her next to him, on that bed, in that moment.

He realised that if he didn't try harder than he ever had he would lose her forever.

When Jonathan was still wondering about in the midst of his thoughts, someone knocked at the door.

Although Sive had never been to his house and she was miles away, he still thought it was her. He jumped off the bed and headed for the door.

It was Michelle.

She was dressed in nothing but a long black jacket and black heels. Before Jonathan could say anything, she unbuttoned the jacket.

Soon, it hit the floor, revealing her body that wasn't exactly one to die for. At least it was a good distraction Jonathan needed before having Sive on billboards as a lost person.

Jonathan ripped off his clothes, and soon he was in his birthday suit. He started kissing her, hard, driving her around the living room, from wall to wall until they landed on the kitchen table.

Jonathan violently wiped off everything on the table with his hand and put her on the table. He made love to her, hard and violently like there was no tomorrow.

He then left her on the table and walked out of the kitchen door to his room. He took his pyjamas, threw them on the bed, and went into the bathroom.

Jonathan wet his body, and slowly rubbed the soap on it. He then started scrubbing his body and when he got to his manhood, he scrubbed it hard until he realised it wasn't worth it. He saw no point of scrubbing all the dirt when Sive was as filthy as sin where she was.

Jonathan sat on the shower floor, letting the warm water rinse over his body. His heart was still so broken, the distraction session only made his pain worse.

He got up and dried up his body. When he emerged from the bathroom door, his eyes caught the sight of Michelle on the bed, covered in a blue towel.

Michelle rose up and went into the bathroom. Jonathan heard the sound of running water and realised that Michelle would take long in the bathroom and he could not wait for her. All he wanted to do was to take a drive to distract all the negative thoughts in his mind.

Chapter 17

It was already past eight when Sive and Gabriel got to the party. People were at the backyard dancing to Cleo's song, Side to Side.

Everyone was enjoying themselves, except for James. He was standing by the front gate, waiting for his best friend. The thought that Sive was poisoning Gabriel's mind was troubling James. Sive noticed that she wasn't James' best person but decided to take it easy and maybe he would come around in time.

James cared so much for Gabriel; all he wanted for him was a reliable, caring and loving woman. Not some gold-digger like Sive. And he told himself he wouldn't stop interfering with his life until he found that woman.

Gabriel knew James loved him so much, although sometimes he found his over-protective behaviour annoying. He loved Sive with every breath he took and all he wanted was for James to be happy for him.

Gabriel pulled out his car next to James' car. He got out and then moved to the other side and opened the car door for his lady. He held Sive's hand and walked towards the gate where James was standing, bored.

James looked away, bored, as the couple approached him and then quickly turned to Gabriel.

"Where've you been, man?" he asked angrily.

"Chill man, we're here now."

"Don't tell me to chill." He glanced at his watch. "It's twenty past eight and the party started at seven…"

"Come on James. What's your problem?" said Gabriel, standing in front of him with his beautiful Sive by his side.

"You! You're my problem. You've changed a lot lately."

"I haven't changed," replied Gabriel, and then walked towards the house, holding Sive's hand with one hand, cell phone and car keys in the other.

Sive and Gabriel were dressed in white tops and black leather jackets. They looked so cute together. Sive looked so happy.

James was watching them walk away. Suddenly, he burst out.

"Ajay is our homeboy, man. You're turning your back on your real friends! For what, a fake!" he said angrily.

Gabriel pulled his hand from Sive and quickly turned to James.

"Did I!" he looked around, "What I see now is myself at Ajay's place, attending his birthday party. So how exactly am I abandoning my friends?" he asked, angrily.

"When the party is almost over!" replied James.

Gabriel glared at him, and then turned and walked away. He patted Sive's shoulder and whispered.

"I'm sorry for this honey."

Sive smiled at him. "It's ok, baby," she said and then tucked her arm under his as they were walking to the house, leaving James standing there. Looking sad.

Sive and Gabriel went into the house and found Ajay talking with some friends in the kitchen, probably his business associates. Everyone looked astonished at the couple entering the kitchen door.

Ajay put his glass of wine on the table and walked to greet his friend.

"Hey, man!" said Ajay, hugging Gabriel.

"Hey man, how're you going?"

"I'm good, man. You?"

Ajay introduced everyone in the room except for the woman who was standing with her back propped against a sick cupboard. She was dressed in a red dress and red heels. She was dark in complexion and looked like a foreigner.

"Nice meeting you guys," said Gabriel, shaking hands. "This is my girlfriend, Sive," he added.

Ajay bulged out his eyes surprisingly.

"Are you kidding me!" exclaimed Ajay, "This, Miss Universe!"

"Well, my Miss Universe," replied Gabriel wrapping his hand around her waist and squeezed her against him.

Ajay was a positive person who only saw a woman that could make his friend happy, and he liked her.

However, there was this confusing feeling he had when he looked at Sive. He could say it was an intimate feeling. But how? She was his best friend's woman.

Ajay shook the thought and smiled at her, opening his arms. "Welcome to the family," he said, hugging her.

James came in when Sive was in Ajay's arms and he just knew he'd accepted her. He went to the woman by the sink, whispered something in her ear, and then went out to join the dancing crowd in the yard.

"I'm coming now honey," said Gabriel running after James, leaving Ajay with his woman. He trusted him.

Ajay was left with the two women as everyone else had already gone outside. He exchanged glances between them in a smile that showed he knew something they didn't. In fact, that Sive didn't know.

At least now, the other woman knew that Gabriel had a woman. She wanted a man to take care of her, and she hoped Gabriel was the one.

"Well, ladies," said Ajay smiling between them.

Sive smiled, took a few steps to the other lady and extended her arm.

"I'm Sive from Cape Town."

"I'm Nancy from Nigeria. But I live in Thembisa," said the lady who wanted Sive to know that she and Gabriel were from the same country.

Sive smiled. "That's nice. How long have you been in South Africa?"

"About eighteen months."

"Nice meeting you, Nancy," said Sive in a beautiful smile that gave Ajay a good perception of her.

"James!" wailed Gabriel. James turned around. Gabriel walked up to him.

"Did you have to do that man, in front of her, after begging?"

James looked so sorry for his earlier behaviour. "I'm so sorry man. I shouldn't have done that, I was out of line," he said, apologising. "But I don't like her," he added.

"You don't have to like her. Just treat her with respect. That's all I'm asking man."

"I'll do that."

"That's my man," said Gabriel hugging his friend. He twisted a naughty smile on his face. "That's all I'm asking man, and leave the liking part to me. I'll do it," said Gabriel and then walked back to the house.

"Oh, by the way, both of the women inside…are yours man," said James walking away.

"What!" said Gabriel surprised, "James, come back here!" he wailed.

James threw his hands in the air, walking away.

"Yes man. I'm going to my boo now," he said leaving him surprised.

169

Gabriel quickly turned and walked into the house. He found his women chatting. Ajay was busy giving a friend on Facebook directions to his house.

Gabriel nervously glanced at them and then went to Ajay. "Come man," he said pulling his arm into the living room.

"I'm giving someone direc…"

"That can wait," he replied closing the door with another hand.

'Please man, don't tell me," he said pointing in the kitchen's direction, "she's the woman he arranged for me."

Ajay smiled naughty, and confirmed. "She is."

"Damn him!" he said angrily, "What's wrong with this guy?" he looked at Ajay, "What am I gonna do with two women?"

Ajay shrugged.

Gabriel stormed out of the door and passed his women in the kitchen flying like a jet. He found James dancing with his girlfriend. He patted him on the shoulder.

"I wanna talk to you, man!" he said angrily.

James could tell from the look on his face that he had stepped on his toes now. Gabriel was so furious.

"Get out of my business, man! Do you hear me, out!"

"What now man? I thought we were cool."

"Cool about what! Messing with my life!" Gabriel twirled and took a few steps forward and then quickly turned to James, "Are you alright!" said Gabriel, poking James's head with his index finger. Angrily. "Why did you bring that woman here?"

"We agreed about bringing her."

Gabriel just glared at him and walked away.

When Gabriel got in the house, Sive was standing against the cupboard waiting for him, and the other woman was sitting on the chair playing with her hands, waiting for him, too.

Sive smiled at him the moment he came in while the other woman was giving him a look full of questions.

Gabriel, touched by Nancy's look, lowered his eyes. Soon, Sive picked up that something was going on between the two, and she got a little jealous. She walked outside. Gabriel grabbed her arm.

"Where're you going babes?"

"Get some fresh air."

"Why?"

Sive just looked at him.

"Please baby, don't do this. Talk to me."

"I'm not a child. I can see that there's something going on between you and her so I'm giving you some space," she replied in a disappointed voice.

Gabriel wasn't sure whether letting her get some fresh air was the right thing to do, but, anyway, he released the grip.

Sive went out and joined the fun on the dance floor. Gabriel turned and looked at the other woman.

After talking for a while, they left. Gabriel didn't want Sive to see him leaving with Nancy. However, when they headed for the front door, Sive came in from the kitchen door and saw them leaving. She turned around and sat on the chair outside.

Sive was lonely and bored, sipping a grape juice. Ajay noticed her. He went to sit next to her. He smiled at her and Sive replied with her sweet smile.

"This is a party not a funeral, young lady," said Ajay jokingly.

A smile faded away from Sive's face.

"That woman you were with in the kitchen is Gabriel's woman?" she asked.

Ajay found himself answering a question with a question, avoiding saying what he should not.

"Why?"

Sive forced a smile on her face. "I'm sorry. I shouldn't be asking you that." she said.

James noticed that Sive was without Gabriel, and he just knew that Gabriel had finally come to his senses. James knew that Gabriel was a good person he wouldn't just ignore Nancy. He walked up to Ajay and Sive just to make sure that Gabriel was with Nancy.

"Where's Gabriel?" he asked.

"He left with Nancy," replied Sive.

James smiled.

"Enjoy the party guys," he said, rubbing his hands together impressively as he went away, dancing.

Ajay stared at him as he was going away, and then put his attention back to Sive.

James didn't care whether Ajay could hit on Sive. He knew he could manage her type, dangerous type.

Ajay was the cutest of them all, and he changed women as often as changing his socks. They called him sex explorer. He posted on Facebook that he had slept with every type of human on earth and he was looking forward to sleeping with an albino.

James was pushing Sive in Ajay's arms to save Gabriel from Sive's claws. He planned to be nice to Sive so he could get her drunk and wake up the next morning in Ajay's bed.

James quickly came back.

"Sive, are you cool? We have a good wine inside."

"Don't worry, I'll take care of her," replied Ajay.

James knew exactly what Ajay meant. He knew he could relax and enjoy the party now. In the morning, Sive and Gabriel would be history.

Ancient history.

Joe Thomas' song, I Wanna Know, came up and every lady was screaming, except for the most beautiful one.

Sive felt like she could dance with Gabriel to that song but, unfortunately, he had left with another woman. When Sive was deep in those thoughts, she heard Ajay said.

"May we have this dance?"

She nodded. "Yes."

Ajay put Sive close to his body. Soon, his body reacted to the closeness without leaving his mind behind.

Suddenly, his soul attached to the creature in front of him.

Ajay felt like Sive was what his soul was yearning for. He felt a contentment he'd never felt with any other woman, and he was so convinced the universe had sent that woman just for him through a friend.

Sive felt emotional and Ajay took advantage of that. He comforted her.

"You are such an amazing woman," said Ajay, starting a conversation with her body close to his the way he wanted.

Sive didn't even want to know why he said that. She just said, "Thank you," still buried in his chest.

James was watching them over his woman's shoulder, happily. He realised that his plan was working.

When Gabriel arrived, the unpleasant view of his woman in another man's arms, welcomed him. It didn't matter it was his best friend.

172

With Ajay's track record of women, even his father wouldn't trust him with his own mother. He was addicted to women.

James saw Gabriel standing, gazing at the dancing couple. He quickly broke from his woman's arms, coming over to stop him from spoiling his perfect plan.

James' girlfriend wailed after him.

"Baby!"

James ignored her.

"Hey man!" James wailed.

Gabriel turned to him.

"Where's she?"

"Who?"

James turned his eyes to Sive dancing in Ajay's arms, and then back to Gabriel again.

"Leave the two alone, they deserve each other. Focus on your life with Nancy, she loves you and she would make a good wife…"

"What! Are you now arranging a marriage for me?" he snapped, and then went to stop the dance between the two.

Gabriel patted Ajay on the shoulder. Ajay quickly woke up from daydreaming. He smiled nervously at Gabriel who wasn't smiling at all.

"Thanks man. I can take it from here," he said, taking Sive's arm that was resting cutely on Ajay's shoulder.

Gabriel was so jealous, and scared of losing her.

Sive looked at Gabriel. "Let us finish this song," she said, going back to Ajay's arms.

Gabriel stood there, watching them. He then rushed to the table to get himself a glass of wine.

Ajay made sure that his arms rested on all the right places on Sive, and Sive decided to forget about Gabriel and enjoy the moment with Ajay.

Gabriel poured a glass of wine and gulped it nervously.

"Easy man, easy. Do you wanna choke yourself to death?" said Vusi, Gabriel's colleague.

Vusi was a South African. He was one of those South Africans who appreciate the presence of foreigners in South Africa.

"What's bothering you my man?" asked Vusi.

Gabriel pulled out a chair, sat down, and gulped the remaining wine in his glass.

Vusi waited for him to make himself comfortable and tell him what was wrong.

"Go and join the fun," said Gabriel, pointing with an empty glass to the happy people on the dance floor, "I'm ok."

Vusi stared at him for a moment. "Although you don't look the Gabriel I know, since you insist, I'll leave," said Vusi dancing his way to join the others.

Gabriel refilled his glass and took a gulp from it.

He was so scared. He didn't know what Sive was thinking, but he was sure that it wasn't good.

When Gabriel was caught in the middle of his fears, the song ended. He didn't even see Sive coming.

"Is she your woman, Gabriel?" Sive dropped the question.

Gabriel's throat suddenly closed. He couldn't speak. The question or the timing caught him off guard and his name in it gave him a shiver. Sive had never called him by his first name before.

Although Gabriel knew that telling the truth was the right thing to do, he didn't want to say anything that could make things worse than they already were.

"Please, tell me the truth. I need to know," she said in a sad, disappointed voice. Sive's unshed tears glittered in her eyes.

When Gabriel saw the glittering of her unshed tears, he felt a sharp pain in his heart. He put his glass on the table, took her hand, and led the way to the house. They went upstairs, in Ajay's bedroom.

Gabriel helped Sive settle on Ajay's bed. He then pulled her against his chest and closed his arms. He murmured.

"You're my life baby, you're my life."

Sive broke away from his arms. She looked into his eyes.

"Tell me. I have the right to know."

Gabriel sighed deeply. "She's the woman James arranged as my date to this party…with my consent, of course," Sive widened her eyes, "It was before I knew you were coming. When you told me that you were coming, I told James to cancel the plans with her. However, he didn't, so I'd to take her home. I didn't want her to get hurt on my account babe," he explained.

"If I didn't come, she would be your date, right?"

"Yes baby. But I wasn't interested in her or any other woman but you."

Sive gave out a sigh of relief.

"I thought you guys had something going on. I was so worried and disappointed," she said, breaking the smile on her face.

Gabriel leaned forward and kissed her.

His lips touched her soft lips. He talked in between the kisses.

"Baby girl," he kissed her, "I won't," another kiss, "deliberately," another kiss, "hurt you," he then pushed his tongue in her mouth.

Gabriel slowly pushed her to lie on the bed. He then made himself comfortable in between her sweet legs, kissing her, passionately.

Ajay walked in on them kissing on his bed. They were so deep in their love that they didn't even notice Ajay in the room.

Ajay's face suddenly covered with sadness.

Sive saw him, and she poked Gabriel. "Baby," she pointed at Ajay with her eyes.

Gabriel quickly moved aside and got up on his feet. He took a few steps towards Ajay, and stood between them.

He noticed that Ajay wasn't happy at all. He just assumed it was because they used his bed without his consent. He had no idea that his best friend was dying of jealousy.

When Ajay realised that he was unconsciously gazing at them, he quickly glanced away.

"I'm sorry man for invading your territory like this. I just quickly needed some privacy," explained Gabriel.

"It's ok man. My house is your house. Just that I didn't expect to run into something like this." He forced a smile on his miserable face. "I'm out guys," he said, closing the door, leaving Gabriel standing in the middle of the room, looking puzzled. Gabriel noticed that something was wrong with Ajay.

Ajay went to the kitchen and poured himself a glass of wine and took a gulp. He was troubled to have such strong feelings for his best friend's girlfriend. He knew getting one was losing the other.

And when he got to that point, he burst out. "Damn!"

"It's your party man. And we don't expect you to curse, but rejoice," said Gabriel standing behind him, holding the hand of the woman who was spinning Ajay's head.

"Don't worry man. I'll be cool. It's nothing," said Ajay trying to shake off the thoughts.

"Ok man. Let me and my woman go and loosen up on the dance floor," he said shaking his body.

Gabriel took a few steps and then turned to Ajay. "How come you don't have a date tonight? It's unlike you," he asked as if he was sensing that he was into his own woman.

Ajay shrugged.

Gabriel and Sive danced their way to join the dancers.

Sive got bubbly and cheerful again, really in the party spirit. She took charge of the dance floor, keeping the party alive. That's what she always did with her friend, Aviwe. Keeping the party in flames throughout the night.

Sive was adored by every male and annoyed every woman at the party. All the guys offered to dance with her, and she wasn't stingy at all. She danced with every man at the party, and that annoyed their partners, including Gabriel.

Ajay made sure that he danced with her more than any other person there did, including Gabriel.

Gabriel was convinced that his woman was still angry with him, and she wanted to punish him. He was so jealous seeing his woman dancing with every X chromosome in the party.

He went to sit at the table, chatting with friends on Facebook. He left her entertaining every guy on the dance floor.

Sive enjoyed all the attention they gave her.

Again, Joe Thomas's song, "I Wanna Know" came up, even better and louder this time. Gabriel wanted to be close to his woman, but again she was already pasted on Ajay's chest.

When Gabriel lifted his eyes, James was standing on the other side of the table. Looking at him.

Gabriel noticed that James wanted to say something.

"What!" he asked.

James glanced at his watch. "It's only a few hours since the party started, but this Cape Town girl has already shown her colours," said James, looking at Sive in Ajay's arms.

Gabriel glanced at him and then placed his eyes on his phone again.

A part of him agreed with James based on Sive's behaviour that evening, but he didn't want to confirm it.

"Ditch this bitch before it's too late. What if you get her pregnant?" James asked.

Gabriel lifted his eyes. "That won't happen."

James pulled out a chair and sat opposite him. "Why?"

"She's not ready for sex."

James laughed sarcastically. "What! And what does that mean?"

Gabriel just bulged out his eyes at him.

"Man, this chick doesn't love you. She is still looking for the right guy."

Gabriel looked at James with eyes full of questions. A part of him knew that James could be right, and he was drawn into his deepest fears.

"You could be right."

"Thanks Lord," said James. He was so happy that Gabriel was getting close to seeing through the witch he called a lover.

"But…"

"No buts man. Get out of this witch's life."

Gabriel stared at Sive in his friend's arms, and then back to James.

"James man, I love this woman with all my heart. I'll settle down with her, or I'll never ever settle down. I'll pay for sex when I need it, for life."

"What if she sleeps with Ajay?" asked James, trying to find out if he could succeed in breaking them up.

"Let's not go there. She hasn't been sleeping with any man, it's just a dance," replied Gabriel. He didn't even want to think about it.

James shrugged. "Don't say I didn't warn you."

Gabriel looked at him, and then lowered his eyes to his wrist. It was half past one in the morning.

"It's time for me to go home," he said.

James stared at his watch, too.

"Ok, I'll see you on Monday," replied James and then walked away.

Although James wanted the two separated, he was worried about how his friend felt.

Gabriel was lonely as usual. All he did was bring other men to his woman and he was so disappointed in Sive, but still loved her. He knew the only way to have her to himself was to take her home.

When the song finished, he went to Sive who was still in Ajay's arms.

"Baby, it's time to go home now."

Ajay glanced at his watch.

"Come on man! It's not even two o'clock yet," he said, probably enjoying Sive's attention.

Gabriel just glared at him. Ajay released his grip and let go.

Sive and Ajay noticed that Gabriel wasn't happy at all. She stood in front of him, feeling guilty.

"Can we please dance together before we leave? I'll ask the DJ to repeat Joe's…"

"If you wanted to dance with me you would've done that already," he said, and then hugged his friends goodbye, except for Ajay.

The crew of guys who was hugging Sive goodbye annoyed Gabriel. Some were even inviting her to their parties.

"You'll meet me in my car," Gabriel said, and then started walking to his car. He was hoping that Sive was going to follow him, but she took long before showing up.

Now Gabriel realised that all James had said was true. However, he was still willing to give their relationship another chance.

Sive got in the car. Gabriel just glanced at her and then drove off.

"What baby?"

"I'm just disappointed in you."

"Baby, it was just an innocent dance."

"Innocent or not. You were supposed to be my date. My woman. You had no right to treat me the way you did."

Sive felt sorry for the way she treated him.

"When you act like that, do you know how it makes me feel, or look?"

"I'm sorry babe. It won't happen again."

"Sure it won't, 'cause there won't be a next time," said Gabriel focusing on the road without blinking like an amateur driver.

Sive bulged out her eyes in surprise. "Are you ditching me?" she asked in a low shocked voice.

Gabriel glanced at her.

"Isn't that what you wanted?"

"Of course not, I was just enjoying myself…"

Gabriel stared at her. "By disrespecting me?"

"I didn't realise that. I'm sorry babe." Gabriel glared at her. "Baby I usually go with my girls to the parties…"

"And is that what you do?"

Sive looked at him for a moment, observing if he was in the mood to handle the truth. However, she was going to tell him nothing but the truth.

"Yes."

There was silence.

Gabriel was even more disappointed than before. Now he observed a character that was contrary to what he saw at the park earlier.

And this was exactly what James had been describing. A loose woman.

"And going home with a different guy each time, right?"

"No, I always go home alone," replied Sive with hidden anger in her voice.

"There's no decent woman that could behave the way you did tonight…"

"So, in your world, descent women are the uptight ones? Once you loosen up, you're labelled a loose woman?"

Gabriel said nothing. He glanced at the window and then brought his attention back to the road.

"I'm sorry. I…I was just, scared. I don't know if I should trust you again."

Sive looked at him quietly, and then stared through the window. Hurting.

After a while, Gabriel looked at her, the sadness written all over her face.

Sive recognised that she was unfair to Gabriel, but his judgment was harsh and unreasonable.

Gabriel pulled his car into his parking lot and turned to her to apologise. She was still looking away.

"I'm sorry, babes," he said, reaching out for her hand.

"No, I am sorry. Too sorry that I'm a woman. That I'm in the spotlight, and every move I make is waiting for someone to label it. That I've got to live my life to please a man, trying to be perfect for him," she said, then grabbed her clutch bag on her bare thighs and opened the door.

When Sive's shoe reached the ground, she turned to Gabriel who was still astonished.

"Well, I'm not perfect…but my mistakes are not worse than yours just because I'm a woman. You took me to the party to enjoy myself, and I did just that."

Sive then got out of the car.

Gabriel walked after her to the house, feeling guilty for being a control freak when he was the one who had two dates.

It wasn't Gabriel's intentions to deprive her of her young fun, but the fear of losing her drove him to the wrong path.

Sive stood in the hallway, next to Gabriel's door. She leaned with her back on the wall, waiting for Gabriel to open the door. Although there was neither a smile nor sadness on her face, she looked more cute than ever in Gabriel's eyes.

The sight of her blew away all of his anger. And the affection in his eyes increased with a decrease in distance.

Instead of opening the door, Gabriel put his leg in between hers and started kissing her. Sive wrapped her free hand around his bald head, replying to his sensual kiss with her moans.

Gabriel soon lifted her into the house. He walked across the room to the end of it where the bed was. He put her on the bed and continued kissing her.

"I love you, baby," Sive confessed in a bedroom voice.

Gabriel's heart throbbed like a drum that was made of animal skin. Once again, his fears faded away and the complete trust for her was reborn, and he had to celebrate the birth of it, in that moment…on that bed. They got tired in each other's arms and fell asleep.

***

Thandi was ironing her clothes to go to church. She was still upset about her daughter's new behaviour. She didn't understand how she could be so unreasonable. She couldn't wait for her return and to sort her out.

Suddenly, someone knocked at the door. She put the iron aside and walked to the door. It was her brother.

"Hey, sis!" he said hugging her.

"Good morning, dear."

Phiwe moved her a bit away to view her face. "You still look not good."

"I didn't sleep well last night. I was thinking about my daughter's behaviour."

"You mean that she's sharing her house with a homosexual?"

Thandi broke away from her brother and went to finish ironing. She slowly moved the iron on her skirt, and then put it aside again. She looked at Phiwe.

"Everything. Where's she?" asked Thandi, bulging out her eyes at her brother. "She's dating Jonathan and now in Johannesburg with another man. That's so unlike the Sive I know."

"Did she tell you she's dating Jonathan?"

180

"That's exactly what I mean. The Sive I know discusses everything with me. She wouldn't just take off to Johannesburg without telling me."

"Wait for her to come back and explain her actions to you."

"Sive doesn't explain anything lately.'

Phiwe shrugged and said. "Finish up, we're going to church together today," he said smiling.

"Thanks."

Thandi finished ironing her clothes, put them on the chair and looked at her brother again, "Have you called Sma to find out whether he has arrived in the US?"

"No. Sma is the one who has to call us first and give us his new contact details."

"Oh yes. I forgot," she chuckled, "This Sive's drastic change of behaviour is disturbing me," she said putting the iron away.

"Sive hasn't done anything bad, sis. You should be grateful to God for giving you such a sweet and smart child. She's old enough now to have a boyfriend and start a family. Don't you want grandchildren?"

Thandi smiled. "I do. Those little boys and girls running around my house when the parents need some quality time…"

"Whoa, sis! You only have one kid so you won't have too many grandchildren."

A smile faded away from Phiwe's face. "But, it's better for you, at least you'll have. Me, I won't," he said sadly.

Thandi looked at her brother, feeling his pain. "Sma might have one…"

"How? Have you ever heard of man getting pregnant?"

"I'm sorry, brother. But, it's not too late for you to have another child."

Phiwe laughed.

"What! Me, at my age? Do you want my niece to lecture me about the disadvantages of a child being born to old parents?"

"Are there any?"

"Wait for my niece to say something about it, and then you'll know."

They both laughed. Phiwe glanced at his watch.

"Hey sis, hurry up. We've got to leave now or we'll get there when they say the last amen."

Thandi laughed, grabbing the clothes and running into the corridor.

***

When Sive woke up in the morning, Gabriel was smiling at her. He watched her when she was asleep, lying next to her, facing each other.

Gabriel grinned when their eyes met. "Good morning, my angel," he said, and it seemed like he forgot all about yesterday's pains.

Sive smiled. "Good morning, baby."

"How did you sleep?" asked Gabriel.

"Like an angel."

"Shame sweetheart, you didn't sleep well."

Sive stretched out her eyes.

"Honey, angels don't sleep. They look over us."

Sive chuckled. "Yes, I didn't sleep. I was watching over you," she said joking.

"Oh, that explains the sweetest sleep I had last night. I slept like morphine was injected into my system," he replied smiling.

"I'm glad my watch over you was like morphine in your system, but don't get addicted…"

"What happens if I do?"

"You'll have to stick with this angel for the rest of your life."

Gabriel smiled. "That's what I want, to stick with this cute angel," he replied, stroking her soft cheek.

Suddenly, silence fell.

"Do you love Ajay?"

Sive shook her head.

"No. I love you," another silence, "Why do you ask?"

"But he has feelings for you?"

Sive shook her head, got up, and went to the bathroom. She didn't want to discuss Ajay with Gabriel so she went to the bathroom.

"Do you want tea?" he asked before Sive got into the bathroom.

"No."

Gabriel made himself a cup of tea and went to sit on the couch.

He knew he wouldn't stand a chance against Ajay and his heart was beating slowly, giving up on Sive. Realising that James was right.

Sive was applying body lotion when Gabriel sniffed, and she lifted up her eyes.

"So, you're keeping it a secret?" he asked.

"What!"

"What you have with my best friend."

"Nothing is between us."

182

"What do you call what you did at that damn party?" he asked angrily, pointing in the opposite direction.

"Baby, can we please focus on us? On things that…"

Gabriel interrupted her. "It's ok! Get dressed and pack your stuff," he said angrily.

"Pack my stuff?" she said, her heart throbbing as if it was going to break out of her rib cage. "Are you kicking me out?" she asked surprised.

"I'm taking you to his place. Ajay's place."

And that was her cue to shut her mouth up. She finished dressing and then started packing her things. Now she was so fed up with Gabriel's insecurities. She missed her house, her girlfriends, Owam, her mother, the kids at the orphanage, her cousin, Bridgette and Smanye…just everyone in her life but Gabriel.

Soon Sive was finished, looking as cute as ever, holding her belongings. She was dressed in a white shorts and a white top.

"Please take me to the airport."

"Why the airport? You've got yourself a new man, right?" said Gabriel getting up from the couch.

"I'm not gonna do this with you, Gabriel. If dancing with your friend is beyond forgiveness, there's nothing I can do. I told you repeatedly that I love you and you're the only one in my heart, but you just couldn't believe me. The foundation of a relationship is trust, and it's exactly what we're lacking here," said Sive, looking fed up.

"Oh, it's my fault now!"

"Definitely yours, Gabriel. You just don't trust me."

Gabriel lowered his voice. "I just don't wanna get hurt again."

"And you're not hurting now?"

Gabriel looked at her pretty face, affectionately. "I don't want you to leave. All I want right now is to hold you in my arms and forget about everything and just love you."

Sive dropped her bags on the floor and replied in a low, sexy voice.

"Why don't you just do that?" she said, looking at him with sexy eyes.

Sive didn't want to go either; she was just fed up with his insecurities.

A cup in Gabriel's hand found its way to the floor. Gabriel covered Sive with his arms. He locked her against his bare, hairy chest. He kept her there for a moment, and then dropped a kiss on her forehead.

"I love you," he murmured and then lowered to pick Sive's luggage up. He lifted his eyes. "The cup is broken," he said.

"What did you expect after treating the poor cup so badly after it's been a loyal servant in your kitchen for so long?" she replied, pretending to be sorry for the loyal cup.

"I hope it understands that the master was in a bad space." He replied and then turned to the broken cup. "Anyway, Rest In Peace my loyal servant," he added.

They both laughed.

Gabriel unpacked Sive's luggage.

Sive chuckled. "You should've done that on Friday when I arrived. Tomorrow at this time, I'll be sweating at work, which means I should be packing now rather than unpacking.

Gabriel glared at her, and then smiled.

"Do you enjoy your job, honey?" he asked, putting her clothes in his wardrobe.

Gabriel knew Sive as a cashier in a grocery store from her Facebook profile, and Sive had never corrected that error. She wanted Gabriel to fall in love with her before she could tell him she was actually a doctor.

Sive nodded. "Yes. Very much."

"Good."

"You?" asked Sive.

"I do. But it will be a problem when we're married 'cause I stay at work."

Deep down, Gabriel believed that he had a future with Sive and somehow, he knew she loved him.

"Oh, you only come home on weekends?"

"Not literally, babes. I just mean, I spend long hours at work."

"Ok."

Sive moved to Gabriel and stood in front of him, looking at his hairy chest, then slowly ran her fingers through the hair, and soon Gabriel breathed out heavily, feeling the magic touch of her hands.

"Don't worry, we will manage," she replied.

Gabriel tucked his hand under her top, stroking her flat tummy.

"Do you think this tiny tummy can carry my seed?"

"Yes, it can. And it will," she replied confidently.

Gabriel moved his hand and cupped her breast.

"And these cute boobs can feed my babies?" he asked, pressing it gently.

184

Sive nodded, and then made sure that there was no gap between them. Gabriel got the message, loud and clear. He then lowered his head and started kissing her.

This time, he made a vow to himself that he would trust her until death do them part.

Gabriel removed his hands from her and then tapped her buttocks.

"I love you, girl," he said and turned to close the wardrobe door. He quickly turned to her again. "You know what, honey?"

Sive bulged out her eyes at him.

"Let's make a healthy breakfast 'cause we gonna live on takeaways for the rest of the day."

Gabriel was leaning against the wardrobe, looking at Sive.

Sive tilted her head. "Why?"

"I wanna spend the last day with my wife-to-be, cosy…"

"In bed."

"Exactly," he said smiling. "Boo, let's get started before you tell me you're hungry."

Sive chuckled. "And I am. I have been since I woke up. I would've told you if you weren't in a bad mood this morning."

Gabriel grabbed her hand and pulled her to him.

"You know I'll do anything for you, even if I'm crying."

They laughed. He then got started with breakfast.

Chapter 18

Ajay was staring at a dirty wall in front of him. The landlord had been making endless postponement on getting it painted. In that moment, all he could see on it was Sive's pretty smile and he asked himself how someone could be that perfect.

Ajay rose up from the couch and walked slowly up the stairs to his bedroom. He threw himself on his back on the bed, staring at the ceiling that wasn't clean either. He was deciding between his childhood friend and the woman he just met. The one who knocked him off his feet.

"What a dilemma!" he screamed, and he decided to keep his feelings for Sive to himself.

***

Gabriel was lying on his back on the bed with his legs bent upwards and Sive on his tummy with her back resting on his legs. They were chatting and laughing.

"You'll make a good husband and daddy one day," said Sive, after a long affectionate stare at Gabriel. She then bent down and kissed him.

When Sive moved her head away, Gabriel followed it until he was in his sitting position. He moved Sive to his thighs, his hands on her waist and Sive's hands around his neck. She wrapped her legs around his waist. He kissed her.

Gabriel gently pushed her to lie on the bed and moved in between her legs, staring at her appetising lips. He licked his big index finger and then ran it on her lips until they were open. He moved downwards and sucked her lower lip, and then pushed his tongue in.

Sive started sucking his tongue like a lollipop.

Suddenly, Gabriel stopped kissing her and looked into her eyes. Sive knew what that look said, and gently nodded.

Gabriel gently pulled off her white top and revealed her cute pair of breasts covered by a sexy red bra, which Gabriel had bought.

Soon, they were both half-naked.

Gabriel kissed her lips, and then moved his smooth muscular tongue down to her neck. He cupped her breast and found out that the bra was a barrier for him to get to all the excitement.

He took it off. The splendour of her naked breasts revealed.

Gabriel lowered his head and started kissing her firm tits while he was stroking the other breast with one hand.

Sive started moaning delightfully. She whispered.

"I love you, babe."

Gabriel moved his tongue smoothly in between her breasts, down her flat belly. When it passed her belly button, moving downwards, Sive stopped him.

***

Monday morning, Gabriel and Sive are at the airport.

"I'm already missing you, babes," she said, burying herself in his arms.

"I hate this moment," said Gabriel, squeezing her body against his.

Sive broke away from him and held his hands. "I'm coming back. Soon," she said smiling.

"Wow! I like the sound of it," he said, pulling her closer to him and wrapped his arms around her body and dropped the most affectionate kiss on her forehead.

He then bent down, picked up her luggage, and gave it to her.

Sive glanced at her wrist, and bulged out her eyes. "Baby, I forgot my watch at your place," she said, but not looking worried.

"I'm sorry, honey. But don't worry; I'll keep it safe for you."

"Thanks, my love," she said and then kissed him on his lips. She smiled naughtily and pulled her luggage.

"What's wrong, babe?" asked Gabriel as she was walking away.

Sive turned and looked at him. "The lipstick on your lips will chase the girls away," she said and continued walking away.

They waved at each other as Sive headed for the gates.

***

Jonathan was standing at the end of the corridor, next to Sive's office when Sive emerged from the corridor.

Sive was dressed in a white dress that revealed all her curves and white heels.

She greeted Jonathan and then went into her office. He followed her, closed the door, and locked it.

"Where were you all weekend?" he asked angrily

"I went to visit Gabriel in Johannesburg," she replied calmly.

Jonathan walked across the room to stand by the window, trying to calm himself down.

"Did you do it with that fool?" he asked, looking through the window.

Sive didn't answer. Jonathan's body was trembling in anger.

"I'm talking to you, damn it!" he said angrily, "Why are you doing this to us?" he asked, his eyes covered with tears. His face was in deep pain.

Sive realised that setting him straight at that moment was the right thing to do if she wanted to claim her life back. A life of being honest with people she loved.

Now, Sive wanted to tell her mother and her girls that she was dating without trying to protect Jonathan's feelings. He was an adult after all, he could deal with the truth…she thought.

Sive lifted her eyes and looked at Jonathan.

"There's no us, Jonathan. I'm in love with Gabriel, not you. Please understand that," she said and walked towards him to open the windows. She then walked to her desk again, "And please, unlock that door. It's time for me to start working," she added.

"Do you know how much I love you?" he said, sadly.

"I love you too, Jonno, but, not the way a woman is supposed to love her man. I love you as a friend," said Sive.

"So, you love him?"

"Yes. He's the man I want to take my virginity and plant his seed in my womb. I'm sorry, Jonno," she said.

A silence fell.

Jonathan read between the lines that she didn't sleep with Gabriel, and that means they still had a chance. He was left with only one option to separate Gabriel and Sive. Desperate measures, for desperate times.

A knock on the door broke the silence.

Sive slipped her hand in Jonathan's jeans pocket, came out with the keys, and opened the door.

It was Michelle. She came to drop off a file for Sive.

"Why was the door locked, baby?" she asked, looking at Jonathan.

"It's none of your business. And please stay out of it," replied Jonathan annoyingly.

"It becomes my problem when my man is locked in some damn office with some woman," she replied angrily.

Sive was quiet; her heart was over the moon for that piece of information. She would use it to get Jonathan off her back.

"I told you too many times that there's only one woman for me, and that's Sive. Are you deaf or something?"

"No, I'm not, but I guess you're the one who's confused here. You claim to love one woman and you keep on sleeping with another…who does that, Jonathan, except for a sick jerk?"

Jonathan was speechless; the cat was out of the bag.

He looked at Sive, and she was staring at him, pretending she was jealous.

"I can explain, baby…"

"And don't forget to explain to her how you made love to me on your kitchen table this weekend," said Michelle, tossing the file on Sive's desk and heading for the door.

"Is it true, Jonno?" asked Sive.

Jonathan nodded. "Yeah, it's true," he confirmed.

"That's great, 'cause, now it seems like we both have partners…"

"Please baby, don't do this. Michelle's not my partner."

Sive glanced at her wrist, forgetting that she left her watch in Johannesburg. She then took a phone from her bag and looked at it. She lifted her eyes to Jonathan who was still in front of her.

"Will you please excuse me? I have to work," she said politely.

Sive felt sorry for Jonathan, but it was about time to do things the right way. Jonno was supposed to stick with Michelle or find another woman.

"The receptionist hasn't sent us folders yet, so we can still talk."

Before Sive could answer, the receptionist came in with a pile of folders and put them on the desk.

"Thanks dear," said Sive smiling at her, and then turned to Jonathan. "And that, is your cue to leave," she said and then called the first patient.

Jonathan left before the patient came in.

***

Sive got a ride home from her colleague. Thandi and Jonathan were waiting at her door.

"Hi, Mom."

"Who are you 'cause you're definitely not my Sive. My Sive is an honest, trustworthy and open person. She doesn't keep things from me," Thandi said.

"Maybe your Sive's grown up now," she murmured.

"What!" asked Thandi.

"Nothing," she replied, smiling.

"I heard you girl. If growing up makes you lose your morals, you better not grow at all."

Sive eyed her mom, surprised, and then stretched her arm to help her get up.

"But, I must admit. You look so gorgeous," she smiled at her. "This look," wagging her finger at her daughter, "says, my little girl has a man."

Sive smiled. "Don't you want grandchildren?" asked Sive, amused.

"I do," she smiled, glancing between Sive and Jonathan. She was convinced that her daughter was dating Jonathan, "Did he promise to marry you?" whispered Thandi.

Sive smiled and then pushed the door open. They went into the house. Jonathan and Thandi made themselves comfortable on either end of a single long couch while Sive was standing behind it.

"How was Johannesburg?" Thandi asked.

Sive and Jonathan nervously exchanged glances. "That's what I heard from," she pursed her lips, "that gay you're staying with," she added.

"His name is Owam, Mom," Sive corrected her mother.

"But baby he is, gay," said Jonathan.

Sive didn't answer him.

Thandi turned to Sive, and there was sadness on her face.

"Why did you turn your house into a Sodom?"

Sive pretended she didn't hear her mom.

"Anything to drink, guys?" she asked.

"Don't you think it ruins your reputation?"

"What reputation Mom?"

"You're respected by everyone…"

Sive interrupted her. "If I won't be respected because I help others, let it be. I don't do things to impress anyone. I do what I feel is right."

Jonathan moved his eyes from Sive to Thandi.

"I don't like it either, Mrs T."

Sive glared at him.

"Your man doesn't like it either. A good wife is the one who listens to her husband," said Thandi.

"I'm not anyone's wife anyway," she murmured.

190

Jonathan heard her and prayed that Thandi didn't hear it. Luckily, his prayer was heard.

"What did you say, baby?" asked Thandi.

Jonathan's fingers were crossed for her not to repeat her words.

"Nothing," she replied, taking off her shoes, "I've been in these shoes all day and now my feet are killing me." She put the shoes in one hand and the purse in the other, "I'm coming now, Mom. I need to be in something more comfortable," she said and disappeared into the corridor.

Sive came back in a pair of black shorts Gabriel had bought her, and they definitely had a sentimental value to her. Thandi and Jonathan were having a conversation. Jonathan was preaching his undying love for her daughter.

Thandi looked at her daughter hoping to see the same smile on her face, but Sive seemed less interested in their conversation.

"Can I get you something to drink?" she said instead.

Jonathan and Thandi asked for tea. Sive brought them tea and then sat in between them, on the couch.

Suddenly, the door opened. It was Owam. The three of them moved their eyes to look at the door.

"I'm so sorry, girl; I didn't know I would take this long. I thought the interview would be over before…"

"Did you say, interview?" Sive asked, jumping up from the couch.

"You heard me, girl," he brushed his dreadlocks with the palm of his hand, "Not just an interview…I got the job. I started today," he said.

"Amen!" said Sive.

"Hallelujah!" he replied, raising his hands up in the air.

"Come here," said Sive with her arms flying up in the air, walking towards Owam.

They hugged each other. Sive held his arms. "I'm proud of you, girl."

"Thanks to you my friend. You such a good friend. As soon as I get paid, I'll move out."

"Who said anything about moving out! I love to have you around. You can stay until your boyfriend gets back."

Owam screamed and hugged her. "Thanks *tshomi*, you're the best person I have ever met…More than family," he said hugging her.

Jonathan and Thandi exchanged glances.

"Baby!" exclaimed Jonathan.

"Shut up, Jonathan! Sive said.

Owam glared at him and when he turned to Sive, he was wearing a naughty smile. They both burst out laughing.

Sive pulled his hand. "Come, sit down. I'll bring you something to drink.

Owam sat where Sive was sitting, between Jonathan and Thandi. He glanced on either side, and neither was welcoming.

Who cares? The owner of the house was so fond of him.

Sive wailed from the kitchen. "Tea or coffee?"

"Juice, girl! I'm not a granny!" he said, making himself comfortable in between the uncomfortable gaze of Jonathan and Thandi.

Sive gave him his glass of juice and patted his legs.

"Open up girl, I wanna get in between these skinny legs."

Sive made herself comfortable on the floor, in between Owam's legs.

"Girl!" said Jonathan, looking surprised, if he wasn't pretending just to stir up a conversation about Owam's sexual orientation.

Both Owam and Sive gave him a glare.

"Do you know why Sodom and Gomorrah were destroyed?" asked Jonathan, staring at Owam. Fortunately, Owam had a powerful attorney in the house.

"Not in my house, Jonathan. This isn't a church. Go find one and insult people there," Sive said.

"Baby, be a true friend to him. Homosexuality is a sin," he said.

"If homosexuality is a sin, let God give his judgement 'cause you're filthy with your own sins…"

"Sive, don't be disrespectful," said her Mom.

Sive glanced at her mom and then looked at Owam.

"*Chomi*, tell me what needs to be done with this," she said, scratching her hair.

"Just a wash and a blow dry my dear," replied Owam. He was so relieved and secured with Sive's love.

"When?" asked Sive.

"Tomorrow."

"Yeah, tomorrow is perfect since tonight I'm visiting my friends," she said and lifted her eyes to the clock on the wall.

"Come on girl, I thought we would catch up over some dessert, you know," he said rolling his eyes.

Sive got up. "Don't worry, we have plenty of time to do all the juicy catching up…"

"Girl, did you say juicy!"

"Dripping juicy… believe me," said Sive, collecting dirty cups from the coffee table.

Thandi got up.

"Baby, let me go home. I just wanted to see if you were ok…and you are," she said touching her chin.

"Let me drop these in the kitchen and walk you out."

Sive opened the door for her mother and they walked to her car.

"Baby, did you fight with Jonathan?"

Thandi caught her off guard. She swallowed hard, trying to gather herself together.

"Yes."

"Sort things out, he seems like a good man," said Thandi getting into her car. She looked at her daughter, smiling, "Mama loves you," she added.

"Love you back, old lady," replied Sive, "Mom, cook on Wednesday. I'll have dinner with you."

"That would be great, baby."

"Can I bring Owam with…"

"No, we need to be alone. I wanna talk to you," replied Thandi.

"You don't like him, do you?" asked Sive, leaning on her hands on the car door, looking at her mother.

Thandi inserted a key and lifted her eyes to her daughter. "I just don't like his influence on you."

"How, Mom?"

Thandi turned the key to run the engine. "You've changed completely since he started living with you."

What Thandi didn't know was that Jonathan was the one who changed her daughter.

"Please mom, don't blame him for my mistakes. He's done nothing wrong. All he needs is love."

"He's gay, baby?"

"You mean gays don't need love?"

"You know what I mean, Sive."

"No, Mom. I don't."

"Exactly what Jonathan said. Homosexuality is a sin."

"It's ok if you and Jonathan think that way…"

"And the rest of the world, Sive!" she said in a high voice.

"Have you asked that…rest of the world, how clean they are?"

Thandi looked at her daughter.

"Yes, Mom. We all commit sins. No one who walks the earth is sinless," she said, and then removed her arms from the car and folded them against her chest, "Don't you think judging others is another sin?" she added.

Thandi smiled at her daughter. She knew that she wouldn't win against her daughter when it comes to defending others.

"Bye, baby," she said, and then drove off.

Sive went into the house. Jonathan was looking at his phone while Owam was watching TV.

"Girl, let me go check on how my friends are doing," she said, as if Jonathan wasn't even there.

"Cool," replied Owam, looking at the TV.

When Sive was wrapping little presents for Bridgette and Smanye in her room, Jonathan went in.

"I need to talk to you," he said.

"I'm sure Michelle is waiting for you."

"Baby. We need to talk about this…work things out."

"What things, Jonno?" she said putting gifts in gift bags.

The silence fell and was interrupted by a knock on the door. It was Owam.

"Can't you see that I'm trying to have a conversation with my woman?" Jonathan snapped at Owam who was bringing Sive's phone.

Owam just glared at him, and then turned to Sive. "Girl, someone on the phone," he said giving her the phone and then glared at Jonathan on his way out.

Sive knew who was on the phone. You could tell from the look on her face that she was madly in love with the person on the other end of the line.

Michelle's incident made Sive not afraid to answer Gabriel's call in front of Jonathan anymore.

"Hey, love!" she said, rising up from the bed to stand against a window.

It was her spot of comfort whenever Chikondi's memories overwhelmed her. She would go and stand at her bedroom window with a beautiful view of the park.

The beautiful trees that trimmed the edge of the park made it more beautiful and natural. Nature had always given her that sense of fulfilment.

The silence fell.

"Baby, are you still there?" she asked.

"Yes, just that I don't know whether I called you at the wrong time," he said, feeling down.

"No baby, you know you can call me anytime…"

"I'm not sure anymore."

"Why?"

"There's a man answering your phone and the other that calls you his woman, but you said you stay alone."

"Baby please, trust me," said Sive.

There was a silence again.

"I do. But I'm scared to lose you," he confessed.

"I'm scared to lose you too. But I trust us." There was a silence. "I believe in us, Gabriel," she added.

Gabriel felt weak at his knees. He was standing by the bed. He balanced with one hand on the bed and lowered himself to sit on the bed.

"Baby, are you still there?" she asked.

"Yes, yes, yes baby," he replied nervously.

"Are you ok?" she asked.

"Yeah, yeah, love," short silence, "Can I ask you something baby?"

"Sure."

"Do you really love me?"

"With all my heart."

"Thanks sweetheart," he said happily.

"Would you please do something for me?" asked Sive.

"Sure. Anything."

"Could you please trust me?"

"Yes, my love. I trust you."

"Thanks babes," she said, moving away the window, "I'm going to see my friends. Let's chat when I get back," she said picking up the little gift bags from the bed.

"Ok, bye. Mother of my five kids," he said teasingly.

"Two, baby."

"Five."

Sive chuckled. "Ok five," she said laughing.

Sive slipped her phone in her pocket and headed for the door. Jonathan grabbed her arm.

"Are you letting that damn foreigner ruin what we have?" he asked angrily.

"I'm not Michelle, Jonathan!"

"Please baby, forgive me for messing up. I love you, not her."

"But she's the one who's recognised by the heavens as your wife, not me," said Sive, using Jonathan's little affair as her scape goat from his claws but they were more tight than she realised.

"What does this foreigner have that I don't?"

Sive looked at him and pulled her arm from him, but the grip was too tight.

Jonathan looked at her for a moment. "Look me in the eyes and tell me you didn't lose your virginity to that fool.

Sive looked him in the eyes. "I'm still a virgin. A virgin, not a stupid, Jonathan," she said.

Jonathan gave out a sigh of relief and pulled her to him. Sive lost the grip of the gifts in her hand and blocked herself from landing on his chest that was so thirsty for her. Unfortunately, Sive's arms missed his body and her body hit his, right where he wanted her to be. On his lean chest.

He wrapped his arms around her waist.

Owam walked in on them in each other's arms, and he went out without them noticing him. He was confused about who Sive was dating… was it Jonathan, or the Johannesburg guy. If Jonathan didn't come around when she was in Johannesburg, he would say Jonathan was the guy she went away with.

When Jonathan and Sive walked past Owam on their way to the door, Owam grabbed Sive's arm.

"I wanna talk to you girl," he whispered.

Sive stretched her eyes for him to speak. Owam glared at Jonathan, and Sive signed him to leave.

Jonathan exchanged glances between them and walked to his car.

"I'll be in my car, sweetheart," he said going through the door.

Sive and Owam moved their eyes from Jonathan and placed them on each other.

"Are you dating him?" asked Owam, pointing at Jonathan.

"What!"

"Are you dating this guy?"

Sive just glared at him and then walked out of the door without saying anything.

"Come on, girl! You owe me at least that piece of information," he wailed from the house.

Sive wailed back as she was walking towards Jonathan's car. "I don't owe you anything."

The gift bags were on Jonathan's lap, and he locked the door on his side. He wanted Sive to get inside the car. Sive stretched her arms to reach out for the bags, but Jonathan put them behind him. Sive eyed him with those big, bright eyes.

"Get in the car, baby," he said.

Sive got in without asking questions, and that gave Jonathan hope that she had realised that they belonged together.

"How I wish we were going on a romantic trip to some romantic Island," he said smiling at her.

"Unfortunately, I'm going to visit my friends."

"Let me drive you." Sive glared at him. "I just want to have quality time with my woman," he added.

"No, I wanna go alone." She glanced at the dashboard for the time. "It's getting late, Jonno."

"I like it when you call me that," said Jonathan, handing over the gift bags.

Sive got out and walked to her car.

Chapter 19

Zuko's phone rang and he went to answer it outside and then tossed it on the couch in front of Mihle on his way to the bathroom. When Mihle checked the call, it was from Sive. He came out, took his phone, slipped it in his jeans pocket, and walked out. Mihle went to get some things from the shop while her kids were playing in their room.

When Zuko came back after few minutes, she saw Sive getting out of her car.

"Hey! Beautiful!" he said cheerfully.

"Hey Zuko, how are you?" she said extending her hand.

"I'm fine, thanks," he scratched his head, "I couldn't hear you when you called earlier," said Zuko.

"I'm sorry, it was one of those pocket calls," she replied smiling.

Mihle was coming from behind, and she didn't hear anything except seeing Sive's annoying smile that used to be inspiring. She was carrying a sachet of milk and a loaf of bread in her hands.

When Mihle saw them together, she concluded that the call was about that meeting and her anger took control.

When Sive saw her friend, she beamed with a smile that was like a sharp sword in Mihle's heart. Her anger went beyond limits.

"Hey girl!" said Sive, moving towards her. Mihle answered with a slap on her face.

Suddenly, her face turned red.

The kids were standing frightened by the door and no one noticed them. They probably saw Sive through the window and went to her.

"You, hypocrite! You pretend to be my friend when you are busy sleeping with my man behind my back."

Sive held her cheek, looking confused. She thought her friend was losing her mind.

"You thought I'd never find out!" she added, throwing a sachet of milk at her.

Soon, white rain fell on Sive. Mihle continued beating her up with bread and then her hands. When Zuko tried to stop her, she went crazy.

"Oh, you're protecting your pathetic little bitch who can't find a man of her own!" Mihle picked up a piece of brick from the edge of her flower garden. "Let me go, Zuko! I wanna teach this pathetic bitch a lesson she won't forget."

Mihle succeeded to break away from Zuko's strong grip and let the brick fly to Sive.

Sive tried to duck but, unfortunately, the brick landed on her elbow and she dropped everything in her hands. She held her bleeding arm and spun in pain and dropped her keys on the ground, and the keys were half buried under the grass.

Mihle picked up another brick and hit Zuko on the head. He fell on the ground with blood all over his face and passed out.

"You both deserve to die!" she screamed, as she was turning to Sive as angry as a hungry lion tearing up its prey.

Sive tried to run, but it was too late. Mihle grabbed her from the back and pulled her on the ground. She kicked her in the stomach.

Sive groaned painfully.

"You don't wanna do this, Mihle," said Sive, moving painfully on the ground.

The girls were standing there, frightened. When Mihle kicked Sive on the back, Bridgette remembered that her mother said she would kill Sive if she came to the house. She cried in a shrill voice,

"Mommy, stop! Don't kill my aunt!"

"Bridgette, baby, take your sister and go back in the house," said Sive. Bridgette just stared at Sive, gaping with tears all over her face. "Now!" Sive insisted.

Bridgette grabbed her sister's arm and ran into the house.

Mihle punched Sive on the flank three times. She then realised that Zuko was regaining his consciousness. She hit him with another brick on the back of his head, his face went back on the ground, and this time, seemed permanent.

"You were on a stupid romantic weekend getaway in Johannesburg, and you have the nerve to come and sneak into my house!"

Mihle laughed hysterically. "Now I'm sending you on a romantic getaway in hell, where you belong," she said turning to Sive, and hit her with a brick on the back, and kicked her several times on her upper body.

"You'll never betray anyone," she said, kicking her on the buttocks, "Is this what you lured my man into your filthy life with?" she kicked her on her breasts, "I'll make sure that he won't recognise you in your next life," she said angrily.

Sive realised that Mihle was killing her. She started talking, but faced down to hide her face.

"Please Mihle, don't kill me."

Mihle bent down. "Oh, you're begging me not to kill you now, after you killed me softly. Pretending to be my friend when you were only after my man?"

"I'm still your friend, girl. Please don't do this to me," she said lifting her head to look at her.

Mihle punched Sive in the nose; soon blood ran out of her nose.

"You have the nerve to tell me that when you're sleeping with my man…the father of my kids," she angrily folded her fist to punch her again on her flank, "That's for making a fool of me," she hit her on the same spot, "and that's for the pain you've caused me and my kids."

Sive hid her face again. Mihle picked up a brick and hit her on the back.

"This is for pretending to love us."

Sive lifted her head again.

"Are you crazy, Mihle! What the hell are you talking about? I'm not sleeping with Zuko…or having an affair with him. How could you even think that?" she said yelling at her, crying.

Sive was now covered everywhere in blood. Mihle got angrier. She beat her up unconsciously. Sive just curled up on the ground.

 Hopelessly.

Bridgette and Smanye were watching through the window after calling Aviwe and told her that their mother was killing Sive. They came running as they saw Aviwe's car come, flying down the road. Their mother was still beating Sive up.

Aviwe quickly got out of the car. "Are you out of your mind! You can go to jail for this, "Aviwe said in her sharp voice, pushing Mihle aside, who was already tired. She fell on her big buttocks on the ground, next to a bleeding Sive.

Blood and dust covered Sive's body. Her pitch-black hair was decorated with grass and sand. She wasn't moving.

Aviwe knelt down next to Sive, calling her name. Slightly patting her back as it was the only place that was free of blood, and she was still.

Aviwe turned to Mihle who couldn't care less about the damage she had done.

"It doesn't look good," said Aviwe.

"She deserved it, and more. Both of them," she replied, "I hope they're dead," she added, pulling herself up the ground.

Aviwe glared at her with her wet eyes.

Soon, the noise of Jonathan's Jeep distracted her. He flew out of the car, leaving the door open. He went out of his mind with the sight of Sive lying on the ground. Aviwe called him as she got the news that Sive was in trouble.

Jonathan bent down to check her pulse. "Let's take her to the hospital," he turned to Mihle who was shaking the dust off her shoes, "I hate you," he added angrily, and then lifted Sive up.

"I called the paramedics. I guess they are on their way now. Put her down," said Aviwe.

"Your bitch is sleeping with my man, and pretending to be my friend," replied Mihle, dropping her shoes on the ground and pushing her feet in.

Jonathan froze and stared at Mihle.

"What! That's a lie. Sive wouldn't do such a thing to a friend, or anyone for that matter. This woman," he said pointing with his head at Sive in his arms, "Won't hurt even a fly."

"Put her down," repeated Aviwe.

Jonathan put Sive back on the ground. He took off his jacket and covered her upper body.

He then went over to Zuko.

"He's bleeding too much, on the head," he said.

Soon the paramedics arrived. They quickly put Sive and Zuko in the vehicle. Aviwe went with Sive and Jonathan followed in his car.

Mihle was left standing with her daughters, surrounded by thrash. Sive's car keys were in that thrash. The book and the chocolate Sive brought for the kids was smashed on the ground, covered with Sive's blood.

Mihle watched the paramedic vehicle disappear around the corner with the man she thought she would spend her whole life with, and her two best friends in it. The only family she ever had. She then lowered her eyes to the ground. Sive's blood on the ground rang the bell that their friendship was gone.

She was all alone.

"What have I done," she murmured.

Suddenly the tears rolled down her cheeks. She slowly went to the house, and her daughters followed. Bridgette looked back where Sive was lying, and then disappeared into the house.

Aviwe called Owam to go and get Sive's car from Mihle's place. She told him to bring the spare key in case he couldn't find the keys. She was afraid that their crazy friend might damage the car as well.

Zuko got stiches on the head. Sive's arm wasn't broken, just badly hurt. Her whole body was badly bruised and in lot of pain.

"Can I take you to your place?" asked Jonathan, helping her walk to the car. Her medication was in his track pants pocket.

Sive shook her head. "No. My mother's place.

Sive asked Aviwe to call her mother, but Thandi didn't pick up. She tried several times with no success.

"Your mom's not picking up," she said, raising up the phone.

Jonathan went to drop Zuko at a friend's place, and then Aviwe at Mihle's place to pick up her car. And Sive's car wasn't there. Sive just looked away when they got to Mihle's place.

"Are you alright?" asked Jonathan.

She nodded.

"What are we gonna do? Your mom is not answering," asked Jonathan.

"Just drive me there. She should be home at this time. She might just be sleeping."

When Sive and Jonathan got to Thandi's place, the house was dark. Jonathan glanced at his watch.

"It's late. She's supposed to be fast asleep," he said, pulling the door open, and went to a locked gate and called Thandi.

"Mrs T! Mrs T! Mrs T!" but there was no response. He called her repeatedly. Still no reply.

Sive popped out of the window. "Say Thandi!" she demanded.

The poor thing, all she needed was a warm bath on her bruised body. Jonathan just glared at her, and then leaned on the cold, iron gate and continued calling, even louder this time.

Still the house was as quiet as a grave.

Jonathan turned and walked back to the car, on Sive's side. "Maybe your voice is what can help here. Let me get you out of the car," he said, opening the door.

202

Sive called for her mom until she was trembling from the cold. Jonathan covered her body with his arms to keep her warm. He enjoyed every bit of it.

Sive lifted her eyes up to Jonathan. "Can I spend the night at your place? My body is getting more painful," Jonathan just gaped at her in surprise, "I'll try my mom in the morning. I'm sure she will respond then," she said with eyes begging for help.

Jonathan gently squeezed her in his arms. "You know I'll do anything for you, including laying down my own life.

They went back into the car and drove off.

Chapter 20

It was after midnight when they got to Jonathan's place. He ran the bath.

"Let me help you take your clothes off," he said.

Sive looked at him, helplessly. She knew Jonathan would take advantage of the situation.

He then started taking her clothes off, slowly, avoiding hurting her. It also gave him enough time to view her incredible body. Soon, Sive was naked, and he looked at her naked body for a moment. He told himself that he could kill someone for losing her.

One way or the other she would be his.

Jonathan put her in a warm bath, and he was enjoying every minute of taking care of his future wife. He ran his hands all over her body cleaning her up and massaging it at the same time.

Jonathan stroked her breasts. They were firm, but soft.

Soon, Jonathan's lips were gaped. His body started sweating, and he was hungry for more than just a touch. All he wanted was to feel his manhood inside her, planting his seed.

His hands moved slowly down to her waist and then, further down to her thighs. He moved his hands inside her thighs, cleaning in between them, using his fingers, gently.

Sive felt uncomfortable and slowly closed her legs. No one had ever touched that area except her mother when she was still at the age of being bathed.

Jonathan used his hand, gently opening her legs. "Relax baby, relax." He whispered, looking into her eyes. He continued rubbing the area with his fingers, and then moved his hands to her legs and feet.

When Jonathan spread the towel on the bed to dry Sive, her phone rang. It was Gabriel.

He took it out of her shorts and answered it outside the room. He didn't want Sive to know that Gabriel called. He wanted her full attention.

"Please, don't interrupt!" he snapped at Gabriel.

"Who's this?" asked Gabriel surprised.

"Jonathan…her man. And please, don't ever call this line again," said Jonathan, and then a short silence, "Sive's carrying my baby…please, just back off," he added, and then dropped the phone.

Jonathan dried Sive up, patted her body gently with a towel.

He tossed the towel on the floor, went into the bathroom again, and came out with a white container of Comfort Cream body cream. He lifted it up.

"I only have this," he said, asking if he could use it on her.

Sive nodded.

Jonathan applied the cream gently on her body.

Sive groaned.

"Am I hurting you?"

"No no, no. it just feels good."

"Is it?" said Jonathan surprised.

Sive nodded. "Yeah."

Jonathan smiled. "I'm glad," he replied, gently rubbing her thighs. "You have a very beautiful body."

"You mean my bruised body," she said, trying not to excite him.

Jonathan lifted his eyes up at her. "You know what I mean. The bruises will be gone soon."

"But now it feels like I've been hit by a train," she said, and they looked at each other and then burst out laughing.

"It's a train now?" said Jonathan, still laughing.

Sive nodded. "Yeah, a train," she replied, smiling, "Dress me up now," she added, looking at Jonathan.

"You don't have clothes here, so you'll get in bed like this," he said, pointing at her naked body.

"No! I can't get in bed with you like this."

"Why?"

Sive just looked at him.

"My dear, I would never force myself on you. I know your first time should be special," an awkward silence fell, "although I'm scared that foreigner might get a chance before me."

"Is that all you care about?" she asked, with sadness on her face.

Jonathan shook his head. "No. I want to be the last, baby…but what if he impregnates you?"

"I'm not that careless, Jonathan."

"I know," he replied and then turned to the closet and took out a T-Shirt and boxers and dressed her.

Jonathan looked at her. "You look good in your future husband's underwear."

They both laughed. Sive looked more relaxed today around Jonathan than any other day.

Jonathan went around the bed to the other side and opened the blankets for her. He lifted her up and put her under the warm blankets. He then turned to the closet again and took out his pyjamas.

He then stood by the couch where Sive could clearly see every bit of his body. He then took off his clothes, every bit of them, trying to seduce her. He revealed his lean, cute body.

Instead of Sive closing her eyes, she enjoyed the show. Jonathan thought she would freak out, but she didn't.

"Do you want me to get in bed like this?" he asked.

There was no reply. Sive looked at his erected manhood.

"Why are you taking your clothes off in front of me?"

"I saw your nakedness, and it would be unfair of me to hide mine," he replied, still standing naked.

"Please dress, Jonno," she said.

Jonathan dressed in his pyjamas and got in bed, next to Sive.

"How do you feel now?"

"Much better, thanks."

"Anytime," he said, moving closer to her. His arm around her waist. He then moved his lips closer to hers.

"Jonno, please," she whispered.

"Baby please, just a kiss. It won't hurt," he said placing his lips to hers.

Sive couldn't block him, her arms were so sore and her neck as well. She just let him entertain himself on her lips.

Jonathan took off her T-Shirt and revealed her breasts. He looked at her eyes.

"Please," he whispered.

Sive became so scared. She thought Jonathan was going to force himself on her. Then tears fell from her eyes. She felt helpless and vulnerable on her back on his bed.

"You can't do this, please."

Jonathan looked into her wet eyes.

"Jonno, please. I can't fall pregnant," she said begging him.

Jonathan chuckled. "Virgins get pregnant from a kiss?" he asked teasing her.

Sive just looked at him, helplessly.

"Baby, I won't go beyond kissing. I won't be that cruel," he promised, and then bent down and kissed her.

Sive didn't respond to his kiss, but that didn't stop Jonathan. He continued. In a moment he felt Sive's lips gaping. She decided to participate so he could be done with it quickly and let her rest.

Jonathan exhaled out of excitement. He pushed his tongue in and cupped her tennis ball-sized breasts. He moved up and knelt with his knees apart. Her sore body was lying in between his knees and his arms were balancing on the bed.

He took pleasure in kissing her. He licked her lips, and then gently bit her lower lip. He lifted his eyes to look at her frightening face.

"I love you," he whispered.

He then moved to her breasts and viewed them for a moment. Suddenly, his manhood took another length.

Jonathan sucked her nipples. Sive moaned. He thought it was out of pleasure. He continued sucking her sore breast. The pain became unbearable for her and she tried to move her painful body.

Jonathan thought it was a reaction from the delightful job of his hands. He then continued kissing her all over her upper body until it was unbearable. Then the tears rolled down her cheeks.

When Jonathan saw the tears on her face, he thought it was a result of her love triangle pain. He pulled her closer to his body and gently held her.

Soon they drifted off to sleep.

***

Aviwe pressed the doorbell at Mihle's house the next morning. She forgot that it hadn't been working for quite some time. She was so angry. Aviwe's life was falling apart and now it was this.

She knocked. Hard.

Mihle was so scared she thought it was the police. She quietly got out of bed and went to a window. She peeped through the curtain. She saw Aviwe wearing a long face on her doorstep, in her work uniform.

"Open this door Mihle, I know you're in there."

Mihle didn't even wear a gown; she hurried to open the door.

"Good morning Av…"

"Don't good morning me after what you did to someone who's always been there for you…your kids. Not to mention a best friend to you."

Mihle was quiet and looked remorseful. Her phone peeped on the table. She just glanced at it, and then looked at Aviwe.

"What came over you!" Aviwe waited for her to defend herself, "Did you even double check your facts?" she asked angrily.

Mihle shook her head. "No." She sniffed tears. "I would undo what I did if I could."

"No, you can't! Her body is covered with bruises," a short silence. Aviwe sniffed tears, "She barely walks," she added with a shaky voice.

Aviwe was more hurt than angry. She was afraid that their friendship would never be the same. She loved both of her friends and she knew something would be missing with the absence of one.

"Do you really believe that Sive is sleeping with Zuko?" she asked, her voice was now low.

Mihle didn't reply.

"Even if that's what you believed, why did you hurt her like that?" Tears fell from Mihle's eyes. "Did you even give her a chance to explain?"

There was no reply. Aviwe hurried out of the door and got into her car. Mihle heard the sound of her car leaving. She wiped her face with her hand and went to her room. When she was about to sit on her bed, she remembered that she got a message on her phone. She went to get it.

The message was from Zuko, and read like this, "I have loved Sive since the first time I laid my eyes on her. Even before we had Bridgette," Mihle's knees got weak. She glanced at the couch, and took a few steps and slowly lowered her big buttocks onto the couch. Staring at the message, "She's the type of woman that I would love to spend my life with, but when I met her, it was too late. I had already slept with her best friend. And I knew she wouldn't even consider dating me…she's a woman of high morals, so I kept my feelings for her untold."

Mihle released a sigh of relief, but her heart was bleeding all types of blood. She closed her wet eyes, opened them again, and carried on with the message that brought her more pain.

"This is the first time I've told someone about my feelings for her, even Sive doesn't know. When I went to my colleague's party, I met another woman. I'm not gonna give you any more details about her since you might hurt her, too. She's the one I went to Joburg with…not Sive. I didn't even know Sive was there before the incident."

Mihle gave out a shrill cry. Her daughters who were supposed to be at school came running from the corridor.

Mihle didn't look at them. She just told them to go back to their room. When she heard them leaving, she dropped her eyes to her phone and continued reading.

"I don't hate you. You're the mother of my beautiful angels and I wish you a good life. Sive was a great friend to you, and I thought you loved her the way she loved you, 'cause if you ever did you would never believe that she could do such a bad thing to you. She wasn't only good to you but to the kids as well. You better go to her and explain why you did what you did. Maybe she will forgive you, though, it won't be easy."

Mihle tried to call Zuko after she finished reading the message, but she lost the courage and dropped the phone before he even had a chance to pick it up. She leaned forward, resting her elbows on either thigh and cupped her face on her hands. Misery was written all over her face. She was regretting what she'd done.

She released a shrill cry, and it filled the whole house. Her kids came running from the corridor, and they stood at the beginning of the corridor, looking at their mom. Pain and confusion covered their cute, little faces.

Mihle lifted up her feet on the couch and curled up in it. Soon, she was asleep. And the girls slept on the carpet, next to her.

Chapter 21

Jonathan pulled his car out behind a red Ferrari, the latest model. No doubt the owner was one of the richest guys in the country.

It was white folk behind the wheel. The passenger and a driver leaned forward, kissing each other.

"Your mom," whispered Jonathan, "in that car," he added pointing with his head.

Sive quickly leaned forward. "Ouch!" she said with a sharp pain on her back.

"Easy baby, easy," said Jonathan helping her to sit back.

The red Ferrari went off and Thandi went to the house without noticing Sive or Jonathan. She was already dressed for work.

Jonathan helped Sive to get out of the car and walked to the house. When Thandi was trying to open the door, she heard footsteps and turned. She saw her daughter walking slowly towards her. She trembled in shock.

"What happened to you, baby?" she said walking towards her, helping Jonathan to get Sive in the house.

Suddenly, what Phiwe said about Jonathan crossed her mind and she quickly turned to Jonathan.

"What the hell happened to my baby? What did you do to her!"

"It's not him…"

"Who?" she said, looking at Sive.

"Her best friend tried to kill her," said Jonathan.

Thandi's mind quickly thought of Owam.

"I knew that filthy gay was up to no good."

"Mom!"

"What!" exclaimed Thandi, knowing that Sive was going to defend him.

"It was Mihle," said Jonathan.

Thandi looked puzzled. "What! But why?" she asked.

Sive shook her head. "I don't know, but she was going on about me sleeping with her man as she was beating me up."

Jonathan helped Sive sit down, and Thandi was staring at them hoping to hear something different.

Sive settled on the couch and then looked at her mother. "I called you last night and you didn't pick it up. And I came over but you weren't home…where were you, Mom?"

Sive caught Thandi off guard. She stammered, without finishing words.

"I…he…we…"

"It seems as if I'm not the only one with secretes here," said Sive, "Simple, you weren't here, Mom. You're dating that white man?"

Thandi looked at her daughter, quietly.

"And what's his name?"

"John."

"Do you love him?"

"Yes. He makes me happy."

"Why did you keep your relationship a secret then?"

Jonathan exchanged glances between them and said. "I have to go now."

Both Sive and Thandi moved their eyes from the door and placed them back on each other.

Thandi didn't have time to thank Jonathan. Sive's question put a frog in her throat.

"I wasn't sure of your reaction."

Sive smiled. "I'm a big girl, Mom." She shrugged. "And you deserve to be happy. And I'm happy for you."

Thandi smiled. "Thank you, baby."

"And we need to invite him over for dinner and formally introduce us to each other."

"That's a good idea," replied Thandi, smiling.

"Let me call work. I can't leave you alone," she said dialling work.

Sive moved her sore muscles to get the phone from her gown pocket. She wanted to call Gabriel. It was strange to her that he didn't call or text her or both the previous night.

The phone slipped through her fingers and fell on the floor. Quickly her mother walked towards her after she finished calling.

211

"Watch out, Mom," she said pointing with her eyes to the floor.

Thandi stopped and lowered her eyes, bent down, picked it up and threw it on the couch.

"Give it here, Mom," she said trying to stretch out her sore arm.

Thandi picked up the phone again and gave it to her. She then placed herself next to her.

"I need water," said Sive after she saw there was no message from Gabriel.

"To drink?" asked Thandi.

"Bath."

"Can you bath yourself?"

Sive shook her head.

Thandi smiled. "So, you didn't bath last night?"

"I did."

"Who bathed you?"

"Jonno."

The smile extended on Thandi's face. "So, it is true that you're dating?"

"I don't wanna talk about that, mom."

"I'm your mother, you should be open with me."

"Could you please stop digging up this thing about Jonno?"

"Fine. Let me go bath you."

A sadness covered Thandi's face as she was undressing her daughter and saw the bruises covering her body. Her body was trembling with anger.

"I'll be fine, Mom," said Sive when noticing a change in her face.

"How could I not be worried when my child is like this," she said pointing at her bruised body. "Why did she do something like this to you?"

Sive shrugged. "Maybe I'm not honest enough about my love life with the people around me," replied Sive.

"Oh please, don't try to take the blame for what happened..."

"No, no, no. I'm not. In fact, I'm furious with her for what she did to me. I know that she's going through a rough patch right now, but that doesn't give her a right to go around hurting others," said Sive with sadness on her face.

Thandi dried her daughter with a pink towel

"This towel was a gift from your paternal granny from the US..."

"Did she send it by post?"

"No. Your father came with a small package from his mother to his first child," she said patting her body softly. "I have few of them kept safely for your first child," she curled up a naughty smile, "And it's not long before I hold my first grandchild in my hands if your boyfriend keeps on bathing you."

Sive chuckled.

"And with that hot romance I saw this morning, it won't be long before I hold my cute baby sis or bro in my arms…"

"What! You gotta be kidding me, at this age!" she said putting her hands on her chest.

Sive slowly nodded her head. "Yeah, that age."

They both laughed.

Thandi gently massaged her daughter's bruised body, in silence. Sive was enjoying the movement of her mother's hands on her sore body.

"Tell me something baby, is Jonathan good to you?"

There was a silence again. Sive was planning to talk about her and Jonathan as a couple just to buy time until she sorted things out with him.

"Yes, although sometimes he's annoying," she replied, lying on her tummy on the bed, with her chin resting on the pillow.

"How?"

"Sometimes we want different things."

"Like?" she asked looking at the movement of her hands on Sive's back.

"Sex."

"And you're not ready?"

"No, I'm not."

"Is it because of your other boyfriend?"

"No, Mom," she said trying to sit up.

Her mother helped her to sit.

"Sex is sacred. It's not something someone can do just for fun. I want to do it when I'm ready."

"I agree," said Thandi, and then went to get her something to wear.

"You must be hungry. What do you want to eat?"

"Just cereal."

Sive looked at her mother. "Thanks Mom for your magical hands. I feel better now."

Thandi smiled. "But not as magical as Jonno's."

"Shut up, old lady."

They both laughed.

When Thandi brought her food, Sive was sitting on the couch. Suddenly, Thandi's phone rang. She picked it up, looked at the screen. It was John. Sive could tell from the look on her face that it was him.

"That's your magical hands, I can tell," said Sive winking at her mother. Thandi stretched her lips even wider and rose up to answer it in private.

When Thandi got back, she found her daughter fast asleep. She went to get her a small blanket and covered her and went to her room.

***

Life seemed not easy at all for Gabriel. He was sitting at his desk, staring at his laptop when James entered. He was hurt…so hurt and trying to forget about Sive. It was so difficult for him to forget about the only woman who made his heart so content. His mind was playing video clips of their sweet memories together, which were interrupted by James entering.

"Even workaholics need to eat," said James dropping two small Steers packages in brown paper on Gabriel's desk and two cans of cold drink. "Steers burger. The way you love them…warm and juicy," said James pulling out a chair opposite his best friend.

James stared at his friend. "Are you ok?"

Gabriel slowly shook his head.

"What's wrong?"

Gabriel paused before answering, leaned backwards. "Sive," said Gabriel looking at James, ready for his insults.

James was calm this time.

"Yes. I don't like Sive but it's so clear that I was right about one thing…she's not good for you. And I hope you see that now," said James in a low dignified voice.

Gabriel pursed his lips in a half smile, looking at James.

"She's pregnant."

James leaned back.

"I'll be damn lying if I say I'm surprised."

Gabriel tilted his head and closed his eyes trying to ease the pain in his heart.

"She didn't have even the slightest decency to tell me. She let me find out the hard way…in a painful way," he said, pain painted on his face.

"How did you find out?" asked James, feeling his friend's pain.

"I called her last night and her phone was answered by her man. He told me to get off her back, she's carrying his baby."

There was silence. Both in pain.

"I hope you're done with this wicked witch."

"I'm trying."

"Don't try. Just do!" said James, trying to encourage his friend to let go of Sive.

Gabriel leaned forward, resting both of his arms on his desk. "Do you know how much I love that woman?"

James took out a burger and took a bite. He placed the food on one side.

"She's not the only woman, man. Nancy loves you so much. Please man, give that girl a chance."

Gabriel wiped his face with his hand and said, "I thought of her…"

"You did!" said James excitedly. All he wanted was his friend to be happy. "And?"

"She's not a bad idea."

"Let me arrange a small function…a braai, and invite her…"

"Whoa man, not so fast. Let me take it one step at a time. All I need now, my friend, is to get over Sive," he closed his eyes for a moment, "If I'll ever be."

"Yes, you will, man. You deserve happiness. And it's Nancy who can give you that."

Gabriel nodded. "I agree."

James pushed the other burger towards his friend.

"Eat before it gets cold."

Gabriel forced a smile on his face and took it.

***

Thandi gave Sive her pills and a glass of water and then sat next to her.

Sive smiled as taking the pills and said, "You're my favourite Mom."

Thandi chuckled. "As if you have other moms."

They both laughed.

"I think I heard someone knocking," said Sive.

The knock continued.

Thandi went to open the door, Aviwe and Owam entered. Thandi hugged Aviwe.

"How are you my child?" she asked, breaking away from her.

Owam stood behind Aviwe, waiting for his hug but Thandi turned to him and just nodded and went to sit down.

"*Chomi!*" said Owam cheerfully, trying to shake off the sadness caused by Sive's mom's cold attitude and squeezed himself in between Thandi and Sive. Thandi moved to another couch, saving her daughter from unnecessary pains.

"You're not bad, girl. I thought I would find your face deformed," he said making actions with his hands.

Sive laughed. "Not so bad my friend," she replied.

"Not so bad! When you can't even bath yourself!" said Thandi with boiling anger. She quickly got up and went to her room.

There was silence.

All the eyes were at the corridor where Thandi had disappeared and they all turned to the knock at the door.

Owam went to answer the door. It was Jonathan.

"How's my future wife?" said Jonathan smiling from ear to ear, probably having sweet memories from the previous night.

"I feel much better now," replied Sive.

"That's great, babe," said Jonathan.

"When are you coming home, *chomi*?" asked Owam.

Sive shrugged. "I don't know. Maybe Monday."

"What! A whole week!" exclaimed Owam.

"I don't know why I was attacked, and I don't know whether she's thinking of finishing me off…"

"I hate hurting a woman, but this," said Jonathan.

"Are you still calling her a woman? No woman can panel beat someone like this. She must be Van Dame or something," said Owam.

They all laughed, including Jonathan.

Sive tried to get up, and Jonathan jumped to help her.

"Please, let me do it myself, Jonno," she said and she managed to get up and walked slowly and stiffly to the bathroom.

Sive wanted to get better. She was planning to visit Gabriel.

"My beautiful Mummy," said Owam pulling his friend's leg.

Sive laughed.

"But this beautiful mummy is hungry," Sive said.

"I'll make her a delicious sandwich," replied Owam going to the kitchen.

Sive slowly came back from the bathroom and placed herself on the couch. She took out her phone and looked for new messages, and still, nothing from Gabriel.

"Are you expecting a message?" asked Jonathan. He knew exactly what she was looking for, and it was a threat to their relationship, at least to him who believed that they had a relationship.

Sive just glanced at him and then back to her phone.

An awkward silence.

"Your mom must have been fast asleep when you got here last night," said Aviwe stirring a conversation.

"Fast asleep is another thing. Mom dearest wasn't even home," replied Sive, curling up a naughty smile.

"At that time, where was she?" asked Aviwe surprised.

Sive chuckled. "You won't believe this," she glanced at Jonathan and back to Aviwe again, "Out."

"Out!" asked Aviwe surprisingly.

"Yeah. With her boyfriend…"

"What! You must be kidding me…or we're not talking about the same person. I mean, Mrs. T!"

Sive blinked twice, and answered. "Yes. Mrs. T has got a man."

Aviwe glanced between Sive and Jonathan.

"He's a white boy," added Jonathan.

"What!" Aviwe exclaimed with Owam entering the room with a tray of food.

Both Sive and Jonathan nodded.

"What is it, guys!" he asked, standing with the food in the middle of the room.

"Girl, I'm dying of hunger here," Sive said.

"Fill me in and I'll feed you, girly," said Owam thirsty for the gossip.

"Mrs. T has got a man…a white boy," answered Aviwe.

"What! No way!" said Owam.

"Yes way. Give me the food," replied Sive.

"Oh no," he said and then laughed, "Mrs. T is now a little gold digger," he added.

There was an awkward silence.

"My mom is definitely not that. She's just in love with the man, I know her," Sive defended her mother.

"Your mom is so cute. Why would she wanna go for a white man if it's not for the money?"

"Who said that white men don't date cute black women?" Sive snapped.

"Come on girl, I hope your wisdom knows that a cross-racial relationship is wrong…"

"No! In fact, it knows that my mom has the same right to date a white man as you have one to date another man," she said, knowing that she was closing the case.

Jonathan and Aviwe were quiet. He was so impressed as to how Sive handled the argument between her and Owam.

There was bad blood between him and Owam. Probably because Jonno didn't want any male near Sive. Gay or not.

"You're right babe, he's the last person to judge others…"

"Stay out of it, Jonno," snapped Sive

Owam teasingly smiled at Jonathan, and Jonathan glared at him.

Sive glanced at her phone again, still nothing. Her constant glancing at her phone explained her grumpiness, and it made Jonathan even more jealous.

Jonathan glanced at Sive's food and then lifted his eyes to her.

"Eat your food, baby."

Owam jumped and took a tray from the coffee table and gently placed it on Sive's lap.

"You are such a nuisance," Jonathan murmured, and sat back. Owam heard him but decided not to answer him.

What was on Owam's mind was a need to apologise to his dear friend. He realised that he stepped on her toes; she had never lost it before, not in his presence. He knew her as Miss. Cool.

Owam placed his tiny buttocks on the edge of the couch and faced Sive's direction.

"I'm sorry girl. I didn't mean to upset you," he said sincerely.

Sive lifted up her stiff arm to put food in her mouth. The unbearable pain was written all over her face.

Jonathan couldn't stand it, watching his lover suffering like that. He jumped up in his seat.

"Let me help you babes," he said.

"No, thanks. I wanna do this. I have to recover," she said and then took a big bite of sandwich. When she tried to lift up a glass of juice, her hand lost its grip and fell on her mother's snow-white fluffy carpet.

Both Owam and Jonathan jumped off their seats to help her. Although they were like cat and dog, they had something in common…they loved Sive.

Of course, in different ways.

"That's it! I'll help you, babe," Jonathan demanded.

Jonathan helped her to get up and walked her to the dinner table. He put the food in front of her, and then went to get her another juice. He pulled up a chair in front of her and started feeding her. Although he hated to see her in such pain, he loved the benefits that came with it.

Owam wailed from the bathroom.

"I can't find anything that I can dry the carpet with!"

"Check outside on the line, an old pink face cloth," replied Sive with her mouth full. Owam came back holding it with two fingertips.

"This new…"

"It's not new. Just clean," said Sive.

"Well, even cleaner than the one I use," he said kneeling down, drying up the carpet, "I need water and some soap or something for this stain to come out," he said looking at Sive who was taking a last bite of her delicious sandwich.

"It was yummy my friend," said Sive smiling at Owam.

Owam smiled back. "I hope we're cool now."

"If you could help me back to the couch, we'll be more than just cool."

Owam dropped the cloth in his hands on the floor and walked towards Sive.

Jonathan glared at him.

"I got this," he snapped.

"But I…"

"Shhh," said Jonathan and lifted her back up to her seat.

Jonathan was getting more emotionally attached to Sive. Now the feeling of holding her up took him to the future when she's his pregnant wife, spoiling her rotten.

Owam stared at Sive.

"What!" Sive asked.

"Soap!" he replied, annoyed by Jonathan.

Sive laughed. "Look in the sink cupboard. Everything you need is in there."

"And stop being jealous," added Jonathan as Owam was walking away.

Owam glared back at Jonathan, and then continued walking. He occupied Owam's seat, next to Sive. He put his hands on her bruised thighs and stroked them.

Owam came back with a bucket of water and a bottle of handy andy. He knelt down and started working on the stain on the carpet.

Sive inhaled deeply, and then gave out a long sigh.

"It feels good," she confirmed.

Jonathan smiled impressively. "Not painful?" he asked smiling tenderly at her.

Sive looked at him with a soft smile on her face that turned Jonathan's world upside down. He wasn't just a step away from the reality of what was going on between them…he was very far. In his own fantasy world. Now, all of this was working in this fantasy's favour, making him more emotionally attached in a way that he would never let her go. He was planning to steal Sive's phone and text Gabriel and break up with him pretending to be Sive.

Jonathan could stoop to any lows to keep Sive in his life.

"Yes, it is. But gently hurting it, feels good," she explained.

Jonathan's smile extended. "Do you want me to stop?" asked Jonathan, wanted to hear her asking for more.

Sive shook her head. Jonathan carried on massaging her thighs.

Owam lifted his eyes. "Get a room!" he screamed at them.

They all laughed.

"Get done so we can go," said Aviwe.

"That's a good idea, leaving these two to turn Mrs. T's house into a brothel," he said throwing the cloth in the bucket and getting up.

Owam lifted the bucket and went out of the room. When he got back, Aviwe rose up in her seat and patted Sive on the shoulder.

"Quick recovery my friend. I'll see you tomorrow."

"And I hope this one," Owam pointed with his eyes at Jonathan, "won't be here."

They left, leaving Sive and Jonathan.

Jonathan knelt down in front of her and continued massaging her thighs with both hands.

Sive moved his hands. "Mom is in her room. She could come out at anytime."

"Mrs T won't mind. Mrs T and I want the same thing."

"Arousing your sexual feelings?"

Jonathan laughed. "No, silly. Your quick recovery. I'm just rubbing your sore body."

"Ok, that's enough."

Jonathan stared at her for a moment, and then got up and sat next to her.

Sive glanced at the clock on the wall. It was half past seven, only thirty minutes until her favourite soap, Generations.

She tried to get up.

"What do you want?" he asked.

"I want to ask my mom to help me bath before Generations."

"But I can do that, babes."

She narrowed her eyes.

"I'll behave, I swear."

"No, thanks," she said dragging her feet to the corridor.

Sive stood at her mother's bedroom door, looking at her lying on her bed.

"Are you awake, Mom?"

"Yes baby," she lifted up her head, "Do you want something?"

"Yes please, help me bath before Generations."

"Ok," Thandi said, getting up.

"Baby!" wailed Jonathan from the living room.

"Go home Jonno!" answered Sive.

Jonathan laughed. "Ok. See you tomorrow, take care."

After bathing, Sive lay on the couch, quietly. She gently rubbed her sore thighs. She wanted to get better soon so she could visit Gabriel before the end of her sick leave.

With the help of her mother and Jonathan, Sive recovered quickly. By the end of the week, she could walk and bath herself.

Chapter 22

On Friday, Sive found herself knocking on Gabriel's door. She noticed that there was no one home. The house was dark, too early to be in bed and too late to still be at work. She decided to sit by the door on her luggage, waiting for him.

A few minutes later, Sive heard Gabriel and James' voices.

"How did you get in?" asked Gabriel.

"No man, that's not the right question. The right question is." He moved his eyes from Gabriel to Sive. "What the hell are you doing here?" James asked.

Nancy was standing next to Gabriel, holding his leather jacket, and Sive felt a bit jealous.

Sive tried to get up, but she lost her balance and fell back on her luggage. Gabriel noticed pain on her face.

"What's wrong, baby! Let me help you get up," he said trying to lift her up.

James pushed Gabriel and he lost hold of Sive, and she fell on the ground.

"Don't be dumb man, this is all an act. Can't you see!" said James annoyed.

"Shut up, man!" replied Gabriel, helping Sive get up.

Sive looked into Gabriel's eyes. "The guy next door let me in," she said.

"Ok," said Gabriel picking up her stuff on the floor and walking inside.

Sive was the last to walk in, and Gabriel noticed that she was walking slowly.

"Don't fall into this conniving witch's scheme," said James.

"There's no scheme here. I got attached…"

"You mean by your boyfriend for cheating on him…well done!" said James.

Gabriel was listening, he wanted to hear her reply but she didn't reply. He was looking at her, and all he could see was her…naked, in that picture with another man.

"Are you cheating on me, Sive?" burst out Gabriel asking.

Sive just gaped at him without a word coming out of her mouth. What was going through her mind was Jonathan all over her naked body. She knew even if she could explain to Gabriel, he wouldn't understand.

"I knew it!" said James.

Sive turned and looked at James.

"You are such a disgusting, filthy witch. You visit another man carrying another man's baby!" said James annoyingly.

Sive bulged out her eyes in surprise and turned to Gabriel.

"Oh please, Sive! Spare me that look!" said Gabriel, "I know you're carrying someone else's baby. How gross is that!"

"Where did you get that?" she asked.

"Does that matter? What matters is that you're not the person I thought you were..."

"Please baby, don't be mad at me. That is all a lie. You're my one and only."

The tears fell off her eyes with the thought of denying Chikondi. Gabriel wasn't the only man in her heart. She loved them both.

Gabriel took out his phone and opened the picture Jonathan had sent him and shoved it into Sive's hands.

"How do you explain this!" said Gabriel with unshed tears.

Sive closed her eyes, and tears fell from her eyes.

"You such a conniving bitch who doesn't deserve my friend!" screamed James.

Sive moved her eyes from James and placed them on Gabriel.

"Baby. It's a long story, but not what it looks like. I swear."

Gabriel moved closer to her.

"Do you know how much I love you?" he asked, forgetting all about Nancy's presence or the picture Jonathan sent.

Sive nodded.

"And I love you more," replied Sive, and they embraced.

"What the hell is wrong with you, man!" burst out James annoyed.

"I love this woman, man," replied Gabriel.

"Even if she's playing you for a fool?"

"She says it's a lie."

"And you believe that? Damn man! How could she be naked in bed with another man?"

Gabriel looked at Sive. "Baby please, tell me what happened."

"I don't trust this woman. She's gonna lie...and there's only one thing that won't lie...a pregnancy test. And I'll go and buy one myself," said James.

Gabriel stared at Sive for confirmation.

She nodded.

James quickly left for the nearby pharmacy to get a pregnancy test. Nancy put Gabriel's jacket on the bed and sat next to it. From the look of things, Nancy realised that her chances of getting this man were slim. Her only hope was the pregnancy test.

The three were quiet. Gabriel was standing with his back leaning on the cupboard, Sive was sitting on a bar chair with her back against the counter. They were all thinking about the same thing, pregnancy test results.

"Here," said James putting it on the table.

Sive slowly went to the bathroom, came out with a pregnancy test with one solid red line, and put it in front of James. She then walked to Gabriel and told him all about the night of the picture Jonathan had sent him.

Gabriel went to sit next to Nancy.

"Nancy, I'm sorry but I'll have to take you home. I didn't know Sive would be here," said Gabriel, not even sure what he was saying was making any sense.

"So, I'll only be with you when she's not around?" asked Nancy.

"I love her. Please understand."

"But…"

"Please, don't make it harder than it already is," said Gabriel and looked at James. "Could you please take her home, man?"

"Take care of your mess, I'm out," said James closing the door behind him.

Gabriel turned to Nancy.

"Let's go," he said and went to whisper something in Sive's ear and kissed her on the forehead and then followed Nancy out of the door.

Gabriel hated himself for how he treated Nancy, but losing Sive was what he couldn't afford. Although pain and tears always accompanied loving her, he chose a life with her rather than Nancy's love.

Gabriel went to drop Nancy at home and went back home where his sweetheart was. When he went inside, he found Sive struggling to put on her pyjamas. Her body wasn't completely healed. The marks on her body were still showing.

"Let me help you, love," he said dropping the keys and the phone on the bed. When he saw the bruises on her body, he gaped.

"What happened, baby?" he asked doubting if it was a woman who beat her like that.

Gabriel just glanced at her and then embraced her. He kept her in his arms for a while, wanted to love her beyond his doubts. He loved Sive although there was something fishy about her.

"Did you tell your mom that you were visiting me this time?" asked Gabriel, still holding her in his arms.

"No,"

"Why?"

She didn't reply.

Gabriel moved her a bit away to see her face.

"Do you think my mom would want me to travel in this state?"

Gabriel pursed his lips as if he said, "I love you anyway."

"I have some leftovers from the previous night," Sive smiled, "but it's only enough for one."

"Then, the one is me," she replied, teasing him.

"It's ok. I'm not hungry anyway," he said going to warm up the food.

Gabriel went to shower while Sive was eating.

When the warm water travelled down his dark skin, waves of affection for his woman hit his heart. He wanted to show her that, beyond everything that was in question about their relationship, he still loved her.

When Gabriel got out of the shower, Sive was rinsing the dishes. He wrapped his lower body with a blue towel. He covered Sive's body in his arms from the back. He cupped her breasts, and he lowered his chin to rest on her shoulder. He kissed her on the neck. He then lifted her up and placed her on the bed, and continued kissing her.

"I love you with every breath I take," he whispered in her ear.

"I love you too…with all my heart."

Suddenly, Gabriel stopped and looked into her eyes.

"Tomorrow, after work we will be leaving for Durban, so I can wash your sore body in big water…"

Sive stretched out her eyes in surprise.

"You're kidding me, right!" she said blissfully.

Gabriel smiled, and shook his head. "I'm not kidding at all. I'm taking my wife, mother of my five kids for the swim of her life."

Sive rolled over him, happily.

"It will definitely be the swim of my life. I have never been to the beach with a man I…"

Suddenly, he realised that her secret that she'd never been with a man before almost slipped out of her mouth.

"Your man has never taken you out to the beach?"

Sive set her seductive eyes on him, escaping his question that she wasn't ready to answer at that time. She lowered her head and let their lips touch.

The magic happened.

Gabriel's body trembled. Thirsty for more than just a kiss, but he didn't want to put any stupid pressure on her that might ruin everything.

He whispered. "Baby, you're waking up the beast,"

She lowered her eyes to look at a bulge below his belt. She laughed and lay aside.

Gabriel turned and faced her.

"Do you love me, Sive?"

Sive looked in his eyes.

"I'd never felt like this before about any person. I love my mom, my family, but what I feel for you is different. My life was perfect without you," Gabriel's eyes widened in fear, "with you, is more perfect…more content."

Gabriel smiled.

He pulled her closer and locked her in his arms. When she felt some movements below his belt, she moved aside wearing a naughty face.

"Let me not wake the beast up."

"Already up and hungry. Why don't you feed it?"

Before Sive answered, her phone rang on the pedestal, next to Gabriel. He picked it up to pass it to Sive.

Suddenly, sadness covered his face.

"What baby!" she asked receiving her phone. Gabriel slipped his feet in his shoes and went out of the door.

Sive's heart throbbed when she saw 'hubby' written on the screen. The only person she saved as that on her phone, was Chikondi…the deceased.

"Hello."

"May I speak with Sive?" said a woman's voice.

"Speaking," Sive replied with a shaking voice.

"I'm Chikondi's mother."

Sive gave out a sigh of relief.

"I hope you're doing well my child."

Sive sighed. "I'm trying. I loved your son, so much."

"I know."

There was a silence.

"I'm calling to tell you that Chikondi left you a note that I found among his stuff a few days ago."

Sive didn't reply.

"I'll keep it for you," she added before ending the call.

Sive put her phone on her chest as if it was Chikondi. She was once again dwelling in her confusing feelings for the deceased.

A part of her was asking if Chikondi was really dead. She just couldn't understand how she could have such deep feelings for a dead person. The sound of Gabriel closing the door woke her from daydreaming.

"Will you ever stop from lying to me, Sive!" he burst out.

Sive didn't reply.

"Why are you here when you're married to someone else?"

"I'm here because I love you…only you."

"Stop lying to me Sive and tell me what's really going on in your life."

"My ex's mother called, using his phone to tell me he left me a note before he died."

"I'm sorry sweetheart, I didn't know."

Sive put her phone down and went to the bathroom.

Gabriel grabbed her arm and pulled her closer to him. He embraced her.

"I know it's hard for you, but I'll take care of you and your son. I'll love him as my own."

"I know. But there's one thing I don't know if you could ever do."

"What is it?"

"Trust me."

Gabriel didn't answer.

She went to brush her teeth and went to bed, leaving Gabriel sitting at the counter, drinking his tea.

Her phone rang, again.

It was a message alert. Aviwe was telling her that her mother postponed for the following weekend. Gabriel took her phone and checked who sent the message.

Unfortunately, this time, it was from a friend.

Gabriel lay on bed next to her. He covered her body until the morning.

***

Sive threw herself on their hotel room bed, and Gabriel placed himself carefully on top of her. He dropped a soft kiss on her lips.

227

"This is the life…being out with the mother of my five kids."

"Thanks babes," she said rolling over him, and kissed him. "What made you think of this trip babe?"

Gabriel smiled. "I guess it's time to do things that could help us bond," he said stroking her smooth face with the back of his left hand, "I love you."

"Me more."

Gabriel held her in his arms for a moment.

"Honey, I had a hectic day at work. I think we should stay in tonight, I need to relax."

She smiled. "As long as I'll be close to you," she said pulling his hand, "Let's go take a bath…a warm relaxing bath. And then, I'll massage your feet."

"And, in return, I'll massage these," he said grabbing her buttocks with both hands.

"That sounds like a good idea," she said pulling him into the bathroom.

Their room was on the twelfth floor, room 112. It stood tall enough to have a beautiful view of the entire city. A beige carpet covered the floor. A king size bed was dressed in snow-white and all the furniture was dark brown. A big window was dressed in maroon.

Gabriel and Sive came out of the bathroom, giggling, naked. She pushed Gabriel and he fell on the bed on his buttocks. She started massaging his body with body lotion.

His attention was on her bare chest. Anxiously waiting for his turn to massage it, and both were comfortable in their nakedness.

Suddenly, Gabriel pulled her on top of him. Started kissing her. Her body was clean for his tongue to make its magic on it.

He looked at her with eyes yearning for every taste of her body. He then lowered his head and kissed her neck. He gently bit her cute cheek, and then dropped a soft kiss on her mouth on his way back to her neck.

When his warm breath hit her neck, Sive groaned. Softly. He gently squeezed her breast and sucked it. His tongue tangled around her tit. She moaned ecstatically and murmured.

"It feels good baby…I like it. Please don't stop, I'm all yours tonight."

Sive felt like it was Chikondi making love to her, and, at that moment, she was ready to share her body with him. She wanted to feel him inside her.

Gabriel was so happy that she was finally ready to take their love to the next level. He slid his tongue down to her flat belly, teasing her belly button. He gently opened her legs, and when his breath hit her crotch, she murmured.

"Make love to me Chikondi…"

Gabriel quickly got up and went to the chest of drawers to get his sleeping clothes. He was so hurt, and all he wanted was to take the next flight back to Johannesburg.

She sat up and her chin rested on her knees. She did not know where to start to explain. Gabriel got into bed and faced away.

"Baby, I can explain."

"Please Sive, keep your lies to yourself," he replied in a low voice.

"Babes…"

Gabriel turned to her.

"Sive, leave me alone! And stop calling me that…my name is Gabriel."

Sive put her arm around his waist, and slowly stroked his tummy until he fell asleep.

Gabriel woke up in the middle of the night and found Sive sitting on a windowsill, crying.

Gabriel covered her in his arms. "It's ok honey, it's ok."

She looked at him with soppy eyes. "It's not ok. I keep on hurting you for someone who's doesn't even exist."

"Is Chikondi the father of your son?"

She nodded.

"It's ok sweetheart, I understand. You share a child with him."

Sive cried even more because she knew if he knew the truth, he wouldn't understand. That she was stuck to someone she didn't even know.

Gabriel lifted her up to bed and covered her in his arms until the morning.

Chapter 23

When Sive woke up in the morning, Gabriel was already dressed for the day. He was watching TV, waiting for her to wake up. She smiled at him and went to brush her teeth.

Soon they went to take a stroll by the beach. Both were dressed in all white. The morning sea breeze washed away their troubles and they felt happy again, and so much in love with each other. They spent all day at the beach, swimming and playing.

After taking a bath that night, Sive and Gabriel sat on the windowsill, viewing the beauty of the city at night.

Sive leaned forward and kissed Gabriel. "Thanks baby. I really enjoyed myself."

Gabriel smiled. "I wish I could travel with you back to Johannesburg."

Sive smiled. "I wish that too. I love you with all my heart."

Gabriel went to take a small little gift, wrapped in red and gave it to her.

She smiled and opened it. It was a key to his place.

Sive smiled.

"You're welcome to my house anytime you want."

Sive wrapped her arms around his neck.

"Thanks, baby. I hope now I'm allowed to call you that."

Gabriel laughed. "Yes honey."

They kissed, and then looked at the sky.

"It's a beautiful night," she said.

Gabriel smiled at her.

"And you're so beautiful," he said, and they leaned forward, kissing.

"Baby, a shooting star!" she said.

"Make a wish," he replied.

"I wish that our love could last forever."

Gabriel kissed her, lifted her to the bed, and continued kissing her.

Although Sive might not manage to walk down the aisle with Gabriel because of her feelings for Chikondi, they had strong feelings for one another. In that moment, Sive felt that, what was in the letter Chikondi left wasn't important anymore. What was important was to make Gabriel trust her and fully commit herself to their relationship.

***

Months after since Sive's accident, Sive heard an announcement through the intercom at work while she was having lunch that she had a visitor. When she emerged from the corridor, she saw Mihle standing against the counter. Sive stood, looking at her in surprise.

"I'm so sorry," said Mihle, shaking her head in pain. Tears racing down her cheeks.

Sive spread out her arms and embraced her friend.

"It's ok honey…it's ok," said Sive, pulled her arm to her office and closed the door. They sat opposite each other at the table.

"I don't know where to start…I know what I did to you is beyond forgiveness." Sive smiled.

"Nothing is beyond forgiveness. We all make mistakes, but I really need to know…why. Why did you attack me? What came over you?"

Mihle shook her head.

"I don't know what blinded me. But now I know that you're the last person that could hurt anyone," she sniffed, "After all I did to you, you're still taking care of my kids. You visit them at school to see if they're doing well."

Sive's eyes widened in surprise. She didn't know that Mihle knew she'd been visiting the kids at school.

Mihle's body was trembling in pain. Sive moved around the table and covered her in her arms.

"It's ok, honey. Let's put all this behind us and start fresh. We can't throw our friendship away over a single mistake."

"Thanks, Sive. You're one of a kind," she said, hugging her.

Sive smiled.

"Now we can resume our friendship, right? Things aren't the same without you…we miss you, Mimz."

Mihle broke a smile on her tight face and nodded.

"I've been missing you guys too …so much."

Sive glanced at her wrist.

"Let me walk you out, girl. It's time to go back to work."

Mihle got up and walked towards the door, Sive behind her. Sive stood at the door, watching her leave.

"Hey!"

Mihle turned.

"I'm gonna see you after work."

Mihle smiled. "I finally moved out last week."

"Is it!"

Sive moved towards her and hugged her again.

"I'm happy for you girl," she said squeezing her. She moved a bit away to view her face. Mihle was crying.

"Come on now…don't cry, baby girl," she said pulling her closer to her again.

"Life is so different without you…I'm lonely."

Sive smiled.

"I'm back now. See you later," Mihle started walking, "Where do you stay now, girl?"

Mihle turned.

"Here, in Mfuleni."

"Is it!" before Mihle replied, "Ok honey, will talk later. Just text me your address."

Mihle nodded, smiled, and then walked away.

Sive called Owam to tell him she would be home late, but she didn't tell him why. She knew how he and her family felt about Mihle. She wanted to tell them in person that she forgave her.

When Sive got to Mihle's place, everything was still upside down. Mihle didn't have time to do anything else besides cry. She helped her in cleaning the house and put everything where it was supposed to be.

"Where are the girls?"

"Their father is picking them up from school today," she glanced at her watch, "They will be home any time now."

Suddenly, they heard the sound of a car. Mihle peeped through the window, "That's them."

Sive quickly stepped out of the door, excited.

When Zuko opened the door for the kids, Bridgette saw Sive standing, smiling on the doorstep.

"Aunt Sive!" she screamed, running to her followed by her sister, then Zuko.

Sive knelt down; both of them clung to her.

"I'm so glad that you came back, Aunt," said Bridgette.

"Me too," added Smanye.

"Thanks, dear, for looking out for my kids," Zuko said, smiling.

Sive lifted her eyes to him.

"They say it takes a village to raise a kid," she replied getting up and hugging Zuko.

"Nice seeing you my dear," he said, squeezing her body.

"Nice seeing you too, Zuko."

She walked back inside with the girls on either hand. Zuko went back to his car.

"Go change, girls," said Sive

The girls went to their room, leaving Aunt Sive and Mihle standing in the middle of a messy sitting room.

Sive glanced around, and then said. "Let's clean the house Mimz."

Mihle shrugged. "Cool."

Sive looked around. "Let's start in the kitchen."

She washed the dishes and Mihle dried them.

"Can I ask you something?"

"Yes girl."

"Do you date someone besides Jonno?"

Although Sive wasn't ready to tell all the truth about her love life, she wanted to extract from its roots from her mind the idea that she slept with her man.

Sive nodded. "He's in Johannesburg."

"Do you love him?"

"Very much."

"Jonno?"

"What about him?"

"Do you love him?"

Sive nodded.

Mihle chuckled. "You, sleeping with two men…"

"Who said anything about sleeping?"

Mihle widened her eyes.

"You mean you still…"

"Yeah," she wiped the table, "I'm not yet ready."

Mihle nodded. "You're right, or you'll end up just like me."

Sive glanced at her, and then continued wiping the table. She threw the dishcloth in the water and smiled at her friend.

"I miss him…so much."

"Jonno?"

Sive shook her head.

"Gabriel."

Mihle broke a beautiful smile.

"Oh, he's Gabriel?"

Sive nodded.

"It's been more than three months since I last saw him."

"Why?"

"I'd been busy, and now he went home."

"Where's home?"

"Nigeria."

Mihle stretched out her eyes. "Do you trust Nigerians?"

Sive smiled. "I trust him."

"Enough about you and your polyandry."

"Shut up!" said Sive, and they both laughed.

"How's Vee?" asked Mihle packing the dishes, "I guess she's avoiding me lately."

"I don't think so. She's going through a lot."

"Losing Sbongile?"

"That included."

"At least you're there for her."

Sive tilted her head. "Some things are deeper, and they need professional help."

"Is it that bad?"

"Yeah. But I hope she'll join us soon."

Mihle raised her shoulders and finished packing up the dishes.

When they finished, Sive made two cups of tea, gave one to Mihle and they went to sit on the couch.

Mihle looked around. "This house looks so different, so clean."

Sive smiled and added. "And beautiful."

"Zuko bought this house for us."

"Is it?"

Mihle nodded.

"That's great, girl," replied Sive.

Sive's phone rang. It was her mother.

"My mom wants me to come over…"

"Is everything ok?"

She raised her shoulders. "I don't know, she didn't tell me why she wants me there…but she sounded a bit nervous," replied Sive getting up from the couch.

***

When Sive got home, Jonathan and Owam were sitting on each end of the couch, focusing on TV. She sat in between them.

"You won't believe what I'm about to tell you," said Sive looking at Owam.

"What is it, my friend?"

"Mrs. T is getting married…"

"Shut up! When?"

"In three months' time."

"Wow, I'm gonna be a bridesmaid."

Jonathan laughed. "You not even her favourite person."

Owam glanced at Jonathan and then gave his friend a puppy look.

Sive smiled at him. "Don't worry my friend, you'll be my bridesmaid."

"Wow! Are you getting married too, girl?"

"Not soon, but eventually I will, and I would like you to be my bride's bitch."

Owam laughed. "Bride's bitch…I love the sound of it."

Jonathan stretched out his eyes. "A guy, as a bride's maid in my wedding, never!"

Owam glared at him. "She will marry Gabriel, not you."

Suddenly, Jonathan's face was covered with anger.

"Sive loves me…not that loser foreigner. She's going to marry me…right, Sive?"

Owam looked at Sive, but she didn't reply.

"Babe, can we please go to Mauritius this weekend?"

Sive shook her head.

"I have a trip this weekend."

Owam gave Jonathan a teasing look.

"Don't tell me you're visiting that foreigner!" Sive rose up from the couch. Jonathan caught her arm, "Please, don't do this to me. You'll be my wife," Sive pulled her arm and walked away, "You have to be. And you will be," he wailed as she disappeared into the corridor.

***

Gabriel opened his house, and switched the lights on. The food aroma filled the house.

"Surprise!"

Gabriel looked at his woman with a tender smile as she was singing a happy birthday for him.

Sive was dressed in a red dress and red heels. Her long hair tied up in a neat ponytail. Her beauty stood out.

"Thanks sweetheart," said Gabriel hugging her. He moved a bit away to view her pretty face, "I missed my stunning wife."

Sive smiled.

"And I missed you too, my love," she replied leaning her head forward kissing him, "And how's everyone at home?"

"Good. And they like you…a lot…"

"Really!"

Gabriel nodded, and then smiled.

"The smell of the food makes me even hungrier."

Sive smiled. "It will be ready in ten."

"Ok, let me go shower. I can't sit next to Miss Universe smelling like this, like a wet dog," he said running to the bathroom.

Sive set the table for two.

Candles and red roses decorated the counter. Gabriel was dressed in beige pants and a red shirt. They sat opposite each other at the counter and started eating.

"What nice food my love!" said Gabriel looking at her.

"Thanks, baby."

Gabriel looked at her for a moment.

"You know what, you are such an amazing woman. No one has ever done anything for my birthday."

"When I said I will love you like I gave birth to you…I meant it."

"And I will take care of you every minute of my life."

Sive smiled. "Thank you, my son."

236

Gabriel laughed. "I feel secure when you call me that."

"Good, 'cause I would never deliberately hurt you. I love you so dearly."

Gabriel took her hand, pulled her to the bed, and kissed her. She whispered in his ear.

"You're spoiling the evening, babe."

"Sweetheart, we're done eating. As for the dishes, they can be cleaned later…"

"The dinner isn't over; get your butt back on that chair young man."

Gabriel laughed and went to sit at the counter. She cleared the table.

"I told you, we were done and…"

Sive glared at him. "Shut up!" said Sive, and then both laughed, "And don't turn around," she added.

"Ok," he whispered.

She disappeared behind him for a moment. She then reappeared with a birthday cake in a shape of a heart, sparkling in thirty burning candles. She dropped it in front of him.

"Happy thirtieth birthday, my king!"

Gabriel stared at the cake, speechless.

"I baked it myself."

The tears rolled down his cheeks.

"Oh babes, don't cry now. I wanna take your pictures," she said wiping his face.

"Thanks baby."

She took pictures of Gabriel cutting the cake.

The next day they spent the afternoon on a picnic, planning their future. By the end of that day, Gabriel was so certain of his future with Sive.

Even Ajay's love for her wasn't an issue to him anymore. He bought her a plane ticket to visit him again the following weekend.

***

Gabriel waited for Sive the whole weekend. He even tried to call her, but her phone was off. On Monday, something in him told him that something wasn't ok. He thought it was just the fear of losing her. He picked up the phone and called James.

"Hey man, what's up!" There was a silence. "I don't think you called me just to say nothing," said James.

Gabriel cleared his throat. "I'm not ok, man."

"What's up?"

A pause.

"After the most wonderful time I had with Sive, she's gone. And I feel it in my soul that it's for good this time."

"I told you so."

"You're not helping."

"It's time for you to forget about her and focus on Nancy." A pause. "Get her pregnant and start a family with her. She's your ticket to happiness."

"You don't know how much I love Sive. She's the air that I breathe. I suffocate without her."

"I know, but she's not good for you. Let her go."

Gabriel sniffed back tears.

"All I want is her to look me in the eyes and tell me it's over."

"That is what you won't get. That conniving little bitch is after her next victim as we speak. I can call Nancy for you if you want…"

"Beer is what you can get me right now."

James glanced at his wrist.

"I'll bring you some after work."

"No Nancy, ok!"

"No Nancy," promised James.

***

Monday afternoon, Sive was reported missing. She was last seen on Friday evening around seven, leaving the shelter. Her car was found parked by the road in Driftsands with a dead dog inside. No one knew the meaning of the dead dog. Some said it was a sign that Sive was no longer alive. When Thandi got home from a shopping spree in London with her fiancé on Tuesday evening, she got the disturbing news.

After several times of Thandi trying to get hold of her daughter, Phiwe knocked once and opened the door. He looked pale and exhausted. Thandi looked at him surprised.

"Why you look like you just woke up from a horrible nightmare?"

Suddenly, unshed tears covered his eyes. He was so hurt, but what hurt him so bad at that moment was the thought of how his sister would handle the news.

"What's wrong? Is Sma okay?"

Phiwe nodded and then took her hand and went to sit on the couch. He held both of her hands.

"You're scaring me now, what happened?"

He closed his eyes and inhaled to block the tears from falling.

"Sive's gone missing."

"What do you mean, missing?"

"She went to work on Friday, and never came home."

"Is she not in Johannesburg?"

Phiwe slowly shook his head.

"There's no records of her leaving the city. Sive wouldn't just bunk off work for pleasure…something bad must have happened."

Thandi's stomach clenched, staring at the air in front of her. Her shoulders trembled in pain.

"Who could want to hurt my little girl?" she said crying.

"Jonathan."

"And you're still sitting here! Go arrest him!" she said angrily, pointing at the door.

"He was arrested last night and got out this morning due to lack of evidence."

Thandi laughed hysterically.

"And your focus is still on him…damn it, Phiwe! While you're busy barking up the wrong tree, the real kidnapper is getting further away with my daughter," she said getting up from the couch.

"This is not my case, sis. As we speak, they're questioning her friend, the one who attacked her months ago."

Thandi grabbed her car key. Phiwe intercepted her.

"Where're you going, sis?"

"To beat the truth out of that filthy, ungrateful pig."

"Please, let the police deal with this in their own way. They know what they're doing."

Thandi broke down and cried. Phiwe sat on the floor next to her and put her on his chest, stroking her back to calm her down.

"I'm so scared, Phiwe…I'm so scared."

"I know. I am too, but it's time for us to trust God. He will never forsake us," he said, rocking his sister.

Sive's disappearance made no sense at all, to anyone. She was everyone's favourite. Who could possibly want to hurt her or, maybe Mihle's apology was nothing but a fake? She just wanted to be closer to her so she could finish what she started.

Mihle was arrested after Sive's earrings and the top she wore the day she went missing were found in her car, under the spare wheel. The top had bloodstains that were later confirmed to be Sive's.

Bridgette and Smanye remained under their father's custody, and their mother, in an orange jumpsuit, behind bars for the disappearance of her best friend whom she tried to kill months ago.

Aviwe, on the other hand, took leave and went to be with her mother who'd never come when she promised she would. She wanted to sort out her life, but it seemed far from being sorted. Her mother got mad when the conversation came to who her father was. All Aviwe knew was that her life had to be changed. She just couldn't end up like her mother. She had lost everything, her dignity, her man, her self-love.

She didn't know that she lost her pillar of strength, too. There was no way that she could have found out, she cut herself from the outside world in the process of finding herself. Owam tried to call her to tell her about Sive's disappearance, but her phone was off.

Now, it seemed like a good friendship reached a sad departure. Sive was missing, Mihle in jail and Aviwe somewhere in Johannesburg…not even sure if she wanted to come back to Cape Town. Thinking maybe moving overseas might be a good idea to start with a clean slate, but the question is, would there ever be a new slate for her?

During the next few days she was in Johannesburg, Aviwe couldn't control her sex craving and slept with her mother's gardener.

Chapter 24

James drove Gabriel home after he barged into his house, drunk and in no state at all to drive.

"My life is over. Sive's gone. And she's not coming back."

"Please man, stop torturing yourself like this. Nancy could save you from destroying yourself."

"To be honest," he threw himself on the couch, next to James, "I don't love Nancy...I love Sive."

"Give her a chance. Maybe, it won't be as bad as you think..."

"A life without Sive, is bad...too bad."

"Well, Sive's gone! You better get used to it. Give Nancy a chance or continue living a miserable life like this," he said pointing at him, drunk on the couch.

"I can't help it. I wrote her name in my heart. And no one can erase it, even if I could marry, she will always be in here," said Gabriel putting his right hand on his chest.

James looked at him for a moment.

"Get up and I'll drive you home," he said, pulling him up.

***

After two months of hearing nothing from Sive, Gabriel started realising that Sive had dumped him and he was forced to go for his second choice, Nancy. The pain of losing her was still sharp in his heart and giving her up was what he would never do.

Gabriel got home one afternoon with nothing on his mind except his beer in the fridge. His stomach clenched as he saw Nancy sitting in the same spot Sive used to sit, waiting for him. The thought that his life was ruined confirmed by the view.

"How did you get in?"

"I asked another woman to let me in."

"How could she do that? She knows it's against the rules," he pushed the door open, "What do you want?"

"You. I love you, Gabriel."

Gabriel tossed the keys on the couch.

"Coffee, tea?"

"Tea."

Gabriel switched on the TV and stared at it, sipping his coffee. Quietly.

He took the last sip of his coffee and then got up.

"I'm going out with the boys tonight," he dropped the cup in the sink, "We can drop you at home on our way…"

"There's no need. She can wait for you, we won't stay up the whole night," replied James, standing at the door.

"No man…"

"Yes man, she's your woman."

Gabriel raised his shoulders in defeat and placed his eyes on Ajay who was standing by the bathroom door as if he was asking for a defence.

Ajay shrugged. "At least you'll be lucky enough to come home to warm blankets," said Ajay.

Ajay and Gabriel were both going through the same pain. Sive's disappearance had cut them deeply.

***

Thandi's wedding had to be postponed, until further notice. She just couldn't move on with her life when her daughter was still missing. Sive'd been gone for almost three months and Thandi lost hope of ever finding her alive.

All she wanted was to bury her and let go.

Thandi took out grocery bags and then pushed the car door closed with her knee.

"Let me help you, sis."

Thandi quickly turned around.

She smiled and handed over the bags to her brother.

"You look better than before, sis."

She stopped and turned to him, her back to the door she was about to open.

"I'm trying to accept that my daughter has been abducted…or even worse."

Phiwe put the bags in one hand and then patted her shoulder.

"All I want now is her body to bury, and let go."

She then opened the door.

"Coffee!" she wailed from the kitchen.

"Yes please."

242

"I want to visit Mihle tomorrow just to tell me where she dumped my baby." She put the cup on the coffee table in front of Phiwe.

Suddenly, her eyes sparkled in unshed teas.

Phiwe looked at her sister. "What if they have arrested the wrong person?"

Thandi glared at him. "Will you just stop with your imagination right now! That heartless woman was found with my daughter's top, covered in blood…Sive's blood and her earrings. What more do you want?" Tears shed, she quickly wiped them. "The same woman who tried to kill her months ago," she added.

"Ok sis, I'll go with you tomorrow," he said and then took a sip of his coffee and put it down. He took his sister's hands and looked into her wet eyes.

"I will look for my niece and bring her home."

"Do you think she's still alive?"

"If Mihle's not the kidnapper, she might be alive."

"But Jonno was in the UK on the day my daughter got lost."

Phiwe looked at her as if he was studying her. "He could get someone to do it for him."

"But it makes no sense. Jonathan's house had been searched, and there was no sign of Sive."

Phiwe shrugged.

"That's what made me think I was barking up the wrong tree at first, but now, I'm investigating him…legally, or illegally."

Thandi just shrugged. Phiwe got up and left.

"Your coffee!" wailed Thandi.

"It won't bring my niece back," he replied opening the door.

"What the hell do you want here?" he said holding the door, looking outside.

"Who's that?"

"It's me, Mrs. T."

Thandi quickly got up and walked to the door.

"Let him in," she said, hoping that he was there to confess kidnapping her daughter.

Suddenly, when their eyes met, Jonathan's tears fell.

"What's wrong, tell me!" Thandi asked.

Phiwe got his hopes up as well, thinking that they were a step closer to finding their child.

"I miss Sive so much," both Phiwe and Thandi gave out a sigh of disappointment. "Could you please give me something that belongs to her that I could hold at night when missing her?"

Thandi and Phiwe's eyes met. Both realising that Phiwe was wrong and the police had the right person.

Thandi disappeared and went to get Sive's gown.

She forced a smile on her miserable face. "She used it on the last night she spent here. I didn't wash it; it still has her body odour."

Jonathan grabbed it with both hands and locked it in his arms on his chest. He trembled in deep pain. He then folded it, his hands were shaking.

"I don't know if I'll ever get over this. Sometimes I feel like taking my own life…"

"No baby, don't do that. What if Sive is found and you're dead?" Thandi said, embracing him.

"Why won't Mihle just tell us where her body is if she killed her. At least burying her would be much better than this torture."

Phiwe sneaked out, unable to handle the guilty feeling of accusing someone who cared so much about his niece.

"Let me go and lay down, Ma'am," he said pulling his body from Thandi. He walked slowly towards the door.

Thandi closed the door and then broke down and cried. Now she was so certain that her daughter was dead and buried in some lonely, shallow grave and she would never see her again. She cursed the day her daughter met Mihle.

***

Thursday morning, Owam madly banged on Thandi's door and windows to open for him. It gave Thandi a fright. She didn't know how he had gotten in since she locked the gates.

Thandi got up and called her brother.

"Mrs. T, please open the door!"

Thandi didn't reply at first. She didn't trust Owam since he was gay. She thought gays were weird people, and she thought that Owam had something to do with Sive's disappearance.

"What do you want, Owam?"

"Please open the door I wanna tell you something."

Thandi opened the door and left the gate locked.

"Say it, what do you want?"

"Please open for me, it's cold."

Thandi closed the door, but Owam grabbed the handle.

"Please don't close the door. Sive's alive…" he said it with Phiwe pulling up his car behind him.

Thandi opened the door and ran to her brother.

"What did he say?" she asked throwing herself at her brother.

Phiwe looked at her and then Owam. The look on Owam's face confirmed real shock.

Phiwe whispered. "Is my niece dead?" he said in a low sad voice.

"No uncle. She's alive."

"What!" he said pushing his sister aside, "Did I hear you correctly?"

Owam nodded excitedly.

He took out his phone from his jeans and quickly logged in on Facebook, opened an inbox message from Jonathan and gave it to Phiwe.

Phiwe looked at it for a moment.

"I knew it…that son of a bitch kidnapped my niece."

Thandi snatched the phone from her brother and nervously read the message aloud.

"It's me, Sive. Jonathan kidnapped me, tell my uncle to follow him after work," Thandi looked up at a dark sky, "Thanks Lord," she whispered.

"Let me go to the station right away. This isn't my case, but I'll go with them. I don't want anything to go wrong." He looked at Owam. "Let me have your phone. You'll get it back when the search is over…"

"Ok, take it as long as I'll have my friend back," Owam looked at the sky, "Thanks Great One!"

The joy on Owam's face brought a dawn of hope on Thandi's face. She stretched her hand.

"Let's go inside and have a warm cup of coffee."

Owam looked at her astonished.

Thandi smiled. He then extended his hand to her, and they walked inside. Owam was in Thandi's good books since that day.

***

Detective Zwane and Arends spied on Jonathan's house that afternoon. They saw him returning home from work but didn't get out.

245

Past eight that evening, Jonathan got out of his house dressed in women's clothes. He took a taxi just around the corner.

Arends called the cops who were waiting in a private car about 400m away. He gave them the details of the car Jonathan got into. They followed it and it stopped by a black BMW with tinted windows. Jonathan got in the car and drove off. They followed him.

When Jonathan realised that he was being followed, it was too late. They were not far from the house where he held Sive hostage. His instincts told him only one thing, to get off the car and vanish into the woods. The cops didn't take long to catch him since he wasn't an expert in moving through the woods.

"Where's Sive Tikolo!" shouted one of the cops.

"I don't know." Tears fell from Jonathan's eyes. "I come here in this place to pray for her safe arrival."

Phiwe laughed.

"Save the lies for another day, boy. You know nothing about God and praying. You're a son of the devil…tell us where my niece is!" said Phiwe angrily.

"Do you have a Facebook account?" asked one of the cops.

He nodded.

The cop took out his phone and gave it to him.

"Log in on Facebook."

Jonathan logged in, and then looked at him.

"Look at your inbox…last night's messages."

Jonathan's heart throbbed as his eyes ran though recent messages. He then lifted his eyes.

"What exactly should I look for?"

Phiwe snatched the phone from him and looked for the message. He nervously looked around.

"There's no message here." He looked at Jonathan angrily. "What did you do to the message, son of a bitch!"

"I guess the boy didn't reply and Sive deleted the message. In that case, it's only the recipient who still has the message…which is the boy's Facebook," said Zwane.

Phiwe passed Owam's phone to Zwane and the message was still there. He gave it to Jonathan.

Jonathan's eyes widened with shock. Fear crawled down his spine.

Phiwe bulged out his eyes at him.

"That filthy gay is lying. He's never liked me, and now is trying to frame me with something like this," said Jonathan trying to turn it all on Owam.

Phiwe slapped him between the eyes.

"Tell us where my niece is, or I'll kill you right now!"

"I swear I don't know where she is…"

"Guys, we not gonna get anything from this guy. By the look of things, we're not far from where she is. Sive's around here. Look, this road has been used recently…by the same tyres," said Arands, staring at the road a few metres from them.

Phiwe went towards him, focusing on the road.

"He's right; this bastard's been using this road."

"Jonathan, you're under arrest for the disappearance of Sive Tikolo. You have the right to remain silent. Anything you say can and will be used against you in a court of law. You have the right to an attorney. If you can't afford an attorney, one will be provided to you," said Zwane putting handcuffs on his wrists.

Jonathan followed Zwane's words. He never opened his mouth ever again.

They put Jonathan in one of the cars and then followed the road. It took them to a big abandoned building. It looked so horrible. They got out and walked towards it, leaving Jonathan with one cop. They went inside the building, and their attention was caught by a room that had a new gate.

Phiwe's heart pounded with high hopes that his niece was just behind that gate. He wailed her name.

"Sive! Sive! Sive!"

No reply. The house was as quiet as a grave.

"Let's go find the keys in his car and see what's inside," said Phiwe.

When Jonathan saw them through the window, carrying the keys, he knew he was done. His life was crashing before his eyes.

As they walked in, Sive was curled up on a single bed…fast asleep. Phiwe hurried up to her.

"Baby!"

Sive heard her uncle in her deep sleep, calling her name. She woke up, but couldn't get up. She was tied up. Phiwe's tears fell as they untied her.

"How could this son of the devil do this to another human being?" he said with his face covered with tears. He knew that Sive was hurt more than what they saw on the outside.

Sive had lost weight, but still looked beautiful. She threw herself on her uncle. They embraced.

"I'd already lost hope of ever being found," she whispered in his ear.

"You're safe now. So safe," replied her uncle.

Jonathan stared at her as she passed by him in the car. Their eyes met. The anger and bitterness was written in her eyes, and she didn't want to say anything. She knew she was done with him.

Tears fell from Jonathan's eyes as he realised that his life was over. The damage he'd done. He wished he could turn back the hands of time and do things differently. But it was already too late.

Jonathan was taken away, and Sive was reunited with her family.

***

Thandi was waiting in her house with Owam. They became good friends in a short period. They cooked Sive her favourite dish. They were so happy that she was coming back home that evening.

Someone knocked at the door while Thandi was in the bathroom. Owam went to open. He screamed.

"Oh my God! Is it really you, girl!" Owam screamed, hugging her.

Thandi came running from the corridor with her arms in the air and wrapped them around her daughter. Phiwe was standing, smiling happily looking at them.

"You're back," said Thandi in a low voice, squeezing her body.

Thandi took her hand and led her to the couch. She sat next to her daughter and Owam on the other side of Sive. Phiwe walked slowly towards them.

"It's been a long day but let me sit and have supper with my family. I can't leave food smelling this good and go eat bread at home," he said taking a seat opposite them.

"You're welcome, the food is enough for all of us." He smiled. "I know you've been starving since your cook went to the US."

"Speaking of him, he's coming back on Sunday."

"Is it!" She turned to Owam. "Why didn't you tell me the good news?"

"I'm sorry Mrs. T, I was carried away by the return of my best friend."

Thandi turned to Sive.

"Why are you so quiet, my darling? You're home now. Safe." She glanced at her wrist. "Let me serve the food now, it's getting late."

"Count me out, I'm not hungry," she said.

"Baby, please eat something…even if it's just little."

Sive just shook her head.

"Did he touch you?"

"That's obvious. He should thank God that he got arrested, otherwise, he'd be cold in a mortuary," Phiwe said.

Sive sighed. "Jonathan didn't rape me."

There was silence.

All three exchanged glances in disbelief.

"Baby, you mean you're still a…"

"Yes mom, I'm still a virgin. Jonathan didn't take that away from me. He said he loved me too much to hurt me that way, although…he did some creepy things to me."

"What are those creepy things?" asked Thandi.

Sive sighed painfully, fighting back the tears.

"Sex without penetration."

Owam narrowed his eyes at her.

"You mean he made you do things to his body?"

"No, he did things to my body…and please, I don't wanna talk about this." She moved her eyes from Owam to Thandi. "Mom, where's my phone?"

"I don't know baby, maybe in police custody."

"No, there was no cell phone in her belongings."

"It was in my purse, in the car before I stopped to help Jonathan."

Phiwe narrowed his eyes at her. "What do you mean, help Jonathan?"

Sive sighed. "I don't wanna talk about this, Uncle. What I want right now is to call Gabriel."

"And, who's that?" asked Phiwe.

"Her boyfriend in Johannesburg," replied Owam excitedly.

Sive smiled for the first time, and raised her shoulders. "If he still is." She moved her eyes to her mother. "Can I use your phone, Mom?"

She nodded.

Sive called Gabriel, and it went straight to voicemail. She kept on trying until the next morning.

She called her mother at work and told her that she would go out with Owam and sleep over at her place. Although her mother wasn't fine with it, she finally agreed.

She then called Owam.

"Pick it up; pick it up." She nervously whispered. "Hey, girl. I need you to do a favour for me."

"Anything, what is it?"

"I want you to take me to the airport tonight. My flight departs at 20:10…"

"To Johannesburg?"

"Yes. And if my Mom calls, please tell her that we have some function to attend…"

"Cool. Girl, let me see you later, I have clients waiting."

"Ok. Girl wait, wait!"

"Yes?"

"I'll hide my luggage in the garden. Put it in the car…and please, not at the back seat where the dead dog was."

Owam laughed. "Now you're scared of a dead dog that's no longer there?"

"It's not that I'm scared, I don't know. Maybe I just hate what happened. Why did he put a dead dog in my car?"

Owam shrugged.

"I don't know, girl. I wish I could tell you why. Hey, have to go now."

Chapter 25

The cab dropped Sive in front of Gabriel's gate at 22:50 on Friday evening. She was dressed in a tracksuit and training shoes. She stood in front of his door, closed her eyes, inhaled, and exhaled deeply.

She then opened the door and flipped the kitchen light on. The house was a mess. Clothes on the floor, dirty dishes piled up in the sink.

Sive was exhausted, all she needed was to bury herself in Gabriel's arms and tell him everything in the morning. She sneaked towards the bed. She didn't want to wake him up.

Suddenly, she stopped, staring at the bed. The tears rolled down her cheeks, and her body trembled.

Gabriel was in bed with Nancy, cuddled up.

Sive gave up. She realised that ten weeks was too long. The two might have a strong connection and Nancy might already be pregnant. Her heart was torn apart. She slowly walked to the couch. She picked up a pillow and a blanket on the floor and curled up on the couch.

After a moment, Nancy started kissing Gabriel. He took off his clothes while Nancy was doing the same. He pulled open a pedestal drawer, took out a condom, and made love to Nancy, while Sive watched.

Sive wanted to scream, but she realised that in spite of how much she loved him, she wasn't at all good for him. Jonathan's sickness and her feelings for Chikondi caused him nothing but pain.

Sive realised that Gabriel needed happiness, and if Nancy was the one who could give him that, she should let it be. However, all the moans they made were like a sharp sword that cut so deep through her soul.

Suddenly, her body felt like it was injected with deadly snake venom that was slowly taking her to death. Soon, she was quiet.

Gabriel woke up the next morning, naked in Nancy's arms. When he saw himself in that manner, all that came to his mind was Sive. He felt so guilty.

When he turned around, Sive was already awake. Their eyes met. Gabriel jumped up like ready toast.

Nancy quickly sat up and looked where Gabriel was looking.

"B-baby," he said moving towards her, and then realised that he was naked.

"You know what, you look disgusting," said Sive getting up off the couch. She had slept in everything, including her shoes.

Gabriel grabbed underwear from the floor and pulled it on.

Sive narrowed her eyes at him while Nancy was laughing.

"What's wrong?" asked Gabriel grabbing his pants from the floor.

Sive shoved him as she walked past him to the bathroom.

"You wear my underwear," said Nancy.

Gabriel quickly looked down.

"Damn," he whispered.

Sive took a shower and then dressed in black skinny jeans, black shirt, black three-quarter leather jacket and black Adidas sneakers. She tied her hair at the back. What scared Gabriel was that there was no smile on her face.

She warmed milk, made herself a bowl of cereal, and then sat down. While she was eating, James entered, bringing Gabriel his phone. He was so shocked to see her.

"And this!" he said pointing at Sive with Gabriel's phone.

Nancy shrugged as she was sitting on the bed, not far from Gabriel who was standing, hopeless. Sive just lifted her eyes at him, quietly.

James looked at Gabriel.

"Man, be man enough and tell this woman to leave," he said pointing at Sive angrily.

"No need, I'm leaving. And I'll never come back."

Her words cut so deep in Gabriel's heart.

"Baby, please, don't do that. Let's talk about this…"

"Hallelujah!" said James.

"Talk about what, hah! That you were sleeping around while I was kidnapped…going through hell, are you serious!"

Silence.

"Kidnapped?" asked Gabriel concerned.

"Oh, please man. Don't tell me you believe this crap."

Gabriel just glanced at James and then focused on Sive.

She sighed and pushed the bowl aside. She closed her eyes, fighting back the tears. She sniffed.

"I lied to you…or, let you believe what wasn't true about me…"

"Amen!" said James clapping his hands. "I told you man…"

"Shut up, James!" said Gabriel, still staring at her.

"I'm not a cashier at Shoprite…"

"You're a gold digging prostitute, and I'll be damned if I will let you milk my friend dry."

Gabriel glared at James and said, "Shut up, James!"

"I'm a doctor at Dr Bob Khabba Clinic."

James laughed mockingly.

"Will you let me finish!" asked Sive angrily.

Gabriel glared at James to stop interfering.

James looked at Gabriel. "To hell with that glare, man. Open your eyes. Your happiness is with Nancy, not this whore."

Gabriel exhaled and then turned to Sive who was getting angrier.

Sive sighed to calm herself down, and then continued.

"I help in a shelter that keeps homeless people. I collect clothes and food from friends and family and donate to the shelter." A gentle smile broke out from underneath her tight skin. "I am also a part of an orphanage in Mfuleni, not far from where I work. I give them 16 hours a month of my time, and 10% of my salary. I was kidnapped coming from dropping food at the shelter…"

"Oh, baby," said Gabriel, touched by her story.

"Come on man. Don't fall for this; this is all a lie…"

"Will you, shut up James!" he asked annoyingly.

"Do you remember when I said I had a stalker?"

Gabriel nodded. "Yes."

She closed her eyes and sighed. The tears fell down.

"He kidnapped me. I saw Jonathan's car by the side of the road. He was standing in the middle of the road, covered in blood. I pulled off and nervously got out."

She covered her face with her hands to block the tears.

"Oh, baby," said Gabriel walking towards her. James grabbed his arm.

Gabriel's eyes were glittering with tears.

"Jonathan was my friend and colleague before." She closed her eyes again. "He grabbed me and then covered my mouth and nose with a damp cloth, and the next thing I woke up in his arms, naked." Her body trembled in pain. "He kept me hostage for ten weeks."

James slowly clapped his hands.

"Bravo! You can write a book…a bestselling one. But you know what, I don't buy this!"

"Who cares what you buy," said Sive and then turned to Gabriel. "You didn't even try to look for me when my phone was off for a long time or haven't been on Facebook for months. All you did was move on…"

"No baby, I didn't move on."

"You made love to another woman, in my presence…my presence, Gabriel! Do you know how much it hurts!"

Tears rolled down his cheeks.

"I'm sorry, baby. So, sorry."

James burst out laughing. "You did what man! That's my boy."

"Shut up, James!"

"Tell her that you're in love with a real woman who makes you happy, not the one who wets your eyes every time."

Gabriel turned to Nancy. "Can you please go home?" he said opening his wallet.

"Nancy's not leaving."

"Stay out of this man."

Gabriel turned to Sive.

"Where would I start looking for you, sweetheart, when I didn't even know where you live in Cape Town?"

"My friends on Facebook could be a lead."

Gabriel looked at Sive. "I'm sorry, love. To be honest, I thought you had dumped me…"

"After everything Gabriel, you still think I would dump you!"

"I'm sorry, honey."

"Do you know how much I loved you?"

Sive's phone rang.

It was her mother. She put it on speaker and placed it on the counter. She knew that her mother would say something that would make James believe that she was speaking the truth.

"Hi baby, how are you?"

"It's over, Mom." Tears welled up in her eyes. "Gabriel has moved on…"

"I haven't sweetheart," he said in a shaky voice.

"Yes, you did," said James.

Gabriel glared at James.

"Baby. You're still a virgin, and vulnerable. You might do what you're not ready for. Just come home and then…"

"Ma'am," he glanced at James and he looked surprised. He walked closer to the phone, "did you say Sive's a virgin? But how, she has a son?"

"Sive's never given birth. Maybe it's just a boy from the orphanage."

"Sive will call you back, Ma'am."

Gabriel ended the call and turned to Sive.

"Why did you lie to me about having a child?"

"In my heart, I do."

Gabriel stretched his eyes.

"I met a guy on Facebook while I was still in college. We fell in love…deeply in love. We chatted every day. I loved him with all my heart and I still do…"

"Go to him then, and leave this couple alone," said James annoyed.

Sive just glanced at him, and then continued.

"He lived in Malawi. We last spoke on my graduation day. Soon after, I got a job. And after six months I went to look for him," she broke out and cried sadly, "But he was dead, leaving behind a four-month old baby boy. A part of me died with him. And I told myself that I would be a parent to the boy, but his mother took him to Zambia, and we lost contact."

James looked at Nancy.

"Take your stuff, we're leaving."

"I'm not…"

"I'll drag you if I have to," James said and then walked out, and Nancy followed.

Sive and Gabriel moved their eyes from the two and placed them on each other.

"Do you still love the guy?"

Tears rolled down her chicks.

"I wish he was still alive. I wouldn't be this hurt right now…yes, I still love him."

Gabriel took her arm, Sive shrugged him off.

"Don't touch me! You smell disgusting," she said, still crying.

"Baby, I'll go and take a quick shower…"

"You don't need a quick shower, you need a lifetime shower," she said heading for her luggage. She quickly turned before reaching it.

"How could you do this to me," her voice was sorrowful, "I thought we had something special…"

"We have, sweetheart."

"Do you call breathing heavily on top of another woman, something special for us?"

"Baby, we can fix this…"

She chuckled.

"This, is beyond repair. I'm leaving…for good." She took out the keys from her purse. "Here are your keys." She threw them at him and walked out of the door.

Gabriel screamed at her to give him another chance but she kept on walking. His heart was completely smashed.

Suddenly, a dark cloud covered his life. Soon, it became meaningless. He remembered nothing about having sex with Nancy. All he remembered was the sweet dream of making love to Sive.

***

Sive was kneeling at Chikondi's grave, crying, hopelessly. She was torn inside.

"I wish you were here. I wish you could hold me right now, make love to me. I wish you could give me the beautiful life we could have lived. Your role in my life ended before it started. Now I can't move on, I'm stuck in a life with you when you're not even there to give me that life."

"My child, come here."

Sive turned around. It was Chikondi's mother.

"Come," she said with open arms, and locked her inside them. She then released the grip, picked up her luggage, then took her hand, and started walking home.

She made tea and sat next to her.

"I can see that you loved my son and he loved you too, otherwise he wouldn't have left you a letter. I didn't read the letter," she took the letter from under a couch cushion and gave it to Sive.

Sive looked at her and took it.

"Thanks, Ma'am."

"Can you tell me what brought you here?"

Sive shrugged. "Love triangle."

"Are you in love with two men?"

"Yes. Gabriel, and your son."

"I'm listening."

"I fell in love with Gabriel. But my feelings for Chikondi have always gotten in the way, and it makes it difficult for me to love him the way a woman is supposed to love her man. And I got kidnapped, and my kidnapper kept me for ten weeks…"

"Oh, my dear, that's bad. I'm so sorry. But, he didn't hurt you?"

Sive shook her head.

"It's ok now." She sighed. "When Gabriel thought that I dumped him he moved on. I went to his place last night. I got in using my keys. I found him in bed with another woman. I slept on the couch..."

"Did he tell you to sleep on the couch?"

Sive shook her head. "He didn't even know that I was there. They were both asleep when I got there."

"Ok."

"He made love to her, while I watched."

The woman broke a soft smile on her face.

"Did you throw everything in the house at them?"

Sive shook her head. "No."

"What did you do?"

"Nothing. Just watched them."

"I'm sorry dear, it must've been painful."

Sive nodded.

Tears fell down her pretty face.

"We argued and I became so angry that death took Chikondi away from me. And I just wanted him closer."

The woman moved closer to her and embraced her trembling body.

"My child, I could see that you and my son had something special. However, he's gone now and you're young, you have to move on. My son was a good man and he wouldn't want to see you like this. He would want you to be happy. Do you love the guy?"

"Yes. But sometimes it feels like I'm betraying my love for Chikondi. I don't even know if I could walk down the aisle with him."

"You're not, my dear. He would want you to be happy. Besides, he will always be here," she said putting her hand on Sive's left breast, "Don't you want to read the letter?"

Sive opened it. It was short.

"My darling Sive, I'm sorry for leaving you like this. I won't make it. My days are numbered, I'm leaving soon. Find a man and love him as you loved me.

So long

Love Chikondi."

Sive broke down and cried. Bitterly.

She took all the money that was in her wallet and gave it to Chikondi's mother.

"Please, put it in your business."

"Thanks, my child."

They hugged.

Sive forced a smile on her miserable but beautiful face.

"Bye," Sive said and pulled her luggage and took the last flight back home.

Chapter 26

It was raining, heavily. Gabriel was sitting on the windowsill, watching the rain pouring and his eyes were doing the same, ignoring every call. He felt so empty without Sive.

Suddenly, Gabriel grew an intense hatred for South Africa. The mean people, crime, police barging into their premises accusing them of selling drugs.

"Why would I stay now, when I have lost the only thing that made South Africa feel like home to me?" he burst out and said.

He then got up and hurried to the wardrobe. He took his big black luggage and started packing his stuff.

There was a knock at the door.

He ignored it.

"Open this door man, I know you're here. I saw your car."

Gabriel carried on packing.

"Open this door," he said banging it.

Gabriel opened the door.

James just hugged his friend. Almost cried too.

"What happened, man?"

"She broke up with me and left just after you. Her phone is off."

"She's just hurt, but she'll come around," James looked around and saw the luggage, "And then?"

"I'm going home…"

"Nigeria!"

He nodded.

"No way, man."

"I'd just lost the only thing that makes me happy in this crazy country…"

"She'll come around, man," Gabriel glared at him, "We'll hunt her down, if it comes to that."

"My mind is made up…and I want to be alone right now," he said opening the door for him.

"Are you kicking me out?"

"Hello! This is a phantom we are talking about. It's Sive who broke up with me, not your favourite Nancy."

"Come on, man…"

"Shut up and leave! If it wasn't for all your damn effort in keeping us apart, things wouldn't have gone this far. I would still have my baby…"

"Geez man…"

"Get out!"

"See you tomorrow," said James leaving.

Gabriel carried on packing. He saw Sive's top among his T-shirts. He grabbed it with both hands and put it against his chest as if it was her. He broke down and cried.

The smell of her perfume on it reminded him of her presence, her beautiful smile, her intellect, her elegance.

Another knock at the door.

Gabriel ignored. It persisted.

"Go away, James!" he said annoyed.

A part of him was blaming James for losing Sive. If he didn't hate Sive the way he did, he wouldn't have shoved Nancy into his arms.

He quickly got up and hurried to the door. He wrenched the door open.

"What do you…"

Gabriel's eyes widened in surprise. He swallowed the rest of the sentence. His heart throbbed. Tears welled up in his eyes. Staring at her, not knowing what to do or say.

Sive was standing wet and dirty in front of Gabriel. Her sneakers and the bottom half of her luggage covered in mud. She was shaking in the cold, staring into Gabriel's eyes.

"I love you, father of my five kids," she said in an angelic voice.

Gabriel gave out a sigh of relief.

He pulled his woman to his chest and covered her in his arms, as wet and dirty as she was.

"I love you more, sweetheart," he said and then dropped a kiss on her cold lips.

He put his palms on either side of her face.

"Let's go shower."

Sive nodded.

They got into bed.

"I thought I had lost you forever, and I was planning to drop everything and go home. I can't live in this country without you."

"I won't leave you."

Gabriel jerked himself up.

"Where did you go?"

She sighed. "Malawi. I wanted closure."

"Did you get it?"

She paused before answering.

"I read the letter."

"What does it say?"

Sive stretched her arm and pulled her purse from the couch. She took the letter and gave it to Gabriel.

He read it. Then lay on his back on the bed, facing the celling.

"I wish you could love me like you loved this guy."

"What if I love you more? Despite what happened, I'm still here and more certain that I still want a life with you."

"I know, baby. I was just being jealous. I'm sorry, sweetheart," he said pulling her onto him.

Sive smiled.

"I was scared; I thought I would find you with her again."

Gabriel shook his head.

"That was a mistake, and it will never be repeated. Not with her, or any other woman."

"How could you call something so special, a mistake?"

"Special?"

"I saw everything. The way you moaned on top of her," she then closed her eyes, blocking the tears.

"Baby, please. Don't do this."

"We need to talk about this," she sat up straight, looking at him. She sighed, "Definitely, you love the woman..."

"No! I love you."

"But she's the one that's recognised by the universe as your wife as we speak."

Gabriel sat up straight and looked into her eyes.

261

"Baby, I was drunk. I don't even remember making love to her. All I remember is a beautiful dream, making love to you."

Sive stared at the air in front of her, quietly.

"What's wrong, sweetheart?"

Sive turned to him.

"Promise me one thing."

"Ok."

"That you'll never let another woman enjoy my goodies."

Gabriel smiled. "Never, ever again."

Sive moved on top of him. She lowered her head. When their lips touched, they both felt like they were kissing for the first time.

She then looked at him.

Gabriel quickly rolled over her. He looked into her eyes, and something in them confirmed that she was the food to his soul.

He kissed her soft, tender lips.

Sive gently pushed him a bit away and started undressing him. She then looked at his nude body.

Strong and muscular.

"Make love to me Gabriel…make me yours."

Gabriel couldn't believe his ears.

"Are you sure?" he asked.

"Positively. It's you that I want…that I want to spend my whole life with. Please, marry me."

Gabriel smiled tenderly.

"I'll make you my wife, and love you for the rest of my life," he said undressing her, revealing her soft, tender, toned body.

Suddenly, the beast announced its hunger as if the stranger didn't feed it the previous night.

Gabriel moved closer and kissed her. Sive felt the movement of the beast against her bare skin and whispered in his ear, "The beast is hungry."

"And you gonna feed it, right?"

"Oh boy, I've got a feast for it," she said gently grabbing her breasts.

Gabriel smiled at his naughty virgin.

He lowered his head and sucked the breasts as Sive was holding them.

She moaned.

Gabriel felt a wave of excitement travel down his spine. He slithered his tongue on her belly down in between her legs. He panted. Sive stretched her legs wider as his warm breath hit her crotch.

Suddenly, Sive's body yearned for his taste.

"Make love to me, babe," she whispered.

Suddenly, Sive felt Gabriel inside her. He gripped her so tight, so divine as the love exploded within him.

"I'll never let you go, baby," he said and then loosened the grip.

***

Sive arrived home at 7:45 on Monday morning. The house was empty and quiet. She assumed that Owam had already left for work. She threw her phone on the couch and went to put her luggage in her room. She heard her phone ringing and hurried to answer it, thinking it was Gabriel.

It was Owam's gay friend. He told Sive that Owam was attacked and she had to come to the bridge behind Khayelitsha Day Hospital.

Sive got in her car and hurried to the place.

Sive's heart pounded as she saw police vehicles and many people standing in a circle. She got out of her car and ran towards them, calling Owam's name. She just wanted to hear his voice. Everyone turned to her and moved to give her a way to see the body that was lying covered with an old duvet cover.

"No, no, no. It can't be him," she said and snatched the duvet cover. She cried hopelessly, looking at her lifeless friend.

Owam was naked, and his manhood cut and shoved in his mouth. A piece of paper was pinned on his forehead written, 'Leviticus 20: 13…If a man lies with a male the same way as with a woman, both of them have committed abomination; they shall surely put to death; their blood is upon them.'

Sive identified the body. Then the police put Owam in a body bag and put him in the vehicle. Sive sadly watched her friend leaving her for good.

***

When Sive got home, Smamkele was standing in her driveway.

"I was trying to call you," he said smiling at her as she was approaching him, "Hey cuz, what's wrong?" he asked embracing her.

Sive continued crying, even more in his arms. Probably thinking how her cousin would take the news.

"Talk to me, cuz."

"Let's go inside," she said.

When they got inside, Smamkele glanced around. "Where's my bitch?"

Sive didn't answer; she just threw herself on the couch. She pulled herself to the edge of the couch, her elbows rested on her thighs. Her face buried in her hands.

Suddenly, her shoulders vibrated.

"Talk cuz. What is it?"

Sive removed her hands from her face, put them in between her thighs, and stared in front of her. "It's Owam."

"What about him? Is he alright?"

Sive shook her head.

"What happened, talk, Sive!"

Sive burst out crying. "He's...dead."

Suddenly, sweat ran down his spine. His throat went dry; he couldn't get out a word for a moment. Tears raced down his cheeks.

Smamkele wiped at his tears.

"I don't understand...how did he die?"

"Killed by crazy homophobes."

"Do you know them?"

Sive shook her head.

"Where's he?"

"Mortuary. State mortuary."

Another silence.

Sive and Smamkele embraced. Rocking each other.

***

It was a warm Spring day when Owam was buried. People were all dressed in dark colours, sitting in front of Sive's house, waiting for Owam's body to arrive.

Pastor Xulu, Owam's stepfather, refused to bury Owam in his home, or have anything to do with his burial, and his submissive wife sided with him.

In the first row, there was Owam's aunt, her husband and a few members of his extended family. In the second row, it was Phiwe, Smamkele, Thandi, Sive, Gabriel, Aviwe and Mihle.

Sive was dressed in a black skirt, charcoal shirt, black tie, black blazer and a black hill. The black hat complimented her skin colour. She put her black clutch bag on her lap.

When Owam's body arrived, Sive's body trembled in pain. Gabriel held her hand and squeezed it to calm her down. Thandi rubbed her back.

Sive was the third speaker. She rose up and slowly walked towards the coffin and stood over it. She cleared her throat.

"Owam was my friend. I loved him with all my heart, for who he was. He was a good person and he didn't deserve to die like this…no one does."

Tears fell from her eyes.

"He was killed, brutally, just because he was gay. I'll say this because I believe that, his killer or someone who knows his murderer or someone who has a passion to murder all homosexuals is here."

Sive took a tissue from her clutch bag and wiped her tears.

She continued.

"If we could carry on following the cruel Old Testament Laws, why did Jesus come? Why did He die on the cross when His death won't bring any change?" she exhaled deeply. "Homophobia and xenophobia have the same roots, lack of love and intolerance of each other's differences. God sent Jesus to teach us love. It's only God who has the authority to judge…not a sinner like you and me."

Now, Sive's voice was getting stronger and louder.

"Before justifying your cruel acts by Moses' cruel laws, think of John 8:7. And analyse what Jesus meant by that."

Sive paused before she continued.

"It's so funny for a person who claims to be in his or her right mind to think that murdering another human being is better than just being a homosexual. Let's just face the reality. Homosexuals and heterosexuals coexist, therefore, you better work on your poor coping skills, they're not going anywhere. When things like this happen, I just wonder how life was before religion became a part of our lives?"

She then covered her eyes with her hand, blocking the tears. Her shoulders were vibrating.

She sniffed tears, and then continued.

"What's so difficult about tolerating behaviour that doesn't harm anyone?"

Sive kissed her hand and then touched the coffin.

"Rest in peace, my dear friend. You'll always be in my heart, and I'll always love you." She said and slowly went to sit down.

***

A month after Owam's burial; Sive, Aviwe, Mihle and the girls went on vacation in Durban. It was an exciting moment for all of them. They lived in the same hotel Sive and Gabriel had lived in when they had visited the city.

"Hurry up guys, it's almost 9:00," said Sive.

It was a bright Saturday morning and they were going out for a picnic by the beach.

Sive was holding Bridgette and Smanye in her hands, Mihle a picnic basket and Aviwe a duvet cover and two pillows. They got in the car and went off.

They found a nice shady spot under a coconut tree to put their stuff.

"Let's go build a sandcastle," said Sive taking the girls' hands.

"Yeee!" said the girls running along with her.

After a moment, they went to join Aviwe and Mihle under the tree, to eat.

When they finished eating, Sive gave the girls a beach ball to play with and then turned to Mihle who looked miles away.

"What's up girl?" she asked, sitting between Aviwe and Mihle on the duvet cover.

"When I was in jail, I didn't think I would ever get this kind of freedom."

"I'm sorry, girl. That was so awful."

Mihle shook her head. "But not as awful as what I did to you."

Sive smiled. "It's all water under bridge now. I know that you were in a bad space. And I know you won't do such a thing ever again."

Mihle shook her head.

"No, especially now that I know how it feels in those filthy orange jumpsuits."

Sive smiled, and then the smile suddenly went away.

"And Jonno is in them…"

"He's so freaking crazy, he belongs there. He kidnaped you and replaced you in your car with a dead, black dog and then framed your friend for…"

Sive intercepted an angry Aviwe.

"I know, but he wasn't all bad. We spent every single night in the same room…under the same blankets but he didn't rape me."

"And if I didn't attack you, he wouldn't have framed me."

Sive smiled.

"I'm sorry, Mimz."

"It's ok girl. I'm free now and back with my kids."

Sive turned to Aviwe.

"And how are you dealing with everything?"

"I went to see the doctor you recommended and I'm starting support group next week…"

"Really! Come here, girl," said Sive, hugging her.

"Support group! For what?" asked Mihle.

"I'm a sex addict."

"Sex addict? What's that?" asked Mihle.

"I can't get enough of sex. I can sleep with three guys in a single day." Mihle's eyes widened in surprise, "And sometimes I sleep with two guys at once."

"How come I didn't know about all that?"

"Because I kept it secret, even Sive found out about it recently."

"So, when was the last time you had sex?" asked Sive.

"The night before I left for this trip, with that guy who left you his business card at the Northern Sun restaurant."

Sive looked confused.

"Oh, the one who was wearing a black shirt," said Mihle.

"Yeah, yeah, that one," confirmed Aviwe.

Then Mihle turned to Sive.

"On the day of choice condoms, girl."

"Oh, I remember him," she laughed, and then looked at Aviwe, "You stole my man."

They all laughed.

Then Sive's face go serious.

"What's up, girl?" asked Mihle thinking that she had feelings for the guy.

"We are finally united, but there's someone missing…Owam."

"How are you holding up?" asked Aviwe.

"I miss him daily, especially when I get home. He kept my house warm."

"I'm sorry girl, I know how much you loved him," said Aviwe.

"With the speech you made at his funeral, definitely, his soul rested in peace," said Mihle.

"Definitely," agreed Aviwe.

"How's your cousin?" asked Mihle.

"He went back to the US…he didn't take it well at all."

"That's life…not always fair," said Mihle.

"Let's leave the past in the past. Now, tell us all about the Malawi story," asked Aviwe.

Sive chucked. "That's the past, too."

"But one that has never been told."

"I told you guys that I found Chikondi dead and buried. What more you want?"

"There was something that you kept a secret about this Malawi story," said Mihle.

Sive sighed.

"I guess the reason why I didn't want to talk about it; I'm still in love with Chikondi. I sometimes feel like dropping Gabriel and moaning for him forever…"

"What!" exclaimed Aviwe.

Sive nodded. "And go join a nun convent…"

Aviwe stretched her eyes.

"What! You, in a convent? Do you think that would suit your personality?" asked Aviwe.

"That's exactly what made me to decide that wasn't an option."

"So, you truly love Gabriel?" asked Mihle.

A short silence.

"Yes. But I don't think the way I love Chikondi."

"And what does that mean?" asked Mihle.

"With these feelings that I have for Chikondi, I don't think I would be able to marry Gabriel."

Silence.

"You can't do that, that poor man loves you," said Mihle.

Sive released a juvenile smile.

"And another secret I kept was that Jonathan was obsessed with me."

"Why would you keep that a secret?" asked Mihle

"I wanted to protect him; I didn't want to embarrass him. I thought he would understand that I wasn't in love with him. I'd never thought that things could go as far as they went."

"So, you weren't in love with him?" asked Aviwe.

Sive shook her head.

"No," she exchanged glances between them, "And the other thing I kept a secret was dating Gabriel."

"Why?"

Sive shrugged.

"It was part of the plan to protect Jonathan."

Aviwe chuckled.

"And if you didn't, Van Dame wouldn't have panel beat you."

They laughed except for Mihle.

Sive touched Mihle's shoulder.

"Girl, if you have a long face each time this fool makes fun of the incident, you'll lose your sense of humour."

"Because I don't see anything funny in all that. I almost killed a person who cares a lot about me, for what? Someone who sees me as just a fat ass."

"We all make mistakes," said Sive hugging her. She then glanced in between them, "If I didn't make the mistake of covering up for a sick man I wouldn't have ended up in that filthy room in the middle of nowhere. You wouldn't have spent two months in jail, or the poor dog killed to make some crazy point, you see. You have to let this go and enjoy the girls' reunion."

They smiled and embraced each other.

"Let me and the girls go and change into our cute swimsuits before they get bored playing with that stupid ball."

Soon, Sive was in a sexy black and white bathing costume and the girls both in red. Their mom liked to buy them similar stuff.

Sive put their clothes in the bag and then stood with her hands on her waist in front of her friends.

"Gabriel bought me this."

"Oh girl, that's so romantic. Did he see how sexy it is on you?" said Mihle.

"Yeah. We spent the whole day swimming and playing at this beach."

"What!" she glanced at Aviwe, and then back to Sive, "Did you guys come here…Durban?"

"Oh yes, and I had the time of my life," replied Sive smiling and then took the girls' arms and ran to the beach.

"Swim time!" they yelled as they were running.

"This conversation isn't over!" yelled Aviwe and then looked at Mihle.

"She spent days with her man at this romantic beach, wearing that," pointing at where Sive went, "sexy costume and still did nothing…what is wrong with her?"

Mihle laughed at her friend.

"Maybe she isn't ready. Or, her love for Chikondi forbids her to open her legs for any guy."

"Oh, please, stuff the dead! Don't you think this not-ready crap is starving the poor guy?"

Mihle burst out laughing.

"What!" she said throwing her hands in the air, "You know I'm right, girl."

"Did you see how fit and muscular that Gabriel is? Sive's still… you know. She might be scared."

"Wow…when I looked at his dark, muscular body I just moved uncomfortably in my seat, imagining him all over my body. Kissing the places before pushing in his big, black snake…"

"Stop!" screamed Mihle closing her ears with her hands.

"What?"

"Hello! He's your best friend's fiancé."

"I know. But I lust over him."

Mihle glared at her.

"You better get the help soon before ripping this friendship apart," she said annoyed and got up and walked to the beach.

*＊＊

That night, Sive bathed the kids, read them bedtime stories, and put them to sleep before joining the girls on the balcony. They were drinking wine.

"Don't look at me like that. I don't have babies, remember?"

Sive chuckled.

"I'm the mama, not you. I know."

"And you're so good at that. Gabriel's so lucky to have you," she said and looked at Aviwe, "Isn't he, Viv?"

"No! He's not. Having a woman that starves you is nothing but bad luck." she said and then sipped her wine.

Sive pulled the chair closer to them with a smile on her face.

"Girls, I'm not a virgin anymore."

"What!" Mihle exclaimed."

"When did that happen?" asked Aviwe.

"When I went to visit him, after the kidnapping."

Aviwe bulged out her eyes.

"And you didn't say anything?"

"Remember I came home to the death of my best friend."

"And, how was it?"

"It was so beautiful, so sacred…so fulfilling," she replied with a beautiful smile on her face. And we did it again when he came for my mother's wedding."

"And you didn't bother telling us. And if he didn't propose at your mother's wedding, I'm sure we wouldn't know that you're engaged."

"Come on, Viv, you were in Johannesburg most of the time and I was grieving. Mimz was getting her life organised. I knew that we had this vacation coming up to unload all the secrets."

Mihle smiled.

"Are you sure there no secrets left?"

"No," she smiled, "Oh, there is. Next week I'm going to Nigeria to meet Gabriel's family. My family loves him; I guess his will love me, too."

"Come on girl, his family loves you, dearly. I saw on Facebook that they are so fond of you," said Mihle.

"So does he," Aviwe added, sipping her wine.

"Guys, those are the youngsters. I'm talking about the elders who know what's good for their son."

"Honey, no one doesn't love virgin Mary…"

"Are you still calling me that? Come on, I know the taste of snake now," replied Sive with a naughty smile.

"I can see from the look on that face that it tastes yummy," said Mihle.

"They say the blacker the berries the sweeter they taste," added Sive.

They all laughed and then continued enjoying the last night of their vacation.

Chapter 27

Sive was dressed in her wedding gown, staring through her bedroom window into her mother's house. All the thoughts of Chikondi that were going through her head were written all over her face. Her eyes glittered with tears.

Their Facebook conversation thread was all Sive had left of Chikondi…memories.

Her friends, who were her bridesmaids, were worried. They thought she was going to call off the wedding.

Mihle went to stand next to Sive, staring at her while she was staring out the window. Then said, "Are you ready, girl?" Sive didn't reply, "People are waiting for you. Gabriel called to find out if everything was ok," she added.

Sive was quiet, looking miles away.

Thandi barged in.

"Girls, are you not ready? People are waiting."

No one answered her.

She looked at her daughter and noticed that something wasn't okay. She slowly walked to her.

"Is everything okay, baby?" she asked.

Tears fell from Sive's eyes.

"Oh baby," said Thandi, hugging her daughter.

Sive broke way and slowly went to sit on her bed and put her laptop on her lap. Everyone was staring at her. They all had one thing in their minds: that Sive was going to take off her wedding gown and call off the wedding.

Sive went through her Facebook conversation with Chikondi. She realised that Chikondi was her past and moving forward with her life was all she needed. She then deleted Chikondi from her friends list.

She closed her laptop and placed both hands on it and exhaled with her eyes closed, fighting back the tears.

Sive entered the church with her uncle. She stopped by the entrance, looking down.

Gabriel could see that there was something wrong with his bride.

James was Gabriel's best man, and you would think from the smile on his face that it was Nancy getting married to Gabriel.

Adam and his granny where sitting in the third row from the entrance. The old lady turned and looked at Sive.

Their eyes met, she smiled. Sive stared at her. All that was going on in her mind was Chikondi's memories.

Suddenly, her mind took her back to Malawi, reading the letter from Chikondi. She smiled.

And then, walked down the aisle…with another man.

www.ingramcontent.com/pod-product-compliance
Lightning Source LLC
Chambersburg PA
CBHW031104260626
47172CB00001B/207